THE CLAY SANSKRIT LIBRARY
FOUNDED BY JOHN & JENNIFER CLAY

GENERAL EDITOR
SHELDON POLLOCK

EDITED BY
ISABELLE ONIANS

WWW.CLAYSANSKRITLIBRARY.ORG
WWW.NYUPRESS.ORG

Artwork by Robert Beer.
Typeset in Adobe Garamond at 10.25 : 12.3 pt.
Editorial input from Dániel Balogh, Ridi Faruque,
Chris Gibbons, Tomoyuki Kono,
Andrew Skilton & Eszter Somogyi.
Printed and Bound in Great Britain by
TJ International, Cornwall on acid free paper

GARLAND OF THE BUDDHA'S PAST LIVES

VOLUME TWO

by ĀRYAŚŪRA

TRANSLATED BY

Justin Meiland

NEW YORK UNIVERSITY PRESS

JJC FOUNDATION

2009

First Edition 2009

The Clay Sanskrit Library is co-published by
New York University Press
and the JJC Foundation.

Further information about this volume
and the rest of the Clay Sanskrit Library
is available at the end of this book and
on the following websites:
www.claysanskritlibrary.org
www.nyupress.org

ISBN 978-0-8147-9583-5

Library of Congress Cataloging-in-Publication Data
Āryaśūra.
[Jātakamālā. English & Sanskrit]
Garland of the Buddha's past lives / by Ārya Śūra ;
translated by Justin Meiland. -- 1st ed.
p. cm.
Miracle stories of the Buddha's past lives.
In English and Sanskrit (romanized) on facing pages;
includes translation from Sanskrit.
Includes bibliographical references and index.
ISBN 978-0-8147-9583-5
1. Buddhist stories, Sanskrit--Translations into English.
2. Aryasura--Translations into English.
I. Meiland, Justin, 1937- II. Title.
BQ1462.E5M47 2009
294.3'82325--dc22
2008046726

CONTENTS

CSL CONVENTIONS

Sanskrit Alphabetical Order

Vowels:	*a ā i ī u ū ṛ ṝ ḷ ḹ e ai o au ṃ ḥ*
Gutturals:	*k kh g gh ṅ*
Palatals:	*c ch j jh ñ*
Retroflex:	*ṭ ṭh ḍ ḍh ṇ*
Dentals:	*t th d dh n*
Labials:	*p ph b bh m*
Semivowels:	*y r l v*
Spirants:	*ś ṣ s h*

Guide to Sanskrit Pronunciation

a	b*u*t
ā, â	f*a*ther
i	s*i*t
ī, î	f*ee*
u	p*u*t
ū, û	b*oo*
ṛ	vocalic *r*, American p*ur*dy or English p*re*tty
ṝ	lengthened *ṛ*
ḷ	vocalic *l*, ab*le*
e, ê, ē	m*a*de, esp. in Welsh pronunciation
ai	b*i*te
o, ô, ō	r*o*pe, esp. Welsh pronunciation; Italian s*o*lo
au	s*ou*nd
ṃ	*anusvāra* nasalizes the preceding vowel
ḥ	*visarga*, a voiceless aspiration (resembling the English *h*), or like Scottish lo*ch*, or an aspiration with a faint echoing of the last element of the preceding vowel so that *taiḥ* is pronounced *taih*[i]
k	lu*ck*
kh	blo*ckh*ead
g	*g*o
gh	bi*gh*ead
ṅ	a*n*ger
c	*ch*ill
ch	mat*chh*ead
j	*j*og
jh	aspirated *j*, he*dgeh*og
ñ	ca*ny*on
ṭ	retroflex *t*, *t*ry (with the tip of tongue turned up to touch the hard palate)
ṭh	same as the preceding but aspirated
ḍ	retroflex *d* (with the tip

	of tongue turned up to touch the hard palate)	*b*	*b*efore
ḍh	same as the preceding but aspirated	*bh*	a*bh*orrent
ṇ	retroflex *n* (with the tip of tongue turned up to touch the hard palate)	*m*	*m*ind
t	French *t*out	*y*	*y*es
th	ten*t h*ook	*r*	trilled, resembling the Italian pronunciation of *r*
d	*d*inner	*l*	*l*inger
dh	guil*dh*all	*v*	*w*ord
n	*n*ow	*ś*	*sh*ore
p	*p*ill	*ṣ*	retroflex *sh* (with the tip of the tongue turned up to touch the hard palate)
ph	u*ph*eaval	*s*	hi*ss*
		h	*h*ood

CSL Punctuation of English

The acute accent on Sanskrit words when they occur outside of the Sanskrit text itself, marks stress, e.g., Ramáyana. It is not part of traditional Sanskrit orthography, transliteration, or transcription, but we supply it here to guide readers in the pronunciation of these unfamiliar words. Since no Sanskrit word is accented on the last syllable it is not necessary to accent disyllables, e.g., Rama.

The second CSL innovation designed to assist the reader in the pronunciation of lengthy unfamiliar words is to insert an unobtrusive middle dot between semantic word breaks in compound names (provided the word break does not fall on a vowel resulting from the fusion of two vowels), e.g., Maha·bhárata, but Ramáyana (not Rama·áyana). Our dot echoes the punctuating middle dot (·) found in the oldest surviving samples of written Indic, the Ashokan inscriptions of the third century BCE.

The deep layering of Sanskrit narrative has also dictated that we use quotation marks only to announce the beginning and end of every direct speech, and not at the beginning of every paragraph.

CSL Punctuation of Sanskrit

The Sanskrit text is also punctuated, in accordance with the punctuation of the English translation. In mid-verse, the punctuation will not alter the sandhi or the scansion. Proper names are capitalized. Most Sanskrit meters have four "feet" (*pāda*); where possible we print the common *śloka* meter on two lines. In the Sanskrit text, we use French *Guillemets* (e.g., *«kva saṃcicīrṣuḥ?»*) instead of English quotation marks (e.g., "Where are you off to?") to avoid confusion with the apostrophes used for vowel elision in sandhi.

SANDHI

Sanskrit presents the learner with a challenge: *sandhi* (euphonic combination). Sandhi means that when two words are joined in connected speech or writing (which in Sanskrit reflects speech), the last letter (or even letters) of the first word often changes; compare the way we pronounce "the" in "the beginning" and "the end."

In Sanskrit the first letter of the second word may also change; and if both the last letter of the first word and the first letter of the second are vowels, they may fuse. This has a parallel in English: a nasal consonant is inserted between two vowels that would otherwise coalesce: "a pear" and "an apple." Sanskrit vowel fusion may produce ambiguity.

The charts on the following pages give the full sandhi system.

Fortunately it is not necessary to know these changes in order to start reading Sanskrit. All that is important to know is the form of the second word without sandhi (pre-sandhi), so that it can be recognized or looked up in a dictionary. Therefore we are printing Sanskrit with a system of punctuation that will indicate, unambiguously, the original form of the second word, i.e., the form without sandhi. Such sandhi mostly concerns the fusion of two vowels.

In Sanskrit, vowels may be short or long and are written differently accordingly. We follow the general convention that a vowel with no mark above it is short. Other books mark a long vowel either with a bar called a macron (*ā*) or with a circumflex (*â*). Our system uses the

VOWEL SANDHI

Final vowels: a	ā	i	ī	u	ū	ṛ	e	ai	o	au	Initial vowels:
' â	" â	y a	y a	v a	v a	r a	e '	ā a	o '	āv a	a
' ā	" ā	y ā	y ā	v ā	v ā	r ā	a ā	ā ā	a ā	āv ā	ā
' ê	" ê	' î	" î	v i	v i	r i	a i	ā i	a i	āv i	i
' ē	" ē	' ī	" ī	v ī	v ī	r ī	a ī	ā ī	a ī	āv ī	ī
' ô	" ô	y u	y u	' û	" û	r u	a u	ā u	a u	āv u	u
' ō	" ō	y ū	y ū	' ū	" ū	r ū	a ū	ā ū	a ū	āv ū	ū
a' r	a" r	y ṛ	y ṛ	v ṛ	v ṛ	' ṝ	a ṛ	ā ṛ	a ṛ	āv ṛ	ṛ
' âi	" âi	y e	y e	v e	v e	r e	a e	ā e	a e	āv e	e
' āi	" āi	y ai	y ai	v ai	v ai	r ai	a ai	ā ai	a ai	āv ai	ai
' âu	" âu	y o	y o	v o	v o	r o	a o	ā o	a o	āv o	o
' āu	" āu	y au	y au	v au	v au	r au	a au	ā au	a au	āv au	au

CONSONANT SANDHI

				Permitted finals:			(Except āḥ/aḥ)			
k	ṭ	t	p	ṅ	n	m	ḥ/r	āḥ	aḥ	*Initial letters:*
k	ṭ	t	p	ṅ	n	ṃ	ḥ	āḥ	aḥ	k/kh
g	ḍ	d	b	ṅ	n	ṃ	r	ā	o	g/gh
k	ṭ	c	p	ṅ	ṃś	ṃ	ś	āś	aś	c/ch
g	ḍ	j	b	ṅ	ñ	ṃ	r	ā	o	j/jh
k	ṭ	ṭ	p	ṅ	ṃṣ	ṃ	ṣ	āṣ	aṣ	ṭ/ṭh
g	ḍ	ḍ	b	ṅ	ṇ	ṃ	r	ā	o	ḍ/ḍh
k	ṭ	t	p	ṅ	ṃs	ṃ	s	ās	as	t/th
g	ḍ	d	b	ṅ	n	ṃ	r	ā	o	d/dh
k	ṭ	t	p	ṅ	n	ṃ	ḥ	āḥ	aḥ	p/ph
g	ḍ	d	b	ṅ	n	ṃ	r	ā	o	b/bh
ṅ	ṇ	n	m	ṅ	n	ṃ	r	ā	o	*nasals* (n/m)
g	ḍ	d	b	ṅ	n	ṃ	r	ā	o	y/v
g	ḍ	d	b	ṅ	n	ṃ	*zero*[1]	ā	o	r
g	ḍ	l	b	ṅ	l̃[2]	ṃ	r	ā	o	l
k	ṭ	c ch	p	ṅ	ñ ś/ch	ṃ	ḥ	āḥ	aḥ	ś
k	ṭ	t	p	ṅ	n	ṃ	ḥ	āḥ	aḥ	ṣ/s
gg h	ḍḍ h	dd h	bb h	ṅ	n	ṃ	r	ā	o	h
g	ḍ	d	b	ṅ/ṅṅ[3]	n/nn[3]	m	r	ā	a[4]	*vowels*
k	ṭ	t	p	ṅ	n	m	ḥ	āḥ	aḥ	*zero*

[1]ḥ or r disappears, and if a/i/u precedes, this lengthens to ā/ī/ū. [2]e.g. tān+lokān=tā̃l lokān.
[3]The doubling occurs if the preceding vowel is short. [4]Except: aḥ+a=o '.

macron, except that for initial vowels in sandhi we use a circumflex to indicate that originally the vowel was short, or the shorter of two possibilities (*e* rather than *ai*, *o* rather than *au*).

When we print initial *â*,	before sandhi that vowel was *a*
î or *ê*,	*i*
û or *ô*,	*u*
âi,	*e*
âu,	*o*
ā,	*ā*
ī,	*ī*
ū,	*ū*
ē,	*ī*
ō,	*ū*
ai,	*ai*
āu,	*au*
’, before sandhi there was a vowel *a*	

When a final short vowel (*a*, *i*, or *u*) has merged into a following vowel, we print ’ at the end of the word, and when a final long vowel (*ā*, *ī*, or *ū*) has merged into a following vowel we print ” at the end of the word. The vast majority of these cases will concern a final *a* or *ā*. See, for instance, the following examples:

What before sandhi was *atra asti*	is represented as *atr' âsti*
atra āste	*atr' āste*
kanyā asti	*kany" âsti*
kanyā āste	*kany" āste*
atra iti	*atr' êti*
kanyā iti	*kany" êti*
kanyā īpsitā	*kany" ēpsitā*

Finally, three other points concerning the initial letter of the second word:

(1) A word that before sandhi begins with *ṛ* (vowel), after sandhi begins with *r* followed by a consonant: *yatha" rtu* represents pre-sandhi *yathā ṛtu*.

(2) When before sandhi the previous word ends in *t* and the following word begins with *ś*, after sandhi the last letter of the previous word is *c*

and the following word begins with *ch*: *syāc chāstravit* represents pre-sandhi *syāt śāstravit*.

(3) Where a word begins with *h* and the previous word ends with a double consonant, this is our simplified spelling to show the pre-sandhi form: *tad hasati* is commonly written as *tad dhasati*, but we write *tadd hasati* so that the original initial letter is obvious.

COMPOUNDS

We also punctuate the division of compounds (*samāsa*), simply by inserting a thin vertical line between words. There are words where the decision whether to regard them as compounds is arbitrary. Our principle has been to try to guide readers to the correct dictionary entries.

Exemplar of CSL Style

Where the Devanagari script reads:

कुम्भस्थली रक्षतु वो विकीर्णसिन्धूररेणुर्द्विरदाननस्य ।
प्रशान्तये विघ्नतमश्छटानां निष्ठ्यूतबालातपपल्लवेव ॥

Others would print:

kumbhasthalī rakṣatu vo vikīrṇasindūrareṇur dviradānanasya /
praśāntaye vighnatamaśchaṭānāṃ niṣṭhyūtabālātapapallaveva //

We print:

kumbha|sthalī rakṣatu vo vikīrṇa|sindūra|reṇur dvirad'|ānanasya
praśāntaye vighna|tamaś|chaṭānāṃ niṣṭhyūta|bāl'|ātapa|pallav" êva.

And in English:

May Ganésha's domed forehead protect you! Streaked with vermilion dust, it seems to be emitting the spreading rays of the rising sun to pacify the teeming darkness of obstructions.

("Nava·sáhasanka and the Serpent Princess" I.3)

INTRODUCTION

In this second volume of the "Garland of the Buddha's Past Lives" (*Jātakamālā*), fourteen further stories recount the Buddha's past lives as a Bodhi·sattva.[1] Although there are key thematic continuities with the first volume—in particular the idealized notion of a virtuous renouncer-king, the anti-householder path of the ascetic, and the Bodhi·sattva's role as a compassionate savior—the division is not entirely an artificial one. Not only does the narrative move on to the third perfection, that of forbearance (*kṣānti*), there are also other shifts in focus as animal stories take precedence and the notion of proper friendship becomes central.

The Perfection of Forbearance

The introduction to the first volume of the "Garland of the Buddha's Past Lives" (Meiland 2009) discussed how stories 1–30 appear to be structured around the first three "perfections" (*pāramitā*) of giving (*dāna*, stories 1–10), virtue (*śīla*, 11–20), and forbearance (*kṣānti*, 21–30). The last four stories (31–34) do not appear to reflect the fourth perfection of vigor (*vīrya*) but instead seem to return to the first three perfections, with stories 33–34 clearly portraying forbearance. According to this analysis, forbearance should therefore be the dominant theme of the present volume (stories 21–34). But, as we shall see, this assumption requires certain qualifications.

"Forbearance" is portrayed in various ways in the "Garland of the Buddha's Past Lives" but perhaps the most paradigmatic tale on the virtue is 'The Birth-Story of Kshanti·vadin' (28), in which the Bodhi·sattva is an ascetic called "Preacher of Forbearance" (Kshanti·vadin). Here a violent and drunken king becomes enraged by Kshanti·vadin, whom he wrongly accuses of attempting to seduce his harem. The ascetic's sermons serve merely to provoke the king further, leading him to mutilate Kshanti·vadin's body and face. Key to the ascetic's practice of forbearance is his control over his emotions (particularly anger) in the face of physical and verbal aggression.

The fine sage felt neither grief nor anger
when the sharp sword fell on his body.
For he knew his body's machinery must end
and had long practiced forbearance toward people.
(28.93 [55])

While such gory depictions may suggest a tendency toward self-mortification or toward the notion of pain as having a purificatory effect, it is important to recognize that pain is usually portrayed negatively in such tales. Indeed it is precisely because the victim does not experience pain that forbearance is demonstrated.

Despite seeing his body being chopped up,
his mind stayed firm in undiminished patience.
He felt no pain but kindness made the saint
suffer at seeing the king's fall from morality. (28.94 [56])

In the "Garland of the Buddha's Past Lives," however, forbearance does not merely involve the overcoming of pain or the control of emotions such as anger. It also involves feeling compassion toward an aggressor or toward people by whom one has been wronged. In 'The Birth-Story of the Shárabha Deer' (25), the Bodhi·sattva thus rescues a king from a pit, even though the king had earlier tried to harm him:

Compassion meant he forgot of him as a foe
and he shared in the king's pain instead. (25.20 [8])

This compassionate type of forbearance can take various forms. In 'The Birth-Story of Kshanti·vadin,' it involves pitying an aggressor for their violation of morality and for the bad karmic effects they are bound to suffer (see 28.94 [56] above).[2] By contrast, in 'The Birth-Story of the Elephant' (30), the Bodhi·sattva's forbearance involves no aggressor at all. Instead, it rests on his compassionate willingness to sacrifice his body for others in distress.[3] The story's maxim thus states: "If it results in the welfare of others, even pain is esteemed by the virtuous as a gain" (30.1).

However, while some stories define forbearance in this extended sense of compassion toward an aggressor or self-sacrifice for others, it would be difficult to argue that forbearance, even under such extended definitions, represents a major theme in every one of the ten stories (21–30) considered to portray the third perfection. The 'Larger Birth-Story of Bodhi' (23) and 'The Birth-Story of Brahma' (29) are, for example, far more concerned with the issue of defeating false doctrines than they are with forbearance, although a minor theme of the former story is that the Bodhi·sattva shows compassion toward a king despite his betrayal of their friendship. Similarly, in 'The Birth-Story of the Goose' (22), although the protagonists do act compassionately toward a traditional enemy (a hunter), the major focus of the story is not on forbearance but on devotion and the need to develop good friendships and virtue (see especially 22.150 [93]–156 [99]). While one might argue that the protagonists' preservation of virtue in a testing situation represents a type of forbearance, or that the geese show forbearance by offering friendship to those who have tried to wrong them, there seems no particular reason why the story should primarily reflect forbearance rather than virtue. It is also noteworthy that the term *kṣānti* ("forbearance") is never mentioned in the narrative itself, including the epilogue's discussion of topics covered by the tale. While forbearance is therefore an important theme in stories 21–30, it is not central to all the narratives and the perfection structure appears weaker here than in the first twenty tales.

Friends, Enemies and Virtuous Company

Connected to the notion of forbearance is the theme of friendship and its related motifs of gratitude, treachery and proper companionship. In numerous stories, friendship and gratitude are extolled while treachery is criticized. 'The Birth-Story of the Great Monkey' (24) offers a typical example, in which a man, inflicted with the karmic punishment of leprosy for betraying the Bodhi·sattva (a monkey), explains to a king the reason for his grotesque appearance:

What you see before you is only
the flower of my betrayal of friendship.
The fruit will surely be different,
something far worse than this.

You should regard treachery
toward friends as a foe
and look affectionately on friends
who are affectionate to you. (24.62 [38]–63 [39])

The Bodhi·sattva's virtue is often the factor that enables enmity to be overcome. In 'The Birth-Story of the Great Monkey' (27), a king's army attacks a tree inhabited by monkeys, "as if eager to attack the inaccessible fortress of an enemy" (27.23). This aggression is dispelled when the king witnesses the Bodhi·sattva's self-sacrifice for his troop of monkeys, giving the following maxim to the story: "Those who act morally can influence the hearts even of enemies." Similarly, in 'The Birth-Story of the Shárabha Deer' (25), a king marvels that a deer whom he tried to kill is still willing to save him from a pit:

How can he show me compassion
when I have clearly treated him as a foe? (25.26 [13])

In some stories the "enemy" is so impressed by the Bodhi·sattva's virtue that he declares not only friendship but also a willingness to offer his life in gratitude: "My life is yours!" (25.40 [21], 26.17 [9]).[4]

However, while enemies are often transformed into friends through virtue, several stories stress the value of proper companionship (rather than just any companionship), since an immoral friend can easily lead a person astray. The notion that moral company facilitates the cultivation of virtue reflects the Buddhist notion of a "good (spiritual) friend" (*kalyāṇa/mitra*) and is expressed, for example, by two verses in 'The Birth-Story of Suta·soma' (31):

Even randomly meeting
a virtuous person just once
creates something firm and enduring,
requiring no constant attention. (31.138 [71])

Never roam far from virtuous people.
Modest in conduct, frequent the good.
For their flower-like virtues spread pollen
which easily touches those nearby.[5] (31.140 [72])

The importance of other people is also relevant to the Bodhi·sattva himself. Although the primary focus of the "Garland of the Buddha's Past Lives" is usually on the Bodhi·sattva and his deeds, his achievement of virtue is not always an entirely solitary task. In the introduction to the first volume, we already had cause to mention the important role played by the Bodhi·sattva's wife, Madri, in 'The Birth-Story of Vishvan·tara' (9). By giving her approval to her husband's extreme gifts, Madri's devotion not only assists the Bodhi·sattva in fulfilling the perfection of giving but also offers a resolution to the conflict between renunciate and social values brought about by the Bodhi·sattva's absolutist moral outlook. The depth of intimacy between the Bodhi·sattva and his wife is highlighted in that story by the god Shakra, who describes their relationship as one of inseparability and interdependence:

I give you back
Madri, your wife.
For moonlight should not
exist apart from the moon. (vol. 1, 9.184 [99])

Such participation by others in the Bodhi·sattva's lives is also emphasized in other stories. In some cases it is expressed in the instrumental or catalytic sense of providing a context for the Bodhi·sattva's performance of virtue. In 'The Birth-Story of the Buffalo' (33), for example, the need for forbearance to have a context in which to operate is expressed by the tale's maxim: "Forgiveness only exists if there is something to forgive, not otherwise." Indeed the Bodhi·sattva of the story (a buffalo) interprets the insults inflicted on him by a mischievous monkey as a benefit, since they provide him with an opportunity to practice forbearance:

There is never a wrong time for forbearance.
But the occasion is rare as it depends on others.
So if another person produces an opportunity,
why would one resort to anger? (33.22 [14])

Other stories move beyond a merely instrumental form of agency to focus extensively on characters other than the Bodhi·sattva. A startling example is provided by 'The Birth-Story of the Goose' (22), in which the main protagonist of the story is in fact not the Bodhi·sattva (a king of geese) but the Bodhi·sattva's general Sumúkha. Sumúkha's prominent role is highlighted by the fact that not only does the prose introduction give a longer description to Sumúkha than to the Bodhi·sattva, but also the story breaks the convention of identifying solely the Buddha's former rebirth by identifying Sumúkha as the former rebirth of the monk Anánda. Moreover, the main focus of the story is on Súmukha's devotion to his king. In fact it is this quality that resolves the conflict in the tale between the geese and their hunters rather than any virtue displayed by the Bodhi·sattva.[6] Accordingly, when the hunter decides to release the geese, he pinpoints Súmukha's virtue as the main factor influencing his actions:

The virtue you have displayed here
in giving your life for your master
would be miraculous even
among humans or gods!

Out of reverence
I will release your king.
For who could wrong him
who is dearer to you than life? (22.95 [52]–96 [53])

In a similar manner to the love shown between the Bodhi·sattva and his wife in 'The Birth-Story of Vishvan·tara' (9), the inseparable companionship between the Bodhi·sattva and his general is again stressed:

The two worked as one in upholding
the body of bliss for the flock of geese,
just as two wings work as one in upholding
the body of a bird flying in the sky. (22.6 [1])

However, while Súmukha receives prominent attention for his own individual morality, it is significant that the virtue for which he is praised is devotion, an attitude that necessarily involves a strong bond of attachment to an object of loyalty, in this case the Bodhi·sattva. The value of Súmukha's moral conduct is therefore never entirely autonomous, however virtuous it is shown to be, but is always dependent on his relationship with the Bodhi·sattva. This is equally true of 'The Birth-Story of Vishvan·tara,' in which the significance of Madri's virtue is based primarily on her devotion to her husband (the Bodhi·sattva). While other characters play an important role in the Bodhi·sattva's lives, the Bodhi·sattva's paramount status is thus always maintained.

This emphasis on devotion picks up on a central theme that was highlighted in the first volume and that is equally important to the present book. Often described as a source of refuge and protection, the Bodhi·sattva's role as a savior is constantly accentuated:[7]

You come to us as Comfort incarnate
as we sink into this mouth of death! (30.22 [10])

Portrayed as offering freedom from fear ("Have no fear! Have no fear!" 26.10), the Bodhi·sattva in various stories saves people from death, suffering and the disastrous consequences of holding immoral views, all of which serve to foreshadow his ultimate attainment of Buddhahood and the end to suffering that will be brought about by this salvific goal. In 'The Birth-Story of the Elephant' (30), the Bodhi·sattva explicitly connects the merit derived from his act of self-sacrifice with his quest to attain Buddhahood. Not only that, in a startling comparison between the corporeal and the soteriological, the body that the Bodhi·sattva sacrifices to save a group of starving people is implicitly compared with the Buddha's teaching of the Dharma that will save the world:[8]

Instead, if I possess any merit from desiring
to rescue these people floundering in the desert,

may I use it to become savior of the world
as it roams the wilderness of samsara. (30.44 [22])

In this intensely devotional context, the intimacy of friendship takes on a heightened role. "A special friend and kinsman" (30.17 [7]), the Bodhi·sattva is portrayed as companion to all, even to strangers or to those who have wronged him:

Be a relative to us bereft of kinsmen!
Be our resort and refuge!
Please save us, illustrious lord,
in whatever way you know best. (30.35 [18])

Though our acquaintance is new,
you have acted towards us
as one would toward a best friend,
following your magnanimous nature. (22.146 [89])

With its emphasis on self-sacrifice, compassion and forbearance, the Bodhi·sattva's practice of virtue thus leads to his depiction as an ultimate "good friend." Offering moral guidance to the world, he saves both friends and foes through a devotional relationship that is both intimate and at the same time based on a hierarchy of savior and saved.

Animals, Ascetics and Kings

A striking aspect of the present volume is the number of animal stories it contains. Eight of the fourteen stories describe the Bodhi·sattva's rebirth as a bird or animal.[9] Animal stories are common in *jātaka* collections and far from unique to the "Garland of the Buddha's Past Lives." However, the fact that they are grouped together in the present volume is noticeable and points to important thematic continuities running through the tales.

There are doctrinal problems involved in depicting the Bodhi·sattva as an animal. According to Buddhist thought, animal rebirth derives from bad karma and thus raises a potential question mark over the purity of the Bodhi·sattva's karmic history. Moreover, while animals have the ability to act morally, their potential for virtue is usually restricted in comparison to humans. The issue of whether the Bodhi·sattva suffers from bad karma is raised by a verse in 'The Birth-Story of the Buffalo' (33.6 [3]): "Some trace of karma must have affected him to be reborn this way." Normally, however, the problem is sidestepped by simply extolling the Bodhi·sattva as a superior being whose virtue transcends the norms of animal nature.[10] 'The Birth-Story of the Great Monkey' (24.4) thus states: "Even though he was a monkey, the Bodhi·sattva had lost none of his moral awareness. Grateful and full of vast fortitude, his nature was devoid of anything lowly." The Bodhi·sattva's virtue is seen as a constant and unchanging attribute, despite his animal rebirth:

The earth with its forests, fine peaks and seas
may through water, fire and wind
perish a hundred times at an eon's end,
but not the great compassion of the Bodhi·sattva.

(24.5 [1])

Numerous references are made to the abnormal quality of the virtue displayed by the Bodhi·sattva as an animal.

Shock is expressed at his ability to speak in an articulate human voice (26.48) and the conceit is often raised that the Bodhi·sattva must be an animal only in appearance and something more superior in substance:

How can animals possess such conduct?
How can they have such wide regard for virtue?
Some design must lie behind your appearance.
You must practice asceticism in an ascetic grove![11]

(33.31 [20])

Far from diminishing his purity, the Bodhi·sattva's rebirth as an animal therefore serves to accentuate his miraculous virtue still further by contrasting his conduct with normal animal nature. Furthermore, the virtue that the Bodhi·sattva displays as an animal throws into relief the immoral conduct of human beings. As the Bodhi·sattva states in 'The Birth-Story of the Antelope' (26.21): "Men's hearts are, after all, usually ruthless and uncontrolled in their great greed."[12] It is thus men who normally act immorally in the narratives, especially by wronging or betraying the Bodhi·sattva, and who thereby display a behavior that is truly animal in quality in contrast to the Bodhi·sattva, whose animal nature is only apparent:

How castigated I feel by
his gentle yet wounding behavior!
It is I who am the animal, the ox.
Who is this creature, a shárabha *but in form?*

(25.27 [14])

The splendor of the Bodhi·sattva's virtue is often paralleled by his physical beauty. Likewise the geographical location of the animal stories is invariably set in forest scenes of exquisite charm. Sometimes compared with a delightful garden (28.9, 28.12), the forest is commonly portrayed as a mysterious realm of refined beauty in which the wild aspects of nature are often tamed.[13]

> *The Bodhi·sattva is said to have once lived as a huge monkey who roamed alone on a beautiful slope on the Hímavat mountain. The body of the mountain was smeared with the ointments of various glistening, multi-colored ores. Draped by glorious dense forests, as if by a robe of green silk, its slopes and borders were adorned with an array of colors and forms so beautifully variegated in their uneven distribution that they seemed to have been purposefully composed. Water poured down in numerous torrents and there was an abundance of deep caves, chasms and precipices. Bees buzzed loudly and trees bearing various flowers and fruits were fanned by a delightful breeze. It was here, in this playground of* vidya·dhara *spirits, that the Bodhi·sattva lived.* (24.3)

Several stories emphasize the forest's remote location and its lack of human contact.[14] The idyllic beauty of the forest is, however, not solely enjoyed by animals. It is also shared with ascetics, whose virtue is said to have a powerful effect on their natural surroundings:

> *The forest effortlessly produced flowers and fruits in every season and its spotless pools of water were adorned by lotuses and lilies. Through his residence there the Bodhi·sattva furnished the area with the auspiciousness of an ascetic grove.* (28.9)

This association between animals and ascetics is a common motif in the "Garland of the Buddha's Past Lives," with various passages comparing the Bodhi·sattva in his animal rebirths to a renunciate yogi.[15] The affinity between ascetics and animals is further accentuated by the fact that they possess a common antagonist: the human being living in ordinary society and, in particular, the king. Clashes between the forest and human society frequently occur in the narratives and are brought about in various ways, depending on how individual stories play on the dialectic between these two opposing, yet interacting, spheres. In 'The Birth-Story of the Great Monkey' (24), a man accidentally enters a remote area of the forest inhabited by the Bodhi·sattva after losing his way because of chasing a stray cow. Whereas in 'The Birth-Story of the Goose' (22), a king intentionally lures a flock of geese closer to the human realm in order to capture them. In the latter story, the motif of idyllic natural beauty takes on an added degree of complexity, as an artificial lake, said to rival the birds' home in both appearance and resources, is built by humans as bait.[16] Here human art, pregnant with connotations of deception and aggression, acts as a dangerous imitation of the natural world.

In other stories, kings come into contact with animals and ascetics through the beauty of the forest itself and the apt setting that this provides for kings to indulge in royal pleasures.[17] Described as "playgrounds of Desire" (21.19 [7]), the same forest scenes that provide an idyllic environment for virtuous animals or ascetics in one context also provide sensual stimulation for licentious kings in another, an affinity particularly expressed by the resemblance between forests and royal gardens.[18] In 'The Birth-Story of Kshanti·vadin' (28), a king thus enjoys wine, women and song among garden-like (28.9, 28.12) forests of exquisite beauty that also happen to be inhabited by an ascetic. The tension inherent in the joint use of the forest by both ascetic and king becomes strained when the king's women, "smitten by the loveliness of the groves" (28.25), accidentally encounter the ascetic and listen to his sermons, the mere sight of him making them "feel overcome by his radiant ascetic power" (ibid.). While the ascetic's intentions are of course entirely virtuous, the story seems keen to probe the conflict between the ascetic and royal spheres (and intensify the contrasting significance placed on the shared motif of forest beauty) by depicting the ascetic's sermons as a form of pious seduction that threatens the king's desire-based outlook. Indeed, it is precisely the king's jealousy that leads him to treat "the ascetic like a foe" (28.55) and assault him.

A similar conflict is expressed in 'The Birth-Story of the Great Monkey' (27), in which a fig-tree, depicted as the centerpiece of an idyllic forest scene, serves as the home of a harmonious community of monkeys in an "area seldom accessed by humans" (27.19). Here again the refined pleasures of a forest inhabited by virtuous animals act as a seduction for human beings driven by the negative emotions of desire, when a fruit from the fig-tree accidentally floats down a river to a royal party and intoxicates a king with its fragrant taste. The contrast between the (superior) pleasures of the forest and the (inferior) pleasures of human society is explored by the story in terms of differing levels of aesthetic and sensual quality:

The combined scent of the bathing ointments,
garlands, liquor and perfume of the women
was dispelled by the fragrance of the fruit,
delightful to smell and swelling with virtues. (27.9 [2])

The king develops such a strong greed for the fruit that he searches for the tree and attacks the monkeys living in it.[19] This conflict between animals and humans (and between forest and society) is only resolved when the Bodhi·sattva saves his herd of monkeys by sacrificing his life to bring about their escape. The king is so impressed that he ceases his attack and the story concludes with the dying monkey instructing him on virtue. A similar resolution occurs in nearly all the stories in which animals or ascetics come into contact with ordinary human society:[20] after an initial conflict, the virtuous conduct of the animal or ascetic wins through and the king (or another human character) is instructed on moral conduct or on the benefits of the renunciate path.

In the previous volume, we already had cause to mention the importance of the theme of kingship in the "Garland of the Buddha's Past Lives." A similar emphasis is shown in the present volume, in which twelve of the fourteen stories either depict some form of instruction of kings or explore the notion of ideal kingship.[21] As is highlighted by 'The Birth-Story of Suta·soma' (31), a central duty of the ideal king (or in this story prince) is to dedicate himself to virtue and to convert the wicked to become good. Taking the Bodhi·sattva's self-sacrificial actions as a paradigm, as portrayed for example in 'The Birth-Story of the Great Monkey' (27), the righteous king should be a model of moral conduct for his people and practice a virtue based on compassion and non-violence, protecting his society and sacrificing himself for his subjects.

Although narratives such as 'The Birth-Story of Ayo·griha' (32) extol asceticism over the householder life, the ascetic life is not viewed as a necessary path for all. The king acts as a moral exemplar for society and is urged, as a layman, to support ascetics and brahmins with gifts (25.50 [29], 28.83 [49]). Nevertheless, the values that form the basis of proper kingship are essentially renunciate virtues based on non-desire and non-violence. As such, they fundamentally grate against conventional notions of kingship which focus on the pursuit of profit (*artha*) and on the acquisition and consolidation of power through violence.[22] In contrast to the Machiavellian type of king who follows the pragmatic teachings of the *Arthaśāstra*, the ideal Buddhist king should eschew politics and military power in favor of virtue:[23]

> *Neither power, treasury nor good policy*
> *can bring a king to the same position*
> *as he can reach through the path of virtue,*
> *however great his effort or expenses.* (22.151 [94])

The reader may well ask whether such an ideal is really possible. Can a king really give up violence and be a paradigm of compassion if he is to maintain power? One way of tackling this matter is to take an alternative approach from simply reading the text in terms of providing straightforward didactic messages. As STEVEN COLLINS has argued (1998: 414ff.), the tension between the ideal and the actual is inherent in the very nature of a renunciate ideology, particularly an ideology expressed through the normative medium of texts. Seeking both to transcend and inform the ordinary world, Buddhist renunciate values are, by necessity, engaged in a constantly oscillating dialectic with human society and kingship, involving both conflict and resolution. Given the inherent complexity of this relationship, while various Buddhist texts do espouse the notion of a non-violent, compassionate king, one need not necessarily take such statements solely at face value. Rather than treating such passages simply as offering genuine alternatives to kingship, one can, as COLLINS suggests, also view them as (often ironical) comments on actual kingship made from an ideological remove.

The "Garland of the Buddha's Past Lives" expresses a similar ambiguity regarding the Bodhi·sattva's virtue in general. In 'The Birth-Story of the Great Monkey' (27), the Bodhi·sattva's self-sacrifice for a community of monkeys is portrayed as a model of virtue to be followed by the king witnessing the event. Elsewhere, however, the text is at pains to stress the miraculous nature of the Bodhi·sattva's unique feats of virtue, asserting that they are "unable to be imitated" by others (Volume 1, preface, v.4). A paragon of virtue, the Bodhi·sattva thus acts both as an ultimate moral standard that shapes and informs the ordinary world and as a transcendent ideal whose exceptional and superior quality serves to inspire the intense devotion that lies at the heart of Arya·shura's work.

The Sanskrit Text

For stories 21–34 I have used HEINRICH KERN's edition (1891) as a base text, which I have then emended by referring to manuscript readings provided by PETER KHOROCHE in his "Towards a New Edition of Ārya·Śūra's Jātakamālā" (1987). I have particularly followed the readings of the earlier manuscripts N and T. For stories 33 and 34, I have benefited greatly from the text-critical comments of MICHAEL HAHN (2001). A list of all emendations made can be found at the end of the volume.

I am very grateful to ANDREW SKILTON for his helpful comments on the introduction and translation.

Notes

1 **Bodhi·sattva**: a person who vows to become a perfectly awakened Buddha by fulfilling the perfections (*pāramitā*). The word *bodhi/sattva* literally means "awakening being." K.R. NORMAN (1997: 104f.) argues that the word is a back formation from the Prakrit *bodhi/satta*, the Sanskrit equivalent of which is either *bodhi/ṣakta* or *bodhi/śakta*. These two compounds can be translated as "aspiring for awakening" (literally "attached to awakening") and "capable of awakening" respectively.

2 See also 28.95 [57]: "Those who are compassionate and great in reason are not afflicted by their own pain as much as by the pain of others."

3 See also 'The Birth-Story of the Great Monkey' (27), in which the Bodhi·sattva endures pain to save his troop of monkeys.

4 In 'The Birth-Story of the Antelope' (26), the Bodhi·sattva is, however, later betrayed by the person who declares these words.

Another notable story in which enmity is overcome by friendship is 'The Birth-Story of the Goose' (22), in which a hunter's aggressive intentions toward a flock of geese cease when he witnesses the devotion shown by a goose for his king (see especially 22.112 [65]). Here the king who ordered the capture of the geese is so impressed by the friendship shown by the pair of geese that he proclaims his own friendship for them (22.144 [88]): "May this friendship never be severed now that it has been embarked upon. Place your trust in me. For a union of noble beings never decays."

5 See also volume 1, 7.42–61 [20–31] and this volume 23.30 [13], 23.117 [62]–118 [63], 26.58 [30], 34.43 [22].

6 The propriety of Súmukha's devotion is, however, debated in a group of verses (22.56 [26]–72 [38]), in which the Bodhi·sattva argues that his general's actions are unpragmatic and will bring no "benefit" (*artha*), whereas Súmukha appeals to the authority of "virtue" (*dharma*). It is noteworthy that this context-free, absolutist form of morality advocated by Súmukha is usually the type of virtue espoused by the Bodhi·sattva in other stories.

7 See, for example, 24.18 [8], 25.40 [21], 26.16 [8]–17 [9], 27.39 [15]–56 [28], 29.68 [47]–69 [48], 30.30 [14], 30.35 [18], 30.44 [22], 31.178 [93].

8 See also the 'Birth-Story of Maitri·bala' (vol. 1, story 8) for a connection between the Bodhi·sattva's sacrifice of his body and his gift of the teaching as a Buddha. There the Bodhi·sattva's blood and flesh, eaten by five demons, is directly compared with the "ambrosia of the teaching of liberation" given by the Buddha at his first sermon to five ascetics (see v. 59 and the epilogue). This theme has particularly been analyzed by REIKO OHNUMA (2007: 199ff.).

9 Stories 22, 24, 25, 26, 27, 30, 33, 34. Stories 33 and 34 are different in style to the other animal stories, a fact that may point to the *Jātakamālā* being incomplete, or to the possibility of interpolation, or simply to a difference in literary technique. Apart from

their noticeably short length, neither story contains a description of the forest or a depiction of a clash between animals and humans, both of which are prominent themes in the other animal stories.

10 See, for example, vol. 1, 6.6–7, 15.6, 16.4 and this volume 22.95 [52], 25.27 [14], 25.32 [17], 27.4.

11 See 30.67 [38]: "This must be an elephant only in appearance. For he seems to uphold the fading conduct of the good!"

12 See also 22.39 (and 22.40 [19]–42 [21]), in which the virtuous goose Súmukha states: "The hearts of men are usually false whenever they display tender compassion. Fabricated courtesies and honeyed words conceal a vicious depravity."

13 See vol. 1, 6.3, 9.76–83, 9.106–107, 15.3 and this volume 21.16–19 [7], 24.3, 25.3, 26.3–5, 27.3–5, 28.9, 28.13 [5]–19 [11], 30.3. The forest is also, however, a place of danger for those unaccustomed to it. It is described, for example, as "terrifying with its wild perils" (24.55 [35]). This dangerous aspect is also expressed in 'The Birth-Story of Suta·soma' (31), where the forest is the home of the cannibal Kalmásha·pada.

14 The introduction to story 25 states: "Quiet from lack of contact with men, the region was home for various hordes of wild animals and abounded with trees and shrubs." See also the introduction to story 30: "A home for forest animals, the woods were blessed by a deep and broad lake, while a vast desert, devoid of trees, shrubs and water, concealed it from human habitation on all sides."

15 See vol. 1, 6.2 and this volume 25.3–5 [1], 33.31 [20], 34.45 [23]. The superiority of the ascetic forest life over the desire-based life of the householder is sometimes expressed through images of beauty. 'The Smaller Birth-Story of Bodhi' states (21.7, 21.16): "Moved by her affection for her husband, his wife also shaved off her hair. Freeing her body from the concerns of wearing superficial ornaments, she became adorned only by the glory of her virtue and natural appearance. [...] [She then] adorned the root

of a tree, illuminating it like a deity with the power of her beauty, focusing on a meditation practice taught by her husband."

16 See 22.19–33.

17 Royal hunts in forests also provide a means for animals or ascetics to encounter human beings. See, for example, story 25.

18 This similarity is conveyed by 'The Birth-Story of Suta·soma' (31), in which the idyllic description of a royal park closely resembles that of forests in other stories (31.10–12 [5]). In this story, there is a reversal of the normal contrast between the serene harmony of the forest and the desire-based violence of human society. Here a king's pleasure trip in his gardens is invaded by the attack of a forest cannibal, thereby conveying a contrast between the civilized pleasures of royal gardens and the unruly wilderness of the forest. The garden-forest motif can therefore vary its significance and function depending on the context. Parks or forests can also take on a divine significance through their association with Nándana, the garden of the gods (28.13 [5]).

19 The invasive nature of the king's actions is highlighted by the fact that his drums terrify the animals living in the forest as he approaches the tree (27.19).

20 These are: stories 21–27, 32. Story 28 is an exception in that the king who assaults the Bodhi·sattva is swallowed up into hell after refusing to lessen his hostility despite hearing the Bodhi·sattva's instruction. Here it is karma that provides a resolution to the conflict. However, a different resolution between the Bodhi·sattva and human beings is achieved at the end of the story when the Bodhi·sattva preaches to the king's ministers, who become his "disciples of virtue" (28.110 [69]). In story 30, the animal realm is again depicted as an idyllic sphere separate from human society, but here the Bodhi·sattva willingly sacrifices himself for a group of starving people and there is no conflict between him and human beings. The stories in which ascetics or animals directly come into contact with kings are: 21–23, 25–28, 32 (while in stories 24 and 30, the Bodhi·sattva as an animal encounters human characters

who are not kings). In story 32, the Bodhi·sattva is a prince who persuades his father to allow him to enter the forest as an ascetic.

21 See especially 22.115 [66]–119 [70], 22.151 [94]–156 [99], 23.118 [63]–128 [73], 24.62 [38]–66 [42], 25.44 [23]–50 [29], 26.76 [38]–83 [44], 27.42 [17]–63 [35], 28.69 [38]–79 [47], 29.71 [49]–80 [58], 30.25 [11]–27 [13], 31.106 [52]–111 [55], 32.33 [21]–64 [48]. Only stories 33 & 34 do not mention kings. While kingship is not a major issue in story 30, the Bodhi·sattva does criticize a king for immoral behavior in 30.25 [11]–27 [13]. In story 24 (24.62 [38]–66 [42]), it is not the Bodhi·sattva who instructs a king, but a man suffering from the bad karma of betraying the Bodhi·sattva's friendship.

22 Some passages refer to the "three pursuits" of virtue, profit and desire (22.119 [70]). However, virtue is always treated as the primary concern. See, for example, 29.75 [53]: "Turn your wealth into an instrument for virtue." The contrast between this ideal form of kingship and conventional kingship is highlighted by the amazed reactions of kings when they witness the Bodhi·sattva's virtue. See, for example, 27.42 [17]: "Ministers and other men serve their king. But it is not for the king to act for their sake. Why then did you sacrifice yourself for the sake of your dependents?"

23 See also 31.106 [52]–111 [55] for an attack on the pragmatic approach of politics (*nīti*).

Select Bibliography

COLLINS, S. 1998. *Nirvana and other Buddhist felicities: Utopias of the Pali Imaginaire*. Cambridge: Cambridge University Press.

EDGERTON, F. 1953. *Buddhist Hybrid Sanskrit Grammar and Dictionary*. 2 vols. New Haven: Yale University Press.

HAHN, M. 2001. 'Text-critical Remarks on Āryaśūra's Mahiṣa- and Śatapattrajātaka.' *Le Parole e i Marmi: Studi in onore di Raniero Gnoli nel suo 70 compleanno*. Ed. RAFFAELE TORELLA Roma:

Istituto Italiano per l'Africa e l'Oriente. Serie Orientale Roma XCII. 377–397.

KERN, H. (ed.). 1891. *The Jātaka-mālā: Stories of Buddha's Former Incarnations, Otherwise Entitled Bodhi·sattva-avadāna-mālā, by Ārya-çūra.* Cambridge: Harvard University Press (repr. 1914, 1943).

KHOROCHE, P. 1987. *Towards a New Edition of Ārya-Śūra's Jātakamālā.* Bonn: Indica et Tibetica Verlag.

——— (trans.). 1989. *Once the Buddha Was a Monkey: Ārya Śūra's Jātakamālā.* Chicago and London: The University of Chicago Press.

MEILAND, JUSTIN. 2009. *Garland of the Buddha's Past Lives.* Vol 1. New York: JJC Foundation and New York University Press.

MONIER-WILLIAMS, M. 1899. *A Sanskrit-English Dictionary.* Oxford: Oxford University Press.

NORMAN, K. R. 1997. *A Philological Approach to Buddhism: The Bukkyō Dendō Kyōkai Lectures 1994.* London: Routledge.

OHNUMA, R. 2007. *Head, Eyes, Flesh, and Blood: Giving Away the Body in Indian Buddhist Literature.* New York: Columbia University Press.

SENART, É (ed.). 1882–97. *Le Mahāvastu.* 3 vols. Paris: Imprimerie Nationale.

SPEYER, J. S. (trans.). 1895. *The Jātakamālā, or Garland of Birth-Stories of Āryaśūra.* London: Henry Frowde.

WELLER, F. (ed.) 1955. *Die Fragmente der Jātakamālā in der Turfansammlung der Berliner Akademie.* Deutsche Akademie der Wissenschaften, Institut für Orientforschung, Veröffentlichung Nr. 24, Berlin.

All Pali text citations refer to editions of the Pali Text Society.

GARLAND OF THE BUDDHA'S PAST LIVES
VOLUME II

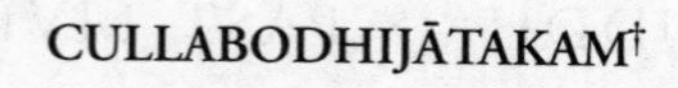

CULLABODHIJĀTAKAM†

STORY 21

THE SMALLER BIRTH-STORY OF BODHI

21.1 KRODHA | VIJAYĀC† chatrūn upaśamayati; vardhayaty eva tv anyathā.

tad|yath" ânuśrūyate.

Bodhisattvaḥ kila Mahā | sattvaḥ kasmiṃś cin mahati brāhmaṇa|kule guṇ'|âbhyāsa|māhātmyād ati|vṛddha|yaśasi pratiniyata|samṛddhi|guṇe rāja|sat|kṛte daivavat† saṃmate lokasya janma pratilebhe.

sa kālānām† atyayen' âbhivṛddhaḥ kṛta|saṃskāra|karmā śruta|guṇ'|âbhyāsād a|cireṇa† vidvat|sadassu prakāśa|nāmā babhūva.

21.5 kīrtir vidvat|sadassv eva viduṣāṃ pravijṛmbhate,
ratna|jñeṣv iva ratnānāṃ, śūrāṇāṃ samareṣv iva. [1]

atha sa mah"|ātmā kṛta|pravrajyā|paricayatvāt† pūrva| janmasu sv|abhyasta|dharma|saṃjñatvāt prajñ"|âvadāta| matitvāc ca na gehe ratim upalebhe. sa kāmān vigraha| vivāda|vaira|vairasya† prācuryād, rāja|caur'|ôdaka|dahana| vipriya|dāyāda|sādhāraṇatvād a|tṛpti|janakatvād an|eka| doṣ'|āyatanatvāc ca sa|viṣam iv' ânnam ātma|kāmaḥ parityajya saṃhṛta|keśa|śmaśru|śobhaḥ kāṣāya|vivarṇa|vāsāḥ parityakta|gṛha|veṣa|vibhramaḥ pravrajyā|vinaya|niyama| śriyam aśiśriyat.

By conquering anger, enemies are quelled. By doing the opposite, enemies are increased. 21.1

Tradition has handed down the following story.

The Bodhi·sattva, that Great Being,* is said to have once taken his birth in an eminent brahmin family that was honored by the king and esteemed by the people as if it were a god. The family's magnificent practice of virtue meant it enjoyed an extremely large fame and secure wealth.

In the course of time the Bodhi·sattva grew up and, after undergoing all the sacred rites, he quickly became renowned among learned assemblies for his dedication to knowledge and virtue.

The fame of the wise expands 21.5
among learned assemblies,
like the fame of gems among jewelers
or the reputation of heroes on battlefields.

The Great One* had become intimate with the ascetic path and had thoroughly developed his moral awareness in his previous lives. This, combined with the fact that his mind was cleansed by wisdom, meant he took no delight in the household life. Desires were full of strife, disagreement, hatred and repugnance. Associated with kings, thieves, floods, fires and hostile kinsmen, they produced discontent and were a source of multiple evils. Desiring spiritual matters instead, he abandoned sensual pleasures as if they were poisoned food. Shaving off his fine hair and beard, he cast aside the illusory graces of his household clothes and put on some dreary-looking saffron robes,

tad|anurāga|vaśa|gā c' âsya patnī keśān avatāry' āhārya|vibhūṣaṇ'|ôdvahana|nirvyāpāra|śarīrā sva|rūpa|guṇa|śobhā|vibhūṣitā kāṣāya|vastra|saṃvīta|tanur anupravavrāja.

atha Bodhisattvas tapo|van'|ânugamana|vyavasāyam asya vidtvā tapo|van'|âdhyāsan'|âyogyatāṃ ca, strī|saukumāryasy' âvocad enāṃ:

«bhadre, darśitas tvay" âyam asmad|anurāga|svabhāvaḥ. tad alam asmad|anugamana|vyavasāyena† te. yatr' âiva tv anyāḥ pravrajitāḥ prativasanti tatra bhavatyā† tābhir eva sārdhaṃ pratirūpaṃ vastuṃ syāt. dur|abhisaṃbhavāni hy araṇy'|āyatanāni. paśya:

21.10 śmaśāna|śūny'|ālaya|parvateṣu
vaneṣu ca vyāla|mṛg'|ākuleṣu
niketa|hīnā yatayo vasanti
yatr' âiva c' âstaṃ ravir abhyupaiti. [2]

dhyān'|ôdyamād eka|carāś ca nityaṃ
strī|darśanād apy apavṛtta|bhāvāḥ.
nivartituṃ tena matiṃ kuruṣva.
ko 'rthas tav' ânena pariśrameṇa?»† [3]

sā niyatam enam anugamana|kṛta|niścayā bāṣp'|ôparudhyamāna|nayanā kiṃ cid īdṛśaṃ pratyuvāca:

committing himself to the glory of ascetic disciplines and restraints.

Moved by her affection for her husband, his wife also shaved off her hair. Freeing her body from the concerns of superficial ornaments, she became adorned only by the glory of her virtue and natural appearance. Clothed in saffron robes, she followed her husband into the ascetic life.

When the Bodhi·sattva realized that his wife intended to follow him into the ascetic forest, he addressed her as follows, knowing that a woman's tender nature is unsuited to a life of austerity in the forest:

"You have shown your innate affection toward me, my lady. But stop being so determined to follow me. It would be more suitable if you lived with other ascetic women. For forests are difficult to dwell in. Consider this:

Abandoning their houses, 21.10
ascetics dwell wherever they are at sunset:
cremation grounds, deserted areas, mountains,
or forests teeming with fierce wild beasts.

Constantly roaming alone, intent on meditation,
they withdraw from the sight of women.
So lend your mind toward turning back.
What need have you for such hardship?"

But his wife had already firmly resolved to follow the Bodhi·sattva and she replied somewhat as follows, her eyes welling with tears:

«yadi me śrama|buddhiḥ syāt
tav' ânugaman'|ôtsave,
kim ity evaṃ prapadyeya
duḥkhaṃ tava ca vi|priyam? [4]

yat tu n' âiva samarth" âsmi
vartituṃ rahitā tvayā,
ity ājñ"|âti|kramam imaṃ
tvaṃ mama kṣantum arhasi!» [5]

21.15 iti sā dvis trir† apy ucyamānā yadā n' âiv' êcchati† sma nivartituṃ, tato Bodhisattva upekṣā|nibhṛta|matir asyāṃ babhūva.

sa tay" ânugamyamānaś cakravāka iva cakravākyā grāma| nagara|nigamān anuvicaran kadā cit kṛta|bhakta|kṛtyaḥ kasmiṃś cit pravivikte śrīmati nānā|taru|gahan'|ôpaśobhite ghana|pracchāye kṛt'|ôpakāra iva kva cit kva cid dinakara| kiraṇa|candrakair nānā|kusuma|rajo|'vakīrṇa|dharaṇi|tale† śucau van'|ôddeśe dhyāna|vidhim anuṣṭhāya sāy'|âhna| samaye vyutthāya samādheḥ pāṃsu|kūlāni sīvyati sma. s" âpi pravrajitā tasy' âiva n' âti|dūre vṛkṣa|mūlam upaśobhayamānā devat" êva svena vapuṣaḥ prabhāveṇa virājamānā tad|upadiṣṭena manas|kāra|vidhinā dhyāyati sma.

atha tatratyo rājā vasanta|kāla|janit'|âbhyadhika|kisalaya| śobhāni bhramad|bhramara|madhukarī|gaṇ'|ôpakūjitāni pramatta|kokila|kula|kilakilāni prahasita|kamala|kuvalay'| âlaṃkṛt'|âbhilaṣaṇīya|jal'|āśayāni vividha|kusuma|saṃmoda|

"If the joy of following you
were a laborious notion,
why would I pursue something
painful to me and disagreeable to you?

But as I am incapable
of living without you,
please pardon me if
I defy your orders!"

21.15 And although he spoke to her this way two or three times, she was still unwilling to turn back. So the Bodhi·sattva decided to show her equanimity.

Followed by his wife as a *chakra·vaka** bird is followed by its mate, he wandered through villages, cities and towns until one day, after he had eaten, he practiced meditation in an isolated spot in the forest. The area was splendid and immaculate and adorned by various trees and thickets. Sun rays, resembling attentive servants, filtered through the thick shade here and there like moonlight, and the ground was sprinkled with the pollen of various flowers. When it turned to evening time, the Bodhi·sattva rose from his meditation and stitched together robes made up of rags from dust-heaps. Not far from him, his ascetic wife adorned the root of a tree, illuminating it like a deity with the power of her beauty and focusing on a meditation practice taught to her by her husband.

At that time a king happened to arrive in the area while making a tour of the forest groves. The spring season had produced an abundance of delightful sprigs and the woods buzzed with swarms of bees roaming around making honey.

gandh'|âdhivāsita|sukha|pavanāny upavanāni samanuvicaraṃs taṃ deśam upajagāma.

vicitra|puṣpa|stabak'|ôjjvalāni
kṛta|cchadān' îva vasanta|lakṣmyā
vācāla|puṃs|kokila|barhiṇāni
saroruh'|ākīrṇa|jal'|āśayāni [6]

samudbhavat|komala|śādvalāni
vanāni matta|bhramar'|ārutāni
ākrīḍa|bhūtāni Manobhavasya
draṣṭuṃ bhavaty eva manaḥ|praharṣaḥ. [7]

21.20 atha sa rājā sa|vinayam abhigamya Bodhisattvaṃ kṛta|pratisaṃmodana|kathas tatr' âik'|ânte nyaṣīdata. sa tāṃ pravrajitām ati|manohara|darśanām abhivīkṣya tasyā rūpa|śobhayā samākṣipyamāṇa|hṛdayo, «nūnam asy' êyaṃ saha|dharma|cāriṇ"» îty avetya lola|svabhāvatvāt tad|apaharaṇ'|ôpāyaṃ vimamarśa.

śruta|prabhāvaḥ sa tapo|dhanānāṃ
śāp'|ârciṣaḥ krodha|hut'|âśanasya
saṃkṣipta|dhairyo 'pi Manobhavena
n' âsminn avajñā|rabhaso babhūva. [8]

tasya buddhir abhavat: «tapaḥ|prabhāvam asya jñātvā śakyam atra tad yuktaṃ pravartituṃ, n' ânyathā. yady ayam asyāṃ saṃrāga|vaktavya|matir, vyaktam asmin na tapaḥ|prabhāvo 'sti. atha tu† vīta|rāgaḥ syān mand'|âpekṣo vā, tato 'smin saṃbhāvyaṃ tapaḥ|prabhāva|māhātmyam.»

Charming ponds were adorned with smiling lotuses and water-lilies, while flocks of wanton cuckoos cried out with joy. Soothing breezes blew, suffused with the fragrant scents of various flowers.

Clusters of multi-colored flowers blazed,
as if draped by the glory of spring.
Male cuckoos and peacocks sang.
Ponds were strewn with lotuses.

Fresh soft grass grew.
Drunken bees hummed.
It captivated the heart to see
these playgrounds of Desire.

The king courteously approached the Bodhi·sattva and sat down to one side after the usual friendly words of greeting had been exchanged. But when he saw the captivating sight of the ascetic lady, his heart was thrown into turmoil by her glorious beauty and his greedy nature made him consider how to kidnap her, even though he realized she was the Bodhi·sattva's companion in virtue. 21.20

Though his composure was destroyed by Desire,
he did not rashly insult the ascetic.
For he had heard of the power of such austerity-rich men,
how their blazing fury could make fiery curses.

"I will only know how to act after I ascertain his ascetic power," the king reflected. "If his mind is ruled by passion for her, then he clearly possesses no ascetic power. But if he is devoid of passion, or shows only little regard for her, then he is likely to have enormous ascetic power."

iti vicintya sa rājā tapaḥ|prabhāva|jijñāsayā Bodhisattvaṃ hit'|âiṣi|vad uvāca:

«bhoḥ pravrajita, pracura|dhūrta|sāhasika|puruṣe 'smiṃl loke na yuktam atra|bhavato nir|ākrandeṣu vaneṣv evaṃ pratirūpay" ânayā saha|dharma|cāriṇyā saha vicaritum. asyāṃ hi te kaś cid aparādhyamāno niyatam asmān apy upākrośa†|bhājanī|kuryāt. paśya:

21.25 evaṃ vivikteṣu tapaḥ|kṛśaṃ tvāṃ
dharmeṇa sārdhaṃ paribhūya kaś cit
imāṃ prasahy' âpahared yadā te,
śokāt paraṃ kiṃ bata tatra kuryāḥ? [9]

roṣa|prasaṅgo hi manaḥ|pramāthī,
dharm'|ôpamardād yaśasaś ca hantā.
vasatv iyaṃ tena jan'|ânta eva.
strī|saṃnikarṣeṇa ca kiṃ yatīnām?» [10]

Bodhisattva uvāca: «yuktam āha mahā|rājaḥ. api tu śrūyatāṃ yad evaṃ|gate 'rthe pratipadyeya:†

syād atra me yaḥ pratikūla|vartī
darp'|ôdbhavād a|pratisaṃkhyayā vā,
vyaktaṃ na mucyeta sa jīvato me,
dhārā|ghanasy' êva ghanasya reṇuḥ.» [11]

atha sa rājā «tīvr'|âpekṣo 'yam asyāṃ, tapaḥ|prabhāva|hīna» ity avajñāya taṃ Mahā|sattvaṃ tad|apāya|nirāśaṅkaḥ kāma|rāga|vaśa|gaḥ strī|saṃdarśinaḥ† puruṣān samādideśa: «gacchat', êmāṃ† pravrajitām antaḥ|puraṃ praveśayat'» êti.

Pondering the matter this way, the king addressed the Bodhi·sattva to ascertain his ascetic power under the pretence of being concerned for his welfare:

"Venerable ascetic, in a world full of rogues and reckless men, it is not right for you to wander these unprotected forests with such a beautiful companion in virtue. For if anyone were to wrong her, I would certainly be blamed. Consider this:

So weakened are you by austerities, 21.25
if someone insulted you and your virtue
and snatched this woman away by force,
what else could you do but grieve?

Attachment to anger destroys the mind,
ruining fame by violating virtue.
Let this woman live in the realm of people.
For what use is female contact to ascetics?"

"Your Majesty speaks fitting words," the Bodhi·sattva replied. "But listen to how I would behave in such circumstances:

If anyone were to offend me
in a surge of pride or thoughtlessness,
they would never escape me while I live,
like dust cannot escape a cloud full of rain."

Concluding that the Bodhi·sattva had a strong regard for the woman and that his ascetic power must be slight, the king formed a low opinion of the Great Being and lost any fear of doing him wrong. Overwhelmed by passion and desire, he ordered the servants in charge of the palace women to go and convey the ascetic lady into his harem.

21.30 tad upaśrutya sā pravrajitā vyāla|mṛg'|âbhidrut" êva vana|mṛgī bhaya|viṣāda|viklava|mukhī bāṣp'|ôparudhyamāna|nayanā gadgadāyamāna|kaṇṭhī tat tad ārti|vaśād vilalāpa:

«lokasya nām' ārti|parājitasya
parāyaṇaṃ bhūmi|patiḥ pit" êva.
sa eva yasya tv a|nay'|āvahaḥ syād,
ākrandanaṃ kasya nu tena kāryam. [12]

bhraṣṭ'|âdhikārā bata loka|pālā!
na santi vā! mṛtyu|vaśaṃ gatā vā!
na trātum ārtān iti ye sa|yatnā.
dharmo 'pi manye śruti|mātram eva! [13]

kiṃ vā surair me, bhagavān yad evaṃ
mad|bhāga|dheyair dhṛta|mauna eva.
paro 'pi tāvan nanu rakṣaṇīyaḥ
pāp'|ātmabhir vipratikṛṣyamāṇaḥ. [14]

‹naśy'!› êti śāp'|âśanin" âbhimṛṣṭaḥ
śailo 'pi yasya† smaraṇīya|mūrtiḥ,
itthaṃ|gatāyām api tasya maunaṃ.
tath" âpi jīvāmy ati|manda|bhāgyā.† [15]

21.35 pāpā kṛpā|pātratarā na c' âham†
evaṃ|vidhām āpadam abhyupetā?
ārteṣu kāruṇyamayī pravṛttis
tapo|dhanānāṃ kim ayaṃ na mārgaḥ? [16]

When the ascetic lady heard this command, her face became distraught with fear and despair, resembling a forest deer chased by a ferocious wild beast. Her eyes welled up with tears and her throat stuttered as she uttered various laments in distress: 21.30

"Like a father, the king protects
people afflicted by distress.
But if the king wrongs a person,
to whom should one appeal then?

The world-guardians must have fallen from office!
Perhaps they do not exist! Or are dead!
For they make no effort to protect the distressed.
Morality itself is, I believe, but a rumor.

But why mention the gods?
My lord stays silent, despite my fate.
When wronged by evil beings,
even a stranger should surely be protected.

He could transform a mountain into a memory
by striking it with his thunder-curse of 'Perish!'.
Yet he stays silent, despite my plight.
Such is the small fortune I have in life.

Perhaps I am evil and unworthy of pity, 21.35
having fallen on this misfortune?
But is it not the path of ascetics to act
with compassion toward those in distress?

śaṅke tav' âdy' âpi tad eva citte,
nivartyamān" âsmi na yan nivṛttā.
tav' â|priyeṇ' âpi may" ēpsitaṃ yad
ātma|priyaṃ, hā tad idaṃ kathaṃ me?» [17]

iti tāṃ pravrajitāṃ karuṇa|vilāp'|ākrandita|rudita|mātra|parāyaṇāṃ te rāja|samādiṣṭāḥ puruṣā yānam āropya paśyata eva tasya Mahasattvasy' ântaḥ|purāya ninyuḥ. Bodhisattvo 'pi pratisaṃkhyāna|balāt pratinudya krodha|balaṃ, tath" âiva pāṃsu|kūlāni niḥ|saṃkṣobhaḥ praśānta|cetāḥ sīvyati sma. ath' âinaṃ sa rāj" ôvāca:

«a|marṣa|roṣ'|âbhinipīḍit'†|âkṣaraṃ
tad uccakair garjitam ūrjitaṃ tvayā!
hṛtāṃ ca paśyann api tāṃ var'|ānanām
a|śakti|dīna|praśamo 'sy avasthitaḥ. [18]

tad darśaya svaṃ bhuja|pauruṣaṃ† vā,
tejas tapaḥ|saṃśraya|saṃbhṛtaṃ vā!
ātma|pramāṇa|grahaṇ'|ân|abhijño
vyartha|pratijño hy adhikaṃ na bhāti!» [19]

21.40 Bodhisattva uvāca: «a|vyartha|pratijñam eva māṃ viddhi, mahā|rāja.

yo 'bhūn mam' âtra pratikūla|vartī,
vispandamāno 'pi sa me na muktaḥ,
prasahya nītaḥ praśamaṃ mayā ca.†
tasmād yath"|ârth" âiva mama pratijñā!» [20]

I fear you still brood over the time
I refused to turn back, against your wishes.
Is this the goal of my desires,
dear to me but unpleasant to you?"

So the ascetic woman grieved: after all, weeping, wailing and pitiful laments were her only recourse. The servants, however, followed the king's orders by placing her on a carriage under the Great Being's very eyes and taking her away to the harem. The Bodhi·sattva, meanwhile, had suppressed any onslaught of anger through the force of his calm equanimity. With a tranquil mind, he continued to sew his ragged robes, as untroubled as before, whereupon the king addressed him with the following words:

"Earlier you uttered high and mighty boasts,
words pummeled by anger and fury!
But when you see this fair lady snatched away,
you remain sad and quiet with impotency!*

Show me the strength of your arms,
or the might of your ascetic power!
For, unaware of their measure,
false vow-makers have no glory at all!"

"You should know that I have kept my vow, great king," the Bodhi·sattva replied. 21.40

"I did not let him go,
though he struggled against me.
Forcefully calming him,
I have kept my vow."

atha sa rājā tena Bodhisattvasya dhairy'|âtiśaya|vyañjakena praśamena samutpādita|tapasvi|guṇa|saṃbhāvanaś cintām āpede: «anyad ev' ânena brāhmaṇen' âbhisaṃdhāya bhāṣitam, tad a|vijñāya c' âsmābhiś† cāpala|kṛtam idam,» iti jāta|pratyavamarśo Bodhisattvam uvāca:

«ko 'nyas tav' âbhūt pratikūla|vartī
yo visphurann eva na te vimuktaḥ,
reṇuḥ samudyann iva toya|dena?
kaś c' ôpanītaḥ praśamaṃ tvay" âtra?» [21]

Bodhisattva uvāca:
21.45 «śṛṇu, mahā|rāja:

jāte na dṛśyate yasminn,
a|jāte sādhu dṛśyate,
abhūn me sa, na muktaś ca
krodhaḥ sv'|āśraya|bādhanaḥ. [22]

yena jātena nandanti
narāṇām a|hit'|âiṣiṇaḥ
so 'bhūn me, na vimuktaś ca
krodhaḥ śātrava|nandanaḥ. [23]

utpadyamāne yasmiṃś ca
sad|arthaṃ na prapadyate,
tam andhī|karaṇaṃ, rājann,
ahaṃ krodham aśīśamam. [24]

The Bodhi·sattva's calmness clearly demonstrated his outstanding fortitude. Filled with respect for the ascetic virtue the Bodhi·sattva displayed, the king had this thought: "This brahmin must have meant something else by his words and I must have acted rashly in ignorance of this." Reflecting this way, he addressed the Bodhi·sattva with the following words:

"Who is this other you did not release,
though he struggled against you,
like rising dust cannot escape a raincloud?
Whom did you compel to be calm just now?"

The Bodhi·sattva replied:
"Listen, Your Majesty: 21.45

When he appears, one is blind.
When he disappears, one can clearly see.
He rose in me but I did not release him.
He is anger, an affliction of his own support.

When he appears in men,
their ill-wishers rejoice.
He rose in me but I did not release him.
He is anger, a delight to one's enemies.

When he surfaces,
no good is done.
Anger causes blindness
and I quelled him.

yen' âbhibhūtaḥ kuśalaṃ jahāti,
prāptād api bhraśyata eva c' ârthāt,
taṃ roṣam ugra|graha|vaikṛt'|ābhaṃ
sphurantam ev' ânayam antam antaḥ. [25]

21.50 kāṣṭhād yath" âgniḥ parimathyamānād
udeti tasy' âiva parābhavāya,
mithyā|vikalpaiḥ samudīryamāṇas
tathā narasy' ātma|vadhāya roṣaḥ [26]

dahanam iva vijṛmbhamāṇa|raudraṃ
śamayati yo hṛdaya|jvaraṃ na roṣam,
‹laghur ayam› iti hīyate 'sya kīrtiḥ
kumuda|sakh" îva śaśi|prabhā prabhāte. [27]

para|jana|dur|itāny a|cintayitvā
ripum iva paśyati yas tu roṣam eva,
vikasati niyamena tasya kīrtiḥ
śaśina iv' âbhinavasya maṇḍala|śrīḥ. [28]

iyam aparā ca roṣasya mahā|doṣatā:

na bhāty alaṃkāra|guṇ'|ânvito 'pi
krodh'|âgninā saṃhṛta|varṇa|śobhaḥ.
sa|roṣa|śalye hṛdaye ca duḥkhaṃ
mah"|ârha|śayy"|âṅka|gato 'pi śete. [29]

21.55 vismṛtya c' ātma|kṣama|siddhi|pakṣaṃ
roṣāt prayāty eva tad utpathena,
nihīyate yena yaśo|'rtha|siddhyā
tāmisra|pakṣ'|êndur iv' ātma|lakṣmyā. [30]

Afflicted by him, one abandons virtue,
losing any benefit one has attained.
Anger is a hideous deformed monster.
I crushed it though it quivered inside me!

When rubbed, wood produces fire, 21.50
leading merely to its own destruction.
So false conceptions stir anger in a man,
leading to his own ruin.

If a man cannot calm the feverous rage
swelling violently like a fire in his heart,
he will be slighted and his reputation will wane,
like moonlight, the friend of lilies, wanes at dawn.

But if, unconcerned by the dangers of others,
a man views anger alone as his enemy,
his reputation will certainly shine
like the glorious sphere of the new moon.

Anger also has these other great faults:

A man is never handsome, however adorned,
when anger's fire steals away his good looks.
When his heart is wounded by anger's barb,
he sleeps uneasily, though on a luxurious bed.

Anger makes him forget how to be happy. 21.55
Traveling along the wrong path instead,
he loses his fame and welfare, like the moon
loses its luster in the dark half of the month.

roṣeṇa gacchaty a|naya|prapātaṃ
nivāryamāṇo 'pi suhṛj|janena.
prāyeṇa vairasya jaḍatvam eti
hit'|â|hit'|âvekṣaṇa|manda|buddhiḥ. [31]

krodhāc ca sātmī|kṛta|pāpa|karmā
śocaty apāyeṣu samā|śatāni.
ataḥ paraṃ kiṃ ripavaś ca kuryus
tīvr'|âpakār'|ôddhata|manyavo 'pi? [32]

antaḥ|sapatnaḥ kopo 'yaṃ, tad evaṃ vidito† mama.
tasy' âvalepa|prasaraṃ kaḥ pumān marṣayiṣyati? [33]

ato na muktaḥ kopo me
visphurann api cetasi;
ity an|artha|karaṃ śatruṃ
ko hy upekṣitum arhati?» [34]

21.60 atha sa rājā tena tasy' âdbhutena praśama|guṇena hṛdaya|grāhakeṇa ca vacas" âbhiprasādita|matir uvāca:

«anurūpaḥ śamasy' âsya
tav' âyaṃ vacana|kramaḥ.
bahun" âtra† kim uktena?
vañcitās tvad|a|darśinaḥ.» [35]

ity abhipraśasy' âinam abhisṛty' âiv' âsya pādayor nyapatad, atyaya†|deśanāṃ ca cakre. tāṃ ca pravrajitāṃ kṣamayitvā vyasarjayat,† paricārakaṃ c' ātmānaṃ Bodhisattvasya niryātayām āsa.

Anger makes him fall into a precipice of ruin,
however his friends try to hold him back.
He often becomes senseless with hatred,
his wits slow in judging good from bad.

Anger makes evil ingrained in him
and he grieves for centuries in hell.
Can enemies do any worse than this,
even when enraged by bitter injuries?

This much I know:
anger is a foe inside us.
Who can endure
its haughty advance?

That is why I did not release my anger,
though it throbbed in my mind,
for who would be indifferent
to such a harmful enemy?"

The king was gladdened by the Bodhi·sattva's virtuous serenity and by his words that so captivated the heart and said: 21.60

"Your words suit
your tranquility.
But why be longwinded?
Blind to you, I was led astray."

Eulogizing the Bodhi·sattva this way, the king went forward, prostrated himself at his feet and confessed his transgression. Begging forgiveness from the ascetic woman, he released her and offered himself to the Bodhi·sattva as a servant.

tad evaṃ, krodha|vijayāc† chatrūn upaśamayati, vardhayaty eva tv anyathā. iti krodha|vijaye† yatnaḥ kāryaḥ.

«evam a|vaireṇa vairāṇi śāmyanti, saṃyamataś ca vairaṃ na cīyate. evaṃ c' ôbhayor arthaṃ caraty a|krodhana,» ity evam|ādiṣu kṣam"|ânuśaṃsā|pratisaṃyukteṣu sūtreṣu vācyam. krodh'|ādīnava|kathāyāṃ Tathāgata|māhātmye c' êti.

In this way, by conquering anger, enemies are quelled. By doing the opposite, enemies are increased. One should therefore strive to quell anger.

This story should be narrated when dealing with discourses that praise forbearance in ways such as the following: "By feeling no hatred enmities are appeased, and by restraining oneself hatred does not accumulate. A man without anger thereby acquires benefit in both regards."* And it should also be narrated when discussing the faults of anger and the magnificence of the Tatha·gata.*

HAṂSAJĀTAKAM

STORY 22

THE BIRTH-STORY OF THE GOOSE

22.1 VINIPĀTA|GATĀNĀM api satāṃ vṛttaṃ n' âlam anukartum† a|sat|puruṣāḥ, prāg eva su|gati|sthānām. tad|yath" ânuśrūyate.

Bodhisattvaḥ kila Mānase mahā|sarasi n'|âika|śata|sahasra|vipula|saṃkhyasya† mahato haṃsa|yūthasy' âdhipatir Dhṛtarāṣṭro nāma haṃsa|rājo babhūva.

tasya nay'|â|naya|parijñāna|nipuṇa|matir viprakṛṣṭa|gocara|smṛti|prabhāvaḥ ślāghanīya|kula|tilaka|bhūto dākṣya|dākṣiṇya|vinaya|bhūṣaṇaḥ sthira|śuci|śīla|vṛtta|cāritraḥ śūraḥ† kheda|sahiṣṇur a|pramādī samara|vidhi|viśāradaḥ† svāmy|anurāga|sumukhaḥ Sumukho nāma haṃsa|senā|patir† babhūva. āry'|Ānanda|sthaviras tena samayena.

22.5 tau paras|para|prema|guṇ'|āśrayāj jvalitatara|guṇa|prabhāvāv† ācārya†|śiṣya|mukhyāv iva pariśeṣaṃ śiṣya|gaṇaṃ, pitṛ|jyeṣṭha|putrāv iva ca śeṣaṃ† putra|gaṇaṃ, tadd haṃsa|yūtham ubhaya|loka|hit'|ôdayeṣv artheṣu samyag|niveśayamānau tat|pratyakṣiṇāṃ deva|nāga|yakṣa|vidyādhara|tapasvināṃ paraṃ vismayam upajahratuḥ.

tāv āsatur haṃsa|gaṇasya tasya
śreyaḥ|śarīr'|ôdvahan'|âika|kāryau,
nabho|gatasy' êva vihaṃ|gamasya
pakṣau śarīr'|ôdvahan'|âika|kāryau. [1]

EVEN WHEN THEY ARE IN TROUBLE, the virtuous behave in ways that cannot be imitated by the bad, let alone when their situation is good. 22.1

Tradition has handed down the following story.

The Bodhi·sattva is said to have once lived as a royal goose named Dhrita·rashtra. Ruling over a huge flock of geese, numbering several hundreds and thousands, he lived in the large lake called Mánasa, "Mind Lake."

Dhrita·rashtra had a general called Súmukha. Expert in discerning right policy from wrong, Súmukha was vigilant over a wide area of land. Like an ornament on the forehead of his exemplary family, he was adorned by cleverness, skill and decency. His conduct was constant, pure and moral and he was able to endure fatigue and was never negligent. Brave, he was skilled in the ways of war and was devoted to his master. This general was the noble venerable Anánda at that time.*

The virtue of these two geese blazed all the more brightly because of the remarkable love they showed each other. Just as a teacher might train his other pupils with his chief disciple, or a father might train his other sons with his eldest son, so they duly guided the flock of geese in matters leading to their increased welfare in both this world and the next, filling the onlooking gods, nagas, yakshas, vidya·dharas, and ascetics with utter wonder.* 22.5

The two worked as one in upholding
the body of bliss for the flock of geese,
just as two wings work as one in upholding
the body of a bird as it flies in the sky.

evaṃ tābhyāṃ tad anugṛhyamāṇaṃ haṃsa|yūthaṃ jagad iva dharm'|ârtha|vistarābhyāṃ parāṃ vṛddhim avāpa. tena ca tat saraḥ parāṃ śobhāṃ babhāra.

kala|nūpura|nādena haṃsa|yūthena tena tat
puṇḍarīka|vanen' êva reje saṃcāriṇā saraḥ. [2]

kva cit pravisṛtair haṃsaiḥ kva cid viṣama|saṃhataiḥ
chinn'|âbhra|lava|citrasya jahāra nabhasaḥ śriyam. [3]

22.10 atha tasya haṃs'|âdhipateḥ sarva|sattva|hita|pravṛtti|sumukhasya† ca senā|pater guṇ'|âtiśaya|prabhāva|vismita|manasaḥ siddha'|rṣi|vidyādhara|daivata|gaṇās tayoḥ kīrty|āśrayābhiḥ kathābhis tatra tatr' âbhiremire:

«uttapta|cāmīkara|saṃnikāśaṃ
śrīmad vapur. vyakta|pad'|âkṣarā vāk.
dharm'|âbhijāto vinayo nayaś ca.
kāv apy amū kevala|haṃsa|veṣau. [4]

guṇa|prakāśair apamatsaraiḥ sā
kīrtis tayor dikṣu vitanyamānā
śraddheyatām ity agaman nṛ|pāṇāṃ
sadassu yat prābhṛtavac cacāra.» [5]

tena ca samayena Brahmadatto nām' ânyatamo Vārāṇasyāṃ rājā babhūva. sa tāṃ haṃs'|âdhipateḥ sa|senā|pater† guṇ'|âtiśay'|āśrayāṃ kathāṃ pratyayit'†|âmātya|dvija|vṛddhaiḥ sadasi saṃstūyamānām a|sakṛd upaśrutya tayor

The flock of geese prospered under their favor, just as the world prospers through a profusion of virtue and wealth. And as a result the lake bore an appearance of great beauty.

The flock of geese roaming
like a floating bed of lotuses,
crooning softly like tinkling anklets,
made the lake look radiant.

As the geese spread out here and there,
clustered in groups of varying size,
the lake took on the beauty of the sky
dappled with pieces of broken cloud.

22.10 Amazed by the power of the exceptional virtue shown by the king of geese and also by his general, who was intent on the welfare of all beings, troops of siddhas,* seers, vidya·dharas and gods delighted in discussing the fame of the two geese:

"Their glorious bodies are like refined gold.
They speak using articulate words.
Their modesty and judgment arise from virtue.
Whatever they are, they are geese only in guise.

Unjealous beings proclaim their virtue,
spreading their fame in every direction
until it roams through assemblies like an offering,
becoming an object of faith for kings."

At that time a king called Brahma·datta ruled in Varánasi. This monarch had repeatedly heard trustworthy ministers and brahmin elders in his assembly eulogize the exceptional virtues of the royal goose and his general and had

darśanaṃ pratyabhivṛddha|kautūhalo 'n|eka†|śāstr'|âbhyāsa|nipuṇa|matīn sacivān uvāca:

«parimṛśyatāṃ tāvad, bhoḥ, prasṛta|nipuṇaḥ† kaś cid upāyo yena nas tau haṃsa|varyau darśana|patham api tāvad upagacchetām iti!»

22.15 atha te 'mātyāḥ svaiḥ svair mati|prabhāvair anusṛtya nīti|pathaṃ rājānam ūcuḥ:

«sukh'|āśā, deva, bhūtāni vikarṣati tatas tataḥ.
sukha|hetu|guṇ'|ôtkarṣa|śrutis tāv ānayed yataḥ. [6]

tad yādṛśe sarasi tāv abhirata|rūpāv anuśrūyete, tad|utkṛṣṭatara|guṇa|śobham iha saraḥ kasmiṃś cid araṇya|pradeśe kārayitum arhati devaḥ... pratyahaṃ ca sarva|pakṣiṇām a|bhaya|pradāna|ghoṣaṇām. api nāma kautūhal'|ôtpādinyā sukha|hetu|guṇ'|âtiśaya|śrutyā tāv ih' ākṛṣyeyātām. paśyatu devaḥ:

prāyeṇa prāpti|virasaṃ
sukhaṃ, deva, na gaṇyate.
parokṣatvāt tu harati
śruti|ramyaṃ sukhaṃ manaḥ.» [7]

atha sa rājā" «âstv etad» ity alpena kālena n' âti|saṃnikṛṣṭaṃ nagar'|ôpavanasya Mānasa|saraḥ|pratispardhi†|guṇa|vibhavaṃ padm'|ôtpala|kumuda|puṇḍarīka|saugandhika|

become increasingly curious to see the two creatures. He therefore addressed his counselors, who were clever and experienced in numerous teachings, saying:

"Well, sirs, devise a clever way for me at least to catch sight of these two fine geese!"

22.15 After the ministers had pondered the path of political strategy with their powerful minds, they gave the king the following reply:

"Hope for happiness draws creatures
away from their various abodes.
The report of a remarkable source
of happiness may therefore lure them.

Your Majesty should have a lake constructed in an area of the wilderness, similar but even more splendid than the lake in which these handsome geese are reported to dwell. And every day you should have it proclaimed that you offer immunity to every bird. Perhaps the rumor that this exceptional lake offers a source of happiness will rouse the curiosity of the geese and draw them here. For Your Majesty should consider that,

once obtained and no longer esteemed,
happiness usually loses its taste.
But happiness made delightful by rumor
captivates the mind by its invisibility."

The king agreed and soon had a huge lake constructed not too near the city park, rivaling Lake Mánasa in the richness of its quality. Captivating the mind, the lake's pure waters were covered by various lotuses and water-lilies, includ-

tāmarasa|kahlāra|samupagūḍha|vimala|salilam† ati|mano|
haraṃ mahat saraḥ kārayām āsa,

22.20 drumaiḥ kusuma|saṃchannaiś calat|kisalay'|ôjjvalaiḥ
tat|prekṣ"|ârtham iv' ôpetaiḥ† kṛta|tīra|parigraham, [8]

vihasadbhir iv' âmbho|jais
taraṅg'|ôtkampa|kampibhiḥ
vilobhyamān'|ākulita|
bhramad|bhramara|saṃkulam, [9]

jyotsnā|saṃvāhan'|ônnidrair
vicitraṃ kumudaiḥ† kva cit
taru|cchāyā|paricchinnaiś
candrikā|śakalair iva, [10]

taraṅg'|âṅguli|saṃkṣiptaiḥ kamal'|ôtpala|reṇubhiḥ
abhyalaṃkṛta|tīr'|ântaṃ hema|sūtrair iva kva cit, [11]

citraiḥ padm'|ôtpala|dalais tatra tatra sa|kesaraiḥ
śriyaṃ pravitatāṃ bibhrad upahāramayīm iva, [12]

22.25 prasanna|stimit'|âmbutvād
vyakta|citra|vapur|guṇaiḥ
vyomn' îva paridhāvadbhir
mīna|vṛndair alaṃ|kṛtam, [13]

ing padmas, útpalas, kúmudas, pundaríkas, saugándhikas, támarasas, and kahláras.

Trees draped with flowers
surrounded the lake's shore
with bright quivering sprigs,
as if come to gaze at the waters. 22.20

Swarms of roaming bees
crowded the lake in disarray,
seduced by lotuses jostled by trembling ripples,
opening their petals as if with a smile.

Over here the lake was adorned by white lilies
sleepless from the touch of moonshine,
resembling splinters of moonlight
fragmented by the canopy of trees.

Over there the shore was decorated by strands
of pollen dust from red and blue lotuses,
pushed there by finger-like waves,
resembling threads of gold.

The bright petals and filaments
of lotuses and water-lilies
made the lake everywhere bear
an expansive beauty like a reverent gift.

So tranquil and still was the water
that shoals of roaming fish decorating
the lake with their fine colorful bodies
were as visible as if they swam in air. 22.25

vicchinna|muktā|hārābhiḥ
kva cid dvirada|śīkaraiḥ
upal'|āsphālan'|ôtkīrṇam
ūrmi|cūrṇām iv' ôdvahat, [14]

vidyādhara|vadhū|snānair mada|sekaiś ca dantinām
rajobhiḥ kusumānāṃ ca sa|vāsam iva kutra cit, [15]

tārāṇāṃ candra|dārāṇāṃ sāmānyam iva darpaṇam,
mudita|dvija|saṃkīrṇaṃ tad|ruta|pratināditam. [16]

tad evaṃ|vidhaṃ saraḥ kārayitvā sarva|pakṣi|gaṇasya c' ân|āvṛta|sukh'|ôpabhogyam etad dattvā pratyahaṃ sarva|pakṣiṇāṃ viśvāsan'|ârtham ity a|bhaya|dāna|ghoṣaṇāṃ kārayām āsa:

22.30 «eṣa padm'|ôtpala|dala|
cchanna|toyam idaṃ saraḥ
dadāti rājā pakṣibhyaḥ
prītyā s'|â|bhaya|dakṣiṇam.» [17]

atha kadā cit saṃhṛta|megh'|ândhakāra|yavanikāsu śarad|guṇ'|ôpahṛta|śobhāsv ālokana|kṣamāsu dikṣu prabuddha|kamala|vana|śobheṣu prasanna|salila|manohareṣu sarassu paraṃ kānti|yauvanam upagate praceya|kiraṇa iva candramasi vividha|sasya|saṃpad|vibhūṣaṇa|dharāyāṃ vasuṃ|dharāyāṃ,

In one area elephants emitted sprays
like broken strings of pearls,
the water seeming to transform into dust,
scattered when pulverized against rocks.

In another area the lake seemed perfumed
by the ointments of vidya·dhara nymphs,
the rut-juices of elephants
and the pollen dust of flowers.

The moon's wives, the stars,
were reflected in the lake like a mirror,
which abounded with joyful birds
and echoed with their warbling.

Such was the lake that the king built as a gift for the entire flock of birds to enjoy with unimpeded pleasure. And to inspire trust in all the birds, he had the following announcement proclaimed every day, granting a gift of immunity:

"Its waters covered by petals
of lotuses and water-lilies,
this lake is joyfully given by the king
along with the gift of immunity." 22.30

One day the season arrived when dark clouds draw aside their curtains and fine autumn doles out her glories. The sky allowed itself to be seen and lakes captivated the mind with their tranquil waters, glistening with clusters of awakened lotuses. The moon seemed to increase the power of its rays and took on an intense youthful splendor, while the earth became adorned by an abundance of crops.

pravṛtte taruṇa|haṃsa|jana|saṃpāte† Mānasāt sarasaḥ śarat|prasannāni dig|antarāṇy anuvicarad anupūrveṇ' ânyatamaṃ haṃsa|mithunaṃ tasmād eva haṃsa|yūthāt tasya rājño viṣayam upajagāma. tatra ca pakṣi|gaṇa|kolāhal'|ônnāditam a|nibhṛta|madhu|kara|gaṇaṃ taraṅga|mālā|viracana†|kṛta|vyāpāraiḥ sukha|śiśirair mṛdubhir anilaiḥ samantato vikṣipyamāṇa|kamala|kuvalaya|reṇu|gandhaṃ, jvalad iva vikacaiḥ kamalair, hasad iva ca sitaiḥ† kumudais tat saro dadarśa.

tasya Mānasa|saraḥ samucitasy' âpi haṃsa|mithunasya tām ati|mano|harāṃ sarasaḥ śriyam abhivīkṣya paro vismayaḥ sva|yūth'|ânusmṛtiś ca prādur|abhūt:† «aho bata, tad api haṃsa|yūtham ih' āgacched» iti.

prāyeṇa khalu lokasya prāpya sādhāraṇaṃ sukham
smṛtiḥ sneh'|ânusāreṇa pūrvam eti suhṛj|janam. [18]

22.35 atha tatra tadd haṃsa|mithunaṃ yathā|kāmaṃ vihṛtya pravṛtte jalada|samaye vidyud|visphurita|śastra|vikṣepeṣu n'|âtighana|vicchinn'|ândhakāra|rūpeṣu samabhivartamāneṣu, daity'|ânīkeṣv iva jala|dhara|vṛndeṣu paripūrṇa|barha|kalāpa|śobheṣu, prasakta|kekā|ninād'|ôtkruṣṭair jala|dhara|vijayam iva saṃrādhayatsu, nṛtta|pravṛtteṣu citreṣu barhi|gaṇeṣu, vācālatām upagateṣu stoka|śakuniṣu, pravicaratsu kadamba|sarj'|ârjuna|ketakī|puṣpa|gandh'|âdhivāsiteṣu

It was the season when young geese take flight. And so it was that a pair of geese from that flock set out from Lake Mánasa, wandering through regions that were bright with the serenity of autumn, until gradually they reached the land of King Brahma·datta. There they saw the lake, blazing with blooming lotuses and smiling with open water-lilies. Resounding with the racket of flocks of birds, the lake buzzed noisily with swarms of bees. Soft, soothing and cool breezes busied themselves by forming garlands of ripples, wafting the fragrance of lotus and lily pollen.

Even though they were accustomed to Lake Mánasa, the two geese were filled with great wonder when they saw the intensely captivating glory of the lake. Remembering their flock, it occurred to them that the other geese should also go there.

When people find
a pleasure to share,
affection first usually turns
their thoughts to friends.

22.35 The pair of geese stayed at the lake, enjoying themselves as they pleased until the monsoon arrived. That is the season when cloud masses advance like demonic armies, their darkness not so thick that it cannot be cut by the sword slashes of quivering lightning bolts. It is the season when colorful flocks of peacocks dance with continuous piercing cries as if praising the triumph of the clouds, glorious as they open their fan of feathers and accompanied by the chatter of smaller birds. It is the time when soothing breezes

sukha|śiśireṣu kānana|viniśvasiteṣv iv' ânileṣu, megha|daśana|paṅktiṣv iv' ālakṣyamāṇa|rūpāsu balākā|yuvatiṣu, gaman'|autsukya|mṛdu|nikūjiteṣu prayāṇa|vyākuleṣu haṃsa|yūtheṣu,

tadd haṃsa|mithunaṃ Mānasam eva saraḥ pratyājagāma. samupetya ca haṃs'|âdhipati|samīpaṃ prastutāsu dig|deśa|kathāsu taṃ tasya saraso guṇa|viśeṣaṃ saṃvarṇayām āsa:†

«asti, deva dakṣiṇena Himavato Vārāṇasyāṃ Brahmadatto nāma nar'|âdhipatiḥ. ten' âtyadbhuta|rūpa|śobham a|nirvarṇya|guṇa|saundaryaṃ mahat saraḥ pakṣibhyaḥ sva|cchanda|sukh'|ôpabhogyaṃ dattam. a|bhayaṃ ca pratyaham avaghuṣyate, ramante c' âtra pakṣiṇaḥ sva|gṛha iva prakṣīṇa†|bhay'|āśaṅkāḥ. tad arhati devo vyatītāsu varṣāsu tatra gantum iti.»

tac chrutvā sarva eva te haṃsās tat|saṃdarśana|samutsukā babhūvuḥ.... atha Bodhisattvaḥ Sumukhaṃ senā|patiṃ paripraśna|vyakt'|ākāraṃ† pratataṃ dadarśa, «kathaṃ paśyas'?» îti c' âvocat. atha Sumukhaḥ praṇamy' âinam uvāca:

«na prāptaṃ tatra devasya gamanam, iti paśyāmi. kutaḥ? amūni tāval lobhanīyāni mano|harāṇy āmiṣa|bhūtāni rūpāṇi. na ca naḥ kena cid† iha parihīyante.† kṛtaka|madhur'|ôpacāra|vacana|pracchanna|tīkṣṇa|daurātmyāni ca prāyeṇa pelava|ghṛṇāni śaṭhāni mānuṣa|hṛdayāni. paśyatu svāmī:

blow like deep breaths from the forest, infused by the fragrance of flowers from kadámba, sarja, árjuna, and kétaki trees.* Or when young cranes stand out like a row of teeth on a cloud and flocks of geese are anxious to migrate, warbling softly in their desire to depart.

When this season arrived, the pair of geese set out for Lake Mánasa. There they approached the king of the geese and while discussing the topic of geography, they praised the special virtues of the lake, saying:

"There is, Your Majesty, a king called Brahma·datta who rules in Varánasi to the south of Mount Hímavat. He has made an offering of a huge and extraordinarily beautiful lake. Indescribable qualities furnish this delightful lake and it is for birds to enjoy at their own pleasure and will. Every day a proclamation of immunity is made in the area and birds take delight in the lake without fear or worry, as if it were their own home. Your Majesty should go there after the rains have passed."

When they heard this, all the geese became eager to see the lake. The Bodhi·sattva then looked at his general Súmukha with an intent expression of inquiry: "What are your views on this?" he asked. Whereupon Súmukha bowed before the Bodhi·sattva and gave the following reply:

"My view is that Your Majesty should not go. Why? Because they are simply enticements—attractive forms set up as baits—and we lack none of such things here. The hearts of men are usually false whenever they display tender compassion. Fabricated courtesies and honeyed words conceal a vicious depravity. Consider this, master:

22.40 vāśit'|ânvartha|hṛdayāḥ† prāyeṇa mṛga|pakṣiṇaḥ.
manuṣyāḥ punar ekīyās tad|viparyaya|naipuṇāḥ. [19]

ucyate nāma madhuraṃ sv|anubandhi nir|atyayam.
vaṇijo 'pi hi kurvanti lābha|siddhy|āśayā vyayam. [20]

yato n' âitāvatā, deva,
visrambhaḥ kṣamate kva cit.
kāry'|ârtham api na śreyaḥ
s'|âtyay'|âpanayaḥ kramaḥ. [21]

yadi tv avaśyam eva tatra gantavyam, gatv" ânubhūya ca tasya saraso vibhūti|rasaṃ† na nas tatra ciraṃ vicarituṃ kṣamaṃ, nivāsāya vā cittam abhināmayitum, iti paśyāmi.»

atha Bodhisattvaḥ prāptāyāṃ vimala|candra|nakṣatra|tārā|vibhūṣaṇāyāṃ† śaradi tena haṃsa|yūthena Vārāṇasī|sarah|saṃdarśanaṃ pratyabhivṛddha|kautūhalena tad|abhigaman'|ârthaṃ punaḥ punar vijñāpyamānas teṣāṃ haṃsānām anuvṛttyā Sumukha|pramukheṇa mahatā haṃsa|gaṇena parivṛtaś candramā iva śarad|abhra|vṛndena tatr' âbhijagāma.

22.45 dṛṣṭv" âiva lakṣmīṃ sarasas tu tasya
teṣāṃ praharṣ'|ākula|vismayānām
citra|prakārā ruci|saṃniveśās
tat|saṃśraye tulya|guṇā babhūvuḥ. [22]

Animals and birds usually
express their hearts through cries.
Humans alone are skilled
in expressing the opposite. 22.40

Their speech is of course pleasant,
coherent and unable to be faulted.
But do merchants not also invest
in the hope of acquiring profit?

You should therefore never place
your trust in them, Your Majesty.
For dangerous and injudicious actions
can never be good, even to acquire a goal.

But if it really is necessary to go there, we should simply go and enjoy the lake's riches. We should not wander there for long, nor incline our minds to staying there. That is my view."

The flock of geese entreated the Bodhi·sattva again and again to go to the Varanási lake, their curiosity to see it growing ever stronger. And so, when autumn arrived and the sky was adorned by a bright moon and stars, the Bodhi·sattva complied with their request and set off for the lake, surrounded by the flock of geese with Súmukha at the front, like the moon attended by a mass of autumn clouds.

As soon as they saw the beauty of the lake,
they were filled with joy mixed with wonder.
Landing radiantly, their splendid forms
rivaled the waters on which they floated. 22.45

yan Mānasād abhyadhikaṃ babhūva
tais tair avasth"|âtiśayaiḥ saras tat,
ataś ciraṃ tad|gata|mānasānāṃ
na Mānase mānasam āsa teṣām. [23]

tatra te tām a|bhaya|ghoṣaṇām upalabhya svasthatāṃ† ca pakṣi|gaṇasya, tasya ca saraso vibhūtyā pramudita|hṛdayās tatr' ôdyāna|yātrām iv' ânubhavantaḥ parāṃ prīti|saṃpadam upajagmuḥ.

atha tasmin sarasy adhikṛtāḥ puruṣās teṣāṃ haṃsānāṃ tatr' āgamanaṃ rājñe nyavedayanta:†

«yādṛśa|guṇa|rūpau, deva, tau haṃsa|varyāv anuśrūyete, tādṛśāv eva kanak'|âvadāta|rucira|patrau tapanīy'|ôjjvalatara| vadana|caraṇa|śobhāv adhikatara|pramāṇa|su|saṃsthita†| dehau n'|âika|haṃsa|śata|sahasra|parivārau devasya saraḥ śobhayitum iv' ânuprāptāv iti.»

22.50 atha sa rājā śākunika|karmaṇi prasiddha|prakāśa|naipuṇaṃ śākunikam anviṣya† tad|grahaṇ'|ârthaṃ s'|ādaram anvādideśa. sa «tath"» êti pratiśrutya tayor haṃsayor gocara| vihāra|pradeśaṃ samyag upalakṣya† tatra tatra dṛḍhān nigūḍhān pāśān nyadadhāt.

atha teṣāṃ haṃsānāṃ viśvāsād apāya|nirāśaṅkānāṃ pramod'|ôddhata|manasāṃ vicaratāṃ sa haṃs'|âdhipatiḥ pāśena caraṇe nyabadhyata.

The lake surpassed Mánasa
in its various fine abodes.
The geese's minds became so attached to it,
they no longer lent a thought to Mind Lake.

On hearing the proclamation of immunity and seeing the ease with which flocks of birds enjoyed the lake, their hearts became gladdened by the glory of the place and they felt utter bliss there, as if enjoying a trip in a park.

Now the men in charge of the lake informed the king that the geese had arrived, saying:

"Divine lord, two fine geese have arrived at Your Majesty's lake, bearing exactly the same features and appearance as the geese we have heard about. Their wings glisten with the purity of gold. Their glorious beaks and feet blaze brightly like molten gold. Their bodies are well-formed and larger than ordinary. Surrounded by several hundreds and thousands of geese, it is as if they have arrived to illuminate the waters."

The king then sought out a fowler who was widely renowned for his fowling skills and eagerly ordered him to capture the geese. The fowler consented and, after duly ascertaining the feeding ground and nesting area of the birds, he laid down various strong and concealed snares. 22.50

The geese had become so trusting that they had lost all fear of danger. And so it was that, one day, when the geese were roaming around, elated with joy, the king of the geese caught his foot in one of the traps.

vismṛt'|âtyaya|śaṅkānāṃ ślakṣṇair† viśvāsana|kramaiḥ
vikaroty eva viśrambhaḥ pramād'|âpanay'|ākaraḥ. [24]

atha Bodhisattvo «mā bhūd anyasy' âpi kasya cid atr' âi-vaṃ|vidho† vyasan'|ôpanipāta» iti viruta|viśeṣeṇa† sa|pra-tibhayatāṃ sarasaḥ prakāśayām āsa. atha te haṃsā† haṃs'|âdhipati|bandhād vyathita|hṛdayā bhaya|virasa|vyākula|virāvāḥ paras|para|nirapekṣā, hata|pravīrā iva sainikā diśaḥ† samutpetuḥ. Sumukhas tu haṃsa|senā|patir† haṃs'|âdhi-pati|samīpān n' âiva vicacāla.

sneh'|âvabaddhāni hi mānasāni
prāṇ'|âtyayaṃ svaṃ na vicintayanti,
prāṇ'|âtyayād duḥkhataraṃ yad eṣāṃ
suhṛj|janasya vyasan'|ārti|dainyam. [25]

22.55 ath' âinaṃ Bodhisattva uvāca:

«gaccha! gacch' âiva, Sumukha!
kṣamaṃ n' êha vilambitum!
sāhāyyasy' âvakāśo hi
kas tav' êtthaṃ|gate mayi?» [26]

Sumukha uvāca:

«n' âik'|ântiko mṛtyur iha sthitasya,
na gacchataḥ syād a|jar"|â|maratvam.
sukheṣu ca tvāṃ samupāsya nityam
āpad|gataṃ, māna|da, kena jahyām? [27]

Subtle confidence-inspiring strategies
make people forget to fear danger.
So trust only brings disaster,
causing heedlessness and imprudence.

To stop any other geese from suffering the same misfortune, the Bodhi·sattva uttered a special cry to announce that the lake was dangerous. The geese were distraught that their king had been snared and, paying no heed to one another, they flew into the sky, uttering shrill and hysterical shrieks out of fear, like soldiers when their leader has been killed. But Súmukha, the general of the geese, did not move from the king's side.

Hearts bound by love do not
consider losing their own life.
For the misery of a friend's suffering
pains them more than losing their life.

The Bodhi·sattva responded to this by saying to Sú mukha: 22.55

"Go! Go, Súmukha!
You should not linger here!
For what scope is there
to help me in this plight?"

Súmukha answered:

"I will not necessarily die if I stay here.
And if I go, I will not escape old age and death.
I always served you in happy times, Your Majesty.
How could I abandon you in distress?

sva|prāṇa|tantu|mātr'|ârthaṃ
tyajatas tvāṃ, khag'|âdhipa,
dhig|vāda|vṛṣṭy|āvaraṇaṃ
kataman me bhaviṣyati? [28]

22.60 n' âiṣa dharmo, mahā|rāja, tyajeyaṃ tvāṃ yad āpadi.
yā gatis tava, sā mahyaṃ rocate, vihag'|âdhipa.» [29]

Bodhisattva uvāca:

«kā nu pāśena baddhasya
gatir anyā mahānasāt?
sā kathaṃ svastha|cittasya
muktasy' âbhimatā tava? [30]

paśyasy evaṃ kam arthaṃ vā
tvaṃ mam' ātmana eva vā
jñātīnāṃ v'' āvaśeṣāṇām,
ubhayor jīvita|kṣaye? [31]

lakṣyate na ca† yatr' ârthas
tamas' îva sam'|â|samam,
tādṛśe saṃtyajan prāṇān
kam arthaṃ dyotayed bhavān?» [32]

22.65 Sumukha uvāca:

«kathaṃ nu, patatāṃ śreṣṭha,
dharme 'rthaṃ na samīkṣase?
dharmo hy apacitaḥ† samyag
āvahaty artham uttamam. [33]

If I abandoned you, king of birds,
just to save the thread of my life,
what shield would I have
against a storm of blame?

It would not be right, Your Majesty, 22.60
for me to abandon you in distress.
Whatever your fate may be,
I am pleased to share it, king of birds."

The Bodhi·sattva replied:

"What fate other than the kitchen
awaits a bird in a snare?
How can that attract you
if you are sane and free?

What benefit do you see
for me, yourself,
or the rest of our kinsmen,
if both of us lose our lives?

What benefit can you reveal
in giving up your life in this situation?
It is as impossible to see as even
or uneven ground in the dark!"

Súmukha said: 22.65

"How can you not see, best of birds,
the benefit in acting virtuously?
For morality, properly revered,
brings the utmost benefit.

so 'haṃ dharmaṃ ca saṃpaśyan
dharmāc c' ârthaṃ samutthitam,
tava, mānada, bhaktyā ca
n' âbhikāṅkṣāmi jīvitam.» [34]

Bodhisattva uvāca:

«addhā dharmaḥ satām eṣa, yat sakhā mitram āpadi
na tyajej jīvitasy' âpi hetor dharmam anusmaran. [35]

22.70 tad arcitas tvayā dharmo,
bhaktir mayi ca darśitā.
yācñām antyāṃ kuruṣv' êmāṃ:
gacch' âiv' ânumato mayā! [36]

api c' âivaṃ|gate kārye
yad ūnaṃ suhṛdāṃ mayā,
tat tvayā, mati|saṃpanna,
bhavet parama|saṃbhṛtam.» [37]

paras|para|prema|guṇād iti saṃjalpatos tayoḥ
pratyadṛśyata naiṣādaḥ sākṣān Mṛtyur iv' āpatan. [38]

atha tau haṃsa|varyau taṃ† niṣādam āpatantam ālokya tūṣṇīṃ babhūvatuḥ. sa ca tadd haṃsa|yūthaṃ vidravantam† ālokya, «nūnam atra kaś cid baddha» iti niścita|matiḥ pāśa|sthānāny anuvicaraṃs tau haṃsa|varyau dadarśa. sa tad|rūpa|śobhayā vismita|manā, «baddhāv» iti manyamānas

It is because I consider virtue
and the benefit arising from virtue
that in devotion to you, honor-giving lord,
I do not hanker after life."

The Bodhi·sattva replied:

"True that, in the morality of the good,
a friend mindful of virtue should not
abandon another friend in distress,
even at the cost of his life.

22.70

You have practiced this virtue
and shown me your devotion.
Now grant me this last request
and leave with my permission!

When matters have reached this state,
it is up to you, wise Súmukha,
to provide a fine substitute
for the role I vacate among our friends."

As the two geese conversed this way
with remarkable mutual affection,
the hunter* appeared,
stalking them like Death incarnate.

At the sight of the hunter rushing upon them, the two fine geese fell silent. The hunter had seen the flock of geese flying away and was certain that one of the birds must have been trapped. So he scoured the different places in which he had set his snares until he spotted the two fine geese. Amazed by the beauty of the birds and assuming that they had both been caught, he unfastened the snares that were

tat|samāsannau† pāśāv udghaṭṭayām āsa. ath' âikaṃ baddham a|baddhen' êtareṇa svasthen' ôpāsyamānam avekṣya vismitatara|hṛdayaḥ Sumukham upety' ôvāca:

«ayaṃ pāśena mahatā
dvi|jaḥ saṃhṛta|vikramaḥ.
vyoma n' âsmāt prapadyeta
mayy apy antikam āgate. [39]

22.75 a|baddhas tvaṃ punaḥ svasthaḥ
sajja|pattra|ratho† balī
kasmāt prāpte 'pi mayy evaṃ
vegān na bhajase nabhaḥ?» [40]

tad upaśrutya Sumukhaḥ pravyakt'|âkṣara|pada|vinyāsena svabhāva|varṇanā|dhairya|guṇ'|âujasvinā svareṇa mānuṣīṃ vācam uvāca:

«śakti|sthaḥ san na gacchāmi yad idaṃ tatra kāraṇam:
ayaṃ pāśa|parikleśaṃ viha|gaḥ† prāptavān iti. [41]

ayaṃ pāśena mahatā saṃyataś caraṇe tvayā,
guṇair asya tu baddho 'ham ato dṛdhatarair hṛdi.» [42]

atha sa naiṣādaḥ parama|vismita|matiḥ saṃhṛṣita|tanū|ruhaḥ Sumukhaṃ punar uvāca:

near them. But when he saw that one trapped goose was attended by another goose who was untrapped and perfectly healthy, he felt even greater amazement and approached Súmukha, saying:

"A large snare stops
this bird from moving.
That is why he does not fly
into the sky, even at my approach.

But you are not trapped. Healthy
and strong, your winged chariot is ready.
Why do you not swiftly take to the sky,
even though I am upon you?"

22.75

On hearing this, Súmukha replied with human words, clearly articulating every syllable, his powerful and brave tone revealing his character:

"Why do I not leave,
even though I can?
Because this bird suffers
the torment of being snared.

You hold him by the foot
with a huge snare.
But I am trapped by the strings
of his virtues gripping tightly on my heart."

The hunter became filled with utter joy at these words. His hair bristled on his body as he addressed Súmukha once more, saying:

22.80 «tyaktv" âinaṃ mad|bhayād anye
diśo haṃsāḥ samāśritāḥ.
tvaṃ punar na tyajasy enaṃ?
ko nv ayaṃ bhavato, dvi|ja?» [43]

Sumukha uvāca:

«rājā mama prāṇa|samaḥ sakhā ca
sukhasya dātā, viṣama|sthitaś ca.
n' âiv' ôtsahe yena vihātum enaṃ
sva|jīvitasy' âpy anurakṣaṇ'|ārtham.» [44]

atha Sumukhaḥ prasāda|vismay'|āvarjita|mānasaṃ taṃ naiṣādam avetya punar uvāca:

«apy asmākam iyaṃ, bhadra,
saṃbhāṣā syāt sukh'|ôdayā!
apy asmān visṛjann adya
dharmyāṃ kīrtim avāpnuyāḥ.» [45]

22.85 naiṣāda uvāca:

«n' âiva te duḥkham icchāmi.
na ca baddho bhavān mayā.
sa tvaṃ gaccha yathā|kāmaṃ!
paśya bandhūṃś ca nandaya!» [46]

Sumukha uvāca:

«no ced icchasi me duḥkhaṃ,
tat kuruṣva mam' ârthanām.
ekena yadi tuṣṭo 'si,
tat tyaj' âinaṃ, gṛhāṇa mām! [47]

"The other geese took to the sky, 22.80
abandoning this bird in fear of me.
Why do you not leave him too?
Who is this goose to you, twice-born?*"

Súmukha answered:

"Equal to my life, he is my king and friend.
He gives me happiness and is now in trouble.
I could therefore never abandon him,
even to protect my own life."

Súmukha saw that the hunter was amazed and becoming benign. So he continued, saying:

"If only our conversation
could produce happiness, sir!
If only you gained a virtuous fame
by releasing us this day!"

The hunter replied: 22.85

"I do not wish to harm you.
It is not you I have trapped.
Go as you please!
See your kin and bring them joy!"

Súmukha said:

"If you really wish me no harm,
then grant my request:
if you are content with one of us,
then release him and take me!

tuly'|āroha|parīṇāhau† samānau vayasā ca nau.
viddhi: niṣkraya ity asya. na te 'haṃ lābha|hānaye. [48]

22.90 tad aṅga samavekṣasva:
gṛddhir bhavatu te mayi!
māṃ badhnātu bhavān pūrvaṃ
paścān muñca† dvij'|âdhipam! [49]

tāvān eva ca lābhas te kṛtā syān mama c' ârthanā,
haṃsa|yūthasya ca prītir, maitrī tena tath" âiva ca. [50]

paśyantu tāvad bhavatā vimuktaṃ
haṃs'|âdhipaṃ haṃsa|gaṇāḥ pratītāḥ
virocamānaṃ nabhasi prasanne
daity'|êndra|nirmuktam iv' ôḍu|rājam!» [51]

atha sa naiṣādaḥ krūrat"|âbhyāsa|kaṭhina|hṛdayo 'pi tena tasya sva|jīvita†|nirapekṣeṇa svāmy|anurāga|ślāghinā kṛtajñatā|guṇ'|âujasvinā dhairya|mādhury'|âlaṃkṛtena vacasā† samāvarjita|hṛdayo vismaya|gaurava|balāt† samānīt'|âñjaliḥ Sumukham uvāca:
«sādhu! sādhu, mahābhāga!

22.95 mānuṣeṣv apy ayaṃ dharma
āścaryo daivateṣu vā
svāmy|arthaṃ tyajatā prāṇān
yas tvay" âtra vidarśitaḥ!† [52]

Equal in height and breadth,
our years are also the same.
Know this: you will lose no profit
by taking me as a ransom for him.

Consider the matter
and covet me instead!
Bind me first and release
this king of birds afterwards!

22.90

You will then still have your gain,
my request will be fulfilled,
and the flock of geese will be joyful
and offer you their friendship.

Let the hordes of geese feel joy
at seeing you release their monarch
so that he glistens in the clear sky
like the star-king released by the demon lord!"*

Although repeated cruelty had hardened the hunter's heart, he was deeply affected by these words which, adorned by bravery and mildness, revealed the goose's indifference to his own life and proclaimed his love for his master, powerfully expressing his gratitude. Overwhelmed by intense feelings of wonder and respect, the hunter therefore addressed Súmukha as follows, his hands cupped in reverence:

"Excellent! Excellent, illustrious bird!

The virtue you have displayed here
in giving your life for your master
would be miraculous even
among humans or gods!

22.95

tad eṣa te vimuñcāmi rājānam anumānayan.
ko hi prāṇa|priyatare tav' âsmin vipriyaṃ caret?» [53]

ity uktvā sa naiṣādas tasya nṛ|pateḥ saṃdeśam an|ādṛtya haṃsa|rājaṃ samanumānayan dayā|sumukhaṃ pāśān mumoca. atha Sumukhaḥ senā | patir haṃsa | rāja | vimokṣāt param'|ānandita|hṛdayaḥ prīty|abhisnigdham udīkṣamāṇo naiṣādam uvāca:

«yathā, suhṛn|nandana, nandito 'smi
tvay" âdya haṃs'|âdhipater vimokṣāt,
evaṃ saha jñāti|gaṇena,† bhadra,
śarat|sahasrāṇi bahūni nanda! [54]

tan mā tav' âyaṃ vi|phalaḥ śramo 'bhūd.
ādāya māṃ haṃsa|gaṇ'|âdhipaṃ ca
sva|sthāv a|baddhāv adhiropya kācam
antaḥ|pure darśaya bhūmi|pāya. [55]

22.100 a|saṃśayaṃ prīta|manāḥ sa rājā
haṃs'|âdhipaṃ s'|ânucaraṃ samīkṣya
dāsyaty a|saṃbhāvita|vistarāṇi
dhanāni te prīti|vivardhanāni.» [56]

atha sa† naiṣādas tasya nirbandhāt, «paśyatu tāvad aty|adbhutam idaṃ haṃsa|yugaṃ sa rāj"» êti kṛtvā te haṃsa|mukhyau kācen' ādāya sva|sthāv a|baddhau rājñe darśayām āsa.

Out of reverence,
I will release your king.
For who could wrong him
who is dearer to you than life?"

Saying this and disregarding the king's command, the hunter paid respect to the royal goose and released him from the snare out of compassion. When the king of geese was released, the general Súmukha was filled with utter joy and addressed the hunter with a gaze of kind affection, saying:

"You have brought joy to your friends!
You have gladdened me today by releasing our king.
May you feel the same joy for thousands of years,
along with crowds of your relatives, good sir!

So that your toil is not fruitless,
take myself and the king of geese,
place us on your pole, unharmed and unbound,
and display us to your king in his palace.

The king will doubtlessly be pleased
at seeing the royal goose and his servant
and give you inconceivable amounts
of wealth to gladden you." 22.100

When Súmukha insisted, the hunter considered that the king really should see this extraordinary pair of geese and so he carried the fine geese on his shoulder-pole, unharmed and unbound, and showed them to the king, saying:

«upāyan'|āścaryam idaṃ draṣṭum arhasi, māna|da:
sa|senā|patir ānītaḥ so 'yaṃ haṃsa|patir mayā!» [57]

atha sa rājā praharṣa|vismay'|āpūrṇa|matir dṛṣṭvā tau haṃsa|pradhānau kāñcana|puñjāv iva śriy" âbhijvalan|manohara|rūpau taṃ naiṣādam uvāca:

«sva|sthāv a|baddhāv amukau
viham|gau bhūmi|cāriṇaḥ
tava hastam anuprāptau
kathaṃ? kathaya vistaram!» [58]

22.105 ity ukte sa naiṣādaḥ praṇamya rājānam uvāca:

«nihitā bahavaḥ pāśā mayā dāruṇa|dāruṇāḥ
vihag'|ākriḍa|deśeṣu palvaleṣu sarassu ca. [59]

atha viśrambha|niḥśaṅkaṃ†
haṃsa|varyaś carann ayam
paricchannena pāśena
caraṇe samabadhyata. [60]

a|baddhas tam upāsīno mām ayaṃ samayācata
ātmānaṃ niṣkrayaṃ kṛtvā haṃsa|rājasya jīvitam, [61]

"Your Majesty should see
this miraculous gift:
I have brought before you
the king of geese and his general!"

The king became filled with joy and wonder when he saw the two fine geese, their captivating forms blazing with glory like heaps of gold. He then addressed the hunter, saying:

"How did you, a land-walker,
get hold of these sky-flying geese,
who are unharmed and unbound?
Tell me in detail!"

22.105 In response, the hunter bowed before the king and addressed him with the following words:

"I set many cruel
and vicious snares
by ponds and lakes
in places where birds play.

This fine goose trapped
his foot in a hidden snare
as he wandered around,
trusting and unfearful.

This other goose attended him.
Though not himself snared,
he begged me to ransom him
for the life of the royal goose.

visṛjan mānuṣīṃ vācaṃ vispaṣṭa|madhur'|âkṣarām,
sva|jīvita|parityāgād yācñām apy ūrjita|kramām. [62]

22.110 ten' âsya vākyena su|peśalena
svāmy|artha|dhīreṇa ca ceṣṭitena
tathā prasanno 'smi, yath" âsya bhartā
mayā samaṃ krūratay" âiva muktaḥ. [63]

atha vihaga|pater ayaṃ vimokṣān
mudita|matir bahudhā vadan priyāṇi
tvad|abhigama iti nyayojayan māṃ,
viphala|guruḥ kila mā mama śramo bhūt. [64]

tad evam ati|dhārmikaḥ
khaga|var'|ākṛtiḥ ko 'py asau
mam' âpi hṛdi mārdavaṃ
janitavān kṣaṇen' âiva yaḥ,
khag'|âdhipati|mokṣaṇaṃ
kṛtam anusmaran mat|kṛte,
sah' âdhipatin" āgataḥ
svayam ayaṃ ca te 'ntaḥ|puram.» [65]

tad upaśrutya sa rājā sa|pramoda|vismayena manasā vividha|ratna|prabh"|ôdbhāsura|rucira†|pādaṃ par'|ârdhy'|āstaraṇa|racan"|âbhirāmaṃ śrīmat|sukh'|âpāśraya†|s'|āṭopam upahita|pāda|pīṭhaṃ rāj'|âdhyāsana|yogyaṃ kāñcanam āsanaṃ haṃsa|rājāya samādideśa, amātya|mukhy'|âdhyāsana|yogyaṃ ca vetr'|āsanaṃ Sumukhāya.

He spoke in a human voice,
using articulate and gentle words,
his request made powerful
by the sacrifice of his life.

Soothed by his elegant words
and the bravery he showed his master,
I released both his lord
and my cruelty as well. 22.110

Overjoyed at the royal bird's release,
the goose spoke many kind words to me,
telling me to go to Your Majesty
so my toil would not be in vain.

This exceptionally virtuous creature,
whatever it is, though in form a fine bird,
has in an instant produced mildness
even in the heart of a man like me.
It is for my sake this goose
comes of his own free will
to your palace with his lord,
grateful I released the royal bird."

The king was filled with joy and astonishment when he heard these words. To the royal goose he gave a throne fit for a king, together with a foot-stool. Padded with a beautiful, soft cushion, the throne was delightfully furnished with a drape of the finest quality and its feet glistened radiantly with the splendor of various jewels. And to Súmukha he gave a cane seat fit for a chief minister.

atha Bodhisattvaḥ kāla idānīṃ pratisaṃmoditum iti nū-pur'|ārāva|madhureṇa svareṇa rājānam ābabhāṣe:

22.115 «dyuti|kānti|niketane śarīre
kuśalaṃ te kuśal'|ârha kac cid asmin?
api dharma|śarīram a|vraṇaṃ te
vipulair ucchvasit' îva vāk|pradānaiḥ? [66]

api rakṣaṇa|dīkṣitaḥ prajānāṃ
samay'|ânugraha|nigraha|pravṛttyā†
abhivardhayase sva|kīrti|śobham
anurāgaṃ jagatāṃ† hit'|ôdayaṃ ca? [67]

api śuddhatay" ôpadhāsv a|saktair
anuraktair nipuṇa|kriyair amātyaiḥ
samavekṣayase hitaṃ prajānāṃ?
na ca tatr' āsi parokṣa|buddhir eva? [68]

naya|vikrama|saṃhṛta|pratāpair
api sāmanta|nṛpaiḥ prayācyamānaḥ
upayāsi dayā|pravṛtti|śobhāṃ†
na ca viśvāsa|mayīṃ pramāda|nidrām? [69]

api dharma|sukh'|ârtha|nirvirodhās
tava ceṣṭā, nara|vīra, saj|jan'|êṣṭāḥ
vitatā iva dikṣu kīrti|siddhyā
ripubhir niśvasitair a|sat|kriyante?» [70]

22.120 ath' âinaṃ sa nṛ|patiḥ pramodād abhivyajyamān'|êndriya|prasādaḥ pratyuvāca:

Reflecting that it was now time to greet the king, the Bodhi·sattva addressed him with a voice as soft as the sound of anklets:

"Your body, full of splendor and beauty, 22.115
I trust is well, health-deserving king?
Is your body of virtue also in good health?
Does it exhale abundant gifts of speech?

Consecrated to protect your subjects
with due rewards and restraints,
do you increase your glorious fame
and the affection and welfare of your people?

Assisted by skilled and affectionate ministers,
their purity making them incapable of deceit,
do you care for the welfare of your subjects?
I hope you do not overlook this matter?

When vassal kings entreat you,
enfeebled by your justice and strength,
do you turn to the glory of compassion
and avoid the sleepy carelessness of credulity?

Do your acts never impede virtue, profit or desire?
Are they approved by the good, hero of men?
Does your fame spread them in all directions?
Can enemies injure them only with sighs?"

The king replied with the following words, his joy revealing the tranquility of his senses: 22.120

«adya me kuśalaṃ, haṃsa, sarvatr' âiva† bhaviṣyati,
cir'|âbhilaṣitaḥ prāpto yad ayaṃ sat|samāgamaḥ. [71]

tvayi pāśa|vaśaṃ prāpte
 praharṣ'|ôddhata|cāpalaḥ
kac cin n' âyam akāriṣīt te
 daṇḍen' âbhirujan rujam? [72]

evaṃ hy amīṣāṃ jālmānāṃ pakṣiṇāṃ vyasan'|ôdaye
praharṣ'|ākulitā buddhir āpataty eva kalmaṣam.» [73]

Bodhisattva uvāca:

22.125 «kṣemam āsīn, mahā|rāja, satyām apy evam āpadi.
na c' âyaṃ kiṃ cid asmāsu śatruvat pratyapadyata. [74]

a|baddhaṃ baddhavad ayaṃ
 mat|snehāt Sumukhaṃ sthitam
dṛṣṭv" âbhāṣata sāmn" âiva
 sa|kautūhala|vismayaḥ. [75]

sūnṛtair asya vacanair ath' āvarjita|mānasaḥ
mām ayaṃ vyamucat pāśād vinayād anumānayan. [76]

"On this day I shall be well
in all respects, good goose.
For I have acquired my wish,
long-desired, to meet the good.

I hope this fellow did not harm you
when you were seized by the snare,
striking you with his stick
and reckless in his joy?

For thus are these vile men:
when birds are in distress,
their minds, confused by joy,
commit an impure sin."

The Bodhi·sattva replied:

"I was safe, Your Majesty,
despite the disastrous event.
This fellow did not at all act
toward me like an enemy.

22.125

When he saw Súmukha standing there,
unbound but resembling one bound,
he was filled with curiosity and surprise
and addressed us with very gentle words.

His heart was moved
by Súmukha's fine words
and he released me from the snare,
honoring me respectfully.

atas ca Sumukhen' êdaṃ
  hitam asya samīhitam:
ih' āgamanam asmākaṃ
  syād asy' âpi sukh'|ôdayam!» [77]

nṛ|patir uvāca:

22.130 «ākāṅkṣit'|âbhyāgamayoḥ† sv|āgataṃ bhavator iha!
atīva prīṇitaś c' âsmi yuṣmat|saṃdarśan'|ôtsavāt! [78]

ayaṃ ca mahat" ârthena
  naiṣādo 'dya sameṣyati.
ubhayeṣāṃ priyaṃ kṛtvā
  mahad arhaty ayaṃ priyam.» [79]

ity uktvā sa rājā taṃ naiṣādaṃ mahatā dhana|vistara|pradānena saṃmānya punar haṃsa|rājam uvāca:

«imaṃ svam āvāsam upāgatau yuvāṃ.
  visṛjyatāṃ tan mayi yantraṇā|vratam.
prayojanaṃ yena yathā, tad ucyatāṃ,
  bhavat|sahāyā hi vibhūtayo mama. [80]

a|śaṅkit'|ôktaiḥ praṇay'|âkṣaraiḥ suhṛt
  karoti tuṣṭiṃ vibhava|sthitasya yām,
na tad|vidhāṃ lambhayate sa tāṃ dhanair.
  mah"|ôpakāraḥ praṇayaḥ suhṛtsv ataḥ.» [81]

That is why Súmukha
wished for this man's welfare.
May our coming here
bring him happiness too!"

The king said:

"I have longed for your arrival. 22.130
Welcome to you both!
I am greatly delighted
by the thrill of seeing you!

This hunter will instantly
be given vast wealth.
For he deserves a reward
in being kind to you both."

Saying these words, the king honored the hunter by giving him a huge amount of wealth and then once again addressed the royal goose, saying:

"This house you are in is your home.
Cease all constraints toward me.
Tell me how I can serve your needs.
For my riches are here to assist you.

The satisfaction a friend gives a rich man
through clear requests exceeds the satisfaction
a rich man gives through offerings of wealth.
For requests among friends are a great benefit."

22.135 atha sa rājā Sumukha|saṃbhāṣaṇa|kutūhala|hṛdayaḥ sa|vismayam abhivīkṣya Sumukham uvāca:

«a|labdha|gādhā nava|saṃstave jane
na yānti kāmaṃ praṇaya|pragalbhatām.
vacas tu dākṣiṇya|samāhit'|âkṣaraṃ
na te na jalpanty upacāra|śībharam? [82]

saṃbhāṣaṇen' âpi yataḥ
kartum arhati no bhavān
sāphalyaṃ praṇay'|āśāyāḥ,
prīteś c' ôpacayaṃ hṛdi.» [83]

ity ukte Sumukho haṃsa|senā|patir vinayād abhipraṇamy' âinam uvāca:

«mah"|êndra|kalpena saha tvayā saṃbhāṣaṇ'|ôtsavaḥ.
iti darśita|sauhārde kasya n' âti|mano|rathaḥ? [84]

22.140 saṃbhāṣamāṇe tu nar'|âdhipe ca
sauhārda|ramyaṃ vihag'|âdhipe ca,
tat|saṃkathā|madhyam upetya dhārṣṭyān
nanv a|kramaḥ preṣya|janasya vaktum? [85]

na hy eṣa mārgo vinay'|âbhijātas.
taṃ c' âiva jānan katham abhyupeyām?
tūṣṇīṃ, mahā|rāja, yataḥ sthito 'haṃ.
tan marṣaṇīyaṃ yadi marṣaṇīyam.» [86]

The king was also curious to converse with Súmukha. 22.135
Looking at him with wonder, he addressed him with the following words:

"Of course one never presumes intimacy
when a new acquaintance has yet to gain depth.
But can one not talk together amiably
with delightful and courteous words?

Merely by talking
with me, good sir,
you would fulfill my hope for intimacy
and increase the joy in my heart."

Addressed this way, Súmukha, the general of the geese, respectfully bowed before the king and said these words:

"It is a joy to speak with you,
a rival to mighty Indra himself.
Who would not feel their desires
exceeded by this display of friendship?

But when a human king and a bird king 22.140
converse with such delightful friendliness,
would it not be wrong for a servant
to interrupt their conversation brashly?

One bred to be polite does not behave this way.
Knowing this, how could I intrude?
That is why I stood here silently, great king.
Forgive me if there is something to be forgiven."

ity ukte sa rājā praharṣa†|vismaya|vikasita|nayanaḥ† saṃrādhayan Sumukham ity† uvāca:

«sthāne bhavad|guṇa|kathā ramayanti lokaṃ!
sthāne 'si haṃsa|patinā gamitaḥ sakhitvam!
evaṃ|vidhaṃ hi vinayaṃ naya|sauṣṭhavaṃ ca
n' âiv' â|kṛt'|ātma|hṛdayāni samudvahanti! [87]

tad iyaṃ prastutā prītir
vicchidyeta yathā na naḥ,
tath" êtaṃ mayi viśrambham.†
a|jaryaṃ hy ārya|saṃgatam.» [88]

22.145 atha Bodhisattvas tasya rājñaḥ parāṃ prīti|kāmatām avetya sneha|pravṛtti|sumukhatāṃ ca saṃrādhayann avocad enam:

«yat kṛtyaṃ parame mitre,
kṛtam asmāsu tat tvayā
saṃstave 'bhinave† 'py asmin
sva|māhātmy'|ânuvartinā. [89]

kasya† nāma, mahā|rāja,
n' âvalambeta† cetasi
saṃmāno vidhin"† ânena
yas tvay" âsmāsu darśitaḥ? [90]

prayojanaṃ nāma kiyat kim eva vā
mad|āśrayaṃ, māna|da, yat tvam īkṣase?
priy'|âtithitvaṃ guṇa|vatsalasya te
pravṛttam abhyāsa|guṇād, iti dhruvam. [91]

The king's eyes widened with joy and astonishment at these words and he replied to Súmukha with the following praise:

"How apt that tales of your virtue delight the world!
How apt that you are friends with this lord of geese!
For those with imperfect hearts cannot display
such modesty, prudence and excellence!

May this friendship never be severed
now it has been embarked upon.
Place your trust in me.
For a union of noble beings never decays."

When the Bodhi·sattva saw the king's desire for friendship and his willingness to show affection, he praised him, saying: 22.145

"Though our acquaintance is new,
you have acted toward us
as one would toward a best friend,
following your magnanimous nature.

Whose heart would not be gripped
by the honor you have shown us?

How much benefit and of what kind
do you see in a friendship with me, king?
Certainly, in your fondness for virtue,
you practice kind hospitality as a habit.

na citram etat tvayi vā jit'|ātmani
prajā|hit'|ârthaṃ dhṛta|pārthiva|vrate
tapaḥ|samādhāna|pare munāv iva.
svabhāva|vṛttyā hi guṇās tvayi sthitāḥ. [92]

22.150 iti praśaṃsā|su|bhagāḥ sukhā guṇā.
na doṣa|dur|geṣu vasanti bhūtayaḥ.
imāṃ viditvā guṇa|doṣa|dharmatāṃ
sa|cetanaḥ kaḥ sva|hit'|ôtpathaṃ vrajet?† [93]

na deśam āpnoti parākrameṇa taṃ,
na kośa|vīryeṇa, na nīti|saṃpadā,
śrama|vyayābhyāṃ nṛ|patir vin" âiva, yaṃ
guṇ'|âbhijātena path" âdhigacchati. [94]

sur'|âdhipa|śrīr api vīkṣate guṇān.
guṇ'|ôditān eva paraiti saṃnatiḥ.
guṇebhya eva prabhavanti kīrtayaḥ.
prabhāva|māhātmyam iti śritaṃ guṇān. [95]

a|marṣa|darp'|ôdbhava|karkaśāny api,
prarūḍha|vaira|sthira|matsarāṇy api
prasādayanty eva manāṃsi vidviṣāṃ
śaśi|prakāś'|âdhika|kāntayo guṇāḥ. [96]

tad evam eva, kṣiti|pāla, pālayan
mahīṃ pratāp'|ānata|dṛpta|pārthivām
a|manda|śobhair vinay'|ādibhir guṇair
guṇ'|ânurāgaṃ jagataṃ prabodhaya. [97]

Nor is this surprising in one so self-mastered.
Devoted to austerity and meditation like a sage,
you uphold royal vows to benefit your people.
For virtues reside in you as a matter of nature.

Virtues bring joy and are blessed by praise. 22.150
There is no such prosperity in the perils of vice.
Knowing the nature of virtue and vice,
what sane man would stray from a path of benefit?

Neither power, treasury nor good policy
can bring a king to the same position
as he reaches through the path of virtue,
however great his effort or expenses.

The glorious king of gods himself heeds virtues.
Humility exists even in those eminent in virtue.
It is from virtues that fame arises.
The majesty of power depends on them.

Virtues are lovelier than the moon's splendor.
They alone can appease the hearts of enemies,
however hardened by anger and pride,
however their envy is entrenched by deep hatred.

Protect the earth, guardian of the land,
her proud kings subdued by your power,
and use your discipline and other bright virtues
to awaken in creatures a passion for morality.

22.155 prajā|hitaṃ kṛtyatamaṃ mahī|pates.
tad asya panthā hy ubhayatra bhūtaye.
bhavec ca tad rājani dharma|vatsale.
nṛ|pasya vṛttaṃ hi jano 'nuvartate. [98]

praśādhi dharmeṇa vasuṃ|dharām ataḥ!
karotu rakṣāṃ tridaś'|âdhipaś ca te!
tvad|antikāt saṃśrita|bhāvanād api
sva|yūthya|duḥkhaṃ tu vikarṣat' îva mām.» [99]

atha sa rājā samabhinandya tat tasya vacanaṃ sa|parṣatkaḥ saṃmānana† | priya | vacana | prayoga | puraḥsaraṃ tau haṃsa | mukhyau visasarja. atha Bodhisattvaḥ samutpatya vimala | khaḍg' | âbhinīlaṃ śarat | prasanna | śobhaṃ gagana | talaṃ pratibimben' êv' ânugamyamānaḥ Sumukhena haṃsa | senā | patinā samupetya haṃsa | yūthaṃ saṃdarśanād eva pareṇa praharṣeṇa saṃyojayām āsa.

kālena c' ôpetya nṛ|paṃ sa haṃsaḥ
par'|ânukampa|vyasanī sa|haṃsaḥ,
jagāda dharmaṃ kṣiti|pena tena
pratyarcyamāno vinay'|ānatena. [100]

tad evaṃ, vinipāta | gatānām api satāṃ vṛttaṃ n' âlam anukartum† a|sat|puruṣāḥ, prāg eva su|gati|ṣṭhānām iti.

22.160 «evaṃ kalyāṇī vāg ubhaya|hit'|āvahā bhavat'» îti kalyāṇa| vacana | praśaṃsāyām apy upaneyam. kalyāṇa | mitra | varṇe 'pi vācyam: «evaṃ kalyāṇa | mitravatāṃ kṛcchre 'py arthāḥ saṃsidhyant'» îti. sthavir'|āry'|Ānanda|pūrva|sa|bhāga|pra-

A king's highest duty is the welfare of his people. 22.155
This path brings prosperity in this world and the next.
It will arise in a king devoted to goodness.
For people tend to follow the behavior of their king.

So rule over the earth justly!
May the king of gods protect you!
Though I prosper from your company,
the suffering of my flock troubles me."

The king and his assembly rejoiced at the Bodhi·sattva's words and, after expressing kind words of respect, the monarch let the two fine geese leave. The Bodhi·sattva then flew into the sky, which was as blue as an unstained sword-blade and radiant with the tranquility of autumn, while Sú-mukha, the general of the geese, followed behind him like a shadow. When the Bodhi·sattva approached the flock of geese, the mere sight of him filled them with the greatest joy.

In his devout compassion for others, the goose
in time returned to the king with his flock,
speaking to him of virtue, while the monarch
honored him with humble submission.

In this way, even when they are in trouble, the virtuous behave in ways that cannot be imitated by the bad, let alone when their situation is good.

This story should be cited in praise of fine speech, saying: "In this way fine words bring benefits to both sides." One should also narrate this speech when eulogizing good friendship, saying: "In this way those who have good friends 22.160

darśane ca vācyam:† «evam ayaṃ sthaviraḥ saha|carita|caraṇo Bodhisattvena cira|kāl'|âbhyasta|prema|bahu|māno 'bhavad» iti.†

gain success even in difficult times." And in order to reveal that the venerable noble Anánda shared in the Buddha's past lives, one should state the following: "So this elder shared in the conduct of the Bodhi·sattva and habitually developed his love and respect for him over a long period of time."

MAHĀBODHIJĀTAKAM

STORY 23

THE LARGER BIRTH-STORY OF BODHI

23.1 A|SAT|KṚTĀNĀM api sat|puruṣāṇāṃ pūrv'|ôpakāriṣv anukampā na śithilī|bhavati, kṛta|jñatvāt kṣamā|sātmyāc ca.

tad|yath" ânuśrūyate.

Bodhisattva|bhūtaḥ kil' âyaṃ bhagavān Bodhir† nāma parivrājako babhūva. sa gṛha|stha|bhāva eva parividita|krama|prayāmo† lok'|âbhimatānāṃ vidyā|sthānānāṃ kṛta|jñāna|kautūhalaś citrāsu ca kalāsu pravrajy"|āśrayāl loka|hit'|ôdyogāc ca viśeṣavattaraṃ dharma|śāstreṣv avahita|matis teṣv ācāryakaṃ padam avāpa.

sa kṛta|puṇyatvāj jñāna|māhātmyāl loka|jñatayā pratipatti|guṇa|sauṣṭhavāc ca yatra yatra gacchati sma, tatra tatr' âiva viduṣāṃ vidvat|priyāṇāṃ ca rājñāṃ rāja|mātrāṇāṃ† brāhmaṇa|gṛhapatīnām anya|tīrthikānāṃ ca pravrajitānām abhigamanīyo bhāvanīyaś ca babhūva.

23.5 guṇā hi puṇy'|āśraya|labdha|dīptayo
gatāḥ priyatvaṃ pratipatti|śobhayā
api dviṣadbhyaḥ sva|yaśo|'nurakṣayā
bhavanti satkāra|viśeṣa|bhāginaḥ. [1]

atha sa mah"|ātmā lok'|ânugrah'|ârtham anuvicaran grāma|nagara|nigama|janapada|rāṣṭra|rājadhānīr anyatamasya rājño viṣay'|ântam† upajagāma. śruta|guṇa|vistara|prabhāvas tu sa rājā tasy' āgamanaṃ dūrata ev' ôpalabhya prīta|manā ramaṇīye svasminn udyāna|vana|pradeśe

EVEN WHEN WRONGED, good men never lessen their compassion toward those who have previously aided them. Such is their gratitude and inherent forgiveness. 23.1

Tradition has handed down the following story.

When he was a Bodhi·sattva, the Lord* is said to have once been a wandering ascetic called Bodhi. While still a householder, he mastered the method and extent of the world-esteemed sciences and was keen to acquire knowledge in the various arts. As an ascetic, his endeavor to benefit the world led him to apply his mind more specifically to the moral treatises,* in which he acquired the status of a master.

The merit he had accumulated, the magnificence of his wisdom, his knowledge of the world and his excellent conduct meant that, wherever he went, he was welcomed and honored by the learned and by kings who were fond of the learned, as well as by royal ministers, brahmins and householders, and ascetics from other sects.

Virtues become splendid when based on merit 23.5
and charming when illuminated by practice.
Even enemies show them exceptional honor,
concerned to protect their reputation.

As he wandered through villages, towns, market-places, countries, kingdoms and royal capitals in his desire to help the world, the Great One arrived in the realm of a certain king. The king had heard of the ascetic's abundant virtue and when he learned of his (albeit still distant) arrival, he was delighted and had a residence built for him in a lovely area of his park. After going to meet him and showing him

tasy' āvasatham kārayām āsa. abhyudgaman'|ādi|satkāra|puraḥsaram c' âinam praveśya sva|viṣayam śiṣya iv' ācāryaṃ paricaraṇa|paryupāsana|vidhinā saṃmānayām āsa.

vibhūti|guṇa|saṃpannam upetaḥ praṇayād gṛham
guṇa|priyasya guṇavān utsav'|âtiśayo 'tithiḥ. [2]

Bodhisattvo 'pi c' âinaṃ śruti|hṛdaya|hlādinībhir dharmyābhiḥ kathābhiḥ śreyo|mārgam anupratipādayamānaḥ pratyaham anujagrāha.

a|dṛṣṭa|bhaktiṣv api dharma|vatsalā
hitaṃ vivakṣanti par'|ânukampinaḥ.
ka eva vādaḥ śuci|bhājan'|ôpame
hit'|ârthini prema|guṇ'|ônmukhe† jane? [3]

23.10 atha tasya rājño 'mātyā labdha|vidvat|saṃbhāvanā labdha|saṃmānāś ca sadasyāḥ pratyaham abhivardhamāna|satkārāṃ Bodhisattvasya guṇa|vibhūtim† īrṣy"|ôpahata|matitvān† na sehire.

sva|guṇ'|âtiśay'|ôditair yaśobhir
jagad|āvarjana|dṛṣṭa|śakti|yogaḥ
racanā|guṇa|mātra|sat|kṛteṣu
jvalayaty eva pareṣv a|marṣa|vahnim. [4]

prasahya c' âinaṃ śāstra|kathāsv abhibhavitum a|śaktā dharma|prasaṅgam a|mṛṣyamāṇāś ca rājñas tena tena krameṇa rājānaṃ Bodhisattvaṃ prati vigrāhayām āsuḥ:

various other acts of honor, the king led the ascetic into his kingdom and venerated him by serving and attending him as a disciple serves a teacher.

There is great joy when
a virtuous guest amiably
arrives at the wealthy house
of a lover of virtue.

Every day the Bodhi·sattva favored the king with moral discourses that gladdened the ear and heart, encouraging him to follow the path to bliss.

In their compassion for others, lovers of virtue
seek to give advice even to the unaffectionate,
let alone to those pure vessels who yearn
for their friendship and wish them well.

23.10 Although the king esteemed his ministers for their learning and treated his advisors with respect, they still could not endure the increasing honor that was paid to the Bodhi·sattva's abundant virtue every day. For their minds were afflicted by envy.

When a person shows ability to inspire the world
through a fame elevated by exceptional virtue,
they ignite a flame of intolerance in other men,
whose esteem rests merely on fabrication.

Incapable of defeating the Bodhi·sattva outright in discussions on the Treatises and intolerant of the king's commitment to virtue, they incited discord between the king and the Bodhi·sattva through strategies such as the following:

«n' ârhati devo Bodhi|parivrājake viśvāsam upagantum. vyaktam ayaṃ devasya guṇa|priyatāṃ dharm'|âbhimukhatāṃ c' ôpalabhya vyasana|pratāraṇā†|ślakṣṇa|śaṭha|vacanaḥ pravṛtti|saṃcāra|hetu†|bhūtaḥ kasy' âpi pratyarthino rājño nipuṇaḥ praṇidhi|prayogaḥ.

tathā hi dharm'|ātmako nāma bhūtvā devam ek'|ântena kāruṇya|pravṛttau hrī|dainye ca samanuśāsty, artha|kām'|ôparodhiṣu ca kṣatra|dharma|bāhyeṣv āsann'|âpanayeṣu dharma|samādāneṣu. day"|ânuvṛttyā ca nāma te kṛtya|pakṣam āśvāsana|vidhin" ôpagṛhṇīte† priya|saṃstavaś c' ânya|rāja|dūtaiḥ. na c' âyam a|vidita|vṛttānto rāja|śāstrāṇām. ataḥ s'|āśaṅkāny atra no hṛdayān' îti.»

23.15 atha tasya rājñaḥ punaḥ punar bhed'|ôpasaṃhitaṃ hitam iva bahubhir ucyamānasya Bodhisattvaṃ prati pariśaṅkā|saṃkocita|sneha|gaurava|prasaram anyādṛśaṃ cittam abhavat.

paiśunya|vajr'|âśani|saṃnipāte
bhīma|svane v" âśani†|saṃnipāte
viśrambhavān mānuṣa|mātra|dhairyaḥ
syān nir|vikāro yadi nāma kaś cit? [5]

atha sa rājā viśrambha|virahān mandī|bhūta|prema|bahu|mānas tasmin Mahā|sattve na yathā|pūrvaṃ sat|kāra|prayoga|sumukho babhūva. Bodhisattvo 'pi śuddha|svabhāvatvāt bahu|kārya|vyāsaṅgā rājāna iti tan manasi

"Your Majesty should not place your trust in this ascetic Bodhi. He is clearly a cunning spy, working for some hostile king. He has learned of Your Majesty's love of virtue and your predilection for morality and now uses smooth and false words to lure you into wickedness, reporting your actions to his king.

Setting himself up as righteous, he instructs Your Majesty to practice pity exclusively and to feel the misery of shame. He encourages you to adopt moral vows that conflict with profit and pleasure and that are irrelevant to the kshatriya law* and entail bad policies. His apparent motivation for exhorting you and telling you how to act is compassion. But he also enjoys a fond friendship with the messengers of other kings. Nor is he unfamiliar with the contents of royal treatises. That is why our hearts are worried about the matter."

After many had addressed the king again and again with such divisive words that were disguised as well-meaning, the king's feelings changed and his free-flowing affection and respect became constricted by suspicion. 23.15

When slander strikes with its thunderbolts,
or lightning strikes with its terrifying sound,
does anyone remain unaffected,
confident and secure in mere human strength?

The king's mistrust meant his love and respect for the Great Being lessened and he no longer felt inclined to honor him. Due to the purity of his nature, the Bodhi·sattva did not take it to heart, reasoning that kings are busy with their many duties. But when he saw that the people around the

cakāra. tat|samīpa|parivartinām† tu vinay'|ôpacāra|śaithilya|saṃdarśanād virakta|hṛdayam avetya rājānaṃ samādāya tri|daṇḍa|kuṇḍik"|ādyāṃ parivrājaka|bhāṇḍikāṃ prakramaṇa|savyāpāraḥ samabhavat. tad upaśrutya sa rājā s' | âvaśeṣa | snehatayā dākṣiṇya | vinay' | ânuvṛttyā c' âinam abhigamya pradarśita|saṃbhramo vinivartayitu|kāma|vad† uvāca:

«asmān a|kasmād apahāya kasmād
gantavya eva praṇatā matis te?
vyalīka|śaṅkā|janakaṃ nu kiṃ cid
dṛṣṭaṃ pramāda|skhalitaṃ tvayā naḥ?» [6]

ath' âinaṃ Bodhisattva uvāca:

23.20 «n' â|kasmiko 'yaṃ gaman'|ôdyamo me.
n' â|sat|kriyā|mātraka|rūkṣitatvāt.
a|bhājanatvaṃ tu gato 'si śāṭhyād
dharmasya. ten' âham ito vrajāmi.» [7]

ath' âsya sa|rabhasa|bhāṣitam ati|vivṛta|vadanam abhidravantaṃ vallabhaṃ śvānaṃ tatr' âbhigatam† abhipradarśayan punar uvāca:

«ayaṃ c' âtra, mahā|rāja, a|mānuṣaḥ s'|âkṣi|nirdeśo dṛśyatām.

ayaṃ hi pūrvaṃ paṭu|cāṭu|karmā
bhūtvā mayi śvā bhavato 'nuvṛttyā
ākāra|gupty|a|jñatayā tv idānīṃ
tvad|bhāva|sūcāṃ bhaṣitaiḥ karoti. [8]

king were acting with less politeness and courtesy toward him, he understood that the monarch had withdrawn his affections. Gathering his trident, waterpot and other ascetic utensils, he made preparations to depart. On hearing the news, the king approached the ascetic, motivated by a remnant of affection as well as by civility and courtesy. Displaying concern and feigning a desire to restrain him, he said:

"Why have you decided you must leave,
deserting us for no obvious reason?
Did you see something offensive or troubling,
some neglectful error on our part?"

The Bodhi·sattva replied with the following words:

23.20

"My desire to leave is not without reason.
Nor is it merely disrespect that grates me.
Your deceit stops you being a vessel of virtue.
That is why I am leaving from this place."

Just at that moment, the king's favorite dog came running up to that spot, barking fiercely and baring its mouth. Pointing to the dog, the Bodhi·sattva again addressed the king, saying:

"Treat this animal as a clear illustration of the matter, great king.

This dog used to be very affectionate
toward me because it imitated you.
But now, not knowing how to hide its feelings,
it shows your true nature through its barks.

tvattaḥ śrutaṃ kiṃ cid anena nūnaṃ
 mad|antare bhakti|vipatti|rūkṣam?
ato 'nuvṛttaṃ dhruvam ity anena
 tvat|prīti|hetor anujīvi|vṛttam.» [9]

23.25 atha sa rājā tat|pratyādeśād vrīḍ"|âvanata†|vadanas tena c' âsya mati|naipuṇyena samāvarjita|matir jāta|saṃvego, n' êdānīṃ śāṭhy'|ânuvṛtti|kāla iti Bodhisattvam abhipraṇamy' ôvāca:

«tvad|āśrayā kā cid abhūt kath" âiṣā
 saṃprastutā naḥ sadasi pragalbhaiḥ;
upekṣitā kārya|vaśān mayā ca.
 tat kṣamyatāṃ, tiṣṭha ca. sādhu mā gāḥ.» [10]

Bodhisattva uvāca: «n' âiva khalv ahaṃ, mahā|rāja, a|sat|kāra|prakṛtatvād a|kṣamayā vā praṇudyamāṇo gacchāmi. na tv ayaṃ, mahā|rāja, avasthāna|kāla; iti na tiṣṭhāmi. paśyatu bhavān:

vimadhya|bhāvād api hīna|śobhe
 yāyāṃ na satkāra|vidhau svayaṃ cet
saṅgād a|gatyā jaḍatā|balād vā,
 nanv ardha|candr'|âbhinay'|ôttaraḥ syām? [11]

prāpta|kramo 'yaṃ vidhir atra, tena
 yāsyāmi, n' â|prīty|abhitapta|cittaḥ.
ek'|âvamān'|âbhihatā hi satsu
 pūrv'|ôpakārā na samī|bhavanti. [12]

Perhaps he heard you say words
harsh and unfriendly toward me?
Now, to please you, he follows them,
in the way that dependents do."

The king responded to this rebuke by lowering his head with shame, his heart stirred by the Bodhi·sattva's intellectual dexterity. Filled with a sense of shock, he decided that this was no longer the time for deceit and instead bowed before the ascetic, saying: 23.25

"Some insolent men did indeed utter
such words about you in my assembly.
I allowed it, pressurized by my duties.
Forgive me. Stay here. Please do not go."

"I am not leaving because I was insulted," the Bodhi·sattva answered. "Nor am I driven by resentment. The reason I cannot stay is because it is inappropriate for me to dwell here, great king. Consider this:

My mediocre status gives me but drab honor.
If due to attachment, lethargy or helplessness
I do not leave of my own accord,
will I not later be forced out by the throat?

This act is right in the circumstances. So I'll go.
But not because my mind burns with displeasure.
For in good men, former favors are not leveled
by the blow of a single act of disrespect.

23.30 a|snigdha|bhāvas tu na paryupāsyas,
toy'|ârthinā śuṣka iv' ôdapānaḥ.
prayatna|sādhy" âpi tato 'rtha|siddhir
yasmād bhaved ākaluṣā kṛśā ca. [13]

prasanna eva tv abhigamya|rūpaḥ
śarad|viśuddh'|âmbu|mahā|hrad'|ābhaḥ
sukh'|ârthinaḥ kleśa|parāṅ|mukhasya
loka|prasiddhaḥ sphuṭa eṣa mārgaḥ. [14]

bhakty|unmukhād yo 'pi parāṅ|mukhaḥ syāt
parāṅ|mukhe c' âbhimukhatva|dīnaḥ
pūrv'|ôpakāra|smaraṇ'|ālaso vā
nar'|ākṛtiś cintya|viniścayaḥ saḥ. [15]

a|sevanā c' âty|upasevanā ca
yācñ"|âbhiyogāś ca dahanti maitrīm.
rakṣyaṃ yataḥ prīty|avaśeṣam etan
nivāsa|doṣād, iti yāmi tāvat.» [16]

rāj" ôvāca: «yady avaśyam eva gantavyam iti niścit" âtra|bhavato matiḥ, tat punar ap' îdānīm ih' āgamanen' âsmān anugrahītum arhati bhavān. a|sevanād api hi prītir anurakṣitavy" âiva.»

23.35 Bodhisattva uvāca: «bahv|antarāyo, mahā|rāja, bah'|ûpadrava|pratyarthikatvāl loka|saṃniveśa, iti na śakyam etad avadhāraṇayā pratijñātum, ‹āgamiṣyām'› îti. sati tv āgamana|kāraṇa|sākalye 'pi nāma punar bhavantaṃ paśyema.»

ity anunīya sa mah"|ātmā taṃ rājānaṃ kṛt'|âbhyanujñā|satkāras tena rājñā tad|viṣayāt pracakrāma. sa tena gṛhi|jana|saṃstaven' ākulita|hṛdayo 'nyatamad araṇy'|āyatanam

One should not frequent unaffectionate people, 23.30
just as a thirsty man should not go to a dry well.
Great effort is needed to benefit from them.
It would be a mixed blessing of meager value.

Those seeking comfort and averse to hardship
should approach people who are serene.
They are like large lakes of pure water in autumn.
This is the clear path proclaimed in the world.

Those who spurn people gazing up in devotion,
or who grieve when friendship is turned away,
or who are lazy in remembering past services,
are men but in form, their identity questionable.

Friendship is destroyed by neglect,
excessive attention and constant requests.
So I'll leave to protect our remaining affection
from the harmful effects of staying here."

The king replied: "If Your Reverence has decided that it is essential to leave, then please favor us by returning here once more. For friendship should indeed be protected from neglect."

"Living in the world involves many hindrances, Your Majesty," the Bodhi·sattva replied. "For it is full of hostile dangers. I therefore cannot promise that I will come again. But if there is a necessary reason for returning, I hope that I will see you once more." 23.35

Conciliating the king with these polite words, the Great One was honored by the monarch and given leave to depart, whereupon he set off from the realm. The Bodhi·sattva felt disturbed by close contact with householders, so he took to

upaśritya dhyān' | âbhiyukta | matis tatra viharann a | cireṇ' âiva catvāri dhyānāni pañca c' âbhijñāḥ† pratilebhe.

tasya samāsvādita|praśama|sukha|rasasya smṛtir anukamp"|ânusāriṇī taṃ rājānaṃ prati prādur|abhūt: kā nu khalu tasya rājño 'vasth" êti. ath' âinaṃ dadarśa tair amātyair yath" | âbhiniviṣṭāni dṛṣṭi | gatāni prati pratāryamāṇam. kaś cid enam amātyo dur|vibhāvya|hetubhir nidarśanair a|hetu| vādaṃ prati pracakarṣa:

«kaḥ padma|nāla|dala|kesara|karṇikānāṃ
saṃsthāna|varṇa|racanā|mṛdut"|ādi|hetuḥ?
patrāṇi citrayati ko 'tra patatriṇāṃ vā?
svābhāvikaṃ jagad idaṃ niyataṃ tath" âiva.» [17]

apara īśvara|kāraṇam asmai sva|buddhi|racitam† upavarṇayām āsa:

23.40 «n' â|kasmikaṃ bhavitum arhati sarvam etad.
asty atra sarvam adhi kaś cid an|anta ekaḥ,
sv'|êcchā|viśeṣa|niyamād ya imaṃ vicitraṃ
lokaṃ karoti ca punaś ca samī|karoti.» [18]

«sarvam idaṃ pūrva | karma | kṛtaṃ sukh' | â | sukham na prayatna|sāmarthyam ast'» îty evam anya enaṃ vigrāhayām āsa:

an area of the forest, where he dwelled focusing his mind on meditation until he soon acquired the four dhyana concentrations and the five transcendent knowledges.*

While the Bodhi·sattva was relishing the joy of tranquility, compassion led him to recall the king and ponder how he was faring. He saw that the ministers were enticing him to follow the false views to which they were variously attached.* One of the ministers proclaimed the doctrine of non-causality, using examples in which causality was hard to perceive:

"What causes qualities such as
form, color, structure and softness
in the stalk, petals, filaments
and pericarp of a lotus?
Who applies the various colors to
the feathers of birds in the world?
The world is therefore fixed
and has an inherent nature."

Another minister eulogized God as a primary cause, an idea he had fabricated in his own mind:

"This entire world cannot be uncaused. 23.40
Some being governs all this, infinite and one.
Through the special application of his will,
he creates the varied world and levels it again."

Another minister tried to persuade the king that everything in the world was created by former actions, whether pleasant or painful, and could not be influenced by any effort:

«evaṃ kariṣyati kathaṃ nu samāna|kālaṃ
bhinn'|āśrayān bahu|vidhān a|mitāṃś ca bhāvān?
sarvaṃ tu pūrva|kṛta|karma|nimittam etat.
saukhya|prayatna|nipuṇo 'pi hi duḥkham eti.» [19]

apara uccheda|vāda|kathābhir enaṃ kām'|ôpabhoga†|prasaṅga eva pratārayām āsa:

«dārūṇi n'|âika|vidha|varṇa|guṇ'|ākṛtīni
karm'|ātmakāni na bhavanti, bhavanti c' âiva.
naṣṭāni n' âiva ca yathā punar udbhavanti,
lokas tath" âyam, iti saukhya|parāyaṇaḥ syāt.» [20]

23.45 apara enaṃ kṣatra|vidyā|paridṛṣṭeṣu nīti|kauṭilya|prasaṅgeṣu nairghṛṇya|malineṣu dharma|virodhiṣv api rāja|dharmo 'yam iti samanuśaśāsa:

«chāyā|drumeṣv iva nareṣu kṛt'|āśrayeṣu
tāvat kṛta|jña|caritaiḥ sva|yaśaḥ parīpset,
n' ârtho 'sti yāvad upayoga|nayena† teṣām.
kṛtye tu yajña iva te paśavo niyojyāḥ.» [21]

"How can anyone create
all the existences at once,
immeasurable and varied,
split into different kinds?
Instead this entire universe
is caused by former actions.
For people still suffer pain,
despite skilled endeavors for happiness."

Another minister, who was attached to the enjoyment of pleasure, enticed the king with discourses on the doctrine of annihilation:

"Pieces of wood differing
in color, quality and form
do not arise from actions
but arise nonetheless.
When they have perished,
they never rise again.
The world is also like this.
One should thus strive for pleasure."

Another minister instructed the king in the teachings of kshatriya science, declaring it to be royal doctrine. Caught up in the crooked ways of politics, these teachings were stained with cruelty and contradicted virtue: 23.45

"By resorting to men as to a shady tree,
one should seek fame through acts of gratitude,
but only while you have no use for them.
When duty calls, use them like sacrificial beasts.

iti te 'mātyās taṃ rājānaṃ tena tena dṛṣṭi|gat'|ônmārgeṇa† netum īṣuḥ.

atha Bodhisattvaḥ pāpa|jana|saṃparka|vaśāt para|pratyaya|neya|buddhitvāc ca dṛṣṭi|gata†|prapāt'|âbhimukham avetya† rājānaṃ tad|anukampā|samāvarjita|hṛdayas tan|nivartan'|ôpāyaṃ vimamarśa.

> guṇ'|âbhyāsena sādhūnām
> kṛtaṃ tiṣṭhati cetasi;
> bhraśyate 'pakṛtaṃ† tasmāj
> jalaṃ padma|dalād iva. [22]

23.50 atha Bodhisattva «idam atra prāpta|kālam» iti viniścitya svasminn āśrama|pade mahāntaṃ vānaram abhinirmāya ṛddhi|prabhāvāt tasya carm' âpanīya śeṣam antar|dhāpayām āsa.

sa tan nirmitaṃ mahad|vānara|carma bibhrat tasya nṛ|pater bhavana|dvāre prādur|abhūt. nivedit'|âbhyāgamanaś ca dauvārikair yathā|kramam āyudhīya|gupta|paryantām amātya|dvija|yodha|dūta|paura|mukhy'|âbhikīrṇāṃ vinīta|dhīr'|ôdātta|veṣa|janāṃ s'|âsi|yaṣṭibhiḥ pratīhārair adhiṣṭhita|pradvārāṃ siṃh'|āsan'|âvasthita|nar'|âdhipām an|ākulāṃ rāja|parṣadam avajagāhe.

In this way, the ministers tried to lead their king along the erring paths of their various false views.

The Bodhi·sattva's heart was stirred by compassion when he realized that the king was about to fall headfirst into the precipice of these false views, partly as a result of keeping company with wicked people and partly because his trust in others meant he was easily led. So he pondered a strategy to restrain him.

Repeated moral practice makes the virtuous
remember good deeds done for them.
But bad deeds slip from their mind
like water from a lotus petal.

After deciding the best course of action in the circumstances, the Bodhi·sattva used his magical power to create the apparition of a huge monkey in his hermitage. Stripping it of its skin, he made the rest of the monkey's body disappear. 23.50

He then appeared at the gate of the king's palace, wearing the skin of the huge monkey that he had created. After the gate-keepers had announced his arrival, he passed in due succession through the outer court, which was guarded by soldiers, until he reached the royal assembly hall, which was teeming with ministers, brahmins, soldiers, envoys and eminent citizens. In this orderly assembly, guarded by gate-keepers bearing swords and staffs, the king was seated on a lion-throne, surrounded by courteous wise men wearing fine clothes.

pratyudgaman'|ādi|vidhinā c' âtithi|jan'|ôpacāreṇa pratipūjyamānaḥ kṛta|saṃmodana†|kathā|satkār'|āsan'|âbhihāraś† ca tena rājñā kautūhal'|ânuvṛttyā vānara|carma|pratilambhaṃ pratyanuyuktaḥ:

«ken' êdam āryāya vānara|carm'|ôpanayatā mahat" ânugraheṇ' ātmā saṃyojita iti?»

Bodhisattva uvāca: «may" âiv' êdaṃ, mahā|rāja, svayam adhigataṃ. n' ânyena kena cid upahṛtam. kuśa|tṛṇa†|mātr'|āstīrṇāyāṃ hi pṛthivyāṃ svabhāva|kaṭhināyāṃ niṣaṇṇena svapatā vā pratapyamāna|śarīreṇa na sukhaṃ dharma|vidhir anuṣṭhīyate. ayaṃ ca may" āśrama|pade mahān vānaro dṛṣṭaḥ. tasya me buddhir abhavat: ‹upapannaṃ bata me dharma|sādhanam: idam asya vānarasya carma! śakyam atra niṣaṇṇena svapatā vā parārdhy'|āstaraṇ'|āstīrṇebhyo rāja|śayanebhyo 'pi nivṛtta|spṛheṇa sva|dharma|vidhir anuṣṭhātum!› iti mayā tasy' êdaṃ carma gṛhītam,† sa ca praśamita iti.»

23.55 tac chrutvā sa rājā dākṣiṇya|vinay'|ânuvṛttyā na Bodhisattvaṃ kiṃ cit pratyuvāca, sa|vrīḍa|hṛdayas tu kiṃ cid avāṅ|mukho babhūva. atha te 'mātyāḥ pūrvam api tasmin Mahā|sattve s'|âmarṣa|hṛdayā labdha|vacan'|âvakāśatvāt pravikasita|smita|vadanā† rājānam udīkṣya Bodhisattvam upadarśayanta ūcuḥ:

The king honored the Bodhi·sattva with the decorum due to a guest by going up to meet him and showing other similar forms of respect. After he had greeted the Bodhi·sattva and respectfully offered him a chair, curiosity then drove the king to ask how he had acquired the monkey-skin:

"Who did themselves the great favor of offering you this monkey-skin, good sir?"

"I acquired it myself, great king," the Bodhi·sattva replied. "No one else offered it to me. I was unable to perform my religious practice properly because my body ached from sitting and sleeping on the hard ground which was strewn only with kusha grass. So when I saw a huge monkey in my hermitage, I had the following thought: 'Aha! Here is a way to aid my moral practice: the skin of this monkey! If I sit or sleep on it, I'll be able to perform my religious practice without even desiring royal couches draped with costly spreads!' With this thought, I took the skin off the monkey as soon as I had quelled it."

23.55 Being polite and well-mannered, the king did not respond to the Bodhi·sattva when he heard these words, but instead hung his head somewhat out of embarrassment. The ministers, on the other hand, held a long-standing grudge against the Great Being. Grasping the opportunity to speak, they looked at the king with faces that beamed with smiles and uttered the following words as they pointed at the Bodhi·sattva:

«aho bhagavato dharm' | ânurāg' | âika | rasā matiḥ! aho dhairyam! aho vyavasāya | sāmarthyam!† āśrama | padam abhigata eva mahān nāma vānara ekākinā tapaḥ|kṣāma|śarīreṇa praśamita, ity āścaryam! sarvathā tapaḥ|siddhir astu!»

ath' âinān a|saṃrabdha eva Bodhisattvaḥ pratyuvāca:

«n' ârhanty atra | bhavantaḥ sva | vāda | śobhā | nirapekṣam ity atr' âsmān† vigarhitum. na hy ayaṃ kramo vidvad|yaśaḥ samudbhāvayitum. paśyantv āyuṣmantaḥ:†

sva|vāda|ghnena vacasā yaḥ parān vijugupsate
sa khalv ātma|vadhen' êva parasy' â|kirtīm icchati.» [23]

23.60 iti sa mah"|ātmā tān amātyān sāmānyen' ôpālabhya pratyekaśaḥ punar upālabdhu|kāmas tam a|hetu|vādinam āmantry' ôvāca:

«svābhāvikaṃ jagad iti pravikatthase tvaṃ.
tattvaṃ ca tad yadi, vikutsayase kim asmān?
śākhā|mṛge nidhanam āpatite sva|bhāvāt
pāpaṃ kuto mama, yataḥ su|hato may" âyam? [24]

atha pāpam asti mama tasya vadhān,
nanu hetutas tad iti siddham idam.
tad a|hetu|vādam imam† utsṛja vā,
vada v" âtra yat tava na yuktam iva. [25]

"Look at how this lordly ascetic delights solely in virtue! Look at his fortitude! Look at his capacity for perseverance! How miraculous that when a monkey—a mighty one no less—entered his hermitage, he quelled it, even though he was alone and his body was emaciated by austerities! May he achieve every success in asceticism!"

Feeling no anger, the Bodhi·sattva replied to the ministers with the following words:

"You should not criticize me on this matter and thereby disregard your own splendid philosophies. That is not the way to increase the glory of your learning. You should consider this, good sirs:

Those who condemn others with words
damaging to their own philosophy
are like people who seek to dishonor
their enemy by destroying themselves."

After thus censuring the ministers in general terms, the Great One sought to attack them further individually. And so he addressed the minister who advocated the doctrine of non-causality as follows: 23.60

"You claim the world has an inherent nature.
If this is true, why accuse me?
If the monkey died due to nature,
what is my crime given I slew him justly?

But if I committed a crime by killing him,
it must have been achieved by some cause.
Reject then this doctrine of non-causality,
or tell me what seems wrong in my argument.

yadi padma|nāla|racan"|ādi ca yat,
 tad a|hetukaṃ nanu sad" âiva bhavet.
salil'|ādi|bīja|kṛtam eva tu tat
 sati tatra saṃbhavati na hy a|sati. [26]

api c', āyuṣman, samyag upadhāraya tāvat:

23.65 na hetur ast' îti vadan sa|hetukam
 nanu pratijñāṃ svayam eva hāpayet!
ath' âpi hetu|praṇay'|âlaso bhavet,
 pratijñayā kevalay" âsya kiṃ bhavet? [27]

ekatra kva cid an|avekṣya yaś ca hetuṃ
 ten' âiva pravadati sarva|hetv|a|bhāvam,
pratyakṣaṃ nanu tad avetya hetu|sāraṃ
 tad|dveṣī bhavati virodha|duṣṭa|vākyaḥ? [28]

na lakṣyate yadi kuha cic ca kāraṇaṃ,
 kathaṃ nu tad dṛḍham a|sad eva bhāṣase?
na dṛśyate sad api hi kāraṇ'|ântarād,
 din'|âtyaye vimalam iv' ârka|maṇḍalam. [29]

nanu ca, bhoḥ,

sukh'|ârtham iṣṭān viṣayān prapadyase,
 niṣevituṃ n' êcchasi tad|virodhinaḥ?
nṛ|pasya sevāṃ ca karoṣi tat|kṛte?
 na hetur ast' îti ca nāma bhāṣase! [30]

23.70 tad evam api ced bhāvān anupaśyasy a|hetukān,
a|hetor vānara|vadhe siddhe kiṃ māṃ vigarhase?» [31]

If the various qualities of a lotus have no cause,
surely they would be found in every situation.
But they are formed by seeds and factors like water.
They arise in these conditions and not others.

You should also carefully consider the following point, good sir:

If people use causal reasoning to declare non-causality, 23.65
surely they discard their own thesis!
But if they are unwilling to use reasoning,
what use is there merely in making a thesis?

If a person says everything lacks a cause
just because they see no cause in a single case,
will they not hate it and abuse it with hostility
when they see it clearly is based on a cause?

If a cause is not perceived in a particular case,
how can you say it definitely does not exist?
Though it exists, it may be invisible for another reason,
like the sun's stainless disc disappears at day's close.

Furthermore, good sir, is it not true that

to gain happiness you seek objects of desire
but you avoid objects that are opposed to it?
Do you not serve the king for this purpose?
And yet still you say there is no causality!

If, despite all this, 23.70
you still maintain that things have no cause,
then the murder of this monkey is causeless.
So how can you censure me?"

iti sa mah"|ātmā tam a|hetu|vādinaṃ viśadair hetubhir niṣ|pratibhaṃ kṛtvā tam īśvara|kāraṇikam āmantry' ôvāca: «āyuṣmān apy asmān n' ârhaty eva vigarhitum. īśvaraḥ sarvasya hi te kāraṇam abhimataḥ. paśya:

kurute yadi sarvam īśvaro,
  nanu ten' âiva hataḥ sa vānaraḥ.
tava k" êyam a|maitra|cittatā,
  para|doṣān mayi yan niṣiñcasi? [32]

atha vānara|vīra|vaiśasaṃ
  na kṛtaṃ tena day"|ânurodhinā,
bṛhad ity avaghuṣyate kathaṃ
  jagataḥ kāraṇam īśvaras tvayā? [33]

23.75 api ca, bhadra, sarvam īśvara|kṛtam iti paśyataḥ,

īśvare prasād'|āśā kā stuti|praṇām'|ādyaiḥ?
sa svayaṃ svayaṃ|bhūs te yat karoti tat karma. [34]

tvat|kṛt" âtha yad' îjyā, na tv asau tad|a|kartā.
ātmano hi vibhūtyā yaḥ karoti, sa kartā. [35]

īśvaraḥ kurute cet pāpakāny akhilāni,
tatra bhakti|niveśaḥ kaṃ guṇaṃ nu samīkṣya? [36]

Stupefying the proponent of non-causality with such clear reasoning, the Great One then addressed the minister who advocated God, saying:

"You too should not accuse me, good sir. For you believe that God is the cause of everything. Consider this:

If God performs everything,
he must be the one who killed the monkey.
How can you have such an unkind heart
as to pour blame on me when another is at fault?

If he did not kill the heroic monkey
because he practices compassion,
then how can you loudly proclaim
the lord as the cause of the world?

Furthermore, good sir, if you hold the view that everything is done by God, 23.75

what hope is there of receiving God's grace
through eulogies, prostrations and other rituals?
For that self-created being
performs your actions himself.

If sacrifices are performed by you,
they are also not unperformed by him.
For an agent is whoever
acts from his own power.

But if God commits every crime,
what value do you see in devotion to him?

tāny a|dharma|bhayād vā yady ayaṃ na karoti,
tena vaktum a|yuktaṃ sarvam īśvara|sṛṣṭam. [37]

23.80 tasya c' ēśvaratā syād dharmataḥ parato vā.
dharmato yadi, na prāg īśvaraḥ sa tato 'bhūt. [38]

dāsat" âiva ca sā syād, yā kriyeta pareṇa.
syād ath' âpi na hetoḥ, kasya n' ēśvaratā syāt? [39]

evam api tu gate bhakti|rāgād a|vigaṇita|yukt'|âyuktasya:

yadi kāraṇam īśvara eva vibhur
jagato nikhilasya tav' âbhimataḥ,
nanu n' ârhasi mayy adhiropayituṃ
vihitaṃ vibhunā kapi|rāja|vadham?» [40]

iti sa mah"|ātmā tam īśvara|kāraṇikaṃ śliṣṭair† hetubhir mūkatām iv' ôpanīya taṃ pūrva|karma|kṛta|vādinam āmantraṇā|sauṣṭhaven' âbhimukhī|kṛty' ôvāca:

23.85 «bhavān apy asmān na śobhate vikutsayamānaḥ. sarvaṃ hi te pūrva|karma|kṛtam ity abhimānaḥ. tena ca tvāṃ bravīmi:

If he does not commit sins
out of fear of immorality,
it is wrong to declare that
everything is created by God.

God's mastery should derive
from either natural law or another cause.
If from natural law,
God did not exist prior to it.

23.80

If from another cause,
it is in fact dependency.
For if dependency does not arise from a cause,
anything at all could be said to have mastery!

Your passion for devotion has made you fail to consider properly what is right and wrong.

If you believe that God alone
causes and rules this entire world,
surely you cannot blame me for the death
of this monkey king if it is ordained by the Lord?"

In this way the Great One made the theist practically speechless through his coherent reasoning. He then turned to the minister who advocated the doctrine that everything is produced from former actions, addressing him skillfully with the following words:

"By accusing me, you also look bad, good sir. For you hold the opinion that everything is produced from former actions. Let me tell you this:

23.85

syāt sarvam eva yadi pūrva|kṛta|prabhāvāc,
chākhā|mṛgaḥ su|hata eva may" âiṣa tasmāt.
dagdhe hi pūrva|kṛta|karma|dav'|âgnin" âsmin
pāpaṃ kim atra mama, yena vigarhase mām? [41]

ath' âsti pāpaṃ mama vānaraṃ ghnataḥ,
kṛtaṃ mayā tarhi, na pūrva|karmaṇā.
yad iṣyate karma ca karma|hetukaṃ,
na kaś cid evaṃ sati mokṣam eṣyati. [42]

bhavec ca saukhyaṃ yadi duḥkha|hetuṣu
sthitasya, duḥkhaṃ sukha|sādhaneṣu vā,
ato 'numīyeta: sukh'|â|sukhaṃ dhruvaṃ
pravartate pūrva|kṛt'|âika|hetukam. [43]

na dṛṣṭam evaṃ ca yataḥ sukh'|â|sukhaṃ,
na pūrva|karm'|âikam ato 'sya kāraṇam.
bhaved a|bhāvaś ca navasya karmaṇas,
tad|a|prasiddhau ca purātanaṃ kutaḥ? [44]

23.90 pūrva|karma|kṛtaṃ sarvam
ath' âivam api manyase,
vānarasya vadhaḥ kasmān
mat|kṛtaḥ parikalpyate?» [45]

iti sa mah"|ātmā nir|anuyojyair hetubhis tasya mauna|vratam iv' ôpadiśya tam uccheda|vādinaṃ smita|pūrvakam uvāca:

«āyuṣmataḥ ko 'yaṃ aty|ādaro 'smad|vigarhāyāṃ, yadi tattvam uccheda|vādaṃ manyase?

If all arises from the power of former actions,
then the monkey was justly killed by me.
For if it was burned by the fire of its former acts,
what crime have I committed to be blamed for?

But if I committed a sin in killing the monkey,
then it was done by me, not by its past actions.
And if karma always causes new karma,
then no-one would ever reach liberation.

If happiness arises in situations causing pain,
or if pain occurs in situations causing happiness,
then one should certainly conclude that
happiness and pain derive only from past acts.

But happiness and pain do not occur this way.
So they are not caused solely by past actions.
And if one never had any new karma,
how could old karma exist in its absence?

But if you still believe that 23.90
all is produced by past actions,
why do you consider the monkey's death
to have been committed by me?"

These incontestable arguments made the minister so speechless he seemed to have taken on a vow of ascetic silence. After instructing him, the Great One went on to address the proponent of annihilation, saying with a smile:

"Why do you show such excessive readiness to accuse me, good sir, when you believe in the doctrine of annihilation?

lokaḥ paro yadi na kaś cana, kiṃ vivarjyaṃ
pāpaṃ? śubhaṃ prati ca kiṃ bahu|māna|mohaḥ?
sva|cchanda|ramya|carito 'tra vicakṣaṇaḥ syād.
evaṃ gate su|hata eva ca vānaro 'yam. [46]

jana|vāda|bhayād ath' â|śubhaṃ
parivarjyaṃ śubha|mārga|saṃśrayāt,
sva|vacaḥ|pratiloma|ceṣṭitair
jana|vādān api n' âtiyāty ayam. [47]

23.95 sva|kṛt'|ânta|pathā|gataṃ sukhaṃ
na samāpnoti ca loka|śaṅkayā.
iti niṣphala|vāda|vibhramaḥ
paramo 'yaṃ nanu bāliś'|âdhamaḥ! [48]

yad api ca bhavān āha:

‹dārūṇi n'|âika|vidha|varṇa|guṇ'|ākṛtīni
karm'|ātmakāni na bhavanti, bhavanti c' âiva.
naṣṭāni n' âiva ca yathā punar udbhavanti.
lokas tath" âyam,› iti ko 'tra ca nāma hetuḥ? [49]

uccheda|vāda|vātsalyaṃ syād evam api te yadi,
vigarhaṇīyaḥ kiṃ hantā vānarasya narasya vā?» [50]

If there is no other world,
why should one avoid sin?
Why be so deluded
as to venerate morality?
The wise would act as they pleased,
following their own whim.
If that is the case,
the monkey was justly slain.

If fear of popular opinion makes a person
reject evil and follow the path of good,
he will not escape scandal
when his actions contradict his words.

If he so fears popular opinion, 23.95
he will gain no happiness on his path to death.
To be led astray by such fruitless doctrine
is the most vile form of foolishness!

And regarding your statement that:

'Pieces of wood differing
in color, quality and form
do not arise from actions
but arise nonetheless.
When they have perished
they never arise again.
The world is also like this.'
What reason is there for saying this?

But if, despite all this,
you still favor the annihilation doctrine,
why should the murderer of a monkey
be accused or even the murderer of a man?"

iti sa Mahā|sattvas tam uccheda|vādinaṃ vispaṣṭa|śobhen' ôttara|krameṇa tūṣṇīṃ|bhāva|parāyaṇaṃ kṛtvā taṃ kṣatra|vidyā|vidagdham amātyam āmantry' ôvāca:†

23.100 «bhavān apy asmān kasmād iti vikutsayate, yadi nyāyyam artha|śāstra|paridṛṣṭaṃ vidhiṃ manyate?†

anuṣṭheyaṃ hi tatr' êṣṭam
  arth'|ârthaṃ sādhv|a|sādhu vā.
ath' ôddhṛtya kil' ātmānam
  arthair dharmaḥ† kariṣyate. [51]

atas tvāṃ bravīmi:

prayojanaṃ prāpya na ced avekṣyaṃ
  snigdheṣu bandhuṣv api sādhu|vṛttam,
hate mayā carmaṇi vānare 'smin
  kā śāstra|dṛṣṭe 'pi naye vigarhā? [52]

dayā|viyogād atha garhaṇīyaṃ
  karm' ēdṛśaṃ duḥkha|phalaṃ ca dṛṣṭam,
yatr' âbhyanujñātam idaṃ nu† tantre,
  prapadyase kena mukhena tat tvam? [53]

23.105 iyaṃ vibhūtiś ca nayasya yatra,
  tatr' â|nayaḥ kīdṛśa|vibhramaḥ syāt?
aho pragalbhaiḥ paribhūya lokam
  unnīyate śāstra|pathair a|dharmaḥ! [54]

a|duṣṭam† ev' âtha tav' âitad iṣṭaṃ
  śāstre kila spaṣṭa|path'|ôpadiṣṭam,
śāstra|prasiddhena nayena gacchan
  na garhaṇīyo 'smi kaper vadhena.» [55]

In this way, the Great Being masterfully reduced the annihilationist to silence with his clear and splendid reasoning. He then addressed the minister who was artful in kshatriya science, saying:

"And why do you accuse me, good sir, when you believe that the method prescribed by political science is right? 23.100

This science allows any act to be performed,
good or bad, if it leads to personal advantage.
Only after a person has raised himself up
should he use his wealth for moral actions.

Let me tell you this:

If, in gaining profit, we need not consider
acting virtuously even toward loving relatives,
why blame me for killing the ape for its skin
when your teachings morally prescribe it?

But if this act is reprehensible,
being cruel and clearly resulting in pain,
why do you follow a system
that allows such conduct?

If your teaching treats this as a great virtue, 23.105
what kind of deviance would it view as vice?
How insolent are those who despise the world
by citing treatises to promote wickedness!

If you accept this action is not sinful,
as your treatises clearly seem to preach,
then I cannot be blamed for killing the monkey
if I follow the morals declared by your teachings."

iti sa mah"|ātmā jita|parṣatkān paricita|prāgalbhyān api ca tān amātyān prasahy' âbhibhūya samāvarjita|hṛdayāṃ ca sa|rājikāṃ parṣadam avetya teṣāṃ vānara|vadha|hṛl|lekha| vinayan'|ârthaṃ rājānam ābabhāṣe:

«n' âiva† khalv ahaṃ, mahā|rāja, prāṇinaṃ vānaraṃ hatavān. nirmāṇa|vidhir ayam. nirmitasya hi vānarasy' êdaṃ carma mayā gṛhītam asy' âiva kathā|kramasya prastāv'| ârtham. tad alaṃ māṃ anyathā grahītum.†»

ity uktvā tam ṛddhy|abhisaṃskāraṃ† pratisaṃhṛtya parayā ca mātray" âbhiprasādita|manasaṃ† rājānaṃ sa|parṣatkam avety' ôvāca:

23.110 «saṃpaśyan hetutaḥ siddhiṃ sva|tantraḥ para|loka|vit
sādhu|pratijñaḥ sa|ghṛṇaḥ prāṇinaṃ ko haniṣyati? [56]

paśya, mahā|rāja:

a|hetu|vādī para|tantra|dṛṣṭir
an|āstikaḥ kṣatra|nay'|ânugo vā
kuryān na yan nāma yaśo|lav'|ârthaṃ,
tan nyāya|vādī katham abhyupeyāt? [57]

dṛṣṭir, nara|śreṣṭha, śubh'|â|śubhā vā
sa|bhāga|karma|pratipatti|hetuḥ.
dṛṣṭy|anvayaṃ hi pravikalpya tat tad
vāgbhiḥ kriyābhiś ca vidarśayanti. [58]

In this way the Great One totally defeated the ministers, even though they controlled the assembly and were accustomed to going about their insolent ways. When he realized that he had turned the hearts of the assembly as well as the king, he addressed the monarch to dispel any unease he may have over the monkey's slaughter:

"I did not actually kill a living monkey, Your Majesty. I simply created an apparition and took the skin from the magically created monkey to form the topic of discussion that we have just had. Do not have the wrong impression of me."

Saying these words, the Bodhi·sattva made the magical monkey skin disappear and, realizing that the king and the assembly were now entirely devoted to him, he said:

"If a person sees that things result from a cause, 23.110
if they are responsible and know the next world exists,
if they are morally aware and compassionate,
would they really kill a living being?

Consider this, Your Majesty:

How can an advocate of morality condone an act
that neither an anti-causalist, nor a believer
in dependency,
nor a nihilist, nor a proponent of political science
would perform even for a sliver of glory?

It is our moral views, whether good or bad,
that determine our conduct and actions, king.
For when we form concepts based on views,
we display them through words and actions.

sad|dṛṣṭir asmāc ca niṣevitavyā,
tyājyā tv a|sad|dṛṣṭir an|artha|vṛṣṭiḥ.
labhyaś ca sat|saṃśrayiṇā kramo 'yam
a|saj|janād dūra|careṇa bhūtvā. [59]

23.115 a|saṃyatāḥ saṃyata|veṣa|dhāriṇaś
caranti kāmaṃ bhuvi bhikṣu|rākṣasāḥ
vinirdahantaḥ khalu bāliśaṃ janaṃ
ku|dṛṣṭibhir dṛṣṭi|viṣā iv' ôragāḥ. [60]

a|hetu|vād'|ādi|virūkṣa|vāśitaṃ
śṛgālavat tatra viśeṣa|lakṣaṇam.
ato na tān arhati sevituṃ budhaś;
caret tad|arthaṃ tu parākrame sati. [61]

loke virūḍha|yaśas" âpi tu n' âiva kāryā
kāry'|ârtham apy a|sadṛśena janena maitrī.
hemanta|durdina|samāgama|dūṣito hi
saubhāgya|hānim upayāti niśākaro 'pi. [62]

tad varjanād guṇa|vivarjayitur janasya
saṃsevanāc ca guṇa|sevana|paṇḍitasya,
svāṃ kīrtim ujjvalaya saṃjanayan prajānāṃ
doṣ'|ânurāga|vilayaṃ guṇa|sauhṛdaṃ ca. [63]

tvayi ca carati dharmaṃ bhūyas" âyaṃ nṛ|lokaḥ
su|carita|su|mukhaḥ syāt svarga|mārga|pratiṣṭhaḥ.
jagad idam anupālyaṃ c' âivam abhyudyamas te.
vinaya|rucira|mārgaṃ dharmam asmād bhajasva. [64]

Good views should therefore be fostered
but bad views rejected, for they rain down ruin.
This path is achieved by frequenting the good
and staying far away from the wicked.

23.115 Undisciplined men, disguised as disciplined,
roam the earth at will. Demon-like monks,
they destroy fools through their false views,
like snakes that poison with a mere look.*

It is their character to howl gratingly
like jackals on doctrines such as non-causality.
A wise man should not consort with them
but act to help them, if he has the strength.

Never make friends with unsuitable people,
even if they are famed, or to achieve a goal.
For even the moon wanes in beauty
when sullied by a gloomy winter's day.

By avoiding those who avoid virtue
and fostering wise men who foster virtue,
illuminate your glory by producing in your people
an end of desire for vice and a love of virtue.

If you act morally, mankind will mostly incline
toward virtue, established on heaven's path.
This world needs protection and you have the energy.
So practice virtue, whose path gleams with discipline.

23.120 śīlaṃ viśodhaya, samarjaya dātṛ|kīrtiṃ.
maitraṃ manaḥ kuru jane sva|jane yath" âiva.
dharmeṇa pālaya mahīṃ ciram a|pramādād.
evaṃ sameṣyasi sukhaṃ tri|divaṃ yaśaś ca. [65]

kṛṣi|pradhānān paśu|pālan'|ôdyatān
mahī|ruhān puṣpa|phal'|ânvitān iva
a|pālayañ jānapadān bali|pradān
nṛ|po hi sarv'|âuṣadhibhir virudhyate. [66]

vicitra|paṇya|kraya|vikray'|āśrayaṃ
vaṇig|janaṃ paura|janaṃ tathā nṛ|paḥ
na pāti yaḥ śulka|path'|ôpakāriṇaṃ
virodham āyāti sa kośa|saṃpadā. [67]

a|dṛṣṭa|doṣaṃ yudhi dṛṣṭa|vikramaṃ
tathā balaṃ yaḥ prathit'|âstra|kauśalam
vimānayed bhū|patir adhyupekṣayā,
dhruvaṃ viruddhaḥ sa raṇe jaya|śriyā. [68]

tath" âiva śīla|śruta|yoga|sādhuṣu
prakāśa|māhātmya|guṇeṣu sādhuṣu
carann avajñā|malinena vartmanā
nar'|âdhipaḥ svarga|sukhair virudhyate. [69]

23.125 drumād yath" āmaṃ pracinoti yaḥ phalaṃ
sa hanti bījaṃ na rasaṃ ca vindati.
a|dharmyam evaṃ balim uddharan nṛ|paḥ
kṣiṇoti deśaṃ na ca tena nandati. [70]

Purify your virtue and acquire fame for giving. 23.120
Be friendly to all people as one would relatives.
May you long guard the earth justly and with
diligence.
You will thus attain happiness, heaven and glory.

By not protecting the people in the countryside—
the farmers and herdsmen who pay tax
resembling trees bearing flowers and fruits—
a king shuts himself off from all his crops.

If he does not protect traders and townsmen,
who live off buying and selling wares
and who help him by paying taxes,
a king shuts himself off from his treasury.

If, by oversight, a king fails to esteem
an army which has no clear faults
and which shows valor and skill in weaponry,
he is certainly impeded from victory in war.

And if a king acts scornfully toward the good
who are virtuous, learned and disciplined
and whose noble qualities are evident,
he is impeded from the joys of heaven.

Just as a man who plucks an unripe fruit 23.125
destroys the seed and finds the fruit tasteless,
so a king who levies an unjust tax
harms his country and gains no joy from it.

yathā tu saṃpūrṇa|guṇo mahī|ruhaḥ
phal'|ôdayaṃ pāka|vaśāt prayacchati,
tath" âiva deśaḥ kṣitip'|âbhirakṣito
yunakti dharm'|ârtha|sukhair nar'|âdhipam. [71]

hitān amātyān nipuṇ'|ârtha|darśinaḥ
śucīni mitrāṇi janaṃ svam eva ca
badhāna† cetassu tad|iṣṭayā girā
dhanaiś ca saṃmāna|nay'|ôpapāditaiḥ. [72]

tasmād dharmaṃ tvaṃ puras|kṛtya nityaṃ
śreyaḥ|prāptau yukta|cetāḥ prajānām,
rāga|dveṣ'|ônmuktayā daṇḍa|nītyā
rakṣaṃl lokān ātmano rakṣa lokān.» [73]

iti sa mah"|ātmā taṃ rājānaṃ dṛṣṭi|gata|kā|pathād† vivecya samavatārya ca san|mārgaṃ sa|parṣatkaṃ tata eva gagana|talaṃ samutpatya prāñjalinā tena janena sa|bahu-māna|praṇatena pratyarcyamānas tad ev' âraṇy'|āyatanaṃ pratijagāma.

23.130 tad evam, a|sat|kṛtānām api sat|puruṣāṇāṃ pūrv'|ôpakā-riṣv anukampā na śithilī|bhavati kṛta|jñatvāt kṣamā|sātmyāc ca. iti n' â|sat|kāra|mātrakeṇa pūrva|kṛtaṃ vismartavyam.

Just as a thriving tree provides
abundant fruits at the time of ripening,
so a country protected by a king provides
a monarch with spiritual and material felicities.

Through pleasing words and respectfully offered
wealth,
form intimate bonds with helpful ministers
who are astute and concerned for your welfare,
as well as with virtuous friends and relatives.

Dedicated to the prosperity of your subjects,
you should therefore always put morality first.
Dispensing justice without passion or hatred,
secure for yourself the heavens by guarding
the people."

In this way the Great One steered the king away from the wrong path of false views and placed him and his assembly on the path of virtue. He then flew into the sky, honored by the people with folded palms and reverent bows, and returned to the same area of the forest.

23.130 In this way, even when wronged, good men never lessen their compassion toward those who have previously aided them. Such is their gratitude and inherent forgiveness. One should therefore not forget a past service just because of an insult.

«evaṃ sa Bhagavān an|abhisaṃbuddho 'pi para|vādān abhibhūya sattva|vinayaṃ kṛtavān» iti Buddha|varṇe 'pi vācyam. «evaṃ mithyā|dṛṣṭir an|anuyoga|kṣamā pāp'|āśrayatvād† a|sevyā c'» êti mithyā|dṛṣṭi|vigarhāyām apy upaneyam. viparyayeṇa samyag|dṛṣṭi|praśaṃsāyām iti.

One should also narrate this story when praising the Buddha, saying: "In this way the Lord, though still unawakened, defeated his opponents' doctrines and disciplined living beings." Furthermore, one should cite this story when criticizing false views, saying: "False views should therefore not be fostered. For they rest on wickedness and cannot stand up to examination." And one should make the reverse statement when praising correct views.

MAHĀKAPIJĀTAKAM

STORY 24
THE BIRTH-STORY OF THE GREAT APE

24.1 N'ĀTMA|DUḤKHENA tathā santaḥ saṃtapyante yath" âpakāriṇāṃ kuśala|pakṣa|hānyā.

tad yath" ânuśrūyate.

Bodhisattvaḥ kila śrīmati Himavat|pārśve vividha|dhātu|rucira|citr'|âṅga|rāge nīla|kauśeya|prāvāra|kṛt'|ôttar'|āsaṅga iva vana|gahana|lakṣmyā prayatna|racitair iv' âneka|varṇa|saṃsthāna|vikalpair vaiṣamya|bhakti|citrair vibhūṣita|taṭ'|ânta|deśe pravisṛta|n'|âika|prasravaṇa|jale gambhīra|kandar'|ântara|prapāta|saṃkule paṭutara|madhukara|ninātde manojña|mārut'|ôpavījyamāna|vicitra|puṣpa|phala|pādape vidyādhar'|ākrīḍa|bhūte mahā|kāyaḥ kapir eka|caro babhūva.

tad|avastham api c' âinam a|parilupta|dharma|saṃjñaṃ kṛta|jñam a|kṣudra|svabhāvaṃ dhṛtyā mahatyā samanvitam anurāga|vaśād iva karuṇā n' âiva mumoca.

24.5 sa|kānanā s'|âdri|varā sa|sāgarā
gatā vināśaṃ śataśo vasuṃ|dharā
yug'|ânta|kāle salil'|ânal'|ânilair;
na Bodhisattvasya mahā|kṛpālutā. [1]

atha sa Mahātmā tāpasa iva vana|taru|parṇa|phala|mātra|vṛttir anukampamānas tena tena vidhinā gocara|patitān prāṇinas tam araṇya|pradeśam adhyāvasati sma.

THE GOOD DO NOT SUFFER so much from their own pain as from their wrongdoers' lapse in morality. 24.1

Tradition has handed down the following story.

The Bodhi·sattva is said to have once lived as a huge monkey who roamed alone on a beautiful slope on the Hímavat mountain. The body of the mountain was smeared with the ointments of various glistening, multi-colored ores. Draped by glorious dense forests, as if by a robe of green silk, its slopes and borders were adorned with an array of colors and forms so beautifully variegated in their uneven distribution that they seemed to have been purposefully composed. Water poured down in numerous torrents and there was an abundance of deep caves, chasms and precipices. Bees buzzed loudly and trees bearing various flowers and fruits were fanned by a delightful breeze. It was here, in this playground of vidya·dhara spirits, that the Bodhi·sattva lived.

But even though he was a monkey, the Bodhi·sattva had lost none of his moral awareness. Grateful and full of vast fortitude, his nature was devoid of anything lowly. As if driven by devotion, compassion never left his side.

The earth with its forests, fine peaks and seas 24.5
may through water, fire and wind
perish a hundred times at an eon's end,
but not the great compassion of the Bodhi·sattva.

So it was that the Great One lived in that forest region, subsisting solely off the leaves and fruits of trees in the forest and showing his compassion in various ways to creatures who happened to enter his foraging area.

ath' ânyatamaḥ puruṣo gāṃ pranaṣṭām anveṣituṃ kṛt'|ôdyogaḥ samantato 'nuvicaran mārga|pranaṣṭo† dig|vibhāga†|saṃmūḍha|matiḥ paribhramaṃs taṃ deśam upajagāma. sa kṣut|pipāsā|gharma|śrama|parimlāna|tanur daurmanasya|vahninā c' ântaḥ pradīpyamāno viṣād'|âti|bhārād iv' ânyatamasmin vṛkṣa|mūle niṣaṇṇo dadarśa paripāka|vaśād vicyutāni paripiñjarāṇi kati cit tindukī|phalāni. sa tāny āsvādya kṣut|parikṣāmatayā parama|svādūni manyamānas tat|prabhav'|ânveṣaṇaṃ pratyabhivṛddh'|ôtsāhaḥ samantato 'nuvilokayan dadarśa prapāta|taṭ'|ânta|virūḍhaṃ paripakva|phal'|ānamita|piñjar'|âgra|śākhaṃ tindukī|vṛkṣam. sa tat|phala|tṛṣṇay" ākṛṣyamāṇas taṃ giri|taṭam adhiruhya tasya tindukī|vṛkṣasya phalinīṃ śākhāṃ prapāt'|âbhipranatām† adhyāruroha, phala|lobhena c' âsyāḥ prāntam upajagāma.

> śākh" âtha sā tasya mahī|ruhasya
> bhār'|âtiyogān namitā kṛśatvāt
> paraśvadhen' êva nikṛtta|mūlā
> sa|śabda|bhaṅgaṃ sahasā papāta. [2]

sa tayā sārdhaṃ mahati giri|dur|ge samantataḥ śaila|bhitti|parikṣipte kūpa iva nyapatat. parṇa|saṃcaya|guṇāt tv asya gāmbhīryāc ca salilasya na kiṃ cid aṅgam abhajyata. sa tasmād uttīrya salilāt samantataḥ parisarpan na kutaś cid uttaraṇa|mārgaṃ dadarśa. sa «niṣ|pratīkāraṃ mar-

One day a man arrived in the area who had lost his way. His sense of direction was totally confused and he was wandering around aimlessly, searching everywhere for a stray cow. His body was withered by hunger, thirst, heat and exhaustion. Tormented by the fire of sorrow that was blazing inside of him, he sat down on the root of a tree, as if burdened by the weight of his despair. There he saw a number of yellow-red tínduki fruits that had fallen to the ground from being ripe. He ate the fruits with delight and was so emaciated by hunger that he imagined they were extremely sweet.* As a result, he became filled with a strong desire to seek out their source. Scouring the forest in every direction, he spotted a tínduki tree growing at the edge of a precipice, the tips of its boughs red with ripe fruits bending the branches down. Lured by his craving for the fruit, he walked up the mountainside and climbed onto the fruit-bearing branch of the tínduki tree that was hanging over the precipice. Indeed so greedy was he for the fruit that he went to the very tip of the branch.

Bent by the excessive weight,
the branch was too weak and fell
suddenly as if chopped by an axe,
snapping with a loud crack.

The man fell with the branch into the vast mountain gorge, which was surrounded on all sides by a wall of rock, resembling a well. But because of the thick foliage and the depth of the water at the bottom, he did not break any bones. Getting out of the water, he crawled around everywhere but could see no way out. Reflecting that he would

tavyam iha mayā na cirād» iti visrasyamāna|jīvit'|āśaḥ śok'|âśru|pariṣikta|dīna|vadanas tīvreṇa daurmanasya|śalyena pratudyamānaḥ kātara|hṛdayas tat tad vilalāpa:†

24.10 «kāntāre dur|ge 'smiñ
jana|saṃpāta|rahite nipatitaṃ mām
yatnād api parimṛgayan
mṛtyor anyaḥ ka iva paśyet? [3]

bandhu|jana|mitra|varjitam
eka|nipānī|kṛtaṃ maśaka|saṃghaiḥ
avapāt'|ānana|magnaṃ
mṛgam iva ko 'bhyuddhariṣyati mām? [4]

udyāna|kānana|vimāna|sarid|vicitraṃ
tārā|vikīrṇa|maṇi|ratna|virājit'|âbhram
tāmisra|pakṣa|rajan" îva ghan'|ândha|kārā
kaṣṭaṃ jagan mama tiras|kurute 'nta|rātriḥ!» [5]

iti sa puruṣas tat tad vilapaṃs tena salilena taiś ca saha nipatitais tinduka|phalair vartayamānaḥ kati cid dināni tatr' âvasat.

atha sa mahā|kapir āhāra|hetos tad vanam anuvicarann āhūyamāna iva mārut" ākampitābhis tasya tindukī|vṛkṣasy' âgra|śākhābhis taṃ pradeśam abhijagāma. samabhiruhya† c' âinaṃ prapātam† avalokayan dadarśa taṃ puruṣaṃ kṣut|parikṣāma|nayana|vadanaṃ paripāṇḍu|kṛśa|dīna|gātraṃ

surely die soon, he lost all hope for his life. Pierced by a sharp barb of sorrow, his despairing face became soaked by tears of grief as he uttered various laments, his heart filled with fear:

24.10

"I've fallen into this trackless forest
devoid of all human contact.
Who but Death can see me,
however intently they search?

Bereft of my relatives and friends,
I am the sole target for swarms of mosquitoes.
Like a wild animal that has plunged
into the mouth of a pit, who will lift me out?

Alas! This night of death
steals the world from my sight,
a darkness as thick as the night
during the dark phase of the moon!
Gone are the beauties of
gardens, forests, groves, rivers,
skies gleaming with the scattered
gems and jewels of the stars!"

Crying out these various laments, the man remained there for some days, living off the water and the fallen tínduka fruits.

One day, however, the great monkey arrived in the area, searching through the forest for food, as if summoned by the wind-jostled branch tips of the tínduki tree. Climbing the tree and noticing the gorge, he spotted the man writhing there in torment, his eyes and face hollow with hunger and his wretched body pale and emaciated. The

paryutsukaṃ tatra viceṣṭamānam. sa tasya paridyūnatayā samāvarjit'|ânukampo mahā|kapir nikṣipt'|āhāra|vyāpāras taṃ puruṣaṃ pratatam īkṣamāṇo† mānuṣīṃ vācam uvāca:

24.15 «mānuṣāṇām a|gamye 'smin prapāte parivartase.
vaktum arhasi tat sādhu: ko bhavān, iha vā kutaḥ?» [6]

atha sa puruṣas taṃ mahā|kapim ārtatayā samabhipraṇamya s'|âñjalir udvīkṣamāṇa† uvāca:

«mānuṣo 'smi, mahā|bhāga, pranaṣṭo vicaran vane
phal'|ârthī pādapād asmād imām āpadam āgamam. [7]

tat suhṛd|bandhu|hīnasya prāptasya vyasanaṃ mahat,
nātha vānara|yūthānāṃ, mam' âpi śaraṇaṃ bhava.» [8]

tac chrutvā sa Mahā|sattvaḥ parāṃ karuṇām upajagāma.

24.20 āpad|gato bandhu|suhṛd|vihīnaḥ
kṛt'|âñjalir dīnam udīkṣamāṇaḥ
karoti śatrūn api s'|ânukampān,
ākampayaty eva tu s'|ânukampān. [9]

ath' âinaṃ Bodhisattvaḥ karuṇāyamāṇas tat kāla|dur|labhena snigdhena vacasā samāśvāsayām āsa:

man's sorrowful condition stirred the monkey's compassion and, putting aside his task of looking for food, the great monkey stared intently at the man and addressed him with human words, saying:

"The gorge you wander in
cannot be accessed by humans.
Please tell me who you are,
good sir, and why you are here." 24.15

In his despair, the man bowed before the great monkey and looked up at him with hands folded in respect, saying:

"I am a human, illustrious being.
I became lost while roaming the forest
and have reached this desperate plight
after trying to get fruit from this tree.

Bereft of friends and relatives,
I have fallen on great misfortune.
You protect troops of monkeys;
please be a refuge for me too."

The Great Being felt great compassion when he heard these words.

A man in distress, without relatives and friends,
gazing up in despair, hands folded in respect,
would make even enemies feel compassion.
Surely he will then stir those with pity. 24.20

Feeling compassion for the man, the Bodhi·sattva consoled him with kind words that were hardly likely to be heard at that moment in time:

«‹prapāta|saṃkṣipta|parākramo 'ham,
a|bāndhavo v"› êti kṛthāḥ śucaṃ mā.
yad bandhu|kṛtyaṃ tava kiṃ cid atra,
kart" âsmi tat sarvam. alaṃ bhayena.» [10]

iti sa Mahā|sattvas taṃ puruṣaṃ samāśvāsya† tataś c' âsmai tindukāny aparāṇi ca phalāni samupahṛtya tad|uddharaṇa|yogyayā puruṣa|bhāra|gurvyā śilay" ânyatra yogyāṃ cakāra. tataś c' ātmano bala|pramāṇam avagamya, ‹śakto 'ham enam etasmāt prapātād uddhartum› iti niścita|matir avatīrya prapātaṃ karuṇayā paricodyamānas taṃ puruṣam uvāca:

«ehi, pṛṣṭhaṃ mam' āruhya
su|lagno 'stu bhavān mayi,
yāvad abhyuddharāmi tvāṃ
sva|dehāt sāram eva ca. [11]

24.25 a|sārasya śarīrasya sāro hy eṣa mataḥ satām,
yat pareṣāṃ hit'|ârtheṣu sādhanī|kriyate budhaiḥ.» [12]

sa tath" êti pratiśruty' âbhipraṇamya c' âinam adhyāruroha.

ath' âbhirūḍhaḥ sa nareṇa tena
bhār'|âtiyogena vihanyamānaḥ
sattva|prakarṣād a|vipanna|dhairyaḥ
pareṇa duḥkhena tam ujjahāra. [13]

"Do not grieve thinking this fall has robbed you
of your strength or that you have no relatives.
I will perform for you every duty
a relative should perform. Cease your fear."

Comforting the man with these words, the Great Being gave him tínduka berries and other fruits. He then went to a different area of the forest to exercise with a rock as heavy as a man with the aim of lifting him from the gorge. After he had determined the measure of his strength, he decided that he was able to lift the man from the gorge. Spurred on by compassion, he then went down to the man and addressed him with the following words:

"Come! Climb onto my back!
And cling to me tightly, good sir,
so I may extract you from this gorge
as well as the real worth from my body.

For the good hold that
the worthless body derives
its worth when the wise
use it to benefit others."

24.25

The man agreed and, bowing reverently, climbed onto the monkey's back.

Though pained by the extreme burden
of carrying the man on his back,
his fine virtue meant his courage never flagged
and he pulled the man out with great difficulty.

uddhṛtya c' âinaṃ parama|pratītaḥ
khedāt parivyākula|khela|gāmī
śilā|talaṃ toya|dhar'|âbhinīlaṃ
viśrāma|hetoḥ śayanī|cakāra. [14]

atha Bodhisattvaḥ śuddha|svabhāvatayā kṛt'|ôpakāratvāc ca tasmāt puruṣād apāya|nirāśaṅko visrambhād enam uvāca:

24.30 «a|vyāhata|vyāla|mṛga|praveśe
vana|pradeśe 'tra samanta|mārge
kheda|prasuptaṃ sahasā nihanti
kaś cit purā māṃ sva|hit'|ôdayaṃ ca, [15]

yato bhavān dikṣu vikīrṇa|cakṣuḥ
karotu rakṣāṃ mama c' ātmanaś ca.
dṛḍhaṃ śramen' âsmi parīta|mūrtis
tat svaptum icchāmi muhūrta|mātram.» [16]

atha sa mithyā|vinaya|pragalbhaḥ: «svapitu bhavān yathā|kāmaṃ sukha|prabodhāya. sthito 'yam ahaṃ† tvat|saṃrakṣaṇāy'» êty asmai pratiśuśrāva. atha sa puruṣas tasmin Mahā|sattve śrama|balān nidrā|vaśam upagate cintām a|śivām āpede:

«mūlaiḥ prayatn'|âtiśay'|âdhigamyair
vanyair yadṛcch"|âdhigataiḥ phalair vā
evaṃ parikṣīṇa|tanoḥ kathaṃ syād
yātr" âpi tāvat, kuta eva puṣṭiḥ? [17]

idaṃ ca kāntāram a|su|pratāraṃ
kathaṃ tariṣyāmi balena hīnaḥ?
paryāpta|rūpaṃ tv idam asya māṃsaṃ
kāntāra|durg'|ôttaraṇāya me syāt. [18]

Though he felt great joy at saving the man,
exhaustion made him reel and stagger.
So, in order to rest, he lay down
on a slab of rock as dark as a raincloud.

Due to his pure nature and because of the service he had just performed, the Bodhi·sattva feared no harm from the man but trustfully addressed him with the following words:

"This forest tract is accessible on all sides. 24.30
Wild animals can enter unimpeded.
To prevent anyone destroying both me
and their welfare as I sleep from exhaustion,

keep a look-out in every direction
and protect both me and yourself.
My body feels completely exhausted.
I would like to sleep for a short while."

Skilled in false politeness, the man agreed, saying: "Sleep as you like, good sir, and wake up at your own ease. I will stand here and watch over you." After the Great Being had fallen asleep through tiredness, the man had the following wicked thought:

"How can I sustain my wasted body,
let alone make it healthy,
with roots found only with great effort
or forest fruits I come across by chance?

How, deprived of my strength,
can I cross this uncrossable forest?
But this animal's meat should be ample
for me to escape from the wild forest.

24.35 kṛt'|ôpakāro 'pi ca bhakṣya eva.
nisarga|yogaḥ sa hi tādṛśo 'sya.
āpat|prasiddhaś ca kil' âiṣa dharmaḥ.
pātheyatām ity upaneya eṣaḥ! [19]

yāvac ca visrambha|sukha|prasuptas,
tāvan mayā śakyam ayaṃ nihantum.
imaṃ hi yuddh'|âbhimukhaṃ sametya
siṃho 'pi saṃbhāvya|parājayaḥ syāt! [20]

tan n' âyaṃ vilambituṃ me kāla.»
iti viniścitya sa dur|ātmā lobha|doṣa|vyāmohita|matir a|kṛta|jño vipanna|dharma|saṃjñaḥ pranaṣṭa|kāruṇya|saumya|bhāvaḥ† paridurbalo 'py a|kāry'|âtirāgān mahatīṃ śilām udyamya tasya mahā|kapeḥ śirasi mumoca.

śil" âtha sā dur|bala|vihvalena
kāry'|âtirāgāt tvaritena tena
atyanta|nidr"|ôpagamāya muktā
nidrā|pravāsāya kaper babhūva. [21]

24.40 sarv'|ātmanā sā na samāsasāda,
mūrdhānam asmān na viniṣpipeṣa.
koṭy|eka|deśena tu taṃ rujantī
śilā tale s" âśanivat papāta. [22]

śil"|âbhighātād avabhinna|mūrdhā
vegād avaplutya tu† Bodhisattvaḥ
‹ken' āhato† 'sm'?› îti dadarśa n' ânyaṃ,
tam eva tu hrīta|mukhaṃ dadarśa, [23]

Though he did me a service, I can still eat him. 24.35
For thus has he been formed by nature.
They say this practice is approved in times of distress.
I can therefore use the monkey as provisions!

But I will only be able to kill him
while he trustfully sleeps in peace.
For even a lion would be expected
to lose in battle against him!

I have no time to squander."

Such was the resolution made by that wicked and ungrateful man, his mind addled by the vice of greed, his moral awareness defunct and his character devoid of compassion or kindness. Despite his weakness and driven by his great desire to commit the crime, he lifted a huge rock and threw it at the head of the great monkey.

But the man staggered from weakness
and his eagerness to act made him rush.
Though aiming to send the ape to eternal sleep,
when released, the rock only woke him.

Failing to strike him with full force, 24.40
the rock did not crush his head.
Hitting the monkey only with an edge,
it fell to the ground, crashing like a thunderbolt.

His head split by the impact of the rock,
the Bodhi·sattva swiftly leapt down,
searching to discover who had hit him.
But he saw only the man, shamefaced.

vailakṣya|pīta|prabham a|pragalbhaṃ
viṣāda|dainyāt paribhinna|varṇam
trās'|ôdayād āgata|kaṇṭha|śoṣaṃ
sved'|ârdram udvīkṣitum apy a|śaktam. [24]

atha sa mahā|kapir asy' âiva tat karm' êti niscita|matiḥ svam abhighāta|duḥkham a|cintayitvā tena tasy' ātma|hita|nirapekṣeṇ' âti|kaṣṭena karmaṇā samupajāta|saṃvega|kāruṇyaḥ parityakta|krodha|saṃrambha|doṣaḥ sa|bāṣpa|nayanas taṃ puruṣam avekṣya samanuśocann uvāca:

«mānuṣeṇa satā, bhadra,
tvay" êdaṃ kṛtam īdṛśam
kathaṃ nāma vyavasitaṃ,
prārabdhaṃ katham eva vā? [25]

24.45 mad|abhidroha|saṃrabdhaṃ
tvaṃ nām' āpatitaṃ param
vinivāraṇa|śauṭīra|
vikramo roddhum arhasi. [26]

duṣ|karaṃ kṛtavān asm' îty abhūn mān'|ônnatir mama.
tvay" âpaviddhā sā dūram ati|duṣkara|kāriṇā. [27]

para|lokād iv' ānito mṛtyor vaktr'|ântarād iva,
prapātād uddhṛto 'nyasmād anyatra patito hy asi! [28]

dhig aho bata dur|vṛttam a|jñāna|mati|dāruṇam,
yat pātayati duḥkheṣu sukh'|āśā|kṛpaṇaṃ jagat! [29]

Timid and pale with embarrassment,
anxiety and despair had changed his color.
Pouring sweat, his throat dried with fear.
he was incapable even of raising his eyes.

When the great monkey realized that the man had done the deed, he no longer gave any thought to the pain he suffered from his injury. Instead he felt sudden compassion for the fact that the man had committed such a terrible act without considering his own welfare. Rejecting any sinful feeling of anger or rage, the monkey looked at the man and grieved for him with the following words, his eyes filled with tears:

"How could you, a human, good sir,
decide on such a deed, let alone perform it?

It was your duty to avert with heroic bravery (24.45)
any foe charging forward, eager to injure me!

I felt a surge of pride
at performing a difficult task.
But you have cast that aside
by doing this exceptionally difficult deed.

I virtually rescued you from the next world,
as if from the mouth of Death.
But once hauled from one precipice,
you have fallen into another!

A curse on that vile and cruel
state of mind called ignorance!
For it hurls the world into suffering,
pitiful in its hope for happiness!

pātito dur|gatāv ātmā,
kṣiptaḥ śok'|ânalo mayi!
nimīlitā yaśo|lakṣmīr,
guṇa|maitrī virodhitā! [30]

24.50 gatvā dhig|vāda|lakṣatvaṃ hatā viśvasanīyatā.
kā nu khalv artha|niṣpattir evam ākāṅkṣitā tvayā? [31]

dunoti māṃ n' âiva tathā tv iyaṃ rujā,
yath" âitad ev' âtra manaḥ kṣiṇoti me:†
gato 'smi pāpe tava yan nimittatāṃ
na c' âham enas tad apohituṃ prabhuḥ. [32]

saṃdṛśyamāna|vapur eva tu pārśvato māṃ
tat sādhv anuvraja, dṛḍhaṃ hy asi śaṅkanīyaḥ,
yāvad bahu|pratibhayād gahanād itas tvāṃ
grām'|ânta|paddhatim anupratipādayāmi [33]

ekākinaṃ kṣāma|śarīrakaṃ tvāṃ
mārg'|ânabhijñaṃ hi vane bhramantam
kaś cit samāsādya purā karoti
tvat|pīḍaṇād vyartha|pariśramaṃ mām.» [34]

iti sa mah"|ātmā taṃ puruṣam anuśocan jan'|ântam ānīya pratipādya c' âinaṃ tan mārgaṃ punar uvāca:

24.55 «prāpto jan'|ântam asi, kānta. van'|ântam etaṃ†
kāntāra|durga|bhayam utsṛja, gaccha sādhu,
pāpaṃ ca karma parivarjayituṃ yatethā:
duḥkho hi tasya niyamena vipāka|kālaḥ.» [35]

You have flung yourself into ruin
and cast the fire of grief on me!
Your glory and reputation have vanished.
All love of virtue has been obstructed!

You have become a target of reproach 24.50
and destroyed any trustworthiness.
What benefit did you expect
would result from this deed?

My physical pain does not torment me
as much as the agonizing thought that
I am the cause of your evil action
but am unable to remove this sin.

Follow by my side. But please stay visible,
for you certainly are not to be trusted.
I will guide you to the village path
away from this dense forest full of dangers

before someone makes
my entire effort meaningless
by attacking you wandering alone,
weak and ignorant of the route."

Grieving this way for the man, the Bodhi·sattva led him to the human realm. And after setting him on his way, he addressed him again, saying:

"You've reached the human realm, my friend. 24.55
Leave the forest, terrifying with its wild perils.
And please endeavor to avoid evil actions.
For, on ripening, they inevitably bring pain."

iti sa mahā|kapis taṃ puruṣam anukampayā śiṣyam iv' ânuśiṣya tam eva vana|pradeśaṃ pratijagāma.

atha sa puruṣas tad ati|kaṣṭaṃ pāpaṃ karma† kṛtvā paścāt|tāpa|vahninā saṃpradīpyamāna|cetā mahatā kuṣṭha|vyādhinā rūp'|ântaram upanītaḥ, kilāsa|citra|cchaviḥ prabhidyamāna|vraṇa|visrav'|ârdra|gātraḥ parama|dur|gandha|śarīraḥ sadyaḥ samapadyata. sa yaṃ yaṃ deśam abhijagāma, tatas tata ev' âinam ati|bībhatsa|vikṛta|darśanaṃ† mānuṣa ity a|śraddheya|rūpaṃ bhinna|dīna|svaram abhivīkṣya puruṣāḥ «sākṣād ayaṃ Pāpm"» êti manyamānāḥ samudyata|loṣṭa|daṇḍā nirbhartsana|paruṣa|vacasaḥ pravāsayām āsuḥ.

ath' âinam anyatamo rājā mṛgayām anuvicaran pretam iv' âraṇye paribhramantaṃ prakṣīṇa|malina|vasanaṃ n'|âti|vasana|praticchanna|kaupīnam† ati|dur|darśanam abhivīkṣya sa|sādhvasa|kautūhalaḥ papraccha:

«virūpita|tanuḥ kuṣṭhaiḥ kilāsa|śabala|cchaviḥ
pāṇḍuḥ kṛśa|tanur dīno rajo|rūkṣa|śiro|ruhaḥ, [36]

24.60 kas tvaṃ? pretaḥ? piśāco vā?
mūrtaḥ Pāpm"? âtha pūtanaḥ?
an|eka|roga|saṃghātaḥ
katamo v" âsi yakṣmaṇām?» [37]

With these words, the great monkey compassionately instructed the man as if he were his disciple and then returned to the same region of the forest.

As for the man, his mind burned with the fire of regret at having committed such a terrible deed and he was suddenly afflicted with leprosy. His body became completely transformed. His skin was mottled with leprous scabs, his limbs were wet with pus oozing from burst sores, and his body stank terribly. Wherever he traveled, his appearance was so hideous and deformed, his body so hardly credible as human, and his voice so abnormal and pitiful, that when people saw him they thought he was the Evil One in person.* Picking up sticks and clods of earth, they drove him away with menacing and harsh words.

One day a king who was out hunting spotted the man wandering around in the jungle like a hungry ghost, his filthy clothes so ragged that they hardly covered his private parts. When he saw the hideous sight, the king was filled with a mixture of alarm and curiosity and asked the man the following questions:

"Your body is deformed by leprosy,
your skin mottled with scabs.
Pale, weak and pitiful,
your hair is soiled with grime.

Who are you? A hungry ghost? A demon? 24.60
The Evil One in person? Or a fiend?
Which of the diseases are you?
For you have assembled many."

sa taṃ dīnena kaṇṭhena samabhipraṇamann uvāca: «mānuso 'smi, mahā|rāja, n' â|mānuṣa iti.» «tat katham imām avasthām anuprāpto 's'?» îti ca paryanuyukto rājñā tad asmai svaṃ duś|caritam āviṣ|kṛty' ôvāca:

«mitra|drohasya tasy' êdaṃ
 puṣpaṃ tāvad upasthitam.
ataḥ kaṣṭataraṃ vyaktaṃ
 phalam anyad bhaviṣyati. [38]

tasmān mitreṣv abhidrohaṃ
 śatruvad draṣṭum arhasi,
bhāva|snigdham avekṣasva
 bhāva|snigdhaṃ suhṛj|janam. [39]

mitreṣv amitra|caritāṃ† parigṛhya vṛttim†
 evaṃ|vidhāṃ samupayānti daśām ih' âiva.
lobh'|ādi|doṣa|malinī|kṛta|mānasānāṃ
 mitra|druhāṃ gatir ataḥ parato 'numeyā. [40]

24.65 vātsalya|saumya|hṛdayas tu suhṛtsu kīrtiṃ
 viśvāsa|bhāvam upakāra|sukhaṃ ca tebhyaḥ
prāpnoti saṃnati|guṇaṃ manasaḥ praharṣaṃ
 dur|dharṣatāṃ ca ripubhis tri|daś'|ālayaṃ ca. [41]

Prostrating himself before the king, the man replied with a pitiful voice: "I am a human, great king, not something inhuman." "How have you reached this plight?" the king asked. Whereupon the man revealed to the king his wicked deed, saying:

"What you see before you is only
the flower of my betrayal of friendship.
The fruit will surely be different,
something far worse than this.
You should regard treachery
toward friends as a foe
and look affectionately on friends
who are affectionate to you.

People suffer such a plight
even in this very life
if they practice unkind
behavior toward friends.
From this you can infer
the destiny in the next world
of those who betray friends,
their minds sullied by vices like greed.

But if one's heart is affectionate
and gentle toward friends,
one attains fame and trustworthiness
and the joy of receiving their favors.
One gains the virtue of humility
and happiness of mind,
protection from enemies
and residence in heaven.

24.65

ime† viditvā, nṛ|pa, mitra|pakṣe
prabhāva|siddhī† sad|a|sat|pravṛttyoḥ,
bhajasva mārgaṃ su|jan'|âbhipannaṃ.
tena prayātam hy† anuyāti bhūtiḥ.» [42]

tad evaṃ, n' ātma|duḥkhena tathā santaḥ saṃtapyante, yath" âpakāriṇāṃ kuśala|pakṣa|hānyā.

iti Tathāgata|māhātmye 'pi† vācyam. sat|kṛtya dharma|śravaṇe kṣānti|kathāyāṃ mitrān abhidrohe pāpa|karm'|ādīnava|pradarśane c' êti.

Knowing the powerful results of good and bad
behavior toward friends, Your Majesty,
follow the path pursued by the good.
For prosperity follows those who travel it."

In this way, the good do not suffer so much from their own pain as from their wrongdoers' lapse in morality.

One should also narrate this story when discussing the Tatha·gata's majesty, likewise when discussing the topic of listening to the Teaching* with respect, or the topic of forbearance, or the topic of treachery toward friends, or when illustrating the evils of immoral deeds.

ŚARABHAJĀTAKAM

STORY 25
THE BIRTH-STORY OF THE SHÁRABHA DEER

25.1 JIGHĀṂSUM APY āpad|gatam anukampanta eva mahā|kāruṇikā n' ôpekṣante.

tad|yath" ânuśrūyate.

Bodhisattvaḥ kil' ânyatamasminn araṇya|vana|pradeśe nir|mānuṣa|saṃpāta|nīrave vividha|mṛga|kul'|âdhivāse tṛṇa|gahana|nimagna|mūla|vṛkṣa|kṣupa|bahule pathika|yāna|vāhana|caraṇair a|vinyasta|mārga|sīm'|ânta|lekhe salila|mārga|valmīka|śvabhra|viṣama|bhūmi|bhāge†

bala|java|varṇa|sattva|saṃpannaḥ saṃhananavat kāy'|ôpapannaḥ śarabha|mṛgo† babhūva. sa kāruṇy'|âbhyāsād an|abhidrugdha|cittaḥ sattveṣu tṛṇa|parṇa|salila|mātra|vṛttiḥ saṃtoṣa|guṇād araṇya|vāsa|nirata|matiḥ praviveka|kāma iva yogī tam araṇya|pradeśam abhyalaṃcakāra.

25.5 mṛg'|ākṛtir mānuṣa|dhīra|cetās
tapasvivat prāṇiṣu s'|ânukampaḥ
cacāra tasmin sa vane vivikte
yog" îva saṃtuṣṭa|matis tṛṇ'|âgraiḥ. [1]

atha kadā cid anyatamo rājā tasya viṣayasy' âdhipatis turaga|var'|âdhirūḍhaḥ sajya|cāpa|bāṇa|vyagra|pāṇir mṛgeṣv astra|kauśalam ātmano jijñāsamānaḥ saṃrāga|vaśāj javena mṛgān anupatann uttama|javena vājinā dūr'|âpasṛta†|hasty|aśva|ratha|padāti|kāyas taṃ pradeśam upajagāma.

IN THEIR COMPASSION, those with great pity never disregard a man in distress, even if he means to kill them. Tradition has handed down the following story. 25.1

The Bodhi·sattva is said to have once lived as a *shárabha* deer* in a wild area of the forest. Quiet from its lack of contact with men, the region was home for various hordes of wild animals and abounded with trees and shrubs, their roots submerged in thick grass. The paths and borders of the forest were undented by the treadmarks of travelers or vehicles and the ground fluctuated unevenly with water channels, anthills and holes.

Robust and full-bodied, the *shárabha* deer was strong, swift, handsome and courageous. Due to his habitual practice of compassion, he felt no malevolence toward other creatures and his virtuous attribute of contentment meant he delighted in living in the forest, living solely off grass, leaves and water. Like a yogi taking pleasure in solitude, he adorned that area of the forest.

Shaped like a deer but intelligent as a human, 25.5
he resembled an ascetic in his pity for beings.
Wandering around the secluded forest,
he was like a yogi satisfied by tips of grass.

One day a certain king, the ruler of the realm, happened to arrive in the area. Mounted on a fine horse, he held his bow and arrow poised and ready, eager to test his archery skills on a deer. Overwhelmed by passion for hunting, he had left his convoy of elephants, cavalry, chariots and footmen far behind as he swiftly pursued deer on his speedy horse.

dūrād eva c' ālokya taṃ Mahā|sattvaṃ hantum utpatita|niścayaḥ samutkṛṣṭa|niśita|sāyako, yena† sa Mahātmā tena turaga|varaṃ saṃcodayām āsa. atha Bodhisattvaḥ samālokỳ âiva turaga|vara|gataṃ s'|āyudham abhipatantaṃ taṃ rājānaṃ śaktimān api pratyavasthātuṃ nivṛtta|sāhasa|saṃrambhatvāt parameṇa† jav'|âtiśayena samutpapāta.

so 'nugamyamānas tena turaṃ|gameṇ' ânumārga|gataṃ† mahac chvabhraṃ goṣ|padam iva javena laṅghayitvā pradudrāva. atha sa tura|gas† ten' âiva mārgeṇa taṃ śarabham anupatann uttamena java|pramāṇena tac chvabhram āsādya laṅghayitum an|adhyavasita|matiḥ sahasā vyatiṣṭhata.

ath' âśva|pṛṣṭhād udgīrṇaḥ s'|āyudhaḥ sa mahī|patiḥ
papāta mahati śvabhre daitya|yodha iv' ôda|dhau. [2]

25.10 nibaddha|cakṣuḥ śarabhe sa tasmin
saṃlakṣayām† āsa na taṃ prapātam.
viśrambha|doṣāc calit'|āsano 'tha
rāj" âśva†|veg'|ôparamāt papāta. [3]

atha Bodhisattvas turaga|khura|śabda|praśamāt «kiṃ nu khalu pratinivṛttaḥ syād ayaṃ rāj"?» êti samutpanna|vitarkaḥ paścād āvarjita|vadanaḥ samālokayan dadarśa tam aśvam an|ārohakaṃ tasmin prapāt'|ôddeśe 'vasthitam. tasya buddhir abhavat:

When he spotted the Great Being in the far distance, the king resolved to kill him. Drawing back a sharp arrow, he spurred on his fine horse to head toward the Great One. But as soon as the Bodhi·sattva saw the armed king charging toward him on the horse, he bounded away with exceptional speed. For although he had the strength to stand up to him, he had rejected violence and rage.

As he was pursued by the horse-riding king, he came across a large pit along the way, which he sprang over as if it were the size of a cow's hoofprint, and then continued his flight. As the horse pursued the *shárabha* with immense speed along the same route, it also had to deal with the pit. But it was taken by surprise and suddenly stopped, disinclined to leap.

The king was thrown off the back
of the horse, weapons and all,
and fell into the large pit
like a demon warrior into the ocean.

His eyes fixed on the *shárabha*, 25.10
the king had not noticed the hole.
Unsuspecting, he was dislodged from his seat
and fell when the horse stopped galloping.

When the thudding of the horse's hooves ceased, the Bodhi·sattva wondered if the king might have turned back. But when he turned his head to look, he saw that the horse was riderless and standing near the pit. He then had this thought:

«niyatam atra prapāte nipatitaḥ sa rājā. na hy atra kiṃ cid viśrāma|hetoḥ† saṃśrayaṇīya|rūpaṃ ghana|pracchāyaṃ vā† vṛkṣa|mūlam asti, nīl'|ôtpala|dala|nīla|vimala|salilam avagāha|yogyaṃ vā saraḥ. na c' âiva vyāla|mṛg'|ânuvicaritam araṇya|madhyam† avagāḍhena yatra kva cid utsṛjya† turaga|varaṃ viśramyate mṛgayā v" ânuṣṭhīyate. na c' âtra kiṃ cit tṛṇa|gahanam api tad|vidhaṃ yatra nilīnaḥ syāt. tad vyaktam atra śvabhre nipatitena tena rājñā bhavitavyam iti.»

tataḥ sa Mahātmā niścayam upetya vadhake 'pi tasmin parāṃ karuṇām upajagāma.

«ady' âiva citra|dhvaja|bhūṣaṇena
vibhrājamān'|āvaraṇ'|āyudhena
rath'|âśva|patti|dvirad'|ākulena
vāditra|citra|dhvaninā balena [4]

25.15 kṛt'|ânuyātro rucir'|ātapatraḥ
parisphurac|cāmara|hāra|śobhaḥ
dev'|êndravat prāñjalibhir jan'|âughair
abhyarcito rājya†|sukhāny avāpya, [5]

ady' âiva magno mahati prapāte
nipāta|vegād abhirugṇa|gātraḥ
mūrch"|ânvitaḥ śoka|parāyaṇo vā.
kaṣṭaṃ bata, kleśam ayaṃ prapannaḥ! [6]

"The king must have fallen into the pit. For there is no shady tree under which he can sit to rest, nor is there a lake for him to dive into with pure waters blue as the petals of a water-lily. Nor, having penetrated the depths of the forest teeming with dangerous beasts, would he release his fine horse so as to rest or pursue his hunt. Nor is there any deep grass in the area in which he might be hiding. The king clearly must have fallen into the pit."

Coming to this conclusion, the Great One was filled with great compassion for the king, even though the king had tried to kill him, thinking:

"On this very day the king
was attended by an army,
adorned by colorful banners,
armor and weapons gleaming,
teeming with chariots, horses,
footsoldiers and elephants,
resounding with a chorus
of various instruments.

Shaded by a bright parasol, 25.15
quivering chowries lending a ravishing beauty,
he enjoyed royal pleasures as if king of the gods,
worshiped by hordes of reverent people.

But now he has plunged into a vast pit,
his limbs broken by force of the fall.
Perhaps he has fainted or is given to grief.
What a terrible misfortune he endures!

kiṇ'|âṅkitān' îva† manāṃsi duḥkhair
 na hīna|vargasya tathā vyathante,
a|dṛṣṭa|duḥkhāny ati|saukumāryād
 yath" ôttamānāṃ vyasan'|āgameṣu. [7]

na c' âyam ataḥ śakṣyati svayam uttartum. yady api s'| âvaśeṣa|prāṇas, tan n' âyam upekṣituṃ yuktam.» iti vitarkayan sa Mahātmā karuṇayā samākṛṣyamāṇa|hṛdayas taṃ prapāta|taṭ'|ântam upajagāma. dadarśa c' âinaṃ tatra reṇu|saṃsargān mṛdita|vārabāṇa|śobhaṃ vyākulit'| ôṣṇīṣa|vasana|saṃnāhaṃ prapāta|patana|nighāta|saṃjanitābhir vedanābhir āpīḍyamāna|hṛdayam āpatita|vaitānyaṃ viceṣṭamānam.

25.20 dṛṣṭv" âtha taṃ tatra viceṣṭamānaṃ
 nar'|âdhipaṃ bāṣpa|parīta|netraḥ
kṛpā|vaśād vismṛta|śatru|saṃjñas
 tad|duḥkha|sāmānyam upājagāma. [8]

uvāca c' âinaṃ vinay'|âbhijātam
 udbhāvayan sādhu|jana|svabhāvam
āśvāsayan spaṣṭa|padena sāmnā
 śiṣṭ'|ôpacāreṇa mano|hareṇa: [9]

«kac cin, mahā|rāja, na pīḍito 'si
 prapāta|pātālam idaṃ prapannaḥ?
kac cin na te vikṣatam atra gātraṃ?
 kac cid rujas te tanutāṃ vrajanti?† [10]

n' â|mānuṣaś c' âsmi, manuṣya|varya.
 mṛgo 'py ahaṃ tvad|viṣay'|ânta|vāsī,
vṛddhas tvadīyena tṛṇ'|ôdakena.
 viśrambham ity arhasi mayy upetum. [11]

Lesser minds are calloused by suffering.
Such people do not suffer the same
as eminent men when disaster falls.
For the eminent are delicate and new to pain.

He is incapable of escaping from the pit himself. If he still has some life left in him, it would not be right to be indifferent toward him."

Reflecting this way, the Great One's heart was gripped by compassion and he went to the edge of the pit. There he saw the king writhing in despair. Dust had removed any gleam from his armor. His turban, clothes and protective gear were in disarray. His heart was tormented by the pain of crashing into the pit.

25.20

The sight of the king writhing
in the pit filled his eyes with tears.
Compassion meant he forgot of him as a foe
and he shared in the king's pain instead.

Revealing his virtuous nature and innate modesty,
he addressed the king, consoling him
with gentle and articulate words
that were charming, polite and courteous:

"I hope Your Majesty is not harmed
by falling into this hell-like pit?
I hope your limbs are not damaged
and that your pain is receding?

I am not a demon, chief among men.
I am an animal inhabiting your realm,
reared by your grass and water.
You should therefore trust me.

prapāta|pātād a|dhṛtiṃ ca mā gāḥ.
  śakto 'ham uddhartum ito bhavantam.
viśrambhitavyaṃ mayi manyase cet,
  tat kṣipram ājñāpaya yāvad aimi.†» [12]

25.25 atha sa rājā tena tasy' âdbhuten' âbhivyāhāreṇa vismay'|āvarjita|hṛdayaḥ saṃjāyamāna|vrīḍo niyatam iti cintām āpede:

«dṛṣṭ'|âvadāne dviṣati kā nām' âsya dayā mayi?
mama vipratipattiś ca k" êyam asminn an|āgasi? [13]

aho madhura|tīkṣṇena
  pratyādiṣṭo 'smi karmaṇā!
aham eva mṛgo gaur vā.
  ko 'py ayaṃ śarabh'|ākṛtiḥ? [14]

tad arhaty ayaṃ praṇaya|pratigraha|saṃpūjanam.»
iti viniścity' âinam uvāca:

25.30 «vārabāṇ'|āvṛtam idaṃ gātraṃ me n' âti|vikṣatam,
prapāta|niṣpeṣa|kṛtāḥ sahyā eva ca me rujaḥ. [15]

prapāta|patana|kleśān na tv ahaṃ pīḍitas tathā
iti kalyāṇa|hṛdaye tvayi praskhalanād yathā. [16]

ākṛti|pratyayād yac ca dṛṣṭo 'si mṛgavan mayā
a|vijñāya sva|bhāvaṃ te, tac ca mā hṛdaye kṛthāḥ.» [17]

Do not despair at falling into this pit.
I am able to lift you out.
If you think you can trust me,
instruct me quickly and I will come."

The king was amazed at the deer's remarkable speech. 25.25
Filled with shame, he had the following earnest thought:

"How can he show me compassion
when I have clearly treated him as a foe?
And how can I act so wrongfully
toward this creature who is pure?
How castigated I feel by
his gentle yet wounding behavior!
It is I who am the animal, the ox.
Who is this creature, a *shárabha* but in form?

I have a duty to honor him by accepting his offer."
Forming this resolution, the king said:

"My body is covered in armor, 25.30
so I am not injured greatly.
I can bear the pain I suffer
from crashing into this pit.

But the pain of my fall
does not afflict me
as much as wronging one
as good-hearted as you.

Because of your appearance
I saw you as a wild animal.
I could not discern your true nature:
please do not take it to heart."

atha sa† śarabhas tasya rājñaḥ prīti|sūcakena ten' âbhivyā-hāreṇ' ânumatam uddharaṇam avetya puruṣa|bhāra|gurvyā śilayā tad|uddharaṇa|yogyāṃ kṛtvā vidit'|ātma|bala|pramāṇas taṃ nṛ|patim uddhartuṃ vyavasita|matir avatīrya taṃ prapātaṃ sa|vinayam abhigamy' ôvāca:

«mad|gātra|saṃsparśam imaṃ muhūrtaṃ
kāry'|ânurodhāt tvam anukṣamasva,
yāvat karomi sva|hit'|âbhipattyā
prīti|prasād'|âbhimukhaṃ mukhaṃ te. [18]

25.35 tad ārohatu mat|pṛṣṭhaṃ mahā|rājaḥ, su|lagnaś ca mayi bhavatv iti.»

sa tath" êti pratiśruty' âinam aśvavad adhyāruroha.†

tataḥ samabhyunnata|pūrva|kāyas
ten' âdhirūḍhaḥ sa nar'|âdhipena
samutpatann uttama|sattva|vegaḥ
khe toraṇa|vyālakavad babhāse. [19]

uddhṛtya dur|gād atha taṃ nar'|êndraṃ
prītaḥ samānīya turaṃ|gameṇa,
nivedya c' âsmai sva|purāya mārgaṃ,
vana|prayāṇ'|âbhimukho babhūva. [20]

atha sa rājā kṛta|jñatvāt tena tasya vinaya|madhureṇ' ôpacāreṇa samāvartita|hṛdayaḥ saṃpariṣvajya śarabham uvāca:

25.40 «prāṇā amī me, śarabha, tvadīyāḥ,
prāg eva yatr' âsti mama prabhutvam.
tad arhasi draṣṭum idaṃ puraṃ me;
satyāṃ rucau tatra ca te 'stu vāsaḥ. [21]

The *shárabha* understood from the king's manifestly friendly words that he agreed to be pulled out of the pit. So he practiced the rescue attempt by lifting a rock that was as heavy as a man. After thus determining the measure of his strength, he steeled himself for rescuing the king. Descending into the pit, he respectfully approached the king, saying:

"In consideration of the task to be done,
please endure touching my body a while
so I can bring myself happiness
by making your face gleam with joy.

Climb onto my back, Your Majesty, and hold on well." 25.35
Agreeing, the king mounted the deer as if he were a horse.

Holding his chest high,
mounted by the king,
he leapt up with great courage and energy,
glorious as a lion-sculpture on a stone arch.

Carrying the king out of the perilous hole,
he joyfully led him back to his horse.
After telling him the way to his city,
he turned to set off for the forest.

The king was so grateful and moved by the deer's modest and tender service that he embraced the *shárabha* and said:

25.40
"My life is yours, *shárabha*,
let alone the power I possess.
So please come and see my city.
If you like it, you can stay there.

vyādh'|âbhikīrṇe sa|bhaye vane 'smin
śīt'|ôṣṇa|varṣ'|ādy|upasarga|duḥkhe
hitvā bhavantaṃ mama nanv a|yuktam
ekasya geh'|âbhimukhasya gantum? [22]

tad ehi, gacchāva iti.»

ath' âinaṃ Bodhisattvaḥ sa | vinaya | madhur' | ôpacāraṃ saṃrādhayan pratyuvāca:

«bhavad|vidheṣv eva, manuṣya|varya,
yuktaḥ kramo 'yaṃ guṇa|vatsaleṣu.
abhyāsa|yogena hi saj|janasya
sva|bhāvatām eva guṇā vrajanti. [23]

25.45 anugrahītavyam avaiṣi yat tu
van'|ôcitaṃ māṃ bhavan'|āśrayeṇa,
ten' âlam. anyadd hi sukhaṃ narāṇām,
anyādṛśaṃ jāty|ucitaṃ mṛgāṇām. [24]

cikīrṣitaṃ te yadi mat|priyaṃ tu,
vyādha|vrataṃ, vīra, vimuñca tasmāt!
tiryaktva|bhāvāj jaḍa|cetaneṣu
kṛp" âiva śocyeṣu mṛgeṣu yuktā. [25]

sukh'|āśraye duḥkha|vinodane ca
samāna|cittān avagaccha sattvān.
ity ātmanaḥ syād an|abhīpsitaṃ yan,
na tat pareṣv ācarituṃ kṣamaṃ te. [26]

Surely it would be wrong to return home alone,
leaving you behind in this forest
teeming with hunters and full of danger,
arduous with cold, heat, rain and other toils.

Come then. Let us go."

Praising the king with polite, soft and courteous words, the Bodhi·sattva replied:

"Your conduct befits a lover of virtue
like yourself, most excellent of men.
For through repeated practice,
virtues become inherent in the good.

But if you think I would be favored 25.45
by living in your palace when used to the forest,
that is wrong. Happiness for men is one thing,
for animals another, as suits their differing birth.

But if you wish to do me a kindness,
then give up hunting, heroic king!
Beasts are dim-witted due to their animal nature.
You should be kind to such pitiful beings.

Be aware that all beings have the same attitude
about pursuing happiness and rejecting pain.
You should therefore not do to others
what you would not want done to yourself.

kīrti|kṣayaṃ sādhu|janād vigarhāṃ
duḥkhaṃ ca pāpa|prabhavaṃ viditvā
pāpaṃ dviṣat|pakṣam iv' ôddharasva.
n' ôpekṣituṃ vyādhir iva kṣamaṃ te. [27]

lakṣmī|niketaṃ yad|apāśrayeṇa
prāpto 'si lok'|âbhimataṃ nṛpatvam,
tāny eva puṇyāni vivardhayethā.
na karśanīyo hy upakāri|pakṣaḥ! [28]

25.50 kāl'|ôpacāra|subhagair vipulaiḥ pradānaiḥ
śīlena sādhu|jana†|saṃgata|niścalena†
bhūteṣu c' ātmani yathā hita|siddhi|buddhyā†
puṇyāni saṃcinu yaśaḥ|sukha|sādhanāni.» [29]

iti sa Mahātmā taṃ rājānaṃ dṛṣṭa|dhārmika|sāṃparāyikeṣv† artheṣv anugṛhya saṃpratigṛhīta|vacanas tena rājñā sa|bahu|mānam avekṣyamāṇas† tam eva van'|ântaṃ praviveśa.

tad evaṃ, jighāṃsum apy āpad|gatam anukampanta eva mahā|kāruṇikā n' ôpekṣanta iti.

karuṇā|varṇe 'pi vācyam. Tathāgata|māhātmye sat|kṛtya dharma|śravaṇe. a|vaireṇa vaira|praśamana|nidarśane ca kṣānti|kathāyām apy upaneyam.

Realizing that wicked deeds produce suffering,
loss of fame and criticism from the good,
you should eradicate evil, as if it were an enemy.
Like a disease, you should never disregard it.

By adhering to pure deeds, you gained kingship,
that abode of prosperity acclaimed in the world.
You should foster such good actions.
For benefactors should not be depleted!

25.50

By giving abundant gifts,
auspicious in being timely and courteous,
by practicing virtuous conduct,
strengthened by association with good people,
and by considering the welfare
of others as much as your own,
you should build up your store of merit,
thereby attaining fame and happiness."

The Great One thus gave helpful advice to the king on matters relating to this life and the next. Embracing his words, the monarch gazed at the deer reverently as he entered the forest.

In this way, in their compassion, those with great pity never disregard a man in distress, even if he means to kill them.

One should also narrate this story when eulogizing compassion, or when discussing the majesty of the Tatha·gata, or when discussing the topic of listening to the Teaching with respect. It should also be cited when illustrating the way in which enmity is quelled by friendship, and when discussing forbearance.

evaṃ tiryag|gatānām api mah"|ātmanāṃ vadhakeṣv anu-krośa | pravṛttiṃ dṛṣṭvā,† ko manuṣya | bhūtaḥ pravrajita | pratijño vā sattveṣv anukrośa | vikalaṃ śobhet', êti prāṇiṣu s'|ânukrośena bhavitavyam.†

After one has observed that, despite being animals, the great-minded have acted compassionately toward would-be murderers, who that is human, or that has taken the vow of renunciation, would wish to appear deficient in compassion toward sentient beings? One should therefore act with compassion toward living creatures.

RURUJĀTAKAM

STORY 26
THE BIRTH-STORY OF THE ANTELOPE

26.1 PARA|DUḤKHAM eva duḥkhaṃ sādhūnām. tadd hi na sahante, n' ātma|duḥkham.

tad|yath" ânuśrūyate.

Bodhisattvaḥ kila sāla | bakula | piyāla | hintāla | tamāla | naktamāla|vidula|nicula|kṣupa|bahule śiṃśapā|tiniśa|śamī| palāśa|śāka|kāśa† |kuśa|vaṃśa|śara|vaṇa|gahane kadamba| sarj' | ârjuna | dhava | khadira | kuṭaja | nicite vividha | vallī | pratān' | âvaguṇṭhita | bahu | taru | viṭape ruru | pṛṣata | sṛmara| camara | gaja | gavaya | mahiṣa | hariṇa | nyaṅku | varāha | dvīpi | tarakṣu|vyāghra|vṛka|siṃha'|rkṣ'|ādi|mṛga|vicarite manuṣya| saṃpāta|virahite mahaty araṇya|vana|pradeśe

tapta|kāñcan'|ôjjvala|varṇaḥ su|kumāra|romā nānā|vidha| padmarāg'|êndranīla|marakata|vaiḍūrya|rucira|varṇa|bindu| vidyotita | vicitra | gātraḥ snigdh' | âbhinīla | vimala | vipula | nayano manimayair iv' â | paruṣa | prabhair viṣāṇa | khura† | pradeśaiḥ parama|darśanīya|rūpo ratn'|ākara iva pāda|cārī ruru|mṛgo babhūva.

26.5 sa jānānaḥ svasya vapuṣo lobhanīyatāṃ† tanu|kāruṇyatāṃ ca janasya nirjana|saṃpāteṣu vana|gahaneṣv abhireme, paṭu|vijñānatvāc ca tatra tatra vyādha|jana|viracitāni yantra| kūṭa | vāgurā | pāś' | âvapāta | lepa | kāṣṭha | nivāpa | bhojanāni

IT IS ONLY WHEN others suffer that the virtuous feel pain. This is what they cannot bear, not their own suffering. Tradition has handed down the following story. 26.1

The Bodhi·sattva is said to have once lived as a *ruru* deer that roamed a large and wild area of the forest, removed from any contact with human beings. *Sala, bákula, piyála, hintála, tamála, nakta·mala, vídula* and *níchula* trees grew abundantly in the area alongside numerous shrubs, and the forest was thick with *shínshapa, tínisha, shami, palásha* and *shaka* trees, as well as *kasha* grass, kusha grass, canes and reeds. Overspread with *kadámba*s, *sarja*s, *árjuna*s, *dhava*s, *khádira*s and *kútaja*s, the branching boughs of the many trees were veiled by various creepers and tendrils.* *Ruru* deer, spotted antelopes, *srímara* deer, yaks, elephants, oxen, buffaloes, *hárina* deer, *nyanku* deer, boars, leopards, hyenas, tigers, wolves, lions, bears and other wild animals frequented the area.

It was here that the *ruru* deer lived, blazing with the color of purified gold. His body was covered with extremely soft fur, its various radiant spots glittering with the color of rubies, sapphires, emeralds and beryls. His large shining eyes were gentle and bright blue and his horns and hooves emitted a soft luminosity, investing his body with such supreme beauty it resembled a treasury of jewels.

Aware of how seductive his beauty was and also how short of compassion humans were, the deer delighted in forest thickets that were devoid of men. Because of his sharp intellect, he carefully avoided traps, nets, snares, pits, poison-smeared baits, sticks, seeds, food, or any device set by hunters, alerting the herds of wild animals that followed 26.5

samyak pariharann anugāminaṃ ca mṛga|sārtham avabodhayann ācārya iva pit" êva ca mṛgāṇām ādhipatyaṃ cakāra.

rūpa|vijñāna|saṃpattiḥ kriyā|sauṣṭhava|saṃskṛtā
sva|hit'|ânveṣiṇi jane kutra nāma na pūjyate? [1]

atha kadā cit sa† Mahātmā tasmin vana|gahane vās'|ôpagatas tat|samīpa|vāhinyā nav'|âmbu|pūrṇayā mahā|vegayā nadyā hriyamāṇasya puruṣasy' ākrandita|śabdaṃ śuśrāva.

«hriyamāṇam a|nātham a|plavaṃ
sarit'|ôdīrṇa|jal'|âugha|vegayā
abhidhāvata, dīna|vatsalāḥ,
kṛpaṇaṃ tārayituṃ javena mām! [2]

na vilambitum atra śakyate
śrama|doṣa|vidheya|bāhunā.
na ca gādham avāpyate kva cit.
tad ayaṃ māṃ samayo 'bhidhāvitum!» [3]

26.10 atha Bodhisattvas tena tasya karuṇen' ākrandita|śabdena hṛd' îva samabhihanyamāno, «mā bhair! mā bhair!» iti janma|śat'|âbhyastāṃ bhaya|viṣāda|śram'|âpanodinīm† āmreḍit'|âbhiniṣpīḍita|spaṣṭa|padām uccair mānuṣīṃ vācaṃ visṛjaṃs tasmād vana|gahanād viniṣpapāta. dūrata eva ca taṃ puruṣam iṣṭam iv' ôpāyanam ānīyamānaṃ salil'|âughena dadarśa.

him as if he were their teacher. Like a father, he ruled over the other animals in the forest.

If one possesses beauty and intellect,
perfected by conduct and virtue,
where will this not be honored
by people seeking welfare?

One day, while residing in that dense forest, the Great One heard the shouts of a man being swept along by the strong current of a river flowing nearby, its waters swollen with fresh rain:

"Swept by this violent torrent of swollen waters,
no one is here to help me! I have no boat!
If you feel any pity for a man in despair,
run over here quickly and save me!

I cannot remain afloat.
My arms are too tired.
I cannot find any ford.
Run over here now!"

26.10 The Bodhi·sattva was so struck by compassion for the man it was as if he had been wounded in the heart. Rushing out of the thicket, with a loud, clear and anxious human voice he repeatedly uttered words that he had used in hundreds of previous rebirths to dispel terror, despair and exhaustion: "Have no fear! Have no fear!" Far in the distance he spotted the man being swept toward him by the torrent of water, as if a coveted present were coming toward him.

tatas tad uttāraṇa|niścit'|ātmā
svaṃ prāṇa|saṃdeham a|cintayitvā
sa tāṃ nadīṃ bhīma|rayāṃ jagāhe,
vikṣobhayan vīra iv' âri|senām. [4]

āvṛtya mārgaṃ vapuṣ" âtha tasya
«mām āśrayasv'» êti tam abhyuvāca.
trās'|āturatvāc chrama|vihval'|âṅgaḥ
sa pṛṣṭham ev' âdhiruroha tasya. [5]

saṃsādyamāno 'pi nareṇa tena
vivartyamāno 'pi nadī|rayeṇa
sattv'|ôcchrayād a|skhalit'|ôru|vīryaḥ
kūlaṃ yayau tasya mano|'nukūlam. [6]

prāpayya tīram atha taṃ puruṣaṃ pareṇa
prīty|udgamena vinivartita|kheda|duḥkhaḥ†
sven' ôṣmaṇā samapanīya ca śītam asya
«gacch'» êti taṃ sa visasarja nivedya mārgam. [7]

26.15 atha sa puruṣaḥ snigdha|bāndhava|suhṛj|jana|durlabhena tena tasy' âty|adbhuten'† âbhyupapatti|saumukhyena† samāvarjita|hṛdayas tayā c' âsya rūpa|śobhayā samutthāpyamāna|vismaya|bahu|mānaḥ praṇamy' âinaṃ tat tat priyam uvāca:

«ā bālyāt saṃbhṛta|snehaḥ
suhṛd bāndhava eva vā
n' âlaṃ kartum idaṃ karma,
mad|arthe yat kṛtaṃ tvayā. [8]

Determined to save him,
disregarding the risk to his own life,
he plunged into the terrifyingly swift river,
like a hero scattering a hostile army.

Blocking the path of the river with his body,
he told the man to hold onto him.
Sick with fear and quivering with fatigue,
the man climbed onto his back.

Although straddled by the man
and jostled by the river current,
the deer's fine courage meant that his power
never faltered and he arrived at the desired bank.

Conveying the man to the bank,
his fatigue and pain dispelled by immense joy,
the deer used his warmth to allay the man's cold
and then released him after telling him the way.

The man's heart was moved by the deer's remarkable will to help others, a quality rarely found even among loving relatives or friends. Feeling amazement and respect at the deer's glorious form, the man bowed before him and said various pleasing words: 26.15

"Even a friend or relative,
affectionate since childhood,
would not be able to perform
the deed you performed for me.

tvadīyās tad ime prāṇās. tvad|arthe yadi nāma me
sv|alpe 'pi viniyujyeran, sa me syād aty|anugrahaḥ. [9]

tad ājñā|saṃpradānena
kartum arhasy anugraham
viniyoga|kṣamatvaṃ me
bhavān yatr' âvagacchati.» [10]

ath' âinaṃ Bodhisattvaḥ saṃrādhayan pratyuvāca:

26.20 «na citra|rūpā su|jane kṛta|jñatā.
nisarga|siddh" âiva hi tasya sā sthitiḥ.
jagat tu dṛṣṭvā samudīrṇa|vikriyaṃ
kṛta|jñat" âpy adya guṇeṣu gaṇyate. [11]

yatas tvāṃ bravīmi. kṛtam idam anusmaratā bhavatā n' âyam arthaḥ kasmai cin nivedyaḥ, «īdṛśen' âsmi sattva|viśeṣeṇ' ôttārita» iti. āmiṣa|bhūta|mati|lobhanīyam idaṃ hi me rūpam paśyāmi.† tanu|ghṛṇāni bahu|laulyād a|nibhṛtāni ca prāyeṇa mānuṣa|hṛdayāni.

tad ātmani guṇāṃś c' âiva māṃ ca rakṣitum arhasi.
na hi mitreṣv abhidrohaḥ kva cid bhavati bhūtaye. [12]

mā c' âivam ucyamāno manyu|praṇaya|virasaṃ hṛdayaṃ kārṣīḥ. mṛgā hi vayam an|abhyasta|mānuṣ'|ôpacāra|śāṭhyāḥ. api ca,

My life is therefore yours.
If it can be used to benefit you,
no matter how small the matter,
I would be immensely favored.

Please do me the favor
of giving me an order
in whatever matter
you see fit, good sir."

The Bodhi·sattva replied to the man with the following words of praise:

"It is no surprise to find gratitude in good men. 26.20
For it is firmly established in their nature.
But on seeing the swirling depravity of the world,
even gratitude is nowadays counted as a virtue.

For this reason, let me tell you this. When you recollect this event, do not inform anyone that you were saved by such a remarkable creature. For I believe my beautiful body is bound to be coveted as prey. After all, men's hearts are usually ruthless and uncontrolled in their great greed.

So guard your virtues
as well as myself.
Betraying one's friends
never brings prosperity.

Please also do not let your heart become angry or lose its affection because I have addressed you this way. We animals are unpracticed in the polite and cunning ways of humans. Besides,

tat kṛtaṃ vañcanā|dakṣair mithyā|vinaya|paṇḍitaiḥ,
yena bhāva|vinīto 'pi janaḥ s'|āśaṅkam īkṣyate. [13]

26.25 tad etat priyaṃ bhavatā saṃpādyamānam icchām' îti.»

sa tath" êti pratiśrutya praṇamya pradakṣiṇī|kṛtya ca taṃ Mahā|sattvaṃ sva|gṛham abhyājagāma.

tena khalu samayena tatr' ânyatamasya rājño devī satya|svapnā babhūva. sā yaṃ yam ātiśayikaṃ svapnaṃ dadarśa, sa tath" âiv' âbhavat. sā kadā cin nidrā | vaśam upagatā pratyūṣa|samaye svapnaṃ paśyati sma sarva|ratna|samāhāram iva śriyā jvalantaṃ siṃh'|āsana|sthaṃ ruru|mṛgaṃ sa|rājikayā parṣadā parivṛtaṃ vispaṣṭ'|âkṣara|pada|vinyāsena† mānuṣeṇa vacasā dharmaṃ deśayantam. vismay'|ākṣipta|hṛdayā ca bhartuḥ prabodha|paṭaha|dhvaninā saha sā vyabudhyata. yathā|prastāvaṃ ca samupetya rājānaṃ labdha|praṇaya|prasara|saṃmānanā†

sā vismay'|ôtphullatar'|ēkṣaṇa|śrīḥ
prītyā samutkampi|kapola|śobhā
upāyanen' êva nṛpaṃ dadarśa
ten' âdbhuta|svapna|nivedanena. [14]

nivedya ca taṃ svapn'|âtiśayaṃ rājñe s'|ādaraṃ punar uvāca:

It is because people are clever in deceit
and skilled in false modesty that
even a genuinely decent person
is viewed with suspicion.

This is the favor I wish you to fulfill."

26.25

Agreeing to his request, the man bowed before the Great Being and circumambulated him before returning to his home.

Now at that time there lived in the region a queen who saw dreams that were true. However extreme the dream she saw, it always came to be. One day, at daybreak, while still under a spell of sleep, she saw a dream: an antelope blazing so beautifully it resembled a heap of every type of jewel. Standing on a lion-throne, the antelope was surrounded by the king and his assembly and was preaching the Teaching with a human voice that clearly expressed every syllable and word. It was at that point, when her heart was struck by wonder, that the queen woke up to the sound of the drums that were used to wake her husband. As soon as was convenient, she approached the king, who always showed her trust, affection and respect.

Her beautiful eyes blooming with wonder,
her graceful cheeks quivering with joy,
she went to see the king, offering the news
of her miraculous dream as if it were a gift.

After informing the king of her exceptional dream, she respectfully addressed him once more, saying:

26.30 «tat sādhu tāvat kriyatāṃ mṛgasya
tasy' ôpalambhaṃ prati, deva, yatnaḥ.
antaḥ|puraṃ ratna|mṛgeṇa tena
tārā|mṛgeṇ' êva nabho virājet.» [15]

atha sa rājā dṛṣṭa | pratyayas tasyāḥ svapna | darśanasya pratigṛhya tad vacanaṃ tat | priya | kāmyayā ratna | mṛg' | âdhigama|lobhāc ca tasya mṛgasy' ânveṣaṇ'|ârthaṃ sarvaṃ vyādha|gaṇaṃ samādideśa. pratyahaṃ ca pura|vare ghoṣaṇām iti kārayām āsa:

«hema|cchavir maṇi|śatair iva citra|gātraḥ
khyāto mṛgaḥ śrutiṣu dṛṣṭa|caraś ca kaiś cit.
yas taṃ pradarśayati, tasya dadāti rājā
grām'|ôttamaṃ paridaśā rucirāḥ striyaś ca.» [16]

atha sa puruṣas tāṃ ghoṣaṇāṃ punaḥ punar upaśrutya

dāridrya|duḥkha|gaṇanā|parikhinna|cetāḥ
smṛtvā ca taṃ ruru|mṛgasya mah"|ôpakāram,
lobhena tena ca kṛtena vikṛṣyamāṇo
dolāyamāna|hṛdayo vimamarśa tat tat: [17]

“Please therefore make an effort
to capture this deer, divine lord.
Your palace will gleam with the jewel-like animal,
just as the sky glitters with the Deer Star.”* 26.30

Experience had taught the king to trust what the queen saw in her dreams and so he took up her request, both because he wanted to please her but also because of his greed to obtain the jewel-like deer. So he instructed his entire troop of hunters to search for the animal. Every day he had the following announcement proclaimed in the capital:

“Gold-skinned, its limbs speckled
as if with hundreds of jewels,
a deer is rumored to exist,
its movements spied by some people.
The king will give to
whoever reveals this deer
a fine village and a total
of ten delightful women.”

The very same man mentioned above happened to hear this repeated proclamation.

Though exhausted by worries
about poverty and suffering,
he recalled the great service
the antelope had done for him.
Torn both by greed
and by gratitude,
he considered various thoughts
with an oscillating heart:

26.35 «kiṃ nu khalu karomi? guṇān† paśyāmy uta dhana|samṛddhim? kṛtam anupālayāmy uta kuṭumba|tantram? para|lokam udbhāvayāmy ath' êmam? sad|vṛttam anugacchāmy ut'|āho loka|vṛttam? śriyam anubhavāmy† āho† svit sādhu|dayitāṃ hriyam?† tadātvaṃ paśyāmy ut' āyatim iti?»

ath' âsya lobh'|ākulita|mater evam abhūt: śakyam adhigata|vipula|dhana|samṛddhinā sva|jana|mitr'|âtithi|praṇayi|jana|saṃmānana|pareṇa sukhāny anubhavatā paro 'pi lokaḥ saṃpādayitum. iti niścita|matir vismṛtya taṃ ruru|mṛgasya mah"|ôpakāraṃ† samupetya rājānam uvāca:

«ahaṃ, deva, taṃ mṛga|varam adhivāsaṃ c' âsya jānāmi. tad ājñāpaya kasmai pradarśayāmy enam iti.»

tac chrutvā sa rājā pramudita|manāḥ, «mam' âiv' âinaṃ, bhadra, pradarśay'!» êty uktvā mṛgayā|prayāṇ'|ânurūpaṃ veṣam āsthāya mahatā bala|kāyena parivṛtaḥ pura|varān nirgamya tena puruṣeṇ' ādiśyamāna†|mārgas taṃ nadī|tīram upajagāma. parikṣipya ca tad vana|gahanaṃ samagreṇa bala|kāyena dhanvī hast'|āvāpī vyavasit'|āpta|puruṣa|parivṛtaḥ sa rājā ten' âiva puruṣeṇ' ādiśyamāna†|mārgas tad vana|gahanam anuviveśa.†

atha sa puruṣas taṃ ruru|mṛgaṃ viśvasta|sthitam ālokya pradarśayām āsa rājñe: «ayam! ayaṃ, deva, sa mṛga|varaḥ! paśyatv enaṃ devaḥ. prayatnaś ca bhavatv iti.»

"What should I do? Should I look to virtues or to opulent riches? Should I safeguard my gratitude or my family loyalties? Should I consider the next world or this one? Should I follow virtue or worldly conduct? Should I enjoy prosperity or follow the sense of shame that is cherished by the good? Should I look to the present or to the future?" 26.35

His mind was so confused by greed that he concocted the following plan: if he gained abundant riches, he could enjoy pleasures and dedicate himself to honoring his relatives, friends, guests and supplicants, while also attaining the next world. His mind made up, the man forgot the great service that the antelope had done for him and approached the king, saying:

"I know this fine deer, divine king. And I know where he lives. Please tell me to whom I should reveal him."

The king was overjoyed at hearing these words and said: "Reveal him to me, good sir!" Putting on his hunting clothes, the king then set out from the capital, accompanied by a large army, and reached the river bank by following the man's directions. After circling the dense forest with his entire army, the king then entered the thick grove, wielding his bow and wearing his hand-guard. Accompanied by determined and trustworthy soldiers, he followed the path directed by the man.

When the man spotted the antelope standing there fearlessly, he pointed him out to the king, saying: "There he is! There is the fine deer, divine lord! Look at him, divine king. And be careful."

26.40 tasy' ônnamayato† bāhuṃ mṛga|saṃdarśan'|ādarāt
prakoṣṭhān nyapatat pāṇir vinikṛtta iv' âsinā. [18]

āsādya vastūni hi tādṛśāni
kriyā|viśeṣair abhisaṃskṛtāni
labdha|prayāmāṇi vipakṣa|māndyāt,
karmāṇi sadyaḥ phalatāṃ vrajanti. [19]

atha sa rājā tat|pradarśitena mārgeṇa ruru|saṃdarśana|kutūhale nayane vicikṣepa.

vane 'tha tasmin nava|megha|nīle
jvalat|tanuṃ ratna|nidhāna|lakṣmyā
guṇair uruṃ taṃ sa ruruṃ dadarśa
śāta|hradaṃ vahnim iv' âbhra|kuñje.† [20]

tad|rūpa|śobh'|āhṛta|mānaso 'tha
sa bhūmi|pas tad|grahaṇ'|âti|lobhāt
kṛtvā dhanur bāṇa|vidaṣṭa|maurvi
vivyatsayā† c' âinam upāruroha. [21]

26.45 atha Bodhisattvaḥ samantato jana|kolāhalam upaśrutya, «vyaktaṃ samantāt parivṛtto 'sm'» îti niścita|matir vyaddhu|kāmam upārūḍhaṃ c' âvetya rājānaṃ, «n' âyam apayāna|kāla» iti viditvā viśada|pad'|âkṣareṇa mānuṣeṇa vacasā rājānam ābabhāṣe:

«tiṣṭha tāvan, mahā|rāja! mā māṃ vyātsīr, nara'|rṣabha!
kautūhalam idaṃ tāvad vinodayitum arhasi. [22]

But as he lifted his arm, 26.40
eager to point out the deer,
his hand fell off his wrist,
as if lopped off by a sword.

For if one acts against an object
so adorned by exceptional conduct,
one's deeds are requited and instantly bear fruit,
there being little virtue to counter them.

Curious to see the antelope, the king cast his eyes along the path indicated by the man.

In that forest, dark as a fresh raincloud,
he saw the deer abounding in virtues,
its body blazing gloriously like a treasure of gems,
like a flame of lightning in the cloud-like grove.

Filled with great desire to seize the deer,
his heart captivated by its beauty,
the king advanced forward to shoot it,
stretching his bow, an arrow biting the string.

When the Bodhi·sattva heard the human commotion all around him, he concluded that he must be surrounded on all sides. And when he saw the king charging forward, eager to shoot him, he realized that he had no time to flee and addressed the king with an articulate human voice: 26.45

"Stop, great king! Don't shoot me!
Please dispel my curiosity, bull among men.

asmin nirjana|sampāte niratam̥ gahane vane
«asāv atra mr̥go 'st'» îti ko nu te mām̥ nyavedayat?» [23]

atha sa rājā tena† tasy' âty|adbhutena† mānuṣen' âbhivyāhāreṇa bhr̥śataram āvarjita|hr̥dayas tam asmai puruṣam̥ śar'|âgreṇa nirdideśa: «ayam asy' âty|adbhutasya no darśayit"» êti. atha Bodhisattvas tam̥ puruṣam̥ pratyabhijñāya vigarhamāṇa uvāca:

«kaṣṭam̥, bhoḥ.

26.50 satya eva pravādo 'yam:
udak'|âugha|gatam̥ kila
dārv eva varam uddhartum̥,
n' â|kr̥ta|jña|matim̥ janam. [24]

pariśramasya tasy' êyam
īdr̥śī pratyupakriyā!
ātmano 'pi na dr̥ṣṭo 'yam̥
hitasy' âpanayaḥ katham?» [25]

atha sa rājā «kim̥ nu khalv ayam evam̥ vikutsayata?»† iti samutpanna|kautūhalaḥ s'|āvegas tam̥ rurum uvāca:

«a|nirbhinn'|ârtha|gambhīram
an|ārabhya|vigarhitam
tad† idam̥ samupaśrutya
s'|ākampam iva me manaḥ. [26]

mr̥g'|âtiśaya, tad brūhi:
kam ārabhy' êti bhāṣase?
manuṣyam a|manuṣyam̥ vā,
pakṣiṇam̥ mr̥gam eva vā?» [27]

Who told you that a deer
such as I was living
in this peopleless place,
delighting in the dense forest?"

The king was intensely moved by the deer's miraculous speech and pointed to the man with the tip of his arrow, saying: "This is the man who guided me to this wonder." Recognizing the man, the Bodhi·sattva chastised him, saying:

"How vile, sir.

26.50

It is true what they say:
better to rescue a log
than an ungrateful man,
if either is caught in a torrent.

This is how he repays
me for my efforts!
How can he not see
the damage he does himself?"

Curious as to why the deer uttered this rebuke, the king avidly asked him the following question:

"When I hear these rebukes,
incomprehensible and deep
with impenetrable meaning,
my mind quivers with alarm.

Tell me, exceptional animal:
to whom do your words refer?
Are they human or non-human,
bird or beast?"

26.55 Bodhisattva uvāca:

«n' âyaṃ vigarh"|ādara eva, rājan.
kuts"|ârham etat tv avagamya karma
n' âyaṃ punaḥ kartum iti vyavasyet,
tīkṣṇ'|âkṣaraṃ tena may" âivam uktam. [28]

ko hi kṣate kṣāram iv' âvasiñced
rūkṣ'|âkṣaraṃ viskhaliteṣu vākyam?
priye tu putre 'pi cikitsakasya
pravartate vyādhi|vaśāc cikitsā. [29]

yam uhyamānaṃ salilena hāriṇā
kṛpā|vaśād abhyupapanna|vāhanam,
tato bhayaṃ māṃ, nṛ|var', êdam āgataṃ.
na khalv a|sat|saṃgatam asti bhūtaye.» [30]

atha sa rājā taṃ puruṣaṃ tīkṣṇayā dṛṣṭyā nirbhartsana|rūkṣam avekṣy' ôvāca: «satyam, are re? purā tvam anen' âivam āpanno 'bhyuddhṛta?» iti.

26.60 atha sa puruṣaḥ samāpatita|bhaya|viṣāda|sveda|vaivarṇya†|dainyo hrī|mandaṃ «satyam» ity avocat.

atha sa rājā «dhik tvām!» ity enam avabhartsayan dhanuṣi śaraṃ saṃdhāy' âbravīt: «mā tāvad bhoḥ!

evaṃ|vidhen' âpi pariśrameṇa
mṛdū|kṛtaṃ yasya na nāma cetaḥ,
tuly'|ākṛtīnām a|yaśo|dhvajena
kiṃ jīvat" ânena nar'|âdhamena?» [31]

The Bodhi·sattva answered: 26.55

"I have no interest in blaming him, Your Majesty.
But when I realized his deplorable action,
I spoke these harsh words hoping that
he would never decide to act this way again.

For who would rub salt into a wound
by speaking harshly to one who has done wrong?
Illness obliges a doctor to apply surgery,
even if the patient is his beloved son.

I rescued this man out of pity
as he was swept away by a forceful current.
Now it is he who puts me in peril, king.
Truly there is no benefit in meeting the bad."

Staring at him fiercely with a violent look of reproach, the king then addressed the man, saying: "What? Is it true that this deer once saved you when you were in distress?"

Terrified and despondent, the distraught man started 26.60 sweating and his face changed color as he replied with words faint with shame: "It is true."

"Shame on you!" the king castigated him. Placing an arrow in his bow, he exclaimed: "This cannot be permitted!

If a man's heart remains unsoftened
when a person makes such effort for him,
he is a badge of dishonor among his own kind.
Why should such a vile person stay alive?"

ity uktvā muṣṭim ābadhya tad|vadh'|ârthaṃ dhanuḥ pracakarṣa. atha Bodhisattvaḥ karuṇayā mahatyā samuparudhyamāna|hṛdayas tad|antarā sthitvā rājānam uvāca:

«alam! alaṃ, mahā|rāja, hataṃ hatvā!

26.65 yad" âiva† lobha|dviṣataḥ pratāraṇāṃ
vigarhitām apy ayam abhyupeyivān,
hatas tad" âiv' êha† yaśaḥ|pariksayād
dhruvaṃ paratr' âpi ca dharma|saṃkṣayāt. [32]

a|sahya|duḥkh'|ôdaya|pīta|mānasāḥ
patanti c' âivaṃ vyasaneṣu mānuṣāḥ
pralobhyamānāḥ phala|saṃpad"|āśayā,
pataṅga|mūrkhā iva dīpa|śobhayā. [33]

ataḥ kṛpām atra kuruṣva, mā ruṣaṃ.
yad īpsitaṃ c' âivam anena kiṃ cana,
kuruṣva ten' âinam a|vandhya|sāhasaṃ.
sthitaṃ tvad|ājñā|pravaṇaṃ hi me śiraḥ.» [34]

atha sa rājā tena tasy' âpakāriṇy api sa|dayatven' â|kṛtakena ca tat|pratyupakār'|ādareṇa parama|vismita|matir jāta|prasādaḥ sa|bahu|mānam udīkṣamāṇas taṃ ruru|varam uvāca:

«sādhu! sādhu, mahā|bhāga!

26.70 pratyakṣ'|ôgr'|âpakāre 'pi dayā yasy' êyam īdṛśī,
guṇato mānuṣas tvaṃ hi; vayam ākṛti|mānuṣāḥ! [35]

Saying this, he gripped his bow tightly and stretched it in order to kill the man. But the Bodhi·sattva's heart was besieged by a feeling of immense compassion. Standing between the two men, he addressed the king, saying:

"Stop, Your Majesty! Stop! Do not destroy a man who is already destroyed!

This man was destroyed when he yielded
to the vile seductions of hostile greed,
losing his reputation in this world
and his merit in the next. 26.65

Thus humans fall on disaster,
their hearts absorbing unbearable suffering,
seduced by the hope of fruitful rewards,
like foolish moths enticed by a lamp's light.

Act therefore with compassion and not anger.
And ensure his reckless act was not in vain,
whatever it was that he desired.
My head is lowered to accept your command."

The king was amazed by the Bodhi·sattva's compassionate and genuine desire to benefit the man, even though he had been wronged by him. Filled with devotion and gazing up at him reverently, the king addressed the supreme antelope, saying:

"Excellent! Excellent, illustrious deer!

To feel such compassion for a man
who clearly brutally wronged you
shows you are a human in virtue
and we are humans but in form! 26.70

yen' ânukampyas tu tav' âiṣa jālmo
  hetuś ca naḥ saj|jana|darśanasya,
dadāmi ten' ēpsitam artham asmai,
  rājye tav' âsmiṃś ca yath"|êṣṭa|cāram.» [36]

rurur uvāca: «pratigṛhīto 'yaṃ may" â|vandhyo mahā|rāja|prasādaḥ. tad ājñāpaya yāvad ih' âbhyāgamana†|prayojanena tav' ôpayogaṃ gacchāma iti.»

atha sa rājā taṃ ruruṃ gurum iva ratha|varam adhiropya† mahatā satkāreṇa pura|varaṃ praveśya kṛt'|âtithi|satkāraṃ mahati siṃh'|āsane niveśya† s'|ântaḥ|puro 'mātya|gaṇa|parivṛtaḥ prīti|bahumāna|saumyam udīkṣamāṇo dharmaṃ papraccha:

«dharmaṃ prati manuṣyāṇāṃ
  bahudhā buddhayo gatāḥ.
niścayas tava dharme tu
  yathā, taṃ vaktum arhasi.» [37]

26.75 atha Bodhisattvas tasya rājñaḥ sa|parṣatkasya sphuṭa|madhura|citr'|âkṣareṇa vacasā dharmaṃ deśayām āsa:

«dayāṃ sattveṣu manye 'haṃ
  dharmaṃ saṃkṣepato, nṛ|pa,
hiṃsā|steya|nivṛtty|ādi|
  prabhedaṃ tri|vidha|kriyam.† [38]

paśya, mahā|rāja:

ātman' îva dayā syāc cet
  sva|jane vā yathā jane,
kasya nāma bhavec cittam
  a|dharma|praṇay'|â|śivam? [39]

But as you think this wretch is worthy of pity,
and since he caused me to see a virtuous being,
I will grant him the object of his desire
and permit you to roam at will in this kingdom."

"I accept your Majesty's blessing," the antelope replied. "It will not be in vain. Tell me your instructions so I can serve you and make use of my coming here."

The king then had the antelope ascend his fine chariot as if he were a guru and transported him to his capital with great honor. After he had paid to the antelope the honor due to a guest, the king placed him on his grand lion-throne and, surrounded by his wives and troop of ministers, he asked the antelope to preach the Teaching, gazing up at him with joy, reverence and tenderness:

"Humans have many opinions on the Teaching.
But you are certain. Tell us your convictions."

So the Bodhi·sattva preached the Teaching to the king and his assembly with words that were clear, pleasant and varied: 26.75

"I believe one can summarize the Teaching
as compassion toward living beings, king.
Performed in three modes,* this path of virtue
divides into non-harm, non-theft and other categories.

Consider this, Your Majesty:

If one felt the same compassion for strangers
as one does for oneself or one's family,
whose mind would be so evil
as to yearn for wickedness?

dayā|viyogāt tu janaḥ paramām eti vikriyām
mano|vāk|kāya|vispandaiḥ sva|jane 'pi jane yathā. [40]

26.80 dharm'|ârthī na tyajed asmād dayām iṣṭa|phal'|ôdayām,
su|vṛṣṭir iva sasyāni, guṇān sā† hi prasūyate. [41]

day"|ākrāntaṃ cittaṃ
na bhavati para|droha|rabhasaṃ.
śucau tasmin vāṇī
vrajati vikṛtiṃ† n' âiva ca tanuḥ.
vivṛddhā tasy' âivaṃ
para|hita|ruciḥ prīty|anusṛtā†
pradāna|kṣānty|ādīn
janayati guṇān kīrty|anuguṇān. [42]

dayālur n' ôdvegaṃ
janayati pareṣām upaśamād.
dayāvān viśvāsyo
bhavati jagatāṃ bāndhava iva.
na saṃrambha|kṣobhaḥ
prabhavati dayā|dhīra|hṛdaye.
na kop'|âgniś citte
jvalati hi dayā|toya|śiśire. [43]

saṃkṣepeṇa dayām ataḥ sthira|dayāḥ†
paśyanti dharmaṃ budhāḥ.
ko nām' âsti guṇaḥ sa sādhu|dayito
yo n' ânuyāto dayām?

But lack of compassion makes
people act in the most warped ways
toward relatives just as strangers,
in mind, speech and body.

Those seeking the Truth should never reject 26.80
compassion which swells with desired rewards.
For it generates virtues,
like a heavy rainfall generates crops.

A mind influenced by compassion
feels no malice or violence against others.
When a man's mind is pure,
his speech and actions are never perverse.
Friendship accompanies his increasing delight
in the welfare of other beings,
generating virtues trailed by fame
such as charity and forgiveness.

A compassionate man never makes
others alarmed, for he is tranquil.
A compassionate man is trustworthy,
like a kinsman to all creatures.
No raging confusion arises in the heart
of a man brave with compassion.
No burning anger blazes in a heart
cool with the waters of compassion.

In brief, wise men strong in pity
perceive the Truth as compassion.
For what virtue cherished by saints
does not follow the steps of compassion?
Show vigorous compassion to your people,

tasmāt putra iv' ātman' îva ca dayāṃ
nītvā prakarṣaṃ jane
sad|vṛttena haran manāṃsi jagatāṃ
rājatvam udbhāvaya.» [44]

atha sa rājā samabhinandya tat tasya vacanaṃ sa|paura|jānapado dharma|parāyaṇo babhūva. a|bhayaṃ ca sarva|mṛga|pakṣiṇāṃ dattvān.

26.85 tad evaṃ, para|duḥkham eva duḥkhaṃ sādhūnām. tadd hi na sahante, n' ātma|duḥkham iti.

karuṇā|varṇe 'pi vācyam. saj|jana|māhātmye khala|jana|kutsāyām apy upaneyam iti.

as you would toward your son or self.
Captivate the minds of living beings
with your virtue and nurture your kingship."

Rejoicing in the Bodhi·sattva's words, the king dedicated himself to the Teaching along with his citizens and countrymen. And he gave immunity to all animals and birds.

26.85 In this way, it is only when others suffer that the virtuous feel pain. This is what they cannot bear, not their own suffering.

This story should also be told when praising compassion. And one should also cite it when discussing the magnanimity of the virtuous or when condemning vile men.

MAHĀVĀNARAJĀTAKAM[†]

STORY 27
THE BIRTH-STORY OF THE GREAT MONKEY*

27.1 DVIṢATĀM API manāṃsy† āvarjayanti sad|vṛtt'|ânuvartinaḥ.

tad|yath" ânuśrūyate.

Bodhisattvaḥ kila śrīmati Himavat|kukṣau vividha|rasa|vīrya|vipāka|guṇair bahubhir oṣadhi|viśeṣaiḥ parigṛhīta|bhūmi|bhāge nānā|vidha|puṣpa|phala|pallava|patra|viṭapa|racanair mahī|ruha|śatair ākīrṇe sphaṭika|dal'|â|mala|salila|prasravaṇe vividha|pakṣi|gaṇa|nāda|nādite vānara|yūth'|âdhipatir babhūva.

tad|avastham api c' âinaṃ tyāga|kāruṇy'|âbhyāsāt pratipakṣa|sevā|virodhitān' îv' ērṣyā|mātsarya|krauryāṇi n' ôpajagmuḥ.

27.5 sa tatra mahāntaṃ nyagrodha|pādapaṃ parvata|śikharam iva vyom' ôllikhantam, adhipatim iva tasya vanasya, megha|saṃghātam iva pratyandhakāra|viṭapam, ākīrṇa|parṇatayā tāla|phal'|âdhikatara|pramāṇaiḥ parama|svādubhir manojña|varṇa|gandhaiḥ phala|viśeṣair ānamyamāna|śākhaṃ niśritya vijahāra.

tiryag|gatānām api bhāgya|śeṣaṃ
  satāṃ bhavaty eva sukh'|āśrayāya
kartavya|saṃbandhi suhṛj|janānāṃ
  videśa|gānām iva vitta|śeṣam. [1]

tasya tu vanas|pater ekā śākhā tat|samīpa|gāṃ nimna|gām abhipraṇat" âbhavat. atha Bodhisattvo dīrgha|darśitvāt tad vānara|yūthaṃ samanuśaśāsa: «asyāṃ nyagrodha|śākhāyāṃ

THOSE WHO ACT morally can influence the hearts even of enemies. 27.1

Tradition has handed down the following story.

The Bodhi·sattva is said to have once ruled over a troop of monkeys in the depths of the Hímavat mountain. Covered by numerous special herbs that were full of different tastes, powers and effects, the region was scattered with hundreds of trees that were decorated with arrangements of flowers, fruits, sprouts, leaves and branches. Water flowed through the area as pure as crystal fragments and there was the constant sound of various flocks of birds.

Despite being born into that state, envy, selfishness and cruelty never afflicted the monkey. For by habitually practicing generosity and compassion, he cultivated their opposites.

The Bodhi·sattva lived in a huge fig-tree. Like a mountain peak tearing through the sky, the tree seemed to rule over the forest, the darkness of its leaf-covered boughs making it resemble a mass of clouds. The tree's branches were bent down by fine fruits of exquisite taste that had a delightful color and scent and were larger than palmyra nuts. 27.5

Even as animals, the virtuous can share
their remaining fortune among friends
to give support to their happiness,
like the leftover wealth of people gone abroad.

One of the branches happened to hang over a river that passed through the area. In his far-sightedness, the Bodhi·sattva had instructed the troop of monkeys to clear away

niṣ|phalāyām a|kṛtāyāṃ na vaḥ kena cid anyataḥ phalam upabhoktavyam» iti.

te tathā cakruḥ.† atha kadā cit tasyāṃ śākhāyāṃ pipīlikābhiḥ parṇa|puṭ'|âvacchāditaṃ taruṇatvān n' âti|mahad ekaṃ phalaṃ na te vānarā dadṛśuḥ. tat krameṇ' âbhivardhamānaṃ varṇa|gandha|rasa|mārdav'|ôpapannaṃ paripāka|vaśāc chithila|bandhanaṃ tasyāṃ nadyāṃ nipapāta, anupūrveṇa c' ôhyamānaṃ† nadī|srotas" ânyatamasya rājñaḥ s'|ântaḥ|purasya tasyāṃ nadyāṃ salila|krīḍām anubhavato jāla|karaṇḍaka|pārśve vyāsajyata.

tat snāna|māly'|āsava|vāsa|gandhaṃ
saṃśleṣa|saṃpiṇḍitam aṅganānām
visarpiṇā svena tiraś|cakāra
ghrāṇ'|âbhirāmeṇa guṇ'|ôdayena. [2]

27.10 tad|gandha|mattāḥ kṣaṇam aṅganās tā
dīrghī|kṛt'|ôcchvāsa|vikuñcit'|âkṣyaḥ
bhūtv" âtha kautūhala|cañcalāni
vicikṣipur dikṣu vilocanāni. [3]

kaūtuhala|prasṛta|lolatara|nayanās tu tā yoṣitas tan nyagrodha|phalaṃ paripakva|tāla|phal'|âdhikatara|pramāṇaṃ jāla|karaṇḍaka|pārśvato vilagnam avekṣya «kim idam?» iti tad|āvarjita|nayanāḥ samapadyanta saha rājñā. atha sa rājā tat phalam ānāyya prātyayika|vaidya|jana|paridṛṣṭaṃ svayam āsvādayām āsa.

adbhutena rasen' âtha nṛ|pas tasya visismiye
adbhutena rasen' êva prayoga|guṇa|hāriṇā. [4]

the fruits from this branch or they would not be allowed to eat the fruit on the other boughs.

The monkeys did as the Bodhi·sattva ordered, but one day they failed to notice one of the fruits. The fruit was not very large because it was still young and was hidden by a leaf that had been rolled up by ants. The fruit gradually grew in size and became colorful, fragrant, tasty and soft. When it was ripe, its stalk loosened and it fell into the river. The current gradually carried the fruit downriver until it became stuck in the side of a net-basket belonging to a king who was playing water games in the river with his wives.

The combined scent of the bathing ointments,
garlands, liquor and perfume of the women
was dispelled by the fragrance of the fruit,
delightful to smell and swelling with virtues.

Sighing deeply and narrowing their eyes, 27.10
the women were instantly intoxicated by the smell.
Restless with curiosity,
they cast their eyes in every direction.

As they searched around in curiosity, the women caught sight of the fig fruit that lay stuck in the side of the net-basket, larger than a palmyra nut. Wondering what it was, their eyes were drawn to the object as were the king's. After he had the fruit brought to him, it was examined by reliable experts, whereupon the king tasted it himself.

The monarch was amazed
by the fruit's extraordinary taste,
just as the wonderful experience of savoring
a fine dramatic performance amazes a spectator.*

a|pūrva|varṇa|gandhābhyāṃ tasy' ākalita|vismayaḥ
yayau tad|rasa|saṃrāgāt parāṃ vismaya|vikriyām. [5]

atha tasya rājñaḥ svādu|rasa|bhojana|samucitasy' âpi tad|rasa|saṃrāga|vaśa|gasy' âitad abhavat:

27.15 «yo nāma n' âmūni phalāni bhuṅkte
sa kāni rājyasya phalāni bhuṅkte?
yasy' ânnam etat tu sa eva rājā
vin" âiva rājatva|pariśrameṇa» [6]

sa tat|prabhav'|ânveṣaṇa|kṛta|matiḥ sva|buddhyā vimamarśa:

«vyaktam ayaṃ taru|vara ito n' âti|dūre nadī|tīre† saṃniviṣṭaś ca, yasy' êdaṃ phalaṃ tathā hy an|upahata|varṇa|gandha|rasam a|dīrgha|kāla|salila|saṃparkād a|parikṣatam a|jarjaraṃ ca, yataḥ śakyam asya prabhavo 'dhigantum.»

iti niścayam upetya tad | rasa | tṛṣṇay" ākṛṣyamāṇo viramya jala|krīḍāyāḥ samyak pura|vare sve rakṣā|vidhānaṃ saṃdiśya yātrā|sajjena mahatā bala|kāyena parivṛtas tāṃ† nadīm anusasāra.

krameṇa c' ôtsādayan sa|śvāpada|gaṇāni vana|gahanāni samanubhavaṃś citrāṇi ras'|ântarāṇi paśyann a|kṛtrima|ramaṇīya|śobhāni van'|ântarāṇi saṃtrāsayan paṭaha|rasitair

His wonder had already been stirred
by the fruit's novel color and scent.
But now his passion for its taste
transformed his wonder to a supreme level.

Despite being used to fine tasting food, the king was so overpowered by desire for the fruit's flavor that he had this thought:

"If a man does not eat fruits like this,
what fruits can he enjoy from his royalty?
A man who has such food is a true monarch,
free from the toils of kingship."

27.15

Deciding to seek out the fruit's origins, the king pondered the matter the following way:

"This fine tree must obviously stand on a river bank that is not far away from here. For the color, smell and taste of its fruit remain unspoilt. It must have been in contact with water for only a short time for it to remain undamaged and intact. It should therefore be possible to discover its origins."

Making this resolution, the king ceased his water games, seduced by his craving for the fruit. After he had given instructions as to how his capital should be guarded, he set off along the river, accompanied by a large army equipped for the journey.

Clearing his way through the dense forests and the hordes of wild animals, the king enjoyed various experiences as he gazed at groves of natural and delightful beauty and terrified the forest animals with the din of his drums. In due

vanya|mṛgān† mānuṣa|jana|dur|gamaṃ tasya vanas|pateḥ samīpam upajagāma.

27.20 taṃ megha|vṛndam iva toya|bhar'|âvasannam
āsanna|śailam api śailavad īkṣyamāṇam
dūrād dadarśa nṛ|patiḥ sa vanaspat'|îndram
ullokyamānam adhirājam iv' ânya|vṛkṣaiḥ. [7]

paripakva|sahakāra|phala|surabhitareṇa ca nirhāriṇā mano|jñena† gandhena pratyudgata iva tasya pādapasya «ayaṃ sa vanas|patir» iti niścayam upajagāma. samupetya c' âinaṃ dadarśa tat|phal'|ôpabhoga|vyāpṛtair an|ekair vānara|śatair† ākīrṇa|viṭapam.

atha sa rājā samabhilaṣit'|ârtha|vipralopinas tān vānarān pratyabhikruddha|matiḥ «hata! hat' âitān! vidhvaṃsayata nāśayata† sarvān vānara|jālmān!» iti sa|paruṣ'|âkṣaraṃ svān puruṣān samādideśa.†

atha te rāja|puruṣāḥ sa|jya|cāpa|bāṇa|vyagra|kar'|âgrā vānar'|âvabhartsana|mukharāḥ samudyata|loṣṭa|daṇḍa|śastrāś c' âpare para|durgam iv' âbhiroddhu|kāmās taṃ vanas|patim abhisasruḥ.

atha Bodhisattvas tumulaṃ tad rāja|balam anila|jav'|ākalitam iv' ârṇava|jalam a|nibhṛta|kalakal'|ārāvam abhipatad āloky' âśani|varṣen' êva ca† samantato vikīryamāṇam taṃ† taru|varaṃ śara|loṣṭa|daṇḍa|varṣeṇa† bhaya|virasa|

course he arrived in the vicinity of the tree, an area seldom accessed by humans.

27.20

Like a mass of clouds
bulging under heavy rain,
or like a mountain,
despite its proximity to real peaks,
the lord of trees was spotted
by the monarch from afar,
gazed up at by other trees
as if it were their king.

When the tree's spreading and captivating scent reached the king, more fragrant than ripe mangoes, he was sure that this must be the tree. But on approaching it, the king saw that its boughs were covered with several hundred monkeys, all busily enjoying its fruits.

Enraged at the monkeys for stealing the objects of his desire, he addressed his men with harsh words, ordering them as follows: "Kill them! Kill them! Annihilate and destroy all these vile monkeys!"

The king's men therefore shouted noisily to scare off the monkeys, their fingers poised on their arrows and strung bows. Others advanced against the tree with raised clods and sticks, as if eager to attack the inaccessible fortress of an enemy.

The Bodhi·sattva, meanwhile, had observed the king's army charging forward noisily, screaming with loud howls like a sea of water whipped up by a swift wind. He saw the fine tree being sprayed on all sides by showers of arrows, clods and sticks as if by a shower of thunderbolts,

virāva|mātra|parāyaṇaṃ ca vikṛta|dīna|mukham unmukhaṃ vānara|gaṇam avekṣya mahatyā karuṇayā samākramyamāṇa|cetās tyakta|viṣāda|dainya|saṃtrāsaḥ samāśvāsya tad vānara|yūthaṃ tat|paritrāṇa|vyavasita|matir abhiruhya tasya vanas|pateḥ śikharaṃ tat|samāsannaṃ giri|taṭaṃ laṅghayitum iyeṣa. ath' ân|eka|praskandana|krama|prāpyam api taṃ giri|taṭaṃ sa Mahā|sattvaḥ sva|vīry'|âtiśayāt khaga iv' âdhiruroha.

27.25 dvābhyām api laṅghana|kramābhyāṃ
gamyaṃ n' âiva tad anya|vānarāṇām
vegena yad antaraṃ tarasvī
pratatār' âlpam iv' âika|vikrameṇa. [8]

kṛpayā hi vivardhitaḥ† sa tasya
vyavasāyaḥ paṭutāṃ jagāma śauryāt
sa ca yatna|viśeṣam asya cakre
manas" êv'† âtha jagāma yatna|taikṣṇyāt. [9]

adhiruhya ca tasya† girer uccataraṃ taṭa|pradeśaṃ tad|antarāl'|âdhika|pramāṇayā mahatyā virūḍhay" â|śithila|mūlayā dṛḍhayā vetra|latayā gāḍham ābadhya caraṇau punas taṃ vanas|patiṃ pracaskanda. viprakṛṣṭatvāt tu tasy' ântarālasya caraṇa|bandhana|vyākulatvāc ca sa Mahā|sattvaḥ kathaṃ cit tasya vanas|pater agra|śākhāṃ karābhyāṃ sam āsasāda.

and watched his troop of monkeys look up at him with disturbed and wretched faces, their sole fallback being to screech shrilly with fear. Overwhelmed by enormous compassion and laying aside any despair, misery or terror, he consoled his troop of monkeys and set his heart on saving them. Climbing to the peak of the tree, he resolved to jump across to the mountain slope nearby. So extraordinary was the Great Being's strength that he landed on the mountain slope like a bird, even though it would normally take several bounds to reach.

Though other monkeys could not
manage the jump even in two bounds,
he mightily sprang across the gap
in a single swift leap as if with ease. 27.25

His resolve was sharpened by courage
and strengthened by his compassion.
Keen in his endeavor, he made a special effort,
reaching the slope as if by sheer will.

Climbing to a higher part of the slope, he found a tall, mature and strong cane that had sturdy roots and was longer in size than the distance between the slope and the tree. Binding the cane tightly around his feet, he leapt back again to the tree. But due to the distance, and because he was encumbered by his bound feet, the Great Being only just managed somehow to grab the tip of the tree's branch with his hands.

tataḥ samālambya dṛḍhaṃ sa śākhām
ātatya tāṃ vetra|latāṃ ca yatnāt,
sva|saṃjñayā yūtham ath' ādideśa:
«drumād ataḥ śīghram abhiprayāta.†» [10]

atha te vānarā bhay'|āturatvād apayāna|mārgam āsādya capalatara|gatayas tad|ākramaṇa|nirviśaṅkās tayā vetra|latayā† svasty apacakramuḥ.

27.30 bhay'|āturais tasya tu vānarais tair
ākramyamāṇaṃ caraṇaiḥ prasaktam
gātraṃ yayau svaiḥ piśitair viyogaṃ,
na tv eva dhairy'|âtiśayena cetaḥ. [11]

tad dṛṣṭvā sa rājā te ca rāja|puruṣāḥ parāṃ vismaya|vaktavyatām upajagmuḥ.

evaṃ|vidhā vikrama|buddhi|saṃpad
ātm'|ân|apekṣā ca dayā pareṣu
āścarya|buddhiṃ janayec chrut" âpi.
pratyakṣataḥ kiṃ punar īkṣyamāṇā? [12]

atha sa rājā tān puruṣān samādideśa:
«bhay'|ôdbhrānta|vānara|gaṇa|caraṇa|parikṣobhita†|kṣata|śarīraś ciram eka|kram'|âvasthānāc ca dṛḍhaṃ pariśrānto vyaktam ayaṃ vānar'|âdhipatiḥ na c' âtaḥ† śakṣyati svayam ātmānaṃ saṃhartum. tac chrīghram asy' âdhaḥ paṭa|vitānaṃ vitatya, vetra|lat" êyaṃ, iyaṃ† ca nyagrodha|śākhā śarābhyāṃ yugapac chidyetām† iti.»

Holding the branch tightly
and trying to stretch the cane,
he used a special signal to tell
the troop to leave the tree quickly.

The monkeys were sick with terror and when they were presented with an escape route, they rushed chaotically to safety along the cane, paying no heed to stepping on their lord.

Sick with fear, the monkeys
trampled him repeatedly,
making him lose some of his flesh,
though his heart never lost its immense fortitude.

27.30

The king and his men were filled with great astonishment when they saw this.

Just hearing of such courage and wisdom,
such self-denying compassion for others,
would in itself inspire wonder.
What if one saw it with one's own eyes?

The king then gave the following orders to his men: "This monkey king's body has been crushed and injured by the feet of his troop who were overwrought with terror. He must be utterly exhausted from staying in one position for so long and surely cannot gather himself on his own. Quickly, spread a blanket beneath him and use your arrows to shoot down the cane and the banyan branch at the same time."

27.35 te tathā cakruḥ. ath' âinaṃ sa rājā śanakair vitānād avatārya mūrchayā vraṇa|vedanā|klam'|ôpajātayā samākramyamāṇa|cetasaṃ mṛduni śayanīye saṃveśayām āsa. sadyaḥ|kṣata|praśamana|yogyaiś ca sarpir|ādibhir asya vraṇān† abhyajya mandī|bhūta|pariśramamaṃ samāśvāsy' âinam abhigamya† sa rājā sa|kautūhala|vismaya|bahumānaḥ kuśala|pariprašna|pūrvakam uvāca:

«gatvā svayaṃ saṃkramatām amīṣāṃ
sva|jīvite tyakta|dayena bhūtvā
samuddhṛtā ye kapayas tvay" ême,
ko nu tvam eṣāṃ? tava vā ka ete? [13]

śrotuṃ vayaṃ ced idam arha|rūpās,
tat tāvad ācakṣva, kapi|pradhāna.
na hy alpa|sauhārda|nibandhanānām
evaṃ manāṃsi prabhavanti† kartum.» [14]

atha Bodhisattvas tasya rājñas tad|abhyupapatti|saumukhyaṃ pratipūjayann ātma|nivedanam anuguṇena krameṇa cakāra:

«ebhir mad|ājñā|pratipatti|dakṣair
āropito mayy adhipatva|bhāraḥ.
putreṣv iv' âiteṣv avabaddha|hārdas
taṃ voḍhum ev' âham abhiprapannaḥ. [15]

27.40 iyaṃ, mahā|rāja, samaṃ mam' âibhiḥ
saṃbandha|jātiś cira|kāla|rūḍhā
samāna|jātitva|mayī ca maitrī
jñāteya|jātā saha|vāsa|yogāt.» [16]

The soldiers did as they were told. The king then gen- 27.35
tly helped the monkey down from the blanket and placed him on a soft couch. The Bodhi·sattva had swooned from fatigue and from the pain brought on by his wounds, but after butter was applied to his injuries and other remedies suitable for soothing fresh wounds, the pain lessened and he revived. The king then approached the monkey, full of curiosity, amazement and respect and after first asking after his welfare, he spoke the following words:

"You rescued these monkeys
by making yourself into a bridge for them,
casting aside concern for your own life.
Who are you to them? And who are they to you?

If I am worthy of hearing it,
please tell me, chief of monkeys.
For the ties of friendship binding your hearts
cannot be small if you are capable of this deed."

The Bodhi·sattva honored in return the kind help the king had shown him and introduced himself in a congenial manner, saying:

"Dedicated to following my orders,
the monkeys entrusted me with kingship.
And I accepted that burden,
my heart bound to them like children.

Such is the bond between me and them, 27.40
developed over a long time, Your Majesty.
Our friendship derives from our kinship.
We share the same birth and we live together."

tac chrutvā sa rājā paraṃ vismayam upetya punar enam uvāca:

«adhip'|ârtham amāty'|ādi,
na tad|arthaṃ mahī|patiḥ.
iti kasmāt sva|bhṛty'|ârtham
ātmānaṃ tyaktavān bhavān?» [17]

Bodhisattva uvāca: «kāmam evaṃ pravṛttā, mahā|rāja, rāja|nītiḥ. dur|anuvartyā tu me† pratibhāti.

a|saṃstutasy' âpy a|viṣahya|tīvram
upekṣituṃ duḥkham atīva duḥkham,
prāg eva bhakty|unmukha|mānasasya
gatasya bandhu|priyatāṃ janasya. [18]

27.45 idaṃ ca dṛṣṭvā vyasan'|ārti|dainyaṃ
śākhā|mṛgān pratyabhivardhamānam
sva|kārya|cint"|âvasar'|ôparodhi
prādudruvan māṃ sahas" âiva duḥkham. [19]

ānamyamānāni dhanūṃsi dṛṣṭvā
viniṣpatat|tīkṣṇa|śilīmukhāni†
bhīma|svana|jyāny a|vicintya, vegād
asmāt taroḥ śailam imaṃ gato 'smi. [20]

vaiśeṣika|trāsa|parīta|cittair
ākṛṣyamāṇo 'ham atha sva|yūthyaiḥ
ālakṣit'|āyāma|guṇāṃ su|mūlāṃ
sva|pādayor vetra|latāṃ nibadhya, [21]

The king was filled with utter amazement at hearing these words and addressed the monkey once more, saying:

"Ministers and others serve their king,
but it is not for a king to act for them.
Why then did you sacrifice yourself
for the sake of your dependents?"

"I accept, great king," the Bodhi·sattva replied, "that this is how royal politics works. But I find it a difficult path to follow.

It is extremely painful to ignore
the severe and unbearable sufferings
even of strangers, let alone dear relatives,
their hearts raised up to you in devotion.

Seeing the terrible pain and grief
overwhelming the monkeys,
a feeling of anguish instantly overtook me,
leaving no scope to worry about my interests.

27.45

When I saw the bows being stretched,
their stone-tipped arrows spraying out fiercely,
I ignored the terrifying twang of bowstrings
and leapt swiftly from the tree to this mountain.

But I was drawn back by my companions,
their hearts stricken with immense fear.
So I bound around my feet
a deep-rooted cane of notable length.

prāskandam asmāt punar eva śailād
imaṃ drumaṃ tārayituṃ sva|yūthyān.
tataḥ karābhyāṃ samavāpam asya
prasāritaṃ pāṇim iv' âgra|śākhām. [22]

samātat'|âṅgaṃ latayā tayā ca
śākh"|âgra|hastena ca pādapasya
amī mad|adhyākramaṇe vi|śaṅkā
niśritya māṃ svasti gatāḥ sva|yūthyāḥ.» [23]

27.50 atha sa rājā pramodya|jātaṃ tasyām apy avasthāyāṃ taṃ Mahā|sattvam avekṣya paraṃ vismayam udvahan punar enam uvāca:

«paribhūy' ātmanaḥ saukhyaṃ para|vyasanam āpatat,
ity ātmani samāropya prāptaḥ ko bhavatā guṇaḥ?» [24]

Bodhisattva uvāca:

«kāmaṃ śarīraṃ, kṣiti|pa, kṣataṃ me,
manaḥ para|svāsthyam upāgataṃ tu:
akāri yeṣāṃ ciram ādhipatyaṃ,
teṣāṃ may" ārtir vinivartit" êti. [25]

jitv" āhave vidviṣataḥ sa|darpān
gātreṣv alaṃkāravad udvahanti
vīrā yathā vikrama|cihna|śobhāṃ,
prītyā tath" êmāṃ rujam udvahāmi. [26]

27.55 praṇāma|satkāra|puraḥsarasya
bhakti|prayuktasya samāna|jātyaiḥ
aiśvarya|labdhasya sukha|kramasya
saṃprāptam ānṛṇyam idaṃ may" âdya. [27]

Leaping once more from mountain to tree,
intent on saving my companions,
I grasped the tip of an extending branch
which was stretched out like an offered hand.

As I lay stretched between the cane
and the branch-tip offered like a hand,
my troop reached safety through my help,
unconcerned about running over me."

The king was utterly astonished when he saw that the Great Being was joyful despite his plight and addressed him once more, saying: 27.50

"But what benefit do you gain
in spurning your own happiness
and taking upon yourself
the calamity afflicting others?"

The Bodhi·sattva replied:

"My body may be wounded, king,
but my mind feels great well-being
at removing the suffering of those
over whom I have ruled a long time.

I bear this pain joyfully, just as heroes
bear on their limbs, like ornaments,
the glorious marks of their bravery
after conquering proud foes in war.

I have on this day paid off my debts 27.55
for the devotion of my kinsmen,
attended by veneration and honor,
and for my lordship and easy way of life.

tan māṃ tapaty eṣa na duḥkha|yogaḥ
suhṛd|viyogaḥ sukha|viplavo vā.
krameṇa c' ânena samabhyupeto
mam' ôtsav'|âbhyāgama† eṣa mṛtyuḥ. [28]

pūrv'|ôpakār'|ān|ṛṇat"|ātma|tuṣṭiḥ
saṃtāpa|śāntir vimalaṃ yaśaś ca
pūjā nṛ|pān nirbhayatā ca mṛtyoḥ
kṛta|jña|bhāva|grahaṇam† ca satsu: [29]

ete guṇāḥ, sad|guṇa|vāsa|vṛkṣa,
prāptā may" âitad vyasanaṃ prapadya.
eṣāṃ vipakṣāṃs tu samabhyupaiti
dayā|vihīno nṛ|patiḥ śriteṣu. [30]

guṇair vihīnasya vipanna|kīrter
doṣ'|ôdayair āvasathī|kṛtasya
gatir bhavet tasya ca nāma k" ânyā
jvāl"|ākulebhyo narak'|ânalebhyaḥ? [31]

27.60 tad darśito 'yaṃ guṇa|doṣayos te
mayā prabhāvaḥ, prathita|prabhāva.
dharmeṇa tasmād anuśādhi rājyaṃ.
strī|cañcala|prema|guṇā hi lakṣmīḥ. [32]

yugyaṃ balaṃ jānapadān amātyān
paurān a|nāthāñ chramaṇa|dvijātīn†
sarvān sukhena prayateta yoktuṃ
hit'|ânukūlena pit" êva rājā. [33]

It is not my physical pain that torments me,
nor separation from friends, nor loss of comfort.
For me the death that has come
is like the arrival of a festival!

The joy of paying off debts for past services,
the quelling of suffering, an untarnished fame,
veneration from a king, fearlessness of death,
and recognition among the good for my gratitude:

these are the virtues I have attained
from this misfortune, tree-like abode of merits!
But a king without compassion for his subjects
acquires the reverse of these virtues.

If a king has no virtues,
if his reputation is ruined
and he is a home for vice,
his only destiny is hell's flaming fires.

27.60

I have shown you, mighty king,
the power of virtue and vice.
Rule therefore your kingdom justly.
For Fortune's love is like that of a fickle woman.

Draught animals, armies, countryfolk, ministers,
citizens, destitutes, ascetics, brahmins:
toward all these a king should act like a father,
striving to give them a beneficial happiness.

evaṃ hi dharm'|ârtha|yaśaḥ|samṛddhiḥ
syāt te sukhāy' êha paratra c' âiva.
praj"|ânukamp"|ârjitayā tvam asmād
rāja'|rṣi|lakṣmyā, nara|rāja, rāja!» [34]

iti nṛ|pam anuśiṣya śiṣya|vad
bahu|mata|vāk|prayatena tena saḥ
rug|abhibhavana|saṃhṛta|kriyāṃ
tanum apahāya yayau tri|viṣṭapam. [35]

tad evaṃ, dviṣatām api manāṃsy āvarjayanti sad|vṛtt'|ânuvartinaḥ. iti lokam āvarjayitu|kāmena† sad|vṛtt'|ânuvartinā bhavitavyam.

27.65 «na samarthās tathā sv'|ârtham api pratipattuṃ sattvā, yathā par'|ârthaṃ pratipannavān sa Bhagavān» iti Tathāgata|varṇe 'pi vācyam. sat|kṛtya dharma|śravaṇe karuṇā|varṇe rāj'|âvavāde ca: «evaṃ rājñā prajāsu day"|āpannena bhavitavyam.» kṛta|jña|kathāyām apy upaneyam: «evaṃ kṛta|jñāḥ santo bhavant'» îti.

Thus a wealth of virtue, profit and fame
will bring you joy here and in the next life.
By showing compassion to your people, king,
may you shine with the glory of royal seers!"

After instructing the king like a pupil,
who listened intently to his revered words,
he entered heaven by leaving his body,
which was seized by overwhelming pain.

In this way, those who act morally can influence the hearts even of enemies. If one wishes to influence people, one should therefore follow the conduct of the good.

One should also tell this story when praising the Tatha·gata, saying: "Living beings cannot achieve even their own welfare in the same way as the Lord was able to achieve the welfare of others." And when discussing the topic of listening to the Teaching with respect, or when eulogizing compassion, or when advising kings, one should say: "A king should therefore behave with compassion toward his subjects." When discussing gratitude, one should also cite this story, saying: "In this way the virtuous are grateful." 27.65

KṢĀNTIVĀDIJĀTAKAM†

STORY 28

THE BIRTH-STORY OF KSHANTI·VADIN

28.1 S'|ĀTMĪ|BHŪTA|KṢAMĀṆĀṂ pratisaṃkhyāna|mahatāṃ n' â|viṣahyaṃ nāma kiṃ cid asti.

tad|yath" ânuśrūyate.

Bodhisattvaḥ kil' ân|eka|doṣa|vyasan'|ôpasṛṣṭam artha|kāma|pradhānatvād an|aupaśamikaṃ rāga|dveṣa|moh'|âmarṣa|saṃrambha|mada|māna|matsar'|ādi†|doṣa|rajasām āpātaṃ pātanaṃ hrī|dharma|parigrahasy' āyatanaṃ lobh'|âsad|grāhasya ku|kārya|saṃbādhatvāt kṛś'|âvakāśaṃ dharmasy' âvetya gṛha|vāsaṃ,†

parigraha|viṣaya|parivarjanāc ca tad|doṣa|viveka|sukhāṃ pravrajyām anupaśyan, śīla|śruta|praśama|vinaya|niyata|mānasas tāpaso babhūva.

28.5 tam a|skhalita|kṣānti|samādānaṃ† kṣānti|varṇa|vādinaṃ tad|anurūpa|dharm'|ākhyāna|kramaṃ vyatītya sve nāma|gotre Kṣāntivādinam ity eva lokaḥ sva|buddhi|pūrvakaṃ saṃjajñe.

aiśvarya|vidyā|tapasāṃ samṛddhir
labdha|prayāmaś ca kalāsu saṅgaḥ
śarīra|vāk|ceṣṭita|vikriyāś ca
nām' âparaṃ saṃjanayanti puṃsām. [1]

NOTHING IS UNBEARABLE for those who have internalized forbearance and are great in equanimity. 28.1

Tradition has handed down the following story.

The Bodhi·sattva is said to have once become an ascetic after he realized that the household life offered meager opportunities for virtue because it thronged with vice. Afflicted by numerous faults and calamities, the household life was devoid of tranquility due to its emphasis on profit and desire. It was a meeting place for wicked taints such as passion, hatred, delusion, intolerance, violence, infatuation, pride and selfishness. Destroying a person's sense of shame and morality, it was an arena for greed and evil.

He saw the renunciate life, on the other hand, as providing a happiness that was removed from these vices, since it shunned possessions and desires. So it was that he became an ascetic, his mind rigorously intent on virtue, learning, tranquility and discipline.

He never deviated from his vow of forbearance. And since he always praised forbearance and preached the Teaching with regard to that virtue, people ignored his personal and family name and created their own name for him, calling him Kshanti·vadin ("preacher of forbearance"). 28.5

A wealth of power, knowledge or asceticism,
or a wide-ranging passion for the arts,
or abnormalities of body, speech or behavior,
can all produce new names for people.

jānan sa tu kṣānti|guṇa|prabhāvaṃ
ten' ātmaval lokam alaṃkariṣyan
cakāra yat kṣānti|kathāḥ† prasaktaṃ,
tat Kṣāntivād" îti tato vijajñe. [2]

svabhāva|bhūtā mahatī kṣamā ca
par'|âpakāreṣv a|vikāra|dhīrā,
tad|artha|yuktāś ca kathā|viśeṣāḥ
kīrtyā muniṃ taṃ prathayāṃ babhūvuḥ. [3]

atha sa Mahātmā pravivikta | ramaṇīyaṃ sarva' | rtu† | sulabha | puṣpa | phalaṃ padm' | ôtpal' | âlaṃkṛta | vimala | salil' | āśayam udyāna | ramya | śobhaṃ vana | pradeśam adhyāvasa-nāt† tapo|vana|maṅgalyatām upanināya.†

28.10 nivasanti hi yatr' âiva
santaḥ sad|guṇa|bhūṣaṇāḥ,
tan maṅgalyaṃ mano|jñaṃ ca,
tat tīrthaṃ, tat tapo|vanam. [4]

sa tatra bahu manyamānas tad|adhyuṣitair devatā|viśeṣair abhigamyamānaś ca śreyo|'bhilāṣiṇā guṇa|vatsalena janena kṣānti | pratisaṃyuktābhiḥ śruti | hṛdaya | hlādinībhir dhar-myābhiḥ kathābhis tasya jana | kāyasya param anugrahaṃ cakāra.

atha kadā cit tatratyo† rājā grīṣma|kāla|prabhāvād abhila-ṣaṇīyatarāṃ salila | krīḍāṃ prati samutsuka | matir udyāna | guṇ' | âtiśaya | niketa | bhūtaṃ taṃ vana | pradeśaṃ s' | ântaḥ | puraḥ samabhijagāma.

Knowing the power of the virtue of forbearance,
keen to adorn the world with it as he did himself,
he repeatedly preached on forbearance
and thus acquired the name Kshanti·vadin.

The vast endurance innate to his nature,
unalterably strong even if others harmed him,
combined with his fine discourses on the topic,
gave him the widespread renown of a sage.

The Great One lived in a region of the forest that was delightfully isolated. Bearing the lovely beauty of a garden, the forest effortlessly produced flowers and fruits in every season and its spotless pools of water were adorned by lotuses and lilies. Through his residence there, the Bodhi·sattva furnished the area with the auspicious nature of an ascetic grove.

28.10

For wherever saints dwell,
adorned by virtuous qualities,
the place becomes auspicious and attractive,
a sacred site or ascetic grove.

Honored by various special deities who lived there, and visited by lovers of virtue who sought bliss, he paid the greatest favor to the crowd by giving religious instructions on the topic of forbearance which gladdened their ears and hearts.

One day the king of the region conceived an urge to play water games, a desire made stronger by the intensity of the hot season. He therefore traveled with his wives to that forest area, which possessed the fine qualities of a garden.

sa tad vanaṃ Nandana|ramya|śobham
ākīrṇam antaḥ|pura|sundarībhiḥ
alaṃ|cakār' êva caran vilāsī
vibhūtimatyā lalit'|ânuvṛttyā. [5]

vimāna|deśeṣu latā|gṛheṣu
puṣpa|prahāseṣu mahī|ruheṣu
toyeṣu c' ônmīlita|paṅka|jeṣu
reme svabhāv'|âtiśayair vadhūnām. [6]

28.15 mäly'|āsava|snāna|vilepanānāṃ
saṃmoda|gandh'|ākulitair dvi|rephaiḥ
dadarśa kāsāṃ cid upohyamānā
jāta|smitas trāsa|vilāsa|śobhāḥ. [7]

pratyagra|śobhair api karṇa|pūraiḥ
paryāpta|mālyair api mūrdha|jaiś ca
tṛptir yath" āsīt kusumair na tāsāṃ,
tath" âiva tāsāṃ† lalitair nṛ|pasya. [8]

vimāna|deśeṣv avasajyamānā†
vilambamānāḥ kamal'|ākareṣu
dadarśa rājā bhramarāyamāṇāḥ
puṣpa|drumeṣu pramad"|âkṣi|mālāḥ. [9]

mada|pragalbhāny api kokilānāṃ
rutāni nṛttāni† ca barhiṇānām
dvi|repha|gītāni ca n' âbhirejus
tatr' âṅganā|jalpita|nṛtta|gītaiḥ. [10]

In that forest as charming as Nándana*,
the king wandered around pleasurably
as if adorning the area with his luxurious play,
his beautiful wives scattered around.

Among the arbors inhabited by creepers,
among the trees with their laughing flowers
and the waters with their expanding lotuses,
he delighted in the women's natural excesses.

The women's graceful reactions of fear 28.15
at bees aroused by the combined scent
of garlands, liquor, ointments and oils
made the king smile as he gazed upon them.

Just as the women were unsated by flowers,
though blossoms of pure beauty covered
their ears and garlands decked their hair,
so the king was never sated by their coquetry.

The king watched as the women's eyes,
themselves like garlands of flowers,
hovered like bees over blossoming trees,
clinging to arbors, tarrying over lotus clusters.

Even the cries of cuckoos, bold with lust,
the dances of peacocks and the song of bees
could not outshine the chattering,
dancing and singing of the women.

payoda|dhīra|stanitair mṛdaṅgair
udīrṇa|kekās tata|barha|cakrāḥ
natā iva svena kalā|guṇena
cakrur mayūrāḥ kṣiti|pasya sevām. [11]

28.20 sa tatra s' | ântaḥ | pura udyāna | vana | vihāra | sukhaṃ prakāmam anubhūya krīḍā | prasaṅga | parikhedān mada | pariṣvaṅgāc ca śrīmati vimāna|pradeśe mah"|ârha|śayanīya| vara|gato nidrā|vaśam upajagāma.

atha tā yoṣitaḥ prastāv' | ântara | gatam avetya rājānaṃ vana | śobhābhir ākṣipyamāṇa | hṛdayās tad | darśan' | â | vitṛptā yathā | prīti | kṛta | samavāyāḥ samākula | bhūṣaṇa | nināda | saṃmiśra | kala | pralāpāḥ samantataḥ prasasruḥ.

tāś chatra|vāla|vyajan'|āsan'|ādyaiḥ
preṣyā|dhṛtaiḥ kāñcana|bhakti|citraiḥ
aiśvarya|cihnair anugamyamānāḥ
striyaḥ svabhāv'|â|nibhṛtaṃ viceruḥ. [12]

tāḥ prāpya rūpāṇi mahī|ruhāṇāṃ
puṣpāṇi cārūṇi ca pallavāni
preṣyā|prayatnān atipatya lobhād
ālebhire svena parākrameṇa. [13]

mārg'|ôpalabdhān kusum'|âbhirāmān
gulmāṃś calat|pallavinaś ca vṛkṣān
paryāpta|puṣp'|ābharaṇa|srajo 'pi
lobhād an|ālupya na tā vyatīyuḥ. [14]

When the drums boomed like thunderclouds,
the peacocks shrieked and spread their fans
like actors using their fine skills
to perform a service for their king.

28.20 After he had enjoyed to his heart's content the pleasures of his women's company in that garden-like grove, the king felt exhausted by this indulgent play and a drunken drowsiness enveloped him, making him fall asleep on a fine and costly couch in a beautiful bower.

When the women saw that the king was occupied with other things, they spread out in various directions, forming groups according to their liking. Drawn by the beauties of the forest—for they were still unsated by its sights—the hum of their chatter mixed with the discordant jangling of their ornaments.

Followed by a parasol, yak-tails,
throne and other marks of sovereignty
carried by maids and gleaming with gold streaks,
the women wandered in natural wantonness.

Ignoring the maids' attempts to stop them,
they greedily grabbed hold of
every pretty flower or lovely sprig
they could grasp from the trees.

Though covered in wreaths and flower ornaments,
the greedy women left unplundered no shrub
with pretty blossoms nor tree with quivering buds
that they encountered along the way.

28.25 atha tā vana | ramaṇīyatay" ākṣipyamāṇa | hṛdayā rāja | yoṣitas tad vanam anuvicarantyaḥ Kṣāntivādina āśrama | padam abhijagmuḥ.† vidita|tapaḥ|prabhāva|māhātmyās tu tasya muneḥ strī | jan' | âdhikṛtā rājño vāllabhyād dur | āsadatvāc ca tāsāṃ n' âināś† tato vārayituṃ prasehire.

abhisaṃskāra|ramaṇīyatarayā c' āśrama|pada|śriyā samākṛṣyamāṇā iva tā yoṣitaḥ praviśy' āśrama | padaṃ dadṛśus tatra taṃ muni|varaṃ praśama|saumya|darśanam api gāmbhīry'|âtiśayād† dur|āsadam, abhijvalantam iva tapaḥ|śriyā, dhyān' | âbhiyogād udāra | viṣaya | saṃnikarṣe 'py a | kṣubhit' | êndriya|naibhṛtya|śobhaṃ, s'|âkṣād dharmam iva maṅgalya| puṇya|darśanaṃ† vṛkṣa|mūle baddh'|āsanam āsīnam.

atha tā rāja | striyas tasya tapas | tejas" ākrānta | sattvāḥ saṃdarśanād eva tyakta | vibhrama | vilās' | āuddhatyā vinaya | nibhṛtam abhigamy' âinaṃ paryupāsāṃ cakrire.

sa tāsāṃ svāgat' | ādi | priya | vacana | puraḥsaram atithi | jana | mano | haram upacāra | vidhiṃ pravartya tat | paripraśn' | ôpapādita | prastāvābhiḥ strī | jana | sukha | grahaṇ' | ârthābhir dṛṣṭāntavatībhiḥ kathābhir dharm'|ātithyam āsāṃ cakāra.

28.25 As the royal women wandered through the forest, their hearts smitten by the loveliness of the groves, they came across the hermitage of Kshanti·vadin. Those in charge of the women did not try to restrain them, even though they knew the sage's ascetic power and illustrious nature. For the king was fond of his women and the women were hard to stand up to.

The women therefore entered the hermitage, as if drawn by the splendor of the site, made all the more beautiful by the ascetic's spiritual accomplishment. There they saw the eminent ascetic sitting cross-legged at the foot of a tree. Auspicious and pure to observe, he was like the personification of Virtue. Although he looked serene and benevolent, his profound nature also made him intimidating; for he seemed almost to blaze with the splendor of his ascetic power. Although his practice of meditation meant he focused on lofty objects of concentration, he still glowed beautifully with the serenity of his untroubled senses.

The mere sight of the ascetic made the women feel overcome by his radiant power. Discarding their frivolous, wanton and overbearing conduct, they approached the ascetic with polite modesty and sat before him respectfully.

The ascetic greeted the women with friendly words of welcome, showing them the proper courtesies that delight guests. Taking advantage of the opportunity offered by their questions, and by way of a hospitality gift, he then preached a sermon, using discourses filled with examples and containing topics that women find easy to grasp.

«a|garhitāṃ jātim avāpya mānūṣīm
an|ūna|bhāvaṃ paṭubhis tath" êndriyaiḥ,
avaśya|mṛtyur na karoti yaḥ śubhaṃ
pramāda|bhāk pratyaham—eṣa vañcyate? [15]

28.30 kulena rūpeṇa vayo|guṇena vā
bala|prakarṣeṇa dhan'|ôdayena vā
paratra n' âpnoti sukhāni kaś cana
pradāna|śīl'|ādi|guṇair a|saṃskṛtaḥ. [16]

kul'|ādi|hīno 'pi tu† pāpa|niḥspṛhaḥ
pradāna|śīl'|ādi|guṇ'|âbhipattimān
paratra saukhyair abhisāryate dhruvaṃ
ghan'|āgame sindhu|jalair iv' ârṇavaḥ. [17]

kulasya rūpasya vayo|guṇasya vā
bala|prakarṣasya dhan'|ôdayasya† vā
ih' âpy alaṃ|kāra|vidhir guṇ'|ādaraḥ
samṛddhi|sūc" âiva tu hema|mālikā. [18]

alaṃ|kriyante kusumair mahī|ruhās,
taḍid|guṇais toya|vilambino ghanāḥ,
sarāṃsi matta|bhramaraiḥ saro|ruhair,
guṇair viśeṣ'|âdhigatais tu dehinaḥ. [19]

a|rogat"|āyur|dhana|rūpa|jātibhir
nikṛṣṭa|madhy'|ôttama|bheda|citratā
janasya c' êyaṃ na khalu sva|bhāvataḥ
par'|āśrayād vā; tri|vidhā tu karmaṇaḥ. [20]

"Those who have a blameless human birth
and have no disabilities, their senses sound,
but who never do good, despite death's necessity,
and are neglectful daily—are they not deceived?

Though they may have noble birth, looks, 28.30
youth, great strength or swelling wealth,
no one enjoys happiness in the next life
unless adorned by giving, morality and the like.

Though lacking qualities such as noble birth,
if one spurns evil and has giving, morality and the like,
one is flooded by happiness in the next life,
just as the sea is flooded by rivers in summer.

Even for those with noble birth, good looks,
youth, great strength or swelling wealth,
a regard for virtue is an ornament in the world,
whereas gold garlands merely indicate wealth.

Trees rising from the earth are adorned by flowers,
clouds bulging with rain are adorned by lightning,
lakes are adorned by lotuses with drunken bees.
But humans are adorned by special virtues.

Humans have low, medium and high levels
of health, lifespan, wealth, looks and birth.
These three types do not derive from character
or external causes; they derive from karma.

28.35 avetya c' âivaṃ niyatāṃ jagat|sthitiṃ
calaṃ vināśa|pravaṇaṃ ca jīvitam
jahīta pāpāni śubha|kram'|āśayād.
ayaṃ hi panthā yaśase sukhāya ca. [21]

manaḥ|pradoṣas tu par'|ātmanor hitaṃ
vinirdahann agnir iva pravartate.
ataḥ prayatnena sa pāpa|bhīruṇā
janena varjyaḥ pratipakṣa|śaṃśrayāt. [22]

yathā sametya jvalito 'pi pāvakas
taṭ'|ânta|saṃsakta|jalāṃ mahā|nadīm
praśāntim āyāti mano|jvalas tathā
śritasya loka|dvitaya|kṣamāṃ kṣamām. [23]

iti kṣāntyā pāpaṃ
pariharati tadd|hetv|abhibhavād.
ataś c' âyaṃ vairaṃ
janayati na† maitry'|āśraya|balāt.
priyaḥ pūjyaś c' âsmād
bhavati sukha|bhāg' êva ca tataḥ,
prayāty ante ca dyāṃ
sva|gṛham iva puṇy'|āśraya|guṇāt. [24]

api ca, bhavatyaḥ, kṣāntir nām' âiṣā:

28.40 śubha|svabhāv'|âtiśaya|prasiddhiḥ†
puṇyena kīrtyā ca parā vivṛddhiḥ
a|toya|saṃparka|kṛtā viśuddhis
tais tair guṇ'|âughaiś ca parā samṛddhiḥ. [25]

Knowing this as the fixed nature of the world 28.35
and that life is changeable and bent on decay,
renounce evil deeds and rely on pure behavior.
For this path will bring glory and happiness.

A corrupt mind is like a fire,
incinerating the welfare of oneself and others.
Those who fear evil should diligently
avoid it by following the reverse.

Just as a fire, however it blazes, quenches
on meeting a mighty river brimming its banks,
so mental flames quench in one of forbearance,
bringing him benefit in this world and the next.

Through forbearance,
one shuns evil by destroying its cause.
Through devotion to kindness,
one never generates hatred.
Loved and honored,
one enjoys happiness.
By practicing purity,
one finally reaches heaven as if it were home.

Furthermore, good ladies, this quality of forbearance

excellently perfects a pure character. 28.40
The highest development of merit and fame,
it is pure without having contact with water
and its many virtues make it full of riches.

par'|ôparodheṣu sad" ân|abhijñā,
vyavasthitiḥ sattvavatāṃ mano|jñā,
guṇ'|âbhinirvartita|cāru|saṃjñā,
‹kṣam"› êti lok'|ârtha|karī kṛpā|jñā. [26]

alaṃ|kriyā śakti|samanvitānāṃ,
tapo|dhanānāṃ bala|saṃpad agryā,
vyāpāda|dāv'|ânala|vāri|dhārā,
prety' êha ca kṣāntir an|artha|śāntiḥ. [27]

kṣamā|maye varmaṇi saj|janānāṃ
vikuṇṭhitā dur|jana|vākya|bāṇāḥ
prāyaḥ praśaṃsā|kusumatvam etya
tat|kīrti|māl"|âvayavā bhavanti. [28]

hant' îti yā dharma|vipakṣa|māyāṃ
prāhuḥ sukhāṃ c' âiva vimokṣa|māyām,
tasmān na kuryāt ka iva kṣamāyāṃ
prayatnam ek'|ânta|hita|kṣamāyām?» [29]

28.45 iti sa Mahātmā tāsāṃ dharm'|ātithyaṃ cakāra.

atha sa rājā nidrā|klama|vinodanāt prativibuddhaḥ s'|âvaśeṣa|mada|guru|nayano madan'|ânuvṛttyā, «kutra devya?» iti śayana|pālikāḥ sa|bhrū|kṣepaṃ paryapṛcchat. «etā, deva, van'|ântarāṇy upaśobhayamānās tad|vibhūtiṃ paśyant'» îti c' ôpalabhya śayana|pālikābhyaḥ sa rājā devī|janasya viśrambha|niryantraṇa|hasita|kathita|drava|viceṣṭita|darśan'|ôtsuka|matir utthāya śayanād yuvati|vidhṛta|cchatra|cāmara|vyajan'|ôttarīya†|khaḍgaḥ sa|kañcukair vetra|daṇḍa|pāṇibhir antaḥ|pur'|âvacaraiḥ kṛt'|ânuyātras tad vanam

A delightful fortitude in the virtuous,
it never takes note of the attacks of others.
Its virtues give it the fair name of 'patience.'
Shrewd in compassion, it acts to benefit the world.

An ornament in the powerful,
the peak of accomplished strength in ascetics,
a torrent of rain on the flaming fires of violence,
it calms all evils in this life and after death.

Worn by the virtuous, the armor of forbearance
blunts the abusive arrows shot by wicked men.
Turning into flowers of praise,
they become a garland of glory.

They describe it as the joy of liberation,
saying it destroys the delusion impeding virtue.
Who would not strive for forbearance
when it always brings welfare?"

Such was the sermon that the Great One offered as a hospitality gift. 28.45

The king had meanwhile woken up, his weariness dispelled by sleep, though his eyes were still heavy with lingering drunkenness. Eager for love-making and furrowing his brow, he asked his female couch-attendants where his queens had gone. When the maids informed him that the queens were adorning other parts of the forest, gazing at its beauty, the king rose from his couch, eager to see his queens' brazen lack of constraint, their laughter and chatter, and their playful behavior. Accompanied by eunuchs from his harem, who wore corsets and bore sticks made of reed, the king wandered into the forest, while young

anuvicacāra. sa tatra yuvati|jan'|â|naibhṛtya|viracitāṃ vividha|kusuma|stabaka|pallava|nikara|prapaddhatiṃ tāmbūla|rasa|rāga|vicitrām anusaraṃs tad āśrama|padam abhijagāma.

dṛṣṭv" âiva tu sa rājā Kṣāntivādinaṃ tam ṛṣi|varaṃ devī|jana|parivṛtaṃ pūrva|vair'|ânuśaya|doṣān mada|paribhramita|smṛtitvād īrṣyā|parābhūta|matitvāc ca paraṃ kopam upajagāma. pratisaṃkhyāna|bala|vaikalyāc ca bhraṣṭa|vinay'|ôpacāra|sauṣṭhavaḥ saṃrambha|pāpm'|âbhibhavād āpatita|sveda|vaivarṇya|vepathur bhrū|bhaṅga|jihma|vivṛtta|sthir'|âbhitāmra|nayano virakta|kānti|lāvaṇya|śobhaḥ pracalat|kanaka|valayau parimṛdnan s'|âṅguli|vibhūṣaṇau pāṇī tam ṛṣi|varam adhikṣipaṃs tat tad uvāca:

«haṃ ho!

asmat|tejaḥ khalī|kṛtya
　　paśyann antaḥ|purāṇi naḥ,
muni|veṣa|praticchannaḥ
　　ko 'yaṃ vaitaṃsikāyate?» [30]

28.50 tac chrutvā varṣavarāḥ sa|saṃbhram'|āvegā rājanam ūcuḥ:

women carried his parasol, yak-tails, fan, cloak and sword. The royal ladies had formed a path made of clusters of flowers and piles of sprigs that they had strewn in their abandon, sprinkled with the dye of betel juice. So the king followed this track until he reached the hermitage.

Now it happened that this king possessed a wicked and deep-seated enmity toward the Bodhi·sattva that derived from past lives. This, combined with the fact that he was overcome by jealousy and his composure was unsteadied by drunkenness, meant that as soon as he saw the eminent ascetic Kshanti·vadin surrounded by the troop of queens, he became filled with utter rage. Lacking all strength of reason and dropping all politeness, courtesy or decency, he became overwhelmed by the evil of rage, making him sweat, change color and quiver. His brows furrowed and his eyes squinted, rolled, glared and turned red. All his good looks and charm disappeared as he ground his gold-ringed hands together, his golden bracelets jangling. Insulting the eminent ascetic, he then said the following words:

"Ha!

Who is this charlatan of an ascetic
who injures my royal splendor
by laying eyes on my palace women,
setting his snare like a bird-catcher?"

When they heard this, the eunuchs were filled with alarm and panic and addressed the king, saying: 28.50

«deva, mā m" âivam! cira|kāla|saṃbhṛta|vrata|niyama|tapo|bhāvit'|ātmā munir ayaṃ Kṣāntivādī nām' êti.»

upahat' | âdhyāśayatvāt tu sa rājā tat teṣāṃ vacanam a|pratigṛhṇann uvāca:

«kaṣṭaṃ bhoḥ!

cirāt prabhṛti loko 'yam
evam etena vañcyate
kuhanā|jihma|bhāvena
tāpas'|â|kumbha|s'|ātmanā? [31]

28.55 tad ayam asya tāpasa|nepathy'|âvacchāditaṃ māyā|śāṭhya|saṃbhṛtaṃ kuhaka | svabhāvaṃ prakāśayām'!» îty uktvā pratihārī†|hastād asim ādāya hantum utpatita|niścayas tam ṛṣi|varaṃ sapatnavad abhijagāma. atha tā devyaḥ parijana|nivedit'|âbhyāgamam† ālokya rājānaṃ krodha|saṃkṣipta|saumya|bhāvaṃ vitānī|bhūta|hṛdayāḥ sa|saṃbhram'|āvega|cañcala|nayanāḥ samutthāy' âbhivādya ca tam ṛṣi|varaṃ samudyat'|âñjali|kuḍmalāḥ śaran|nalinya iva samudgat'|âika|paṅkaj'|ânana|mukulā rājānam abhijagmuḥ.

tat tāsāṃ samudācāra|līlā|vinaya|sauṣṭhavam
na tasya śamayām āsa krodh'|âgni|jvalitaṃ manaḥ. [32]

"Please do not say this, Your Majesty! Please! This is a sage who has purified himself through an accumulation of long-practiced vows, disciplines and austerities. He is called Kshanti·vadin."

But the king's mind was confounded. Taking no heed of the eunuchs' words, he exclaimed:

"My word!

How long should the world
be fooled by the crooked deceit
of this fellow styling himself
as an ascetic and not a lady's man?*

28.55 Well, I'll expose the cheating nature he hides under his ascetic costume, full of deceitful guile!" With these words, he took the sword from the hand of his female attendant and advanced on the ascetic like a foe, intent on slaying him. The queens had been informed of the king's arrival by their attendants, and when they saw that rage had dispelled all gentleness from the king, they felt distraught and their eyes rolled with panic and alarm. Standing up and paying their respects to the eminent seer, they approached the king and raised folded hands to their heads, so that their faces peered through like lotus buds emerging from their sheaths in autumn.

But their graceful, modest
and charming behavior
could not pacify the king's mind
as it burned with anger's fire.

labdhatara|praṇaya|prasarās† tu tā devyaḥ sa|saṃrambha| vikāra|samudācāra|rūkṣa|kramaṃ s'|āyudham abhipatantaṃ tam udīkṣya rājānaṃ tam ṛṣi|varaṃ prati vivartit'|âbhiniviṣṭa|dṛṣṭiṃ samāvṛṇvatya ūcuḥ:

«deva, mā! mā khalu sāhasaṃ kārṣīḥ! Kṣāntivādī bhagavān ayam iti.»

praduṣṭa|bhāvatvāt† tu sa rājā «samāvarjita|bhāvā nūnam anen' êmā» iti suṣṭhutaraṃ kopam upetya sphuṭataraṃ bhrū|bhaṅgair asūyā|samāveśa|tīkṣṇais tiryag|avekṣitais tat tāsāṃ praṇaya|prāgalbhyam avabhartsya sa|roṣam avekṣamāṇaḥ strī|jan'|âdhikṛtāñ chiraḥ|kampād ākampamāna| kuṇḍala|mukuṭa|viṭapas tā yoṣito 'bhivīkṣamāṇa uvāca:

28.60 «vadaty eva kṣamām eṣa,
 na tv enāṃ pratipadyate.
tathā hi yoṣit|saṃparka|
 tṛṣṇāṃ na kṣāntavān ayam. [33]

vāg anyath", âny" âiva śarīra|ceṣṭā.
 kaṣṭ'|āśayaṃ† mānasam anyath" âiva.
tapo|vane ko 'yam a|saṃyat'|ātmā
 dambha|vrat'|āḍambara|dhīram āste?» [34]

atha tā devyas tasmin rājani krodha|saṃrambha|karkaśa| hṛdaye pratyāhata|praṇayāḥ prajānānāś ca tasya rājñaś caṇḍatāṃ dur|anuneyatāṃ ca, vaimanasya|dainy'|ākrānta| manasaḥ, strī|jan'|âdhikṛtair bhaya|viṣāda|vyākulitair hasta|

Fury had made the king's conduct become violent and when they saw him charging forward, weapon in hand, glaring at the eminent seer with a rigid stare, the queens took the opportunity to entreat him and blocked his way, saying: "Divine king! Please stop! Please do not be rash! This is illustrious Kshanti·vadin."

In his wickedness, however, the king assumed that the ascetic had won over the queens' hearts, making him even more angry. His furrowed brow and his fierce and jealous sidelong glances made his disapproval of their audacious request all too apparent. Casting his eyes at the attendants in charge of the women, he shook his head, making the tips of his crown and earrings tremble. He then turned his glare onto the women, addressing them with the following words:

"He only speaks of forbearance
but he does not practice it.
For he could not forbear the desire
to have contact with women. 28.60

His words are one thing, his actions another.
His pernicious mind is again something else.
Who is this dissolute man sat in the ascetic forest,
brazenly banging away about his deceitful vows?"

The women were filled with despondency when the king struck down their entreaties, his heart hardened by fury and violence. For they were well-acquainted with the king's ferocious and implacable nature. Grieving for the eminent ascetic, they lowered their heads with shame and withdrew

saṃjñābhir apasāryamāṇā vrīḍ"|âvanata|vadanās tam ṛṣi|varaṃ† samanuśocantyas tato 'pacakramuḥ.

«asman|nimittam aparādha|vivarjite 'pi
dānte tapasvini guṇa|pratite 'py amuṣmin
ko vetti kām api vivṛtya vikāra|līlāṃ
ken' âpi yāsyati pathā kṣiti|pasya roṣaḥ? [35]

kṣit'|īśa|vṛttiṃ pratilabdha|kīrtiṃ
tanuṃ muner asya tapas|tanuṃ ca
amūny an|āgāṃsi ca no manāṃsi
tulyaṃ nihanyād† api nāma rājā!» [36]

28.65 iti tāsu devīṣv anuśocita|viniḥśvasita|mātra|parāyaṇāsv apayātāsu sa rājā tam ṛṣi|varaṃ saṃtarjayan roṣa|vaśān niṣkṛṣya khaḍgaṃ, svayam eva cchettum upacakrame. nir-vikāra|dhīram a|saṃbhrānta|sva|stha|ceṣṭitaṃ ca taṃ Mahā|sattvam āsādyamānam apy avekṣya sa|saṃrambhataram† enam uvāca:

«dāṇḍājinikat" ânena prakarṣaṃ gamitā yathā
udvahan kapaṭ'|âṭopaṃ munivan mām ap' īkṣate!» [37]

atha Bodhisattvaḥ kṣānti|paricayād a|vicalita|dhṛtis ten' â|sat|kāra|prayogeṇa taṃ rājānaṃ roṣa|saṃrambha|virūpa|ceṣṭitaṃ bhraṣṭa|vinay'|ôpacāra|śriyaṃ vismṛt'|ātma|hit'|â|hita|patham āgata|vismayaḥ kṣaṇam abhivīkṣya

from the area, obeying the hand signals made by the attendants in charge of the women, who were also distraught with fear and despair.

"We have caused the king's anger against
this innocent, disciplined and virtuous ascetic.
Who knows what perverse whim he will follow,
or what path his rage will take?

If he harms the sage's body, thin from austerities,
he will also harm his own royal standing
and the renown he has acquired from it,
and afflict our own innocent minds!"

28.65 So the queens departed, able to do nothing more than lament and sigh, at which point the king approached the eminent seer, reviling him and drawing his sword in anger, intent on slaying him with his very own hands. But when he saw that the Great Being bravely remained unchanged, despite the attack, his demeanor unwavering and composed, the king addressed him with even greater rage:

"How perfectly he plays
the role of an ascetic!
Parading his deceitful arrogance,
he even looks at me like a sage!"

But the Bodhi·sattva was so familiar with forbearance that his steadiness remained unruffled by this act of disrespect. Although surprised, he instantly recognized that the king's hideous behavior was so fuelled by anger and rage that he had dropped all refinements of politeness or courtesy and had lost sight of what would bring him harm or benefit. Feeling pity for the king and intending to advise

karuṇāyamānaḥ samanuneṣyan niyatam īdṛśaṃ kiṃ cid uvāca:

«bhāgy'|âparādha|janito 'py avamāna|yogaḥ†
 saṃdṛśyate jagati, tena na me 'tra cintā.
duḥkhaṃ tu me yad ucit" âbhigateṣu vṛttir
 vāc" âpi na tvayi mayā kriyate yath"|ârham. [38]

api ca, mahā|rāja,

28.70 a|sat|pravṛttān pathi saṃniyokṣyatām
 bhavad|vidhānāṃ jagad|artha|kāriṇām
na yukta|rūpaṃ sahasā pravartitum,
 vimarśa|mārgo 'py anugamyatāṃ yataḥ. [39]

a|yuktavat sādhv api kiṃ cid īkṣyate,
 prakāśate '|sādhv api kiṃ cid anyathā.
na kārya|tattvaṃ sahas" âiva lakṣyate
 vimarśam a|prāpya viśeṣa|hetuṣu.† [40]

vimṛśya kāryaṃ tv avagamya c' ârthataḥ†
 prapadya dharmeṇa ca nīti|vartmanā
mahānti dharm'|ârtha|sukhāni sādhayañ
 janasya tair eva na hīyate nṛ|paḥ. [41]

vinīya tasmād ati|cāpalāṃ† matiṃ
 yaśasyam ev' ârhasi karma sevitum.
atiprathante† hy abhilakṣit'|ātmanām
 a|dṛṣṭa|pūrvāś cariteṣv atikramāḥ. [42]

tapo|vane tvad|bhuja|vīrya|rakṣite
 pareṇa yan nāma kṛtaṃ na marṣayeḥ,
hita|kram'|ônmāthi tad† ārya|garhitaṃ
 svayaṃ, mahī|nātha, kathaṃ vyavasyasi? [43]

him, he earnestly addressed him with words somewhat as follows:

"To be disrespected is common in the world.
Fate or sin may cause it; it is of no concern.
What pains me is that I have not treated you
as one should a visitor, not even a greeting.

Besides, great king,

Men like you who act for the welfare of beings 28.70
and direct wrongdoers onto the right path,
should not act out of rash violence.
For they should follow the path of reason.

Even virtue can sometimes be seen as wrong,
while evil can sometimes appear other than it is.
The right way to act cannot be seen instantly
unless one considers the specific conditions.

But if he ponders his task, understands reality,
and puts into action a policy that is just,
a king will gain great spiritual and material joy,
both for his people and also for himself.

So discipline your unsteady mind
and pursue actions leading to glory.
For scandals arise when men of note
commit unexpected transgressions.

In an ascetic grove protected by your mighty arms,
you would never allow a person to destroy
moral conduct in a way deplored by noble men.
So how can you decide to do it yourself, king?

28.75 striyo 'bhiyātā yadi te mam' āśramaṃ
yad|ṛcchay" ântaḥ|pura|rakṣibhiḥ saha,
vyatikramas tatra ca no bhavet kiyān
ruṣā yad evaṃ gamito 'si vikriyām? [44]

ath' âpy ayaṃ syād aparādha eva me,
kṣam" âtra† śobheta tath" âpi te, nṛ|pa.
kṣamā hi śaktasya paraṃ vibhūṣaṇaṃ
guṇ'|ânurakṣā|nipuṇatva|sūcanāt. [45]

kapola|lola|dyuti|nīla|kuṇḍale
na mauli|ratna|dyutayaḥ pṛthag|vidhāḥ
tath" âbhyalaṃkartum alaṃ nṛpān, yathā
kṣam"—êti n' âinām avamantum arhasi. [46]

tyaj' â|kṣamāṃ nityam a|saṃśraya|kṣamāṃ.
kṣamām iv' ārakṣitum arhasi kṣamām.
tapo|dhaneṣv abhyucitā† hi vṛttayaḥ
kṣit'|īśvarāṇāṃ bahu|māna|peśalāḥ.» [47]

ity anunīyamāno 'pi sa rājā tena muni|vareṇ' ân|ārjav'|ôpahata|matis tam anyath" âiv' âbhiśaṅkamānaḥ punar uvāca:

28.80 «na tāpasa|cchadma bibharti ced bhavān,
sthito 'si vā sve niyama|vrate yadi,
kṣam"|ôpadeśa|vyapadeśa|saṃgataṃ
kim artham asmān† a|bhayaṃ prayācase?» [48]

Bodhisattva uvāca: «śrūyatāṃ, mahārāja, yad|artho 'yaṃ mama prayatnaḥ.

If your women happened to come
to my hermitage with their attendants,
what crime have I committed
to make you so transformed by rage? 28.75

And even if I did commit some crime,
it would befit you to forbear, my king.
The chief ornament in a man of power,
forbearance shows acuity in guarding virtue.

Neither blue earrings flashing against cheeks,
nor various bright gems embedded in crowns
can adequately adorn kings like forbearance.
Please therefore do not show contempt for it.

Renounce impatience; it cannot be relied on.
Instead guard forbearance like the earth.*
For the conduct of kings toward ascetics
should be proper and adorned with respect."

But despite this advice, the king's mind remained afflicted by wickedness and he continued to view the eminent sage with false suspicion, replying:

"If you are not disguised as an ascetic
and really are established in restraint,
why do you ask me for safety
under the pretext of teaching forbearance?" 28.80

"Please hear the reason for my exhortations, Your Majesty," the Bodhi·sattva replied.

‹an|āgasaṃ pravrajitam avadhīd brāhmaṇaṃ nṛ|paḥ.›
iti te mat|kṛte mā bhūd yaśo vācya|vijarjaram. [49]

martavyam iti bhūtānām
ayaṃ naiyamiko vidhiḥ
iti me na bhayaṃ tasmāt
sva|vṛttaṃ† c' ânupaśyataḥ. [50]

sukh'|ôdarkasya dharmasya
pīḍā mā bhūt tav' âiva tu,
kṣamām ity avadaṃ tubhyaṃ
śreyo|'dhigamana†|kṣamām. [51]

28.85 guṇānām ākaratvāc ca doṣāṇāṃ ca nivāraṇāt
prābhṛt'|âtiśaya|prītyā kathayāmi kṣamām aham.» [52]

atha sa rājā sūnṛtāny api tāny an|ādṛtya tasya muner vacana|kusumāni s'|âsūyaṃ tam ṛṣi|varam uvāca: «drakṣyāma idānīṃ te kṣānty|anurāgam!» ity uktvā nivāraṇ'|ârtham īṣad|abhiprasāritam abhyucchrita|pratanu|dīrgh'|âṅguliṃ tasya muner dakṣiṇaṃ pāṇiṃ niśiten' âsinā kamalam iva nāla|deśād vyayojayat.

chinne 'gra|haste 'pi tu tasya n' āsīd
duḥkhaṃ tathā kṣānti|dṛḍha|vratasya,
sukh'|ôcitasy' â|pratikāra|ghoraṃ
chettur yath" āgāmi samīkṣya duḥkham. [53]

"People would say the king had murdered
an innocent ascetic, a brahmin.
And I did not want to be the reason
your fame was ruined by a shameful act.

It is the fixed nature of things
that all creatures have to die.
I therefore feel no fear
as I review my own conduct.

It was to stop you violating virtue,
the origin of happiness,
that I spoke to you of forbearance
since it leads to acquiring bliss.

I described forbearance to you
with the joy of offering a fine gift.
For it is a mine of virtues
and a defense against vices."

28.85

But the king disregarded these kind and true flowers of speech and addressed the eminent seer with indignation, saying: "Let's see how much you love forbearance!" At these words, the sage slightly extended his right hand to stop the king, his long and slender fingers raised, but the king cut off the ascetic's hand with his sharp sword, as if severing a lotus from its stalk.

But though his hand was cut off,
his vow was so firm he felt less pain at this
than at seeing the inevitable hideous anguish
his well-to-do slayer would suffer in future.

atha Bodhisattvaḥ «kaṣṭam! atikrānto 'yaṃ sva|hita|maryādām a|pātrī|bhūto 'nunayasy'» êti vaidya|pratyākhyātam āturam iv' âinaṃ samanuśocaṃs tūṣṇīṃ babhūva.

ath' âinaṃ sa rājā saṃtarjayan punar uvāca:

28.90 «evaṃ c' ācchidyamānasya
nāśam eṣyati te tanuḥ.
muñca dambha|vrataṃ c' êdam
khala|buddhi|pralambhanam!» [54]

Bodhisattvas tv anunay'|â|kṣamam enaṃ viditv" «âyaṃ ca nām' âsya nirbandha» iti n' âinaṃ kiṃ cid uvāca. atha sa rājā tasya Mahātmano dvitīyaṃ pāṇim ubhau bāhū karṇa|nāsaṃ caraṇau ca† tath" âiva nicakarta.

patati tu niśite 'py asau śarīre
na muni|varaḥ sa śuśoca no cukopa
parividita|śarīra|yantra|niṣṭhaḥ
paricitayā ca jane kṣam"|ânuvṛttyā. [55]

gātra|cchede 'py a|kṣata|kṣānti|dhīraṃ
cittaṃ tasya prekṣamāṇasya sādhoḥ
n' āsīd duḥkhaṃ, prīti|yogān nṛ|paṃ tu
bhraṣṭaṃ dharmād vīkṣya saṃtāpam āpa. [56]

pratisaṃkhyāna|mahatāṃ
na tathā karuṇ"|ātmanām
bādhate duḥkham utpannaṃ
parān eva yathā śritam. [57]

"Alas!" he reflected, "This man has gone beyond the bounds of his welfare and is no longer capable of receiving advice." Grieving over him this way as if over a sick patient rejected by doctors, the Bodhi·sattva stayed silent.

Abusing him further, the king addressed the ascetic once more, saying:

"I'll keep chopping you this way
until your body is destroyed.
Give up your fraudulent vow
and your wicked deceit!" 28.90

The Bodhi·sattva made no reply, knowing that the king was incapable of being advised and would remain obstinate. So the king cut off the Great One's other hand, as well as his two arms, ears, nose and feet.

The fine sage felt neither grief nor anger
when the sharp sword fell on his body.
He knew his body's machinery must end
and had long practiced forbearance toward people.

Despite seeing his body being chopped up,
his mind stayed firm in undiminished patience.
He felt no pain but kindness made the saint
suffer at seeing the king's fall from morality.

Those who are compassionate
and strong in intelligence
are not afflicted by their own pain
as much as by the pain of others.

28.95 ghoraṃ tu tat karma nṛ|paḥ sa kṛtvā
sadyo jvareṇ' ânugato 'gnin" êva.
vinirgataś c' ôpavan'|ânta|deśād
gāṃ c' âvadīrṇāṃ sahasā viveśa. [58]

nimagne tu tasmin rājani bhīma|śabdam avadīrṇāyāṃ vahni|jvāl'|ākulāyāṃ samudbhūte mahati kolāhale samantataḥ prakṣubhite vyākule rāja|kule tasya rājño 'mātyā jānānās tasya munes tapaḥ|prabhāva|māhātmyaṃ tat|kṛtaṃ ca rājño dharaṇī|tala|nimajjanaṃ manyamānāḥ, «pur" âyam ṛṣi|varas tasya rājño doṣāt sarvam imaṃ† jana|padaṃ nirdahat'» îti jāta|bhaya|śaṅkāḥ† samabhigamya tam ṛṣi|varam abhipraṇamya kṣamayamāṇāḥ kṛt'|âñjalayo vijñāpayām† āsuḥ:

«imām avasthāṃ gamito 'si yena
nṛ|peṇa mohād ati|cāpalena,
śāp'|ânalasy' êndhanatāṃ sa eva
prayātu te, mā puram asya dhākṣīḥ! [59]

strī|bāla|vṛddh'|ātura|vipra|dīnān
an|āgaso n' ârhasi dagdhum atra!
tat sādhu deśaṃ kṣiti|pasya tasya
svaṃ c' âiva dharmaṃ, guṇa|pakṣa, rakṣa!» [60]

ath' âinān† Bodhisattvaḥ samāśvāsayann uvāca:
28.100 «mā bhaiṣṭ', āyuṣmantaḥ!

But as soon as he did that terrible deed
the king was struck by a fire-like fever.
Stepping beyond the edge of the forest,
he suddenly entered a gaping hole in the earth. 28.95

There was a terrifying noise as the earth tore open, full of fiery flames, and swallowed the king. A huge din arose on all sides and the royal party became disturbed and distraught. The king's ministers knew the strength and might of the ascetic's spiritual power. Assuming that this must be the reason why the king had sunk into the earth, they worried with fear and alarm whether the eminent seer would burn up the entire country because of the king's crime. Approaching the great seer, they prostrated themselves before him and, with hands folded in respect, they begged him for forgiveness, saying:

"In his rashness and ignorance,
it was the king who brought you to this state.
May he be the sole fuel for your blazing curse!
Please do not incinerate his city!

Please do not burn the innocent people here:
women, children, elderly, sick, brahmins and the distressed.
Please conserve the king's country
and your own morality, virtuous ascetic!"

The Bodhi·sattva then comforted them, saying:
"Have no fear, good people! 28.100

sa|pāṇi|pādam asinā karṇa|nāsam an|āgasaḥ
chinnavān yo 'pi tāvan me vane nivasataḥ sataḥ, [61]

kathaṃ tasy' âpi duḥkhāya cintayed api mad|vidhaḥ?
ciraṃ jīvatv asau rājā! mā c' âinaṃ pāpam āgamat! [62]

maraṇa|vyādhi|duḥkh'|ārte
  lobha|dveṣa|vaśī|kṛte
dagdhe duś|caritaiḥ śocye
  kaḥ kopaṃ kartum arhati? [63]

syāl labhya|rūpas tu yadi kramo 'yaṃ,
  mayy eva pacyeta tad asya pāpam!
duḥkh'|ânubandho hi sukh'|ôcitānāṃ
  bhavaty a|dīrgho 'py a|viṣahya|tīkṣṇaḥ. [64]

28.105 trātuṃ na śakyas tu mayā yad evaṃ
  vinirdahann ātma|hitaṃ sa rājā,
utsṛjya tām ātma|gatām a|śaktiṃ
  rājñe kariṣyāmi kim ity asūyām? [65]

ṛte 'pi rājño maraṇ'|ādi|duḥkhaṃ
  jātena sarveṇa niṣevitavyam.
janm' âiva ten' âtra na marṣaṇīyaṃ.
  tan n' âsti cet, kiṃ ca kutaś ca duḥkham? [66]

kalpān a|saṃkhyān† bahudhā vinaṣṭaṃ
  śarīrakaṃ janma|paraṃparāsu.
jahyāṃ kathaṃ tat|pralaye titikṣāṃ
  tṛṇasya hetor iva ratna|jātam? [67]

Though he cut off with a sword
my hands, feet, ears and nose
as I dwelled virtuously
in the forest without sin,

how could someone such as I
even think of doing him any harm?
May the king live long!
May no evil fall upon him!

How can one be angry toward the pitiful
who suffer death, disease and suffering,
enslaved by greed and hatred
and consumed by wicked deeds?

If only it were possible that
his wicked action had its result in me!
For any association with suffering, however brief,
is harsh and unbearable for those used to comfort.

It is impossible for me to save this king 28.105
who has burned up his own welfare.
So why give up my helpless state
and feel resentment toward him?

Aside from the king, every being
must experience suffering such as death.
It is birth one should not tolerate in this world.
Without it, what is suffering? How would it arise?

For incalculable eons and over successive lives
my body has been destroyed in numerous ways.
Why give up forbearance at my body's ruin,
like giving up a jewel for a piece of straw?

vane vasan pravrajita|pratijñaḥ
kṣam"|âbhidhāyī na cirān mariṣyan
kim a|kṣamāyāṃ praṇayaṃ kariṣye?
tad bhaiṣṭa mā. svasti ca vo 'stu. yāta.» [68]

iti sa muni|varo 'nuśiṣya tān
samam upanīya† ca sādhu|śiṣyatām,
a|vicalita|dhṛtiḥ kṣam"|āśrayāt
samadhiruroha divaṃ kṣam"|āśrayāt. [69]

28.110 tad evaṃ, s' | ātmī | bhūta | kṣamāṇāṃ pratisaṃkhyāna | mahatāṃ n' â|viṣahyaṃ nāma kiṃ cid ast' îti.† kṣānti|guṇa|saṃvarṇane munim upanīya vācyam. cāpal'| â|kṣānti|doṣa|nidarśane rājānam upanīya kām'|ādīnava|kathāyām api vācyam: «evaṃ kāma|hetor duś|caritam āsevya vinipāta|gāmino† bhavant'» îti. saṃpadām a|nityatā|pradarśane† c' êti.

Dwelling in the forest, following my ascetic vow,
preaching forbearance and soon about to die,
why would I feel a desire to be indignant?
So do not fear. Be well. And now go."

Thus instructing them, the ascetic
initiated them as disciples of virtue.
Dedicated to forbearance, his constancy unaltered,
he ascended to heaven from his abode on earth.

28.110 In this way, nothing is unbearable for those who internalize forbearance and are great in equanimity.

One should narrate this story when praising the virtue of forbearance, citing the sage as an example. Likewise, one should narrate this story when illustrating the flaws of reckless behavior and impatience, or when discussing the perils of desire, citing the king as an example, saying: "Those who practice evil for the sake of desire thus fall upon ruin." And similarly when demonstrating the impermanence of wealth.

BRAHMAJĀTAKAM

STORY 29

THE BIRTH-STORY OF BRAHMA

29.1 MITHYĀ|DṚṢṬI|paramāṇy a|vadyān', îti viśeṣen' ânukampyāḥ† satāṃ dṛṣṭi|vyasana|gatāḥ.

tad|yath" ânuśrūyate.

Bodhisattva|bhūtaḥ† kil' âyaṃ Bhagavān dhyān'|âbhyās'|ôpacitasya kuśalasya karmaṇo vipāka|prabhāvād Brahma|loke janma pratilebhe. tasya tan mahad api dhyāna|viśeṣ'|âdhigataṃ Brāhmaṃ sukhaṃ pūrva|janmasu kāruṇya|paricayān n' âiva para|hita|karaṇa|vyāpāra|nirutsukaṃ manaś cakāra.

viṣaya|sukhen' âpi parāṃ
pramāda|vaktavyatāṃ vrajati lokaḥ.
dhyāna|sukhair api tu satāṃ
na tiras|kriyate para|hit'|êcchā. [1]

29.5 atha kadā cit sa Mahātmā karuṇ"|āśraya|bhūtaṃ vividha|duḥkha|vyasana|śat'|ôpasṛṣṭam utkṛṣṭa†|vyāpāda|vihiṃsā|kāma|dhātuṃ kāma|dhātum avalokayan† dadarśa Videha|rājam Aṅgadinnaṃ nāma ku|mitra|saṃparka|doṣād a|san|manas|kāra|paricayāc ca mithyā|dṛṣṭi|gahane paribhramantam.

«n' âsti para|lokaḥ, kutaḥ śubh'|âśubhānāṃ karmaṇāṃ phala|vipāka†» ity evaṃ sa niścayam upetya praśānta|dharma|kriy"|âutsukyaḥ pradāna|śīl'|ādi|sukṛta|pratipatti|vimukhaḥ saṃrūḍha|paribhava|buddhir dhārmikeṣv a|

EXTREME FALSE VIEWS are reprehensible. That is why the virtuous show particular pity toward those who hold such disastrous views. 29.1

Tradition has handed down the following story.

When our Lord was a Bodhi·sattva, he is said to have taken his birth in the Brahma Realm as a result of a ripening of good karma that he had accumulated through practicing dhyana meditation.* But despite attaining the great happiness of a Brahma deity, which is only reached through exceptional meditation, the Bodhi·sattva was so used to practicing compassion in his previous births that he did not lose his urge to be active in benefiting others.

In their enjoyment of pleasures,
people become deplorably reckless.
But the good never lose the will to help others,
though they experience the joys of meditation.

One day the Great One was surveying the Sphere of Desire*, the proper place for compassion since it is afflicted by hundreds of pains and misfortunes and involves extreme ruin, violence and sensuality. There he spotted the King of Videha, who was called Anga·dinna. Due to keeping company with bad friends, and also due to his habitual regard for evil, this king was wandering aimlessly in a thicket of false views. 29.5

The king had reached the conclusion that the next world did not exist, let alone the ripening of the fruit of pure or impure deeds. As a result, any longing he may have felt for religious practices had been quashed. Turning his back on moral behavior such as giving or virtue, he felt a deep con-

śraddhā|rūkṣa|matir dharma|śāstreṣu parihāsa|cittaḥ para|loka|kathāsu śithila|vinay'|ôpacāra|gaurava|bahu|mānaḥ śramaṇa|brāhmaṇeṣu kāma|sukha|parāyaṇo babhūva.

«śubh'|â|śubhaṃ karma sukh'|â|sukh'|ôdayaṃ
dhruvaṃ paratr'» êti virūḍha|niścayaḥ
apāsya pāpaṃ yatate śubh'|āśraye.†
yath"|êṣṭam a|śraddhatayā tu gamyate. [2]

atha sa Mahātmā deva'|rṣis tasya rājñas tena dṛṣṭi|vyasan'|ôpanipāten' âpāyikena lok'|ânarth'|ākara|bhūtena samāvarjit'|ânukampas tasya rājño viṣaya|sukh'|ākalita|mateḥ śrīmati pravivikte vimāna|deśe 'vatiṣṭhamānasy' âbhijvalan Brahma|lokāt purastāt samavatatāra. atha sa rājā tam agni|skandham iva jvalantaṃ, vidyut|samūham iva c' âvabhāsamānaṃ, dina|kara|kīraṇa|saṃghātam iva ca parayā dīptyā virocamānam abhivīkṣya tat|tejas" âbhibhūta|matiḥ sa|saṃbhramaḥ prāñjalir enaṃ pratyutthāya sa|bahu|mānam udīkṣamāṇa ity uvāca:

«karoti te bhūr iva saṃparigrahaṃ
nabho 'pi, padm'|ôpama|pāda, pādayoḥ!
vibhāsi saurīm iva c' ôdvahan prabhāṃ.
vilocan'|ānandana|rūpa, ko bhavān?» [3]

29.10 Bodhisattva uvāca:

tempt for the pious and his lack of belief meant he held harsh opinions on religious teachings. Ridiculing stories about the next world, he showed little politeness, courtesy, respect or honor toward ascetics or brahmins and was devoted to sensual pleasures.

If convinced that good and bad deeds have
happy and unhappy results in the next life,
one avoids evil and strives for purity.
But non-believers follow their whims.

The king's pernicious false view was an affliction that spelled ruin, bringing calamity on the world. As a result, the Great One, that divine seer, felt compassion for the king. So, one day, while the monarch was staying in a beautiful and secluded grove, caught up in sense pleasures, the Great One descended from the Brahma Realm and blazed in front of him. At the sight of the deity blazing like a heap of fire, flashing like a mass of lightning bolts and shining with immense splendor like the sun's rays combined, the king was overwhelmed by the Great One's brilliance. Cupping his hands in veneration and filled with alarm, he rose up and addressed the Great One, gazing at him reverently:

"Lotus-footed god,
your feet rest on the sky as if it were ground!
You shine radiantly with sunny splendor.
Your beauty delights the eyes: who are you?"

The Bodhi·sattva replied: 29.10

«jitvā dṛptau śātrava|mukhyāv iva saṃkhye,
rāga|dveṣau citta|samādhāna†|balena,
Brāhmaṃ lokaṃ ye 'bhigatā, bhūmi|pa, teṣāṃ
deva'|ṛṣīṇām anyatamaṃ māṃ tvam avehi.» [4]

ity ukte sa rājā sv|āgat'|ādi|priya|vacana|puraḥsaraṃ pādy'|ârghya|satkāram asmai samupahṛtya sa|vismayam enam abhivīkṣamāṇa uvāca:

«āścarya|rūpaḥ khalu te, mārṣa,† ṛddhi|prabhāvaḥ.

prāsāda|bhittiṣv a|viṣajjamānaś†
caṃkramyase vyomni yath" âiva bhūmau.
śata|hrad'|ônmeṣa|samṛddha|dīpte,
pracakṣva tat kena tav' êyam ṛddhiḥ!» [5]

29.15 Bodhisattva uvāca:

«dhyānasya śīlasya ca nir|malasya
varasya c' âiv' êndriya|saṃvarasya
s'|ātmī|kṛtasy' ânya|bhaveṣu, rājann,
evaṃ|prakārā phala|siddhir eṣā.» [6]

rāj" ôvāca: «kiṃ satyam ev' êdam asti paraloka iti?»
Brahm" ôvāca: «ām, asti, mahā|rāja, para|lokaḥ.»
rāj" ôvāca: «kathaṃ punar idaṃ, mārṣa, śakyam asmābhir api śraddhātuṃ syāt?»

29.20 Bodhisattva uvāca: «sthūlam etan, mahā|rāja, pratyakṣ'|ādi|pramāṇa|yukti|grāhyam āpta|jana|nidarśita|kramaṃ parīkṣā|krama|gamyaṃ ca. paśyatu bhavān:

"Know me, king, as a divine seer
who has attained the Brahma Realm
by quashing greed and hate through meditation
as if defeating proud enemy chiefs in war."

Addressed this way, the king spoke to the Bodhi·sattva with words of welcome and other friendly greetings and showed him hospitality by offering water for his feet. Gazing at him with amazement, he then spoke to him as follows, :

"The might of your supernatural power is indeed wondrous to see, good sir.

You walk on air as if it were ground,
not even holding the palace walls.
Shining brightly with a hundred lightning flashes,
tell me the source of your powers!"

The Bodhi·sattva replied: 29.15

"Powers such as these, Your Majesty,
are the fruit of meditation, stainless virtue,
and supreme restraint of the senses,
all realized in my other existences."

"Is it true that the next world exists?" the king asked.

"Yes, great king. The next world exists," Brahma answered.

"But how can someone such as I believe in this, good sir?"

"It is an ostensible fact, Your Majesty. It can be grasped by reason, using measurements of proof such as direct perception. Its nature has been illustrated by trustworthy people and it can be proved by tests. You should consider this: 29.20

candr'|ârka|nakṣatra|vibhūṣaṇā dyaus
tiryag|vikalpāś ca bahu|prakārāḥ—
pratyakṣa|rūpaḥ para|loka eṣa.
mā te 'tra saṃdeha|jaḍā matir bhūt. [7]

jāti|smarāḥ santi ca tatra tatra
dhyān'|âbhiyogāt smṛti|pāṭavāc ca.
ato 'pi lokaḥ parato 'numeyaḥ.
sākṣyaṃ ca nanv atra kṛtaṃ may" âiva? [8]

yad buddhi|pūrv" âiva ca buddhi|siddhir,
‹lokaḥ paro 'st'› îti tato 'py avehi.
ādyā hi yā garbha|gatasya buddhiḥ,
s" ân|antaraṃ pūrvaka|janma|buddheḥ. [9]

jñey'|âvabodhaṃ ca vadanti buddhiṃ.
janm'|ādi buddher viṣayo 'sti tasmāt.
na c' āihiko 'sau nayan'|ādy|a|bhāvāt,
siddhau yadīyas tu paraḥ sa lokaḥ. [10]

29.25 pitryaṃ sva|bhāvaṃ vyatiricya dṛṣṭaḥ
śīl'|ādi|bhedaś ca yataḥ prajānām,
n' ākasmikasy' âsti ca yat prasiddhir,
jāty|antar'|âbhyāsa|mayaḥ sa tasmāt. [11]

paṭutva|hīne 'pi mati|prabhāve
jaḍa|prakāreṣv api c' êndriyeṣu
vin" ôpadeśāt pratipadyate yat
prasūta†|mātraḥ stana|pāna|yatnam, [12]

The sky adorned by moon, sun and stars
and the many diverse forms of animals:
these are the next world in its perceptible form.
Do not be paralyzed by doubt about this.

There are some who can remember past lives
through meditation and sharp memories.
Thus one can infer there is a world hereafter.
Surely I myself offer evidence for your eyes?

An intellect develops from a former intellect.
Thus you can realize that the next world exists.
For the initial intellect of an embryo links
directly with the intellect of a former birth.

They say that intellect is
awareness of the knowable.
So the sphere of the intellect
must exist from conception.*
It cannot be of this world:
a fetus has no eyes or other senses.
It must consequently
belong to the other world.

In distinctions of virtue and other factors, 29.25
parents and children clearly differ in nature.
Since this cannot occur for no reason,
it must arise from habits formed in other births.

Though their mental powers lack acumen
and though their senses are still numb,
newborn children desire to drink from breasts,
without requiring any instruction.

āhāra|yogyāsu kṛta|śramatvaṃ
tad darśayaty asya bhav'|ântareṣu.
abhyāsa|siddhir hi paṭū|karoti
śikṣā|guṇaṃ karmasu teṣu teṣu. [13]

tatra cet para | loka | saṃpratyay' | â | paricayāt syād iyam āśaṅkā bhavataḥ:

‹yat saṃkucanti vikasanti ca paṅka|jāni,
kāmaṃ tad anya|bhava|ceṣṭita|siddham eṣām.†
no cet, tad iṣṭam atha kiṃ stana|pāna|yatnaṃ
jāty|antarīyaka|pariśrama|jaṃ karoṣi?› [14]

29.30 sā c' āśaṅkā n' ânuvidheyā niyam' | â | niyama | darśanāt prayatn'|ân|upapatty|upapattibhyāṃ ca.

dṛṣṭo hi kāla|niyamaḥ kamala|prabodhe
saṃmīlane ca, na punaḥ stana|pāna|yatne.
yatnaś ca n' âsti kamale, stana|pe tu dṛṣṭaḥ.
sūrya|prabhāva iti padma|vikāsa|hetuḥ. [15]

tad evaṃ, mahā|rāja, samyag upaparīkṣamāṇena śakyam etac chraddhātum: ‹asti para|loka› iti.»

This shows that in other existences
they already endeavored to find food.
For habitual practice sharpens learning
in a variety of different tasks.

Perhaps your lack of familiarity with belief in the other world may lead you to have the following doubt:

'Then the opening and closing of lotuses
must also result from acts in other existences.
But if not, why do you claim that the desire
to breastfeed is due to efforts in other births?'

One should, however, reject this doubt by noticing that in the one instance there is external compulsion, whereas in the other instance there is no external compulsion, and in the one instance there is no endeavor, whereas in the other instance there is endeavor. 29.30

The opening and closing of lotuses
are clearly regulated by time.
But this is not the case regarding
the desire to drink from breasts.
There is no endeavor in a lotus,
but in a breast-suckler endeavor is clear.
It is the power of the sun that
causes the opening of lotuses.

That is why, Your Majesty, if one examines the matter properly, one can believe that there is another world."

atha sa rājā mithyā|dṛṣṭi|parigrah'|âbhiniviṣṭa|buddhitvād upacita|pāpatvāc ca tāṃ para|loka|kathāṃ śrutv" â|sukhāyamāna uvāca:
«bho! maha"|rṣe!

29.35 lokaḥ paro yadi na bāla|vibhīṣik" âiva,†
grāhyaṃ may" âitad iti vā yadi manyase tvam,
ten' êha naḥ pradiśa niṣka|śatāni pañca,
tat te sahasram aham anya|bhave pradāsye.» [16]

atha Bodhisattvas tad asya prāgalbhya|paricaya|nirviśaṅkaṃ mithyā|dṛṣṭi|viṣ'|ôdgāra|bhūtam a|samudācāra|vacanaṃ yukten' âiva krameṇa pratyuvāca:

«ih' âpi tāvad dhana|saṃpad|arthinaḥ
prayuñjate n' âiva dhanaṃ dur|ātmani
na ghasmare n' â|nipuṇe na c' âlase.
gataṃ hi yat tatra tad|antam eva† tat. [17]

yam eva paśyanti tu sa|vyapatrapaṃ
śam'|âbhijātaṃ vyavahāra|naipuṇam,
ṛṇaṃ prayacchanti raho 'pi tad|vidhe.
tad|arpaṇaṃ hy abhyuday'|āvahaṃ dhanam. [18]

kramaś ca tāvad|vidha eva gamyatām
ṛṇa|prayoge, nṛ|pa, pāralaukike.
tvayi tv a|sad|darśana|duṣṭa|ceṣṭite
dhana|prayogasya gatir na vidyate. [19]

But the king's mind was entrenched in its attachment to wrong views, and because of the evil he had accumulated, he felt displeased when he heard this sermon about the next world and said:

"Well, great seer!

If the next world is not a bogey man for children, 29.35
and if you think I should believe in it,
then give me five hundred nishkas*
and I'll return you a thousand in another life!"

Although the king, in his customary audacity, had spoken indecently and without any qualms, as if vomiting the poison of his wrong views, the Bodhi·sattva answered with the following proper words:

"Even in this world, wealth-seekers
do not offer money to the wicked,
nor to the greedy, fools or indolents.
For whatever goes there comes to ruin.

But if they see someone who is modest,
naturally calm and skilled in business,
they will give him a loan, even without witnesses.
For money entrusted to such a man brings reward.

The same procedure for giving a loan
should be used for the next world, king.
But it would be improper to entrust money to you;
for your conduct is corrupted by wicked views.

29.40 ku|dr̥ṣṭi|doṣa|prabhavair hi dāruṇair
nipātitaṃ tvāṃ narake sva|karmabhiḥ
vi|cetasaṃ niṣka|sahasra|kāraṇād
ruj"|āturaṃ kaḥ praticodayet tadā?† [20]

na tatra candr'|ârka|karair dig|aṅganā
vibhānti saṃkṣipta|tamo|'vaguṇṭhanāḥ.
na c' âiva tārā|gaṇa|bhūṣaṇaṃ nabhaḥ
saraḥ prabuddhaiḥ kumudair iv' ēkṣyate. [21]

paratra yasmin nivasanti nāstikā,
ghanaṃ tamas tatra himaś ca mārutaḥ,
karoti yo 'stiny api dārayan rujaṃ.
tam ātmavān kaḥ praviśed dhan'|ēpsayā? [22]

ghan'|ândhakāre kaṭu†|dhūma|dur|dine
bhramanti ke cin narak'|ôdare ciram
sva|vadhra†|cīra|pravikarṣaṇ'|āturāḥ
paraspara|praskhalan'|ārta|nādinaḥ. [23]

viśīryamāṇaiś caraṇair muhur muhur
Jvalatkukūle narake tath" âpare
diśaḥ pradhāvanti tad|unmumukṣayā,
na c' ântam āyānty a|śubhasya, n' âyuṣaḥ. [24]

29.45 ātakṣya takṣāṇa iv' âpareṣāṃ
gātrāṇi raudrā viniyamya Yāmyāḥ
nistakṣṇuvanty eva śit'|ôgra†|śastrāḥ
s'|ārdreṣu dāruṣv iva labdha|harṣāḥ. [25]

Who would harass you for a thousand nishkas 29.40
when you lie in hell, senseless, sick with pain,
brought there by your own actions
caused by the evil of your false views?

In hell, the darkness-veiled directions will
not shine with the rays of the sun and moon.
You will see no sky adorned by constellations
like a lake adorned by lotuses in bloom.

In the next world, where nihilists live,
a thick darkness and icy wind tortures
people by tearing through their very bones.
What prudent man would go there to get money?

Some wander a long time on the belly of hell,
a thick darkness, a misery of acrid smoke.
Miserably dragging rags fastened by thongs,
they holler with pain as they fall over each other.

In Hell of Blazing Chaff, others repeatedly run
everywhere with broken feet, eager to escape.
They never find an end to their misfortune,
nor an end to their lifespans.

Like carpenters, hideous servants of Yama 29.45
strap down and chop up the limbs of others,
fashioning them gleefully with fierce sharp knives,
carving them as if they were fresh timber.

samutkṛtta|sarva|tvaco vedan"|ārtā
vimāṃsī|kṛtāḥ ke cid apy asthi|śeṣāḥ
na c' āyānti nāśaṃ dhṛtā duṣ|kṛtaiḥ svais
tath" âiv' âpare† khaṇḍaśaś chidyamānāḥ. [26]

jvalita|pṛthu|khalīna|pūrṇa|vaktrāḥ
sthira|dahanāsu mahīṣv ayomayīṣu
jvalana|kapila|yoktra|totra|vaśyāś
ciram apare jvalato rathān vahanti. [27]

Saṃghāta|parvata|samāgama|piṣṭa|dehāḥ
ke cit tad|ākramaṇa|cūrṇita|mūrtayo 'pi
duḥkhe mahaty a|virale† 'pi ca no mriyante
yāvat parikṣayam upaiti na karma pāpam. [28]

droṇīṣu ke cij jvalan'|ôjjvalāsu
lauhair mahadbhir musalair jvaladbhiḥ
samāni pañc' âpi samā|śatāni
saṃcūrṇyamānā visṛjanti n' âsūn. [29]

29.50 tīkṣṇ'|āyasa|jvalita|kaṇṭaka|karkaśeṣu
tapteṣu vidruma|nibheṣv apare drumeṣu
pāṭyanta ūrdhvam adha eva ca kṛṣyamāṇāḥ
krūrai ravair a|puruṣaiḥ puruṣair Yamasya. [30]

jvaliteṣu tapta|tapanīya|nibheṣv
aṅgāra|rāśiṣu mahatsv apare
upabhuñjate sva|caritasya phalaṃ
vispandit'|ārasita|mātra|balāḥ. [31]

Others suffer their entire skin being torn off.
Stripped of flesh, all that remains is bones.
Sustained by their evil actions, they cannot perish,
just as those who are chopped into pieces.

Others drag blazing chariots for an age
on an iron ground burning with constant fires.
Tamed by flaming red harnesses and whips,
their mouths are filled with large burning bits.

Others are crushed by Sanghāta's clashing peaks,*
their bodies pulverized by the onslaught.
But despite the immense and incessant pain,
they cannot perish until their bad karma ends.

For no less than five hundred years,
others are pounded in blazing troughs
by huge burning iron pestles.
But still they do not die.

Yama's bellowing demon servants 29.50
shred others to pieces, dragging them
up and down scorching trees, red as coral,
jagged with sharp, burning iron thorns.

Able only to writhe and wail,
others enjoy the fruit of their conduct
by lying on blazing heaps of embers
resembling molten gold.

ke cit tīkṣṇaiḥ śaṅku|śatair ātata|jihvā
jvālā|mālā|raudratarāyāṃ† vasu|dhāyām
rāraṭyante tīvra|ruj"|āviṣṭa|śarīrāḥ
pratyāyyante te ca tadānīṃ para|lokam. [32]

āveṣṭyante loha|paṭṭair jvaladbhir.
niṣkvāthyante loha|kumbhīṣv ath' ânye.
ke cit tīkṣṇaiḥ śastra|varṣaiḥ kṣat'|âṅgā
nis|tvaṅ|māṃsā vyāla|saṅghaiḥ kriyante. [33]

ke cit klāntā vahni|saṃsparśa|tīkṣṇaṃ
kṣāraṃ toyaṃ Vaitaraṇyāṃ viśanti,
saṃśīryante yatra māṃsāni teṣāṃ,
no tu prāṇā duṣ|kṛtair dhāryamāṇā. [34]

29.55 Aśucikuṇapam abhyupeyivāṃso
hradam iva dāha|pariśram'|ārta|cittāḥ,
a|tulam anubhavanti tatra duḥkhaṃ
krimi|śata|jarjarit'|âsthibhiḥ śarīraiḥ. [35]

jvalana|parigatā jvalac|charīrāś
ciram apare 'nubhavanti dāha|duḥkham
jvalana|parigat'|āyasa|prakāśāḥ;
sva|kṛta|dhṛtā na ca bhasmasād bhavanti. [36]

chidyante† krakacair jvaladbhir apare,
ke cin niśātaiḥ kṣuraiḥ.
ke cin mudgara|vega|piṣṭa|śirasaḥ
kūjanti śok'|āturāḥ.
pacyante pṛthu|śūla|bhinna|vapuṣaḥ
ke cid vidhūme 'nale.
pāyyante jvalit'|âgni|varṇam apare
lauhaṃ rasanto rasam. [37]

Others scream loudly, afflicted by fierce pain,
hundreds of sharp nails stretching their tongues
on a ground fiercely burning with rings of fire.
Then they come to believe in the next world.

Some are wrapped in blazing iron turbans.
Others are boiled to a broth in iron pots.
Others are cut by showers of sharp weapons,
their skin and flesh ripped by hordes of beasts.

Tired, others enter Váitarani's acrid waters*,
which scorches them on contact like flames.
Their flesh wastes away but not their lives,
for they are sustained by their evil deeds.

Exhausted by the flames, others enter 29.55
Hell of Impure Corpses, as if entering a lake.
There they suffer unparalleled anguish
as hundreds of worms decompose their bodies.

Surrounded by flames, their bodies ablaze,
resembling irons enveloped by fire,
others suffer the pain of burning for an age.
Sustained by their deeds, they never turn to ash.

Some are sliced by burning saws,
others by sharpened razors.
Others wail, stricken with grief,
their heads crushed by pounding mallets.
Some are cooked on a smokeless fire,
their bodies spiked by broad spits.
Others scream as they are forced to drink
liquid iron the color of blazing flames.

apare śvabhir bhṛśa|balaiḥ śabalair
 abhipatya tīkṣṇa|daśanair daśanaiḥ
parilupta|māṃsa|tanavas tanavaḥ
 prapatanti dīna|virutā virutāḥ. [38]

evaṃ|prakāram a|sukhaṃ nirayeṣu ghoraṃ
 prāpto bhaviṣyasi yadā† sva|kṛta|praṇunnaḥ,
śok'|āturaṃ śrama|viṣāda|parīta|cittaṃ
 yāced ṛṇaṃ ka iva nāma tadā bhavantam? [39]

29.60 lauhīṣu dur|jana|kaḍevara†|saṃkulāsu
 kumbhīṣv abhijvalita|vahni|dur|āsadāsu
prakvātha|vega|vaśa|gaṃ vi|vaśaṃ bhramantaṃ
 yāced ṛṇaṃ ka iva nāma tadā bhavantam? [40]

yac c' āyasa|jvalita|kīla|nibaddha|dehaṃ
 nirdhūma|vahni|kapile vasudhā|tale vā
nirdahyamāna|vapuṣaṃ karuṇaṃ rudantaṃ
 yāced ṛṇaṃ ka iva nāma tadā bhavantam? [41]

prāptaṃ parābhavaṃ taṃ duḥkhāni
 mahānti kas tad" ânubhavantam
yāced ṛṇaṃ bhavantaṃ prativacanam
 api pradātum a|prabhavantam? [42]

viśasyamānaṃ hima|mārutena vā
 nikūjitavye 'pi vipanna|vikramam
viśīryamāṇ'|âsthi|†śat'|ārti|nādinaṃ†
 paratra kas tv" ârhati yācituṃ dhanam? [43]

Others are attacked by spotted dogs
of great strength, biting them with sharp teeth.
Their flesh ripped away, they fall down,
wasted and screaming cries of misery.*

When you acquire this horrific anguish in hell,
dispatched there by your own actions,
stricken with grief, seized by fatigue and despair,
who would ask you for your debt then?

When you swirl helplessly, boiled in iron pots 29.60
crammed full of the corpses of sinners,
forbidding access through blazing flames,
who would ask you for your debt then?

When blazing iron nails fasten your body
to the ground red with smokeless flames
and you wail pitifully as your body burns,
who would ask you for your debt then?

When you suffer this calamity
and experience these vast woes,
who would ask you for your debt
if you are unable even to answer?

When you are lacerated by an icy wind
and lack the strength even to groan,
when you scream a hundred cries as bones shatter,
who in the next world would ask you for money?

vihiṃsyamānaṃ puruṣair Yamasya vā
  viceṣṭamānaṃ jvalite 'tha v" ânale
śva|vāyasair vā hṛta†|māṃsa|śoṇitaṃ
  paratra kas tvā dhana|yācñayā tudet?† [44]

29.65 vadha|vikartana|pāṭana|tāḍanair†
  dahana|takṣaṇa|peṣaṇa|bhedanaiḥ
viśasanair vividhaiś ca sad" āturaḥ
  katham ṛṇaṃ pratidāsyasi me tadā?» [45]

atha sa rājā tāṃ niraya | kathām ati | bhīṣaṇāṃ samupaśrutya jāta|saṃvegas tyakta|mithyā|dṛṣṭy|anurāgo labdha|saṃpratyayaḥ para|loke, tam ṛṣi|varaṃ praṇamy' ôvāca:

«niśamya tāvan narakeṣu yātanāṃ
  bhayād idaṃ vidravat' îva me manaḥ.
kathaṃ bhaviṣyāmi nu† tāṃ sameyivān
  vitarka|vahnir dahat' îva māṃ punaḥ. [46]

mayā hy a|sad|darśana|naṣṭa|cetasā
  ku|vartmanā yātam a|dīrgha|darśinā.
tad atra me sādhu|gatir gatir bhavān!
  parāyaṇaṃ tvaṃ śaraṇaṃ ca me, mune! [47]

yath" âiva me dṛṣṭi|tamas tvay" ôddhṛtaṃ,
  divā|kareṇ' êva samudyatā tamaḥ,
tath" âiva mārgaṃ tvam, ṛṣe, pracakṣva me
  bhajeya yen' âham ito na dur|gatim.» [48]

When Yama's servants injure you
and you writhe on a blazing fire,
when dogs and crows eat your flesh and blood,
who in the next world would vex you for money?

Continuously afflicted by different tortures, 29.65
whether beatings, cuts, rips or poundings,
bites, chops, pummelings or hacks,
how could you pay me back your debt?"

The king felt alarmed when he heard this terrifying account of hell. Abandoning his attachment to wrong views and acquiring faith in the next world, he bowed before the eminent seer and said:

"My mind almost runs wild with fear
at learning of the punishments in hell.
It practically burns with blazing thoughts
regarding my plight on meeting that fate.

Shortsightedly I trod the wrong path,
my mind destroyed by evil views.
Be then my path, recourse of the good!
Be my resort and refuge, sage!

As you dispelled the darkness of my views
like the rising sun dispels night,
so tell me, seer, the path I should follow
to avoid a bad rebirth after this life."

29.70 ath' âinaṃ Bodhisattvaḥ saṃvigna|mānasam ṛjū|bhūta| dṛṣṭiṃ dharma|pratipatti|pātra|bhūtam avekṣya pit" êva putram ācārya iva ca śiṣyam anukampamāna iti samanuśaśāsa:

«sac|chiṣya†|vṛttyā śramaṇa|dvijeṣu
pūrve guṇa|prema yathā vivavruḥ†
nṛ|pāḥ sva|vṛttyā ca dayāṃ prajāsu,
kīrti|kṣamaḥ sa tri|divasya panthāḥ. [49]

a|dharmam asmād bhṛśa|dur|jayaṃ jayan
kadarya|bhāvaṃ ca dur|uttaraṃ taran
upaihi ratn'|âtiśay'|ôjjvalaṃ jvalan
divas|pateḥ kāñcana|gopuraṃ puram. [50]

manasy a|sad|darśana|saṃstute 'stu te
ruci|sthiraṃ saj|jana|saṃmataṃ matam.
jahīhi taṃ bāliśa|rañjanair janaiḥ
pravedito '|dharma|viniścayaś ca yaḥ. [51]

tvayā hi sad|darśana|sādhun" âdhunā,
nar'|êndra, vṛttena yiyāsatā satā
yad" âiva citte guṇa|rūkṣatā kṣatā,
tad" âiva te mārga|kṛt'|āspadaṃ padam. [52]

29.75 kuruṣva tasmād guṇa|sādhanaṃ dhanaṃ
śivāṃ ca loke sva|hit'|ôdayāṃ dayām
sthiraṃ ca śīl'|êndriya|saṃvaraṃ varaṃ.
paratra hi syād a|śivaṃ na tena te. [53]

The Bodhi·sattva saw that the king was deeply moved, that his views had been corrected and that he had become a suitable vessel for learning the Teaching, so he compassionately instructed him as follows, like a father instructs a son or a teacher instructs a pupil: 29.70

"Past kings revealed their love of virtue,
acting like good pupils to ascetics and brahmins
and showing pity to their subjects as they should.
This is the path leading to heaven and fame.

Conquer vice, so difficult to vanquish!
Pass beyond greed, so difficult to overcome!
You will thus reach the gleaming gold-gated city
of the king of heavens, ablaze with fine gems.

May your mind, which once praised evil views,
firmly cherish the creeds valued by good men.
Abandon immoral beliefs proclaimed
by those eager to pleasure fools.

Your present desire to practice
the good conduct of right views
has destroyed your abrasiveness toward virtue,
thereby establishing you on the path.

Use your wealth as an instrument for virtue. 29.75
Show kind pity to the world; it will benefit you.
Be firm in the fine moral restraints of the senses.
You will thus suffer no harm in the next life.

sva|puṇya|lakṣmyā, nṛ|pa, dīptay" āptayā
su|kṛtsu śuklatva|manojñay" ājñayā
car' ātmano 'rtha|pratisaṃhitaṃ hitaṃ
jagad|vyathāṃ kīrti|mano|haraṃ haran. [54]

tvam atra san|mānasa|sārathī rathī.
sva eva deho guṇa|sūr atho rathaḥ
a|rūkṣat"|âkṣo dama|dāna|cakravān
samanvitaḥ puṇya|manīṣay" ēṣayā. [55]

yat'|êndriy'|âśvaḥ smṛti|raśmi|saṃpadā
mati|pratodaḥ śruti|vistar'|āyudhaḥ
hry|upaskaraḥ saṃnati|cāru|kūbaraḥ
kṣamā|yugo dākṣa|gatir dhṛti|sthiraḥ. [56]

a|sad|vacaḥ|saṃyamanād a|kūjano
manojña|vāṅ|manda|gambhīra|nisvanaḥ
a|mukta|saṃdhir niyam'|â|vikhaṇḍanād
a|sat|kriyā|jihma|vivarjan'|ārjavaḥ. [57]

Through the majestic splendor
of your meritorious deeds,
and through your commands
charming the good with their purity,
may you act for your welfare
and personal advantage,
dispelling the world's anguish
and gaining the delights of fame.

You ride a chariot.
Moral thoughts are its driver.
Your body is the chariot,
giving rise to virtues.
Meekness is its axle,
restraint and giving its wheels.
Virtuous intentions
are the chariot-pole.

The senses are its horses,
tamed by the reins of awareness.
The mind is its goad,
broad learning its weaponry.
Shame is its furnishings,
modesty its lovely frame.
Patience is its yoke, skillfulness
its movement and fortitude its steadiness.

If you hold back evil words,
your chariot will not rattle.
If you use charming speech,
its sound will be deep and smooth.
If you never break your disciplines,

29.80 anena yānena yaśaḥ|patākinā
day"|ânuyātreṇa śam'|ôcca|ketunā
caran par'|ātm'|ârtham a|moha|bhāsvatā
na jātu, rājan, nirayaṃ gamiṣyasi.» [58]

iti sa Mahātmā tasya rājñas tad a|sad|darśan'|ândhakāraṃ bhāsvarair vacana|kiraṇair vyavadhūya prakāśya c' âsmai su|gati|gamana|mārgaṃ† tatr' âiv' ântar|dadhe. atha sa rājā samupalabdha|para|loka|vṛttānta|tattvaḥ pratilabdha|samyag|darśana|cetāḥ s'|âmātya|paura|jānapado dāna|dama|saṃyama|parāyaṇo babhūva.

tad evaṃ, mithyā|dṛṣṭi|paramāṇy a|vadyān', îti viśeṣen' ânukampyāḥ satāṃ dṛṣṭi|vyasana|gatāḥ.

«evaṃ sad|dharma|śravaṇaṃ paripūrṇāṃ śraddhāṃ paripūrayat'» îty evam apy upaneyam. «evaṃ parato dharma|śravaṇaṃ samyag|dṛṣṭy|utpāda|pratyayo bhavat'» îty evam apy upaneyam. «evam avasādanām† api santas tadd|hit'|ôpadeśena pratinudanti kṣamā|paricayān na pāruṣyeṇ'» êti sat|praśaṃsāyāṃ kṣāmā|varṇe 'pi vācyam. «saṃvegād evam

the joints of the chariot will not loosen.
If you shun the crooked path of vice,
the chariot will travel straight.

With glory as its banner, 29.80
pity as its retinue
and tranquility as
its lofty flag, king,
if you travel in this chariot
glittering with wisdom
to benefit others and yourself,
you will certainly not enter hell."

After he had dispelled the darkness of the king's wrong views with the splendid rays of his speech and shown him the path toward good rebirth, the Great One disappeared there and then. The king, for his part, grasped the truth about the next world. Accepting the right view into his heart, he became devoted toward giving, discipline and self-restraint, as did his ministers, citypeople and countryfolk.

In this way, extreme false views are reprehensible. That is why the virtuous show particular pity toward those who hold such disastrous views.

One should also draw the following conclusion: "In this way, hearing the Good Teaching fills people with faith." And also: "In this way, hearing the Teaching from another person produces a belief that gives rise to right view." And one should also tell this story when eulogizing the virtuous or praising forbearance, saying: "In this way, the virtuous ward off the attacks of others by pointing out what is for

āśu śreyo|'bhimukhatā bhavat'» îti saṃvega|kathāyām api vācyam iti.

their good." And one should narrate this story when discussing the topic of spiritual alarm, saying: "In this way, the experience of spiritual alarm quickly makes a person intent on the good."

HASTIJĀTAKAM

STORY 30
THE BIRTH-STORY OF THE ELEPHANT

30.1 Para|hit'|ôdarkaṃ duḥkham api sādhavo lābham iva bahu manyante.

tad|yath" ânuśrūyate.

Bodhisattvaḥ kil' ânyatamasmin nāga|vane puṣpa|phala| pallav'|ālakṣita|śikharair alaṃ|kṛta iva tatra taru|vara|taruṇair vividha|vīrut|tṛṇa†|pihita|bhūmi|bhāge vana|rāmaṇīyaka|nibaddha|hṛdayair an|utkaṇṭhitam adhyāsyamāna iva parvata|sthalair āśraya|bhūte vana|carāṇāṃ gambhīra| vipula|salil'|āśaya|sanāthe mahatā nirvṛkṣa|kṣupa|salilena kāntāreṇa samantatas tiras|kṛta|jan'|ânte mahā|kāya eka| caro hastī babhūva.

sa tatra taru|parṇena bisena salilena ca
abhireme tapasv" îva saṃtoṣeṇa śamena ca. [1]

30.5 atha kadā cit sa Mahā|sattvas tasya vanasya paryante vicaran yatas tat kāntāraṃ tato jana|śabdam upaśuśrāva. tasya cintā prādur abhūt: «kiṃ nu khalv idam? na tāvad anena pradeśena kaś cid deś'|ântara|gāmī mārgo 'sti. evaṃ mahat kāntāraṃ ca vyatītya mṛgay" âpi na yujyate, prāg eva mahā| samārambha|parikhedam asmat|sva|yūthya†|grahaṇam.

vyaktaṃ tv ete paribhraṣṭā mārgād vā mūḍha|daiśikā
nirvāsitā vā kruddhena rājñā sven' â|nayena vā. [2]

IF IT RESULTS IN the welfare of others, even pain is esteemed by the virtuous as a gain. 30.1

Tradition has handed down the following story.

The Bodhi·sattva is said to have once lived as an enormous elephant who wandered alone in an elephant forest. Fine young trees seemed to adorn the forest like ornaments, their crests conspicuous with flowers, fruits and sprays. The ground was covered by a variety of plants and grasses and mountain plateaus seemed to preside contentedly, their hearts enthralled by the forest's beauty. A home for forest animals, the woods were blessed by a deep and broad lake, while a vast desert, devoid of trees, shrubs and water, concealed the forest from human habitation on all sides.

Delighting in the forest like an ascetic
with contentment and tranquility,
he was satisfied by leaves,
lotus-stalks and water.

One day, as he wandered the edges of the forest, the Great Being heard the sound of humans in the desert. "What can this be?" he wondered. "This area has no path leading to another region. A hunting party would never have crossed this huge desert, let alone suffer the exhaustion of such an immense enterprise just to capture my relatives. 30.5

Muddled over their directions,
clearly they must have lost their way.
Perhaps they were exiled by an angry king,
or by their own misconduct.

tathā hy ayam an|ojasko naṣṭa|harṣ'|ôddhava|dravaḥ
keval'|ārti|balaḥ śabdaḥ śrūyate rudatām iva. [3]

taj jñāsyāmi tāvad enam.»

iti sa Mahā|sattvaḥ karuṇayā samākṛṣyamāṇo yataḥ sa jana|nirghoṣo babhūva tataḥ prasasāra. viṣpaṣṭatara|vilāpaṃ ca viṣāda|dainya|virasaṃ tam ākrandita|śabdam upaśṛṇvan kāruṇya|paryutsuka|manāḥ sa Mahātmā drutataraṃ tato 'bhyagacchat. nirgamya ca tasmād vana|gahanān nirvṛkṣa|kṣupatvāt tasya deśasya dūrata† ev' âvalokayan dadarśa sapta|mātrāṇi puruṣa|śatāni kṣut|tarṣa|pariśrama|manda|mandāni† tad vanam abhimukhāni prārthayamānāni.

30.10 te 'pi ca puruṣās taṃ Mahā|sattvaṃ dadṛśur jaṅgamam iva hima|giri|śikharaṃ nīhāra|puñjam iva śarad|valāhakam iva ca† pavana|bal'|āvarjitam abhimukham āyāntam. dṛṣṭvā ca viṣāda|dainya|parītā «hant', êdānīṃ naṣṭā vayam» iti bhaya|grasta|manaso 'pi kṣut|tarṣa|pariśrama|vihat'|ôtsāhā n' âpayāna|prayatna|parā babhūvuḥ.

te viṣāda|parītatvāt kṣut|tarṣa|śrama|vihvalāḥ
n' âpayāna|samudyogaṃ bhaye 'pi pratipedire. [4]

atha Bodhisattvo bhītān avety' âinān:† «mā bhaiṣṭa! mā bhaiṣṭa! na vo bhayam asti matta!» iti samucchritena snigdh'|

The noise I hear is feeble,
strong only in anguish.
Lacking all joy, glee or fun,
it sounds like people crying.

I will find out what it is."

So the Great Being made for the human sound, drawn by his compassion. When he heard the laments more clearly, shrill with despair and misery, the Great Being picked up his speed, moved by ardent compassion. As soon as he emerged from the dense jungle, the area was so empty of trees and shrubs that, even though he was very far away, his scanning eyes immediately spotted seven hundred men heading longingly for the forest and becoming gradually weaker from hunger, thirst and exhaustion.

30.10 The men likewise spotted the Great Being heading toward them, resembling a moving peak of Mount Hímavat, or a mass of fog, or an autumn cloud driven by the force of a wind. The sight filled them with despair and misery. But though they feared they would perish, their energy was so depleted by hunger, thirst and fatigue that they made no effort to run away.

Seized by despair, afflicted
by hunger, thirst and fatigue,
they made no effort to flee,
despite being filled with fear.

Noticing their fear, the Bodhi·sattva consoled them by lifting his trunk, the tip of which was soft, red and broad, and by crying out: "Do not be afraid! Do not be afraid! You

âbhitāmra|pṛthu|puṣkareṇa kareṇa samāśvāsayann abhigamya karuṇāyamāṇaḥ papraccha:

«ke 'tra|bhavantaḥ? kena c' êmāṃ daśām anuprāptāḥ stha?

rajaḥ|sūry'|âṃśu|saṃparkād
vivarṇ'|ākṛtayaḥ kṛśāḥ
śoka|klam'|ārtāḥ ke yūyam?
iha c' âbhigatāḥ kutaḥ?» [5]

30.15 atha te puruṣās tasya tena mānuṣeṇ' âbhivyāhāreṇ' â|bhaya|pradān'|âbhivyañjakena c' âbhyupapatti|saumukhyena pratyāgata|hṛdayāḥ samabhipraṇamy' âinam ūcuḥ:

«kop'|ôtpāt'|ânilen' êha
kṣiptāḥ kṣiti|pater vayam
paśyatāṃ śoka|dīnānāṃ
bandhūnāṃ, dvirad'|âdhipa. [6]

asti no bhāgya|śeṣas tu
Lakṣmīś c' âbhimukhī dhruvam,
suhṛd|bandhu|viśiṣṭena
yad dṛṣṭā bhavatā vayam. [7]

nistīrṇām āpadaṃ c' êmāṃ
vidmas tvad|darśan'|ôtsavāt.
svapne 'pi tvad|vidhaṃ dṛṣṭvā
ko hi n' āpadam uttaret?» [8]

ath' âinān sa dvirada|vara uvāca: «atha kiyanto 'tra|bhavanta?» iti.

have nothing to fear from me!" Approaching them, he then compassionately asked them:

"Who are you gentlemen? How have you come to this plight?

The dust and rays of the sun
have made you pale and weak.
Who are you, stricken with grief and fatigue?
And why have you come here?"

30.15 When the men heard the Bodhi·sattva express his harmless intentions through human speech and when they saw his friendly disposition, they regained their confidence and bowed before him, saying:

"Ruler of elephants,
we were hurled here
by the blast of our king's anger,
our distraught kinsmen looking on.

But we must still possess some luck
and Fortune must still incline toward us,
if we have been spotted by you,
a special friend and kinsman.

The joy of seeing you makes us
sure we have crossed this calamity.
For who would not escape misfortune
at seeing someone like you, even in a dream?"

"So how many of you gentlemen are there?" the fine tusker asked.

30.20 manuṣyā ūcuḥ:

«sahasram etad vasudh"|âdhipena
tyaktaṃ nṛṇām atra, manojña|gātra.
a|dṛṣṭa|duḥkhā bahavas tatas tu
kṣut|tarṣa|śok'|âbhibhavād vinaṣṭāḥ. [9]

etāni tu syur, dvirada|pradhāna,
sapt' âvaśeṣāṇi nṛṇāṃ śatānim
nimajjatāṃ mṛtyu|mukhe 'tra† yeṣāṃ
mūrtas tvam Āśvāsa iv' âbhyupetaḥ!» [10]

tac chrutvā tasya Mahā|sattvasya kāruṇya|paricayād aśrūṇi prāvartanta. samanuśocaṃś c' âinān niyatam īdṛśaṃ kiṃ cid uvāca:

«kaṣṭaṃ bhoḥ!

30.25 ghṛṇā|viyuktā† bata nir|vyapatrapā
nṛ|pasya buddhiḥ para|loka|nirvyathā!
aho taḍic|cañcalayā nṛpa|śriyā
hṛt'|êndriyāṇāṃ sva|hit'|ân|avekṣitā. [11]

avaiti, manye, na sa mṛtyum agrataḥ
śṛṇoti pāpasya na vā dur|antatām.
aho bat' â|nāthatamā nar'|âdhipā
vimarśa|māndyād vacana|kṣamā na ye. [12]

dehasy' âikasya nām' ârthe
roga|bhūtasya nāśinaḥ
idaṃ sattveṣu nairghṛṇyaṃ!
dhig aho bata mūḍhatām!» [13]

To which the men replied: 30.20

"We were one thousand, handsome lord,
when the king abandoned us here.
But, unused to suffering, many died
from hunger, thirst and anguish.

The survivors, chief of tuskers,
should be about seven hundred now.
You come to us as Comfort incarnate
as we sink into this mouth of death!"

It was the Great Being's habit to feel compassion and so tears rolled from his eyes when he heard these words. Grieving for the men, he addressed them with firm words somewhat as follows:

"For shame!

How removed from pity, how unabashed, 30.25
how unbothered by the next world is this king's mind!
See how his senses disregard his own welfare,
captivated by royal glories as fickle as lightning!

I assume he does not understand death is near.
Or maybe he has not heard of evil's terrible end.
Kings who never yield to counsel,
weak in judgment, are most helpless of all!

For shame! See how cruel
the stupid are to living creatures,
just for the sake of a single,
decaying, disease-ridden body!"

atha tasya dvirada|pates tān puruṣān karuṇā|snigdham avekṣamāṇasya cintā prādur abhūt:

«evam amī kṣut|tarṣa|śrama|pīḍitāḥ paridurbala|śarīrā nir|udakam a|pracchāyam an|eka|yojana|śat'|āyataṃ† kāntāram a|pathy|adanāḥ† kathaṃ vyatiyāsyanti? nāga|vane 'pi ca kiṃ tad asti yen' âiṣām ek'|âham api tāvad a|parikleśena vārtā syāt? śaknuyuḥ† punar ete madīyāni māṃsāni pātheyatām upanīya, dṛtibhir iva ca mam' ântraiḥ salilam ādāya kāntāram etan nistarituṃ, n' ânyathā.

30.30 karomi tad idaṃ dehaṃ bahu|roga|śat'|ālayam
eṣāṃ duḥkha|paritānām āpad|uttaraṇa|plavam. [14]

svarga|mokṣa|sukha|prāpti|
samarthaṃ janma mānuṣam
dur|labhaṃ ca, tad eteṣāṃ
m" âivaṃ vilayam āgamat. [15]

sva|gocara|sthasya mam' âbhyupetā
dharmeṇa c' ême 'tithayo bhavanti.
āpad|gatā bandhu|vivarjitāś ca
mayā viśeṣeṇa yato 'nukampyāḥ. [16]

cirasya tāvad bahu|roga|bhājanaṃ
sad" āturatvād vividha|śram'|āśrayaḥ
śarīra|saṃjño 'yam an|artha|vistaraḥ
par'|ârtha|kṛtye viniyogam eṣyati.» [17]

A thought then occurred to the lord of elephants as he gazed at the men with tender compassion:

"These men are afflicted by hunger, thirst and fatigue and their bodies are extremely weak. The desert stretches for hundreds of yójanas* and provides neither water nor shade. How can they cross it without provisions for the road? What is there for them in the elephant forest, even for one day, without incurring great toil? But my flesh could serve as their provisions. And if they use my bowels as bags, they could take water and cross the desert. There is no other answer.

I will use this body, 30.30
this home of a hundred ills,
as a raft to save from calamity
these men suffering anguish.

A human birth is rare.
Through it one can attain
the happiness of heaven and liberation.
May they not lose it!

Having visited me in my foraging area,
they are justly my guests.
Bereft of relatives, they are in distress.
I should show them special compassion.

After long being a vessel for many illnesses,
a home for toils caused by constant sickness,
this assemblage of evils we call a body
will finally be of use in benefiting others."

ath' âinam anye kṣut|tarṣa|śrama|gharma|duḥkh'|ātura|śarīrāḥ kṛt'|âñjalayaḥ s'|âśru|nayanāḥ samabhipraṇamy' ārtatayā hasta|saṃjñābhiḥ pānīyam† ayācanta:

30.35 «tvaṃ no bandhur a|bandhūnāṃ!
tvaṃ gatiḥ śaraṇaṃ ca naḥ!
yathā vetsi, mahā|bhāga,
tathā nas trātum arhasi!» [18]

ity enam anye sa|karuṇam ūcuḥ. apare tv enaṃ dhīratara|manasaḥ salila|pradeśaṃ kāntāra|dur|g'|ôttaraṇāya† ca mārgaṃ papracchuḥ:

«jal'|āśayaḥ śīta|jalā sarid vā
yad yatra vā nairjharam asti toyam
chāyā|drumaḥ śādvala|maṇḍalaṃ vā,
tan no, dvi|pānām adhipa, pracakṣva. [19]

kāntāraṃ śakyam etac ca nistartuṃ manyase yataḥ
anukampāṃ puras|kṛtya tāṃ diśaṃ sādhu nirdiśa. [20]

saṃbahulāni hi dināny atra naḥ kāntāre paribhramatām. tad arhasi naḥ, svāmin, nistārayitum iti.»

30.40 atha sa Mahātmā taiḥ karuṇaiḥ prayācitais teṣāṃ bhṛśataram ākledita|hṛdayo yatas tat kāntāraṃ śakyaṃ nistartuṃ babhūva, tata eṣāṃ parvata|sthalaṃ saṃdarśayann abhyucchritena bhujaga|vara|bhoga|pīvareṇa kareṇ' ôvāca:

At this point, some of the men, pained by hunger, thirst, fatigue and heat, folded their hands in supplication and prostrated themselves wretchedly before the Bodhi·sattva, using hand signals to beg for water, tears welling in their eyes. Others addressed him pitifully, saying:

30.35

"Be a relative to us bereft of kinsmen!
Be our resort and refuge!
Please save us, illustrious lord,
in whatever way you know best!"

Others possessed stronger minds and asked him where they could find water and to show them the escape route out of the treacherous desert.

"If there is some pond, or stream
with cool waters, or waterfall perhaps,
some shady tree or grassy area,
please tell us, lord of elephants.

If you think it is possible
to escape this wilderness,
please show us pity
and tell us the way.

We have been wandering in this desert for many days. Please help us to escape it, lord."

30.40

The Great One's heart was softened even more by these pitiful requests. Lifting his trunk, the coils on which were as fat as a great snake's, he pointed to the mountain plateau as the way to escape the desert, saying:

«asya parvata|sthalasy' âdhastāt padm'|ôtpal'|âlaṃkṛta| vimala|nīla†|salilam asti mahat saraḥ. tad anena mārgeṇa gacchata. tatra ca vyapanīta|gharma|tarṣa|klamās tasy' âiva n' âti|dūre 'smāt parvata|sthalāt patitasya hastinaḥ śarīraṃ drakṣyatha. tasya māṃsāni pāthey'|ârtham† ādāya† dṛtibhir iva ca† tasy' ântraiḥ salilam upagṛhy' ânay" âiva diśā yātavyam. evam alpa|kṛcchreṇa kāntāram idaṃ vyatiyāsyatha.»

iti sa Mahātmā tān puruṣān samāśvāsana|pūrvakaṃ tataḥ prasthāpya tato drutataram anyena mārgeṇa tad giri|śikharam adhiruhya† tasya janasya† nistāraṇ'|âpekṣayā svaṃ śarīraṃ† tato mumukṣur niyatam iti praṇidhim upabṛṃhayām āsa:

«n' âyaṃ prayatnaḥ su|gatiṃ mam' āptuṃ,
n' âik'|ātapatrāṃ manuj'|êndra|lakṣmīm,
sukha|prakarṣ'|âika|rasāṃ na ca dyāṃ,
Brāhmīṃ śriyaṃ n' âiva, na mokṣa|saukhyam. [21]

yat tv asti puṇyaṃ mama kiṃ cid evaṃ
kāntāra|magnaṃ janam ujjihīrṣoḥ,
saṃsāra|kāntāra|gatasya tena
lokasya nistārayitā bhaveyam.» [22]

30.45 iti viniścitya sa Mahātmā pramodād a|vigaṇita†|prapāta| niṣpeṣa|maraṇa|duḥkhaḥ† svaṃ śarīraṃ† tasmād giri|taṭād yath"|ôddeśaṃ mumoca:

reje tataḥ sa nipatañ charad' îva meghaḥ,
paryasta|bimba iva c' Âsta|gireḥ śaś'|âṅkaḥ,
Tārkṣyasya† pakṣa|pavan'|ôgra|jav'|âpaviddhaṃ
śṛṅgaṃ girer iva ca tasya him'|ôttarīyam. [23]

"There is a large lake beneath that mountain plateau. Its pure blue waters are adorned by lotuses and lilies. Follow that route. When you have dispelled your heat, thirst and fatigue, you will see an elephant's body that has fallen from the mountain not far from that spot. Take its flesh as your provisions and use its bowels as bags to carry water. Then continue in the same direction. You will thus easily cross the desert."

Consoling the men this way, the Great One sent them on their way and hastily climbed the mountain peak by another route. Intent on giving up his body to rescue those people, he then strengthened his Bodhi·sattva vow by saying:

"My endeavor is not for a good rebirth,
nor for the glory of my royal parasol,
nor for heaven with its fine undiluted pleasures,
nor for Brahma's splendor, nor liberation's joy.

Instead, if I possess any merit from desiring
to rescue these people floundering in the desert,*
may I use it to become savior of the world
as it roams the wilderness of samsara."

Making this resolution, the Great One did as he intended and joyfully hurled his body down the mountain-side, paying no heed to the painful death he would suffer from being crushed in the gorge. 30.45

His falling body resembled an autumn cloud,
or the moon's orb dropping behind Mount Sunset*,
or a snow-cloaked mountain peak,
driven by the fierce gust of Gáruda's wings.

ākampayann atha dharāṃ dharaṇī|dharāṃś ca
  Mārasya ca prabhu|mad'|âdhyuṣitaṃ sa† cetaḥ,
nirghāta|piṇḍita|ravaṃ nipapāta bhūmāv
  āvarjayan druma|latā† vana|devatāś ca. [24]

a|saṃśayaṃ tad|vana|saṃśrayās tadā
  manassu visphārita|vismayāḥ surāḥ
vicikṣipur vyomni mud"|ôttanūruhāḥ
  samucchrit'|âik'|âṅguli|pallavān bhujān. [25]

su|gandhibhiś candana|cūrṇa|rañjitaiḥ
  prasaktam anye kusumair avākiran,
a|tāntavaiḥ kāñcana|bhakti|rājitais
  tam uttarīyair apare vibhūṣaṇaiḥ. [26]

30.50 stavaiḥ prasāda|grathitais tath" âpare
  samudyataiś c' âñjali|padma|kuḍmalaiḥ
śirobhir āvarjita|cāru|maulibhir
  namas|kriyābhiś ca tam abhyapūjayan. [27]

su|gandhinā puṣpa|rajo|vikarṣiṇā†
  taraṅga|mālā|racanena vāyunā
tam avyajan ke cid, ath' âmbare 'pare
  vitānam asy' ôpadadhur ghanair ghanaiḥ. [28]

tam arcituṃ bhakti|vaśena ke cana
  vyahāsayan† dyāṃ sura|dundubhi|svanaiḥ,
a|kāla|jaiḥ puṣpa|phalaiḥ sa|pallavair
  vyabhūṣayaṃs tatra tarūn ath' âpare. [29]

Shaking the earth and her mountains
and Mara's power-intoxicated mind,
he fell to the earth, crashing like a whirlwind,
making creepers and forest deities lie prostrate.

Without doubt, the gods in the forest
burst with wonder and bristled with joy,
throwing their hands into the air,
their twig-like fingers extending upwards.

Some constantly scattered him with flowers,
fragrant and tinged with sandal powder,
others with ornaments and garments
of unknown weave, gleaming with gold streaks.

Some worshiped him with devout hymns, 30.50
reverently raising cupped hands like lotus buds.
Others honored him with acts of homage,
lowering their beautifully crowned heads.

Some fanned him with a breeze
forming lines of ripples on water,
fragrant with pollen drawn from flowers.
Others draped him with a canopy of dense clouds.

With devout praise, some made the heavens
laugh with the rumbling of divine drums.
Others decorated the trees with fruits,
flowers and sprays out of season.

diśaḥ śarat|kānti|mayīṃ dadhuḥ śriyaṃ.
raveḥ karāḥ prāṃśutarā iv' âbhavan.
mud" âbhigantuṃ tam iv' āsa c' ârṇavaḥ
kutūhal'|ôtkampita|vīci|vikramaḥ.† [30]

atha te puruṣāḥ krameṇa tat saraḥ samupetya tasmin vinīta|gharma|tarṣa|klamā yathā|kathitaṃ tena Mahātmanā tad|avidūre hasti|śarīraṃ a|cira|mṛtaṃ† dadṛśuḥ. teṣāṃ buddhir abhavat:

30.55 «aho! yath" âyaṃ sadṛśas tasya dvirada|pater hastī!

bhrātā nu tasy' âiva† mahā|dvipasya
syād? bāndhavo v" ânyatamaḥ? suto vā?
tath" âiva† khalv asya sit'|âdri|śobhaṃ
saṃcūrṇitasy' âpi vibhāti rūpam. [31]

kumuda|śrīr iv' âika|sthā jyotsnā puñjī|kṛt" êva ca
chāy" êva khalu tasy' êyam ādarśa|tala|saṃśritā.» [32]

atha tatr' âikeṣāṃ nipuṇataram anupaśyatāṃ buddhir abhavat:

«yathā paśyāmaḥ sa eva khalv ayaṃ dig|vāraṇ'|êndra|pratispardhi|rūp'|âtiśayaḥ kuñjara|vara āpad|gatānām a|bandhu|suhṛdām asmākaṃ nistāraṇ'|âvekṣayā† giri|taṭād asmān nipatita iti.»

The sky displayed a glorious autumnal beauty.
The sun's rays seemed to exceed their length.
The ocean's rough waves appeared to surge
with curiosity at the joy of visiting him.

The men gradually arrived at the lake. After its waters had dispelled their heat, thirst and exhaustion, they spotted the recently deceased body of an elephant nearby, just as the Great One had described to them. They then had this thought:

"My word! How similar this elephant is to the lord of tuskers we just met! 30.55

Could it be the brother of that huge elephant?
Or a relative? Or one of his sons?
Though crushed, he too looks
as glorious as a white mountain.

Like a beautiful cluster of water lilies,
or a mass of accumulated moonshine,
he resembles the other elephant
reflected in a mirror."

Some of them, however, considered the matter more shrewdly, thinking:

"As far as we can see, this fine elephant, whose exceptional beauty rivals the lordly elephants who stand in the sky,* has hurled himself down this mountain-side in order to save us from our distress, even though we are neither his relatives nor friends." Reflecting this way, they then said:

30.60 «yaḥ sa nirghātavad abhūt
kampayann iva medinīm,
vyaktam asy' âiva patataḥ
sa c' âsmābhir dhvaniḥ śrutaḥ. [33]

etad vapuḥ khalu tad eva mṛṇāla|gauraṃ
candr'|âṃśu|śukla|tanu|jaṃ tanu|bindu|citram.
kūrm'|ôpamāḥ sita|nakhāś caraṇās ta ete
vaṃśaḥ sa eva ca dhanur madhur'|ānato 'yam. [34]

tad eva c' êdaṃ mada|rāji|rājitaṃ
su|gandhi|cārv†|āyata|pīṇam ānanam.
samunnataṃ śrīmad an|arpit'|âṅkuśaṃ
śiras tad etac ca bṛhac|chiro|dharam. [35]

viṣāṇa|yugmaṃ tad idaṃ madhu|prabhaṃ
sa|darpa|cihnaṃ taṭa|reṇun" âruṇam.
ādeśayan mārgam imaṃ ca yena naḥ
sa eṣa dīrgh'|âṅguli|puṣkaraḥ karaḥ. [36]

āścaryam aty|adbhuta|rūpaṃ bata khalv idam!

30.65 a|dṛṣṭa|pūrv'|ânvaya|śīla|bhaktiṣu
kṣateṣu bhāgyair a|pariśruteṣv api
suhṛttvam asmāsu bat' êdam īdṛśaṃ,
suhṛtsu vā bandhuṣu v" âsya kīdṛśam? [37]

“The noise we heard 30.60
like a whirlwind,
seeming to shake the earth,
was surely made by this elephant’s fall.

This is clearly the same body:
yellow-white like lotus-fibers,
dappled with small spots,
its hair white as moonbeams.
The feet are the same:
tortoise-like with white nails.
And the backbone is identical:
smoothly curved like a bow.

It is the same face: gleaming with ichor streaks,
fragrant, handsome, long and plump.
And here is the same head: lofty and glorious,
untouched by a goad, borne by a huge neck.

Here are the same two tusks: bright as honey,
red with a proud mark of dust from the slope.
And here is the same trunk he used
to show us the path, its tip like a long finger.

What a miraculous wonder this is!

If he is so friendly to us fate-crippled people, 30.65
though he has never heard of us before
nor knows our family, character or faith,
what affection would he show friends or relatives?

sarvathā namo 'stv asmai mahā|bhāgāya!

āpat|parītān bhaya|śoka|dīnān
asmad|vidhān abhyupapadyamānaḥ
ko 'py eṣa, manye, dvirad'|âvabhāsaḥ
sīdat† satām uddharat' îva† vṛttam. [38]

kva śikṣito 'sāv atibhadratām imām?
upāsitaḥ ko nv amunā gurur vane?
‹na rūpa|śobhā ramate vinā guṇair›
jano yad ity āha, tad etad īkṣyate. [39]

aho svabhāv'|âtiśayasya saṃpadā
vidarśit" ânena yath"|ârtha†|bhadratā!
him'|âdri|śobhena mṛto 'pi khalv ayaṃ
kṛt'|ātma|tuṣṭir hasat' îva varṣmaṇā! [40]

30.70 tat ka idānīm asya snigdha|bāndhava|suhṛt|prativiśiṣṭa|vātsalyasy' âivam abhyupapatti|sumukhasya svaiḥ prāṇair apy asmad|artham upakartum abhipravṛttasy' âti|sādhu|vṛttasya māṃsam upabhoktuṃ śakṣyati? yuktaṃ tv asmābhiḥ pūjā|vidhi|pūrvakam agni|satkāreṇ' âsy' ānṛṇyam upagantum iti.»

atha tān bandhu|vyasana iva śok'|ânuvṛtti|pravaṇa|hṛdayān s'|âśru|nayanān gadgadāyamāna|kaṇṭhān avekṣya kāry'|ântaram avekṣamāṇā dhīratara|manasa ūcur anye:

«na khalv evam asmābhir ayaṃ dvirada|varaḥ saṃpūjitaḥ sat|kṛto vā syāt. abhiprāya|saṃpādanena tv ayam asmābhir yuktaḥ pūjayitum iti paśyāmaḥ.

Let us pay every homage to this illustrious being!

He helped men like us seized by misfortune,
distraught with terror and misery.
This must be an elephant only in appearance.
For he seems to uphold the fading conduct of the good!

Where did he learn this great goodness?
What teacher did he sit by in the forest?
One sees in him the truth of the proverb:
'Beauty never delights without virtues.'

He displayed his truly auspicious quality
by fulfilling his exceptional nature!
Even in death he seems to smile contentedly,
his body gleaming like a snowy mountain!

Who could possibly eat the flesh of this virtuous being, who was so determined to help us that he sacrificed his very life for our benefit, showing us greater affection than a loving relative or friend? We should instead repay our debt to him by honoring him with a cremation and due rites of worship." 30.70

So it was that the hearts of some of the men inclined to sorrow, their eyes filling with tears and their voices stuttering with grief as if at the disaster of a relative. Others, however, were of firmer minds and saw the matter differently. Observing the other men, they remarked:

"We would not worship or honor this fine elephant if we acted that way. Our view is that we will honor him properly if we fulfill his wishes.

asman|nistāraṇ'|âpekṣī sa hy a|saṃstuta|bāndhavaḥ
śarīraṃ tyaktavān etad† iṣṭam iṣṭatar'|âtithiḥ. [41]

abhiprāyam atas tasya†
yuktaṃ samanuvartitum
anyathā hi bhaved vyartho
nanu tasy' âyam udyamaḥ. [42]

30.75 snehād udyatam ātithyaṃ
sarva|svaṃ tena khalv idam.
a|pratigrahaṇād vyarthāṃ
kuryāt ko nv asya sat|kriyām? [43]

guror iva yatas tasya
vacasaḥ saṃpratigrahāt
sat|kriyāṃ kartum arhāmaḥ,
kṣemam ātmana eva ca. [44]

nistīrya c' êdaṃ vyasanaṃ samagraiḥ
pratyekaśo vā punar asya pūjā
kariṣyate nāga|varasya sarvaṃ,
bandhor atītasya yath" âiva kṛtyam.» [45]

atha te puruṣāḥ kāntāra|nistāraṇ'|âvekṣayā† tasya ca† dvirada|pater abhiprāyam anusmarantas tad vacanam a|pratikṣipya tasya Mahā|sattvasya māṃsāny ādāya dṛtibhir iva ca tad|antraiḥ salilaṃ, tat|pradarśitayā diśā svasti tasmāt kāntārād viniryayuḥ.

tad evaṃ, para|hit'|ôdarkaṃ duḥkham api sādhavo lābham iva bahu manyante.

For it was to save us that
this unknown kinsman
sacrificed his dear body,
his guests dearer to him still.

We should then fulfill his wishes,
or his efforts will be in vain.

Such was his affection he gave
all he had as his guest-offering.
Who would invalidate this act
of honor by not accepting it?

30.75

We will honor him
if we accept his words
just as if they came from a guru.
We will also thus acquire our safety.

After we have escaped this calamity,
we can worship him together or individually.
Every rite will be done for this fine elephant,
just as if he were a dead relative."

Eager to escape the desert and bearing in mind the wishes of the lordly elephant, the men did not ignore his instructions. Taking the Great Being's flesh, they used his bowels as bags to carry water and left the desert safely, following the route indicated by the elephant.

In this way, if it results in the welfare of others, even pain is esteemed by the virtuous as a gain.

30.80 iti sādhu|jana|praśaṃsāyāṃ vācyam, Tathāgata|varṇe 'pi, sat | kṛtya dharma | śravaṇe ca. bhadra | prakṛti | niṣpādana | varṇe 'pi vācyam: «evaṃ bhadrā prakṛtir abhyastā janm' | ântareṣv apy† anuvartata» iti. tyāga|paricaya|guṇa|nidarśane 'pi vācyam: «evaṃ dravya|tyāga|paricayād ātma|sneha|parityāgam apy a|kṛcchreṇa karot'» îti.

yac c' ôktaṃ Bhagavatā parinirvāṇa|samaye samupasthiteṣu divya|kusuma|vāditr'|ādiṣu: «na khalu punar, Ānanda, etāvatā Tathāgataḥ sat|kṛto bhavat'» îti, tac c' âivaṃ nidarśayitavyam: «evam abhiprāya|saṃpādanāt pūjā kṛtā bhavati, na gandha|māly'|ādy|abhihāreṇ'» êti.

One should narrate this story when praising the virtuous, or when eulogizing the Tatha·gata, or when discussing the topic of listening to the Teaching with respect. One should also tell this story when praising the cultivation of an auspicious nature, saying: "In this way, an ingrained auspicious nature follows a person even through other lives." And when demonstrating the virtue of habitual generosity, one should state: "In this way, by habitually giving up material objects, a person can easily give up even love for themselves." 30.80

When the Lord was entering complete nirvana,* attended by divine flowers, music and other forms of worship, he said: "This is not the way to honor the Tatha·gata, Anánda."* This story should be used to illustrate the Lord's words by saying: "In this way, a person honors the deceased by fulfilling their wishes, not by giving perfumes, garlands or other offerings."

SUTASOMAJĀTAKAM

STORY 31
THE BIRTH-STORY OF SUTA·SOMA

31.1 ŚREYAḤ SAMĀDHATTE yathā tath" âpy upanataḥ sat|saṃgama iti śreyo|'rthinā saj|jan'|âpāśrayeṇa† bhavitavyam. tad|yath" ânuśrūyate.

Bodhisattva|bhūtaḥ kil' âyaṃ bhagavān yaśaḥ|prakāśa|vaṃśe guṇa|parigraha|prasaṅgāt† sātmī|bhūta|praj"|ânurāge pratāp'|ānata|dṛpta|sāmante śrīmati Kauravya|rāja|kule janma pratilebhe.

tasya guṇa|śata|kiraṇa|mālinaḥ Somavat† priya|darśanasya sutasya Sutasoma ity evaṃ pitā nāma cakre. sa śukla|pakṣa|candramā iva pratidinam abhivardhamāna|kānti|lāvaṇyaḥ

31.5 kāla|kramād avāpya s'|âṅgeṣu s'|Ôpavedeṣu ca Vedeṣu vaicakṣaṇyaṃ, dṛṣṭa|kramaḥ s'|ôttara|kalānāṃ kalānāṃ lokyānāṃ, loke prema†|bahu|māna|niketa|bhūtaḥ samyag|abhyupapatti|saumukhyād abhivardhamān'|âdarāt paripālana|niyamāc ca bandhur iva guṇānāṃ babhūva.

śīla|śruta|tyāga|dayā|damānāṃ,
tejaḥ|kṣamā|dhī|dhṛti|saṃnatīnām,
anunnati|hrī|dyuti†|kānti|kīrti|
dākṣiṇya|medhā|bala|śuklatānām, [1]

VIRTUOUS COMPANY produces felicity, however it comes about. Those who seek felicity should therefore associate with the good. 31.1

Tradition has handed down the following story.

When he was a Bodhi·sattva, our Lord is said to have been born in the glorious lineage of the Káurava kings, a dynasty of celebrated renown. Their commitment to virtue meant that their subjects loved them with an innate devotion and their splendor made proud neighboring kings bow their heads before them.

The Bodhi·sattva's father named him Suta·soma. For he was as lovely to behold as Soma* and hundreds of virtues emanated from him like a garland of rays. Just as the moon waxes in the bright half of the month, so he grew more handsome and charming every day.

31.5 In due course he gained expertise in the Vedas, the Vedángas and the Upavédas,* and became knowledgeable in the popular arts, including their advanced levels. An object of love and respect for his people, he was eager to give effective help, showed an ever-increasing consideration for others, and possessed a disciplined sense of custodianship, all of which made him like a kinsman of the Virtues.

Morality, learning, generosity, pity, discipline,
vigor, forbearance, wisdom, bravery, humility,
modesty, shame, splendor, beauty, renown,
skill, intelligence, might and impeccability:

teṣāṃ ca teṣāṃ sa guṇ'|ôdayānām
alaṃ|kṛtānām iva yauvanena
viśuddhat"|audārya|manoharāṇāṃ
candraḥ kalānām iva saṃśrayo 'bhūt. [2]

ataś c' âinaṃ sa rājā loka|paripālana|sāmarthyād a|kṣudra|bhadra|prakṛtitvāc ca yauvarājya|vibhūtyā saṃyojayām āsa.

vidvattayā c' āsur† atīva tasya
priyāṇi dharmyāṇi su|bhāṣitāni.
ānarca pūj"|âtiśayair atas taṃ,
su|bhāṣitair enam upāgamad yaḥ. [3]

31.10 atha kadā cit sa Mahātmā kusuma|māsa|prabhāva|viracita|kisalaya|lakṣmī|mādhuryāṇi pravikasat|kusuma|manojña|prahasitāni pravitata|nava|śādvala|kutha†|sanātha|dharaṇī|talāni kamal'|ôtpala|dal'|āstīrṇa|nirmala†|salilāni bhramad|bhramara|madhukarī|gaṇ'|ôpagītāny a|nibhṛta|parabhṛta|barhi|gaṇāni mṛdu|surabhi|śiśira|sukha|pavanāni manaḥ|prasād'|ôdbhāvanāni nagar'|ôpavanāny anuvicaran anyatamad† udyāna|vanaṃ n' âti|mahatā bala|kāyena parivṛtaḥ krīḍ"|ârtham upanirjagāma.

sa tatra puṃs|kokila|nādite vane
mano|har'|ôdyāna|vimāna|bhūṣite
cacāra puṣp'|ānata|citra|pādape
priyā|sahāyaḥ su|kṛt" îva Nandane. [4]

these were his various fine virtues,
almost adorned by his youth,
and made attractive by his purity and nobility,
just as the moon combines different phases.

Due to his ability to protect the world, as well as his good and noble nature, the king conferred on the Bodhi·sattva the mighty status of heir apparent.

Because of his wise nature,
religious maxims were particularly dear to him.
He treated with exceptional honor
anyone who came to him with fine sayings.

31.10 One day, accompanied by a small group of soldiers, the Great One set out on a pleasure trip to one of the calm-inducing parks that surrounded the city. The blossoming season had decorated the gardens with lovely and delightful sprays. Blooming flowers made the parks smile captivatingly and the ground was protected by a carpet of fresh grass. Ponds of pure water were strewn with the petals of blue and white lotuses, while swarms of buzzing honey-making bees roamed around. There were flocks of noisy cuckoos* and peacocks, and a soft breeze blew, fragrant, cool and soothing.

So he roamed in that grove echoing with cuckoos,
adorned by captivating gardens and bowers,
its various trees bending under blossoms,
like one enjoying merit in Nándana with dear ladies.

gīta|svanair madhura|tūrya|rav'|ânuviddhair
nṛttaiś† ca hāva|caturair lalit'†|âṅga|hāraiḥ
strīṇāṃ mad'|ôpahṛtayā ca vilāsa|lakṣmyā
reme sa tatra vana|cārutayā tayā ca. [5]

tatra|sthaṃ c' âinam anyatamaḥ su|bhāṣit'|ākhyāyī brāhmaṇaḥ samabhijagāma. kṛt'|ôpacāra†|satkāraś ca tad|rūpa|śobh"|âpahṛta|manās tatr' ôpaviveśa. iti sa Mahā|sattvo yauvan'|ânuvṛttyā puṇya|samṛddhi|prabhāv'|ôpanataṃ krīḍā|vidhim anubhavaṃs tad|āgamanād utpanna|bahu|māna eva tasmin brāhmaṇe su|bhāṣita|śravaṇād an|avāpt'|āgamana|phale sahas" âiv' ôtpatitaṃ gīta|vāditra|svan'|ôparodhi krīḍā|prasaṅga|janita|praharṣ'|ôpahantṛ pramadā|jana|bhaya|viṣāda|jananaṃ kolāhalam upaśrutya, «jñāyatāṃ kim etad» iti s'|ādaram antaḥ|pur'|âvacarān samādideśa. ath' âsya dauvārikā bhaya|viṣāda|dīna|vadanāḥ sa|saṃbhramaṃ drutataram upetya nyavedayanta:

«eṣa sa, deva, puruṣ'|âdaḥ Kalmāṣapādaḥ Saudāsaḥ s'|âkṣād iv' Ântako nara|śata|kadana|karaṇa|paricayād rākṣas'|âdhika|krūratara|matir ati|mānuṣa|bala|vīrya|darpo rakṣaḥ|pratibhaya|raudra|mūrtir mūrtimān iva jagat|saṃtrāsa ita ev' âbhivartate.

Taking pleasure in
the beauty of the forest,
he delighted in the drunken
playful charms of the women,
in their singing punctuated by
the lovely music of instruments,
and in the skillful coquetry
and graceful moves of their dance.

While he was there, a brahmin approached him. A reciter of fine sayings, the brahmin was received respectfully and with due courtesy and sat down, captivated by the prince's beauty. Even though he was enjoying the youthful games that derived from his store of rich merit, the Great Being had great regard for the brahmin's visit. But before the brahmin could reap any reward from reciting his wise sayings, a tumultuous noise suddenly interrupted the singing and music, destroying the party's enjoyment of their indulgent play. The commotion filled the women with fear and despair and, concerned at the noise, the Great Being directed the harem supervisors to discover what had occurred. Running up to him anxiously, their faces wretched with fear and despair, the wardens informed him as follows:

"It is Sudása's son, the cannibal Kalmásha·pada, Your Majesty. Like Death incarnate, he habitually kills hundreds of men. His mind is more brutal than an ogre's and his strength, vigor and pride are superhuman. As frightful and vicious as a demon, he is coming to this very place like the Terror of the World in person.

31.15 vidrutaṃ ca nas tat|saṃtrāsa|grasta|dhairyam udbhrānta|ratha|turaga|dvirada|vyākula|yodhaṃ balam. yataḥ pratiyatno bhavatu devaḥ, prāpta|kālaṃ vā saṃpradhāryatām iti.»

atha Sutasomo jānāno 'pi tān uvāca: «bhoḥ ka eṣa Saudāso nāma?»

te taṃ procuḥ: «kim etad devasya na viditaṃ, yathā Sudāso nāma rājā babhūva? sa mṛgayā|nirgato 'śv'|âpahṛto† vana|gahanam anupraviṣṭaḥ siṃhyā sārdhaṃ saṃyogam† agamat. āpanna|sattvā ca sā siṃhī saṃvṛttā, kāl'|ântareṇa ca kumāraṃ suṣuve.† sa vana|carair gṛhītaḥ Sudāsāy' ôpanītaḥ. ‹a|putro 'ham› iti ca kṛtvā Sudāsena saṃvardhitaḥ.

pitari ca sura|puram upagate svaṃ rājyaṃ pratilebhe. sa mātṛ|doṣād āmiṣeṣv abhisaktaḥ. ‹idam idaṃ rasa|varaṃ māṃsam› iti† mānuṣaṃ māṃsam āsvādya sa† paurān eva hatvā† bhakṣayitum upacakrame. atha paurās tad|vadhāy' ôdyogaṃ cakruḥ. tato† 'sau bhītaḥ Saudāso nara|rudhira|piśita|bali|bhugbhyo bhūtebhya upaśuśrāva: ‹asmāt saṃkaṭān mukto 'haṃ rāja|kumāra|śatena vo† bhūta|yajñaṃ kariṣyām'!› îti. so 'yaṃ tasmāt saṃkaṭān muktaḥ. prasahya† c' ânena bahu|rāja†|kumār'|âpaharanaṃ kṛtam.

so 'yaṃ devam apy apahartum† āyātaḥ! śrutvā devaḥ pramāṇam iti.»

Our army has fled, its courage consumed by fear. The chariots, horses and elephants are in disarray and the troops are in turmoil. Your Majesty should employ a countermeasure or consider what needs to be done." 31.15

"Who is this son of Sudása, gentlemen?" Suta·soma asked, even though he already knew the answer.

"Does Your Majesty not know of King Sudása?" they replied. "King Sudása once went on a hunting expedition on horseback, penetrating the dense forest. There he copulated with a lioness. The lioness became pregnant and after some time gave birth to a baby boy. Some forest dwellers took the child and brought him to Sudása and, since he was childless, Sudása raised him.

When his father passed away, departing for the city of the gods, the son took over the kingship. But because of his mother's nature, he was addicted to raw meat. On tasting human flesh, he found it had an excellent flavor and so he began to murder people in his very own city so as to eat them. The people in the city then tried to kill him. Terrified, the son of Sudása made a vow to goblins that eat offerings of human flesh and blood, saying: 'If I escape this plight, I will sacrifice one hundred royal princes to you!' He escaped his plight and therefore violently kidnapped many royal princes.

This man has now come to snatch away Your Majesty too! Now that you have heard this, we will let Your Majesty be the judge."

31.20 atha† Bodhisattvaḥ pūrvam eva vidita|śīla|doṣa|vibhramaḥ Saudāsasya kāruṇyāt tac|cikitsā|vahita|matir āśaṃsamānaś c' ātmani tac|chīla|vaikṛta†|praśamana|sāmarthyaṃ priy' | ākhyāna iva ca Saudās' | âbhiyāna | nivedane prītiṃ pratisaṃvedayan niyatam ity avocat:†

«rājyāc cyute 'smin nara|māṃsa|lobhād
unmāda|vaktavya iv' â|sva|tantre
tyakta|sva|dharme hata|puṇya|kīrtau
śocyāṃ daśām ity anuvartamāne [6]

ko vikramasy' âtra mam' âvakāśa
evaṃ|gatād vā bhaya|saṃbhramasya?
a|yatna|saṃrambha|parākrameṇa
pāpmānam asya prasabhaṃ nihanmi. [7]

gatv" âpi yo nāma may" ânukampyo,
mad|gocaraṃ sa svayam abhyupetaḥ.
yuktaṃ may" ātithyam ato 'sya kartum.
evaṃ hi santo 'tithiṣu pravṛttāḥ. [8]

tad yath"|âdhikāram atr' âvahitā bhavantu bhavantaḥ.»

31.25 iti sa tān antaḥ|pur'|âvacarān anuśiṣya viṣāda|vipulatara|pāriplav'|âkṣam āgadgada|vilulita|kaṇṭhaṃ mārg'|āvaraṇa|s'|ôdyamam āśvāsana|pūrvakaṃ vinivartya yuvati|janaṃ, yatas tat kolāhalaṃ tataḥ prasasāra. dṛṣṭv" âiva ca vyāyat'|ābaddha|malina|vasana|parikaraṃ valkala|paṭṭa|viniyata|

The Bodhi·sattva already knew of the errant and morally corrupt nature of Sudása's son and, in his compassion, he desired to cure him. Since he considered that he was capable of quelling that man's moral aberration, he felt as joyful at hearing of the son of Sudása's arrival as if he had received welcome news. Resolutely addressing the men, he therefore said: 31.20

"In his greed for human flesh,
this man has fallen from royalty.
Like a vile maniac,
he has lost all self-control.
His morality is abandoned,
his merit and fame destroyed.
His condition is a lamentable one.

Is it appropriate for me to attack such a man,
or shudder in fear when he suffers this plight?
I will instead destroy his evil utterly
without effort, violence or force.

I would pity him even if he were departing,
but in fact he approaches me himself.
I should therefore offer him hospitality.
For this is how the good act toward guests.

Attend therefore to your normal duties, gentlemen."

Instructing the supervisors of the harem this way, he turned to the women who were preparing to block the path of the man-eater, their eyes agitated and wide with despair, their throats choked with distress. After he had comforted them, the prince advanced toward the noise. There he saw the son of Sudása pursuing the fleeing royal army. A loose 31.25

reṇu† | paruṣa | pralamba | vyākula | śiro | ruhaṃ prarūḍha | śmaśru|jāl'|âvanaddh'|ândhakāra|vadanaṃ roṣa|saṃrambha| vyāvṛtta | raudra | nayanam udyat' | âsi | carmāṇaṃ Saudāsaṃ vidravad anupatantaṃ rāja | balaṃ, vigata | bhaya | sādhvasaḥ samājuhāva:

«ayam aham are Sutasomaḥ! ito† nivartasva. kim anena kṛpaṇa|jana|kadana†|prasaṅgen' êti?»

tat|samāhvāna|śabd'|ākalita|darpas tu Saudāsaḥ siṃha iva tato nyavartata. nir|āvaraṇa|praharaṇam ekākinaṃ prakṛti| saumya | darśanam abhivīkṣya ca Bodhisattvam, «aham api tvām eva mṛgayām'!» îty uktvā nir|viśaṅkaḥ sahasā saṃrambha | drutataram abhisṛty' âinaṃ skandham āropya pradudrāva.

Bodhisattvo 'pi c' âinaṃ saṃrambha | darp' | ôddhata | mānasaṃ sa|saṃbhram'|ākulita|matiṃ rāja|bala|vidrāvaṇād upārūḍha|praharṣ'|âvalepaṃ s'|âbhiśaṅkam avetya, «n' âyam asy' ânuśiṣṭi|kāla» ity upekṣāṃ cakre. Saudāso 'py abhimat'| ârtha|prasiddhyā param iva lābham adhigamya pramudita| manāḥ svam āvāsa|durgaṃ praviveśa.

hata|puruṣa|kaḍevar'†|ākulaṃ,
  rudhira|samukṣita|raudra|bhū|talam,
paruṣam† iva ruṣ"|âvabhartsayat
  sphuṭa|dahanair a|śivaiḥ śivā|rutaiḥ, [9]

hanging girdle tied up his filthy clothes and a long matted beard darkly covered his face. His straggly disheveled hair was coarse with dust and held back by a strip of bark. Wielding a sword and shield, his terrifying eyes rolled with furious rage. Feeling no fear or terror, the prince challenged the son of Sudása, saying:

"Hey! I am Suta·soma! Come over here! Why are you busy killing these wretched men?"

The son of Sudása's pride was stirred by this challenge and he turned around like a lion. When he saw the Bodhi·sattva bearing his natural kind looks and standing all alone without armor or weapon, he cried out: "You are exactly what I am hunting for!" Without hesitating, he rushed up to him violently, hastened by his rage. Placing the prince on his shoulder, he then ran away.

The Bodhi·sattva, for his part, observed with some concern that the son of Sudása's mind was still whipped up with anger and pride and surging with rage. His gleeful arrogance had also been increased by routing the royal troops. The prince therefore continued to show him indifference, judging that now was not the right moment to instruct him. The son of Sudása, on the other hand, had acquired what seemed to him a very fine taking. Joyful at fulfilling his desire, he entered his impregnable home.

Heaving with the corpses of slaughtered men,
its hideous ground drenched with blood,
the dwelling seemed to make harsh angry threats
with its bright fires and ominous jackal howls.

31.30 gṛdhra|dhvāṅkṣ'|âdhyāsana|rūkṣ'|âruṇa|parṇaiḥ
kīrṇaṃ vṛkṣair n'|âika|citā|dhūma|vivarṇaiḥ,
rakṣaḥ|pret'|ānartana|bībhatsam a|śāntaṃ
dūrād dṛṣṭaṃ trāsa|jaḍaiḥ sārthika|netraiḥ. [10]

samavatārya ca tatra Bodhisattvaṃ tad|rūpa|saṃpadā vinibadhyamāna|nayanaḥ pratataṃ īkṣamāṇo† viśaśrāma. atha Bodhisattvasya su|bhāṣit'|ôpāyan'|âbhigataṃ brāhmaṇam a|kṛta|satkāraṃ tad|udyāna|nivartana†|pratīkṣam† āś"|âvabaddha|hṛdayam anusmṛtya cintā prādur|abhūt:
«kaṣṭaṃ bhoḥ!

su|bhāṣit'|ôpāyanavān āśayā dūram āgataḥ
sa maṃ hṛtam upaśrutya vipraḥ kiṃ nu kariṣyati? [11]

āśā|vighāt'|âgni|parīta|cetā
vaitānya|tīvreṇa pariśrameṇa
viniśvasiṣyaty anuśocya vā māṃ,
sva|bhāgya|nindāṃ pratipatsyate vā.» [12]

31.35 iti vicintayatas tasya Mahā|sattvasya tadīya|duḥkh'|âbhitapta|manasaḥ kāruṇya|paricayād aśrūṇi prāvartanta. atha Saudāsaḥ s'|âśru|nayanam abhivīkṣya Bodhisattvaṃ samabhiprahasann uvāca:

Covered by trees discolored
with the smoke of various pyres,
their rough dark-red leaves
inhabited by vultures and crows,
the evil dwelling terrified
with its dancing demons and ghosts,
making the eyes of travelers become
fixed with fear when seen from afar. 31.30

After placing the Bodhi·sattva on the ground, the son of Sudása took some rest and stared at the prince continuously, captivated by his beauty. The Bodhi·sattva, however, recalled the unhonored brahmin who had come with his gift of wise sayings and who would still be waiting expectantly for the prince's return to the park. Filled with anxiety, he thought:

"Alas!

That brahmin came from afar,
offering wise sayings with hope.
What will his reaction be
when he hears of my capture?

Seized by the fire of disappointment,
afflicted by fatigue bitter with despair,
he will sigh and grieve for me,
or blame his own fortune."

31.35 So deep-seated was the Great Being's compassion that he shed tears as he pondered these thoughts, his mind tormented by the brahmin's suffering. When he saw the Bodhi·sattva's eyes welling with tears, the son of Sudása laughed and addressed him, saying:

«mā tāvad bhoḥ!

dhīra ity asi vikhyātas
tais taiś ca bahubhir guṇaiḥ,
atha c' âsmad|vaśaṃ prāpya
tvam apy aśrūṇi muñcasi. [13]

su|ṣṭhu khalv idam ucyate:

āpatsu vi|phalaṃ dhairyaṃ, śoke śrutam apārthakam.
na hi tad vidyate bhūtam āhataṃ yan na kampate. [14]

31.40 iti tat satyaṃ tāvad brūhi.

prāṇān priyān atha dhanaṃ sukha|sādhanaṃ vā
bandhūn nar'|âdhipatitām atha v" ânuśocan
putra|priyaṃ pitaram aśru|mukhān sutān† vā
smṛtv" êti s'|âśru|nayanatvam upāgato 'si?» [15]

Bodhisattva uvāca:

«na prāṇān pitarau na c' âpi† tanayān
bandhūn na dārān na ca
n' âiv' āiśvarya|sukhāni saṃsmṛtavato
bāṣp'|ôdgamo 'yaṃ mama.
āśāvāṃs tu su|bhāṣitair abhigataḥ
śrutvā hṛtaṃ māṃ dvi|jo
nairāśyena sa dahyate dhruvam, iti
smṛtv" âsmi s'|âsr'|ēkṣaṇaḥ. [16]

"Don't be like that, good fellow!

Your many fine virtues
make you famed for bravery.
Yet you shed tears
on entering my home!

It is true what they say:

In calamity, bravery has no reward.
In grief, learning is useless.
For there exists no living being
who does not tremble when afflicted.

So tell me the truth. 31.40

Do you grieve for your dear life,
or for pleasure-bringing wealth,
or for your relatives,
or for lordship over men?
Do tears cover your face
from remembering
your dear son, your father,
or your weeping children?"

The Bodhi·sattva answered:

"I do not shed tears
from considering my life,
parents, children, relatives,
wives or royal pleasures.
I weep from recalling a brahmin who
came to me hopeful with wise sayings.
Surely when he hears of my capture,
he will be consumed with disappointment.

tan mām† visarjayitum arhasi, tasya yāvad
āśā|vighāta|mathitaṃ hṛdayaṃ dvi|jasya
saṃmānan'|âmbu|pariṣeka|navī|karomi
tasmāt su|bhāṣita|madhūni ca saṃbibharmi. [17]

31.45 prāpy' âivam ānṛṇyam ahaṃ dvi|jasya
gant" âsmi bhūyo 'n|ṛṇatāṃ tav' âpi
ih' āgamāt prīti|kṛta|kṣaṇābhyāṃ
nirīkṣyamāṇo bhavad|īkṣaṇābhyām. [18]

mā c' ‹âpayātavya|nayo 'yam asy'› êty
evaṃ viśaṅk'|ākula|mānaso bhūḥ.
anyo hi mārgo, nṛ|pa, mad|vidhānām,
anyādṛśas tv anya|jan'|âbhipannaḥ.» [19]

Saudāsa uvāca:

«idaṃ tvayā hy ādṛtam ucyamānaṃ
śraddheyatāṃ n' âiva kathaṃ cid eti.
ko nāma mṛtyor vadanād vimuktaḥ
svasthaḥ sthitas tat punar abhyupeyāt? [20]

dur|uttaraṃ mṛtyu|bhayaṃ vyatītya
sukhe sthitaḥ śrīmati veśmani sve
kiṃ nāma tat kāraṇam asti yena
tvaṃ mat|samīpaṃ punar abhyupeyāḥ?» [21]

31.50 Bodhisattva uvāca: «katham evaṃ mahad api mam' āgamana|kāraṇam atra|bhavān n' âvabhudhyate? nanu mayā pratijñātam† ‹āgamiṣyām'› îti? tad alaṃ māṃ khala|jana|saṃbhāvanay"† âivaṃ viśaṅkitum.† Sutasomaḥ khalv aham.

Please therefore let me go.
Sprinkling him with the water of honor,
I can revive his heart crushed by lost hope
and receive his sweet wise sayings.

After I have paid my debt to him, 31.45
I will return to pay my debt to you,
the sight of my arrival
bringing joy to your eyes.

Do not suspect that
this is a ruse to escape.
Men such as I follow a path
different from others, king."

The son of Sudása replied:

"Your earnest words
quite beggar belief.
Who would return when released
safely from the jaws of death?

If you survive death's peril,
so difficult to escape,
why return to me again
once in your cozy fine palace?"

"How can you not know my weighty reason for returning, good sir?" the Bodhi·sattva asked. "Have I not promised that I will return? You should not suspect that I am some rogue. I am Suta·soma. 31.50

lobhena mṛtyoś ca bhayena satyaṃ
satyaṃ yad eke tṛṇavat tyajanti.
satāṃ tu satyaṃ vasu jīvitaṃ ca
kṛcchre 'py atas tan na parityajanti. [22]

na jīvitaṃ yat sukham âihikaṃ vā
satyāc cyutaṃ rakṣati dur|gatibhyaḥ.
satyaṃ vijahyād iti kas tad|arthaṃ
yac c' ākaras tuṣṭi†|yaśaḥ|sukhānām. [23]

saṃdṛśyamāna|vyabhicāra|mārge tv
a|dṛṣṭa|kalyāṇa|parākrame vā
śraddheyatāṃ n' âiti śubhaṃ tathā ca
kiṃ vīkṣya śaṅkā tava mayy ap' îti? [24]

tvatto bhayaṃ yadi ca nāma mam' âbhaviṣyat,
saṅgaḥ sukheṣu karuṇā|vikalaṃ mano vā,
vikhyāta|raudra|caritaṃ nanu vīra|mānī
tvām udyata|praharaṇ'|āvaraṇo 'bhyupaiṣyam? [25]

31.55 tvat|saṃstavas tv ayam abhīpsita eva me syāt.
tasya dvi|jasya sa|phala|śramatāṃ vidhāya
eṣyāmy ahaṃ punar api svayam antikaṃ te.
n' âsmad|vidhā hi vitathāṃ giram udgiranti.» [26]

atha Saudāsas tad Bodhisattva|vacanaṃ vikatthitam† iv' āmṛṣyamāṇaś cintām āpede:

«suṣṭhu khalv ayaṃ satya|vāditayā ca dhārmikatayā ca vikatthate. tat paśyāmi tāvad asya saty'|ânurāgaṃ dharma|priyatāṃ ca. kiṃ ca tāvan mam' ânena naṣṭen' âpi syāt? asti hi me sva|bhuja|vīrya|pratāpād vaśī|kṛtaṃ śata|mātraṃ kṣatriya|kumārāṇām. tair yath"|ôpayācitaṃ bhūta|yajñaṃ kariṣyām'» îti vicintya Bodhisattvam uvāca:

True that out of greed or fear of death
some reject truth as if it were chaff.
But truth is the wealth and life of the virtuous.
They will never abandon it, even in peril.

Neither life nor worldly pleasures can protect
one from bad rebirth if one falls from truth.
Truth is a mine of satisfaction, fame and joy.
Who would sacrifice it for these other pursuits?

If a person clearly walks the path of evil,
or shows no proof of striving for good,
one cannot trust in their moral purity.
But what have you seen in me to mistrust?

If I had feared you, or lacked pity,
or had been attached to pleasures,
would I not have faced one so famed for cruelty
with sword and armor, haughty with bravery?

Perhaps I wanted to be acquainted with you. 31.55
After ensuring the brahmin's effort bears fruit,
I will return to you again of my own accord.
For men such as I do not utter falsehoods."

Irritated by the Bodhi·sattva's seeming boasts, the son of Sudása thought:

"This fellow really does brag about speaking the truth and being righteous. Well, let's see how attached he is to the truth and how fond he is of virtue. What does it matter if I lose him anyway? I already have a total of one hundred warrior princes, subdued by the mighty strength of my arms. I can use them to sacrifice to the goblins, as requested." Thinking this, he said to the Bodhi·sattva:

«tena hi gaccha. drakṣyāmas te satya|pratijñatāṃ dhārmikatāṃ ca!

gatvā kṛtvā ca tasya tvaṃ dvi|jasya yad abhīpsitam
śīghram āyāhi yāvat te citāṃ sajjī|karomy aham!» [27]

31.60 atha Bodhisattvas «tath"» êty asmai pratiśrutya sva|bhavanam abhigataḥ pratinandyamānaḥ svena janena tam āhūya brāhmaṇaṃ tasmād gāthā|catuṣṭayaṃ śuśrāva. tac chrutvā su|bhāṣit'|âbhiprasādita|manāḥ sa Mahā|sattvaḥ saṃrādhayan priya|vacana|satkāra|puraḥsaraṃ sāhasrikīṃ gāthāṃ kṛtvā samabhilaṣiten' ârthena taṃ brāhmaṇaṃ pratipūjayām āsa.

ath' âinaṃ tasya pit" â|sthān'|âtivyaya|nivāraṇ'|ôdyata|matiḥ prastāva|kram'|āgataṃ s'|ânunayam ity uvāca:

«tāta, su|bhāṣita|pratipūjane sādhu mātrāṃ jñātum arhasi. mahā|janaḥ khalu te bhartavyaḥ, kośa|saṃpad|avekṣiṇī† ca rāja|śrīḥ. ataś ca tvāṃ bravīmi:

śatena saṃpūjayituṃ su|bhāṣitaṃ
paraṃ pramāṇaṃ. na tataḥ paraṃ kṣamam.
ati|pradātur hi kiyac ciraṃ bhaved
Dhaneśvarasy' âpi dhan'|ēśvara|dyutiḥ? [28]

samartham arthaḥ paramaṃ hi sādhanaṃ,
na tad|virodhena yataś caret priyam.
nar'|âdhipaṃ śrīr na hi kośa|saṃpadā
vivarjitaṃ veśa|vadhūr iv' ēkṣate.» [29]

"Well, go then! Let's see your virtue and how true you are to your promises!

Leave and fulfill
the brahmin's desire.
And come back quickly.
I'll be preparing a pyre for you!"

31.60 "So be it," the Bodhi·sattva agreed and returned to his palace, where he was joyfully received by his people. Summoning the brahmin, the Bodhi·sattva heard him recite four verses. On hearing them, the Great Being's heart was gladdened and he pleased the brahmin with kind words and acts of honor, valuing each verse at a thousand coins and venerating him with whatever rewards he desired.

The Bodhi·sattva's father was, however, intent on restraining the prince from any excessive and inappropriate expense. When an opportunity arose to broach the topic, he politely addressed the Bodhi·sattva, saying:

"My son, it would be good if you could recognize some measure when honoring wise sayings. Your people are many and need support. A king's majesty depends on the wealth of his treasury. Let me tell you this:

To honor a wise saying with a hundred coins
already is a high reckoning. More is not fit.
Even if he is Kubéra, if he gives too much,
how long can a king's splendid riches last?*

Wealth is the chief power and means to success.
If one obstructs it, one cannot live by desire.
Like a harlot, Fortune shows
no regard for a king without riches."

31.65 Bodhisattva uvāca:

«argha|pramāṇaṃ yadi nāma kartuṃ
śakyaṃ bhaved, deva, su|bhāṣitānām,
vyaktaṃ na te vācya|pathaṃ vrajeyaṃ
tan|niṣkrayaṃ rājyam api prayacchan. [30]

śrutv" âiva yan nāma manaḥ prasādaṃ
śreyo|'nurāga|sthiratāṃ† ca yāti
prajñ"|âbhivṛddhyā† vitamaskatāṃ ca
krayyaṃ nanu syād api tat sva|māṃsaiḥ! [31]

dīpaḥ śrutaṃ moha|tamaḥ|pramāthī
caur'|ādy|a|hāryaṃ paramaṃ dhanaṃ ca
saṃmoha|śatru|vyathanāya śastraṃ
nay'|ôpadeṣṭā paramaś ca mantrī. [32]

āpad|gatasy' âpy a|vikāri mitram,
a|pīḍanī śoka|rujaś cikitsā,
balaṃ mahad doṣa|bal'|âvamardi,
paraṃ nidhānaṃ yaśasaḥ śriyaś ca. [33]

31.70 sat|saṃgame prābhṛta|śībharasya,
sabhāsu vidvaj|jana|rañjanasya,
para|pravāda|dyuti|bhāskarasya,
spardhāvatāṃ kīrti|mad'|âpahasya [34]

prasanna|netr'|ānana|varṇa|rāgair,
a|saṃstutair† apy ati|harṣa|labdhaiḥ,
saṃrādhana|vyagra|kar'|âgra|deśair
vikhyāpyamān'|âtiśaya|kramasya, [35]

The Bodhi·sattva replied: 31.65

"But if one could set a value
on wise sayings, divine king,
I would certainly not be blamed
if I gave my very kingdom to buy them.

Hearing such words calms the heart,
strengthening its love of goodness,
its darkness dispelled through increased wisdom.
One would use one's very flesh to buy them!

Knowledge is a lamp destroying dark ignorance.
Thieves and the like cannot gain this chief wealth.
A weapon for toppling the foe that is delusion,
it is our principal advisor, teaching the right way.

An unchanging friend even in calamity,
knowledge is a painless cure for grief's ills.
A mighty army to crush the forces of evil,
it is the chief receptacle of fame and glory.

Knowledge is the basis of elegant speech. 31.70
A charming gift in good company,
eloquence delights the wise in assemblies.
Shedding light on hostile doctrines,
it dispels the proud fame of rivals.

The superiority of eloquence is proclaimed
by the bright eyes and glowing faces
even of strangers thrilled with great joy,
their praise extending to their fingertips.

vispaṣṭa|hetv|artha|nidarśanasya,
vicitra|śāstr'|āgama|peśalasya,
mādhurya|saṃskāra|manoharatvād
a|kliṣṭa|mālya|prakar'|ôpamasya, [36]

vinīta|dīpta|pratibh"|ôjjvalasya,
prasahya kīrti|pratibodhanasya,
vāk|sauṣṭhavasy' âpi viśeṣa|hetur
yogāt prasann'|ârtha|gatiḥ śruta|śrīḥ. [37]

śrutvā ca vairodhika|doṣa|muktaṃ
tri|varga|mārgaṃ samupāśrayante.
śrut'|ânusāra|pratipatti|sārās
taranty a|kṛcchreṇa ca janma|dur|gam. [38]

31.75 guṇair an|ekair iti viśrutāni
prāptāny ahaṃ prābhṛtavac chrutāni
śaktaḥ kathaṃ nāma na pūjayeyam?
ājñāṃ kathaṃ vā tava laṅghayeyam? [39]

yāsyāmi Saudāsa|samīpam asmād.
artho na me rājya|pariśrameṇa
nivṛtta|śaṅkena† guṇ'|ôpamarde
labhyaś ca yo doṣa|path'|ânuvṛttyā.» [40]

ath' âinaṃ pitā snehāt samutpatita|saṃbhramaḥ s'|ādaram uvāca: «tav' âiva khalu, tāta, hit'|âvekṣiṇā may" âivam abhihitam. tad alam atra te manyu|vaśam evam† anubhavitum. dviṣantas te Saudāsa|vaśaṃ gamiṣyanti! ath' âpi pratijñātaṃ tvayā tat|samīp'|ôpagamanam, ataḥ saty'|ânurakṣī tat saṃpādayitum icchasi, tad api te n' âham anujñāsyāmi. a|pātakaṃ hi sva|prāṇa|parirakṣā|nimittaṃ guru|

By skillfully citing treatises and teachings,
eloquence reveals meaning by clear reason.
Through its captivating charm and refinement,
it resembles a garland of unwithered flowers.

Blazing with bright and controlled light,
eloquence gives direct rise to fame.
When applied, the glory of knowledge
thus provides a clear path to success.

Listeners of knowledge follow the three pursuits,*
a path free from the obstacles of vice.
By behaving in accord with knowledge,
they easily cross the perilous realm of rebirth.

Renowned this way for many virtues, 31.75
I have received these teachings like a gift.
How can I not honor them if able to?
But, then, how can I ignore your command?

I will therefore go to the son of Sudása.
I have no desire for the toil of kingship,
nor for the result of following evil
if I neglectfully violate my virtue."

Affection made the father fill with anxiety. "My son," he said with concern. "It was solely out of regard for your welfare that I spoke these words. Do not be so upset about it. Let your enemies go and submit themselves before the son of Sudása! Although you have promised to return to him, and though you wish to fulfill your vow because you cherish the truth, I will not allow it. Men who know the Vedas say that there is no offence in falsehood if it is done to save

jan'|ârthaṃ c' ân|ṛtam āhur Veda|vida† iti. tat|parihāra|śrameṇa te† ko 'rthaḥ?

artha|kāmābhyāṃ ca virodha†|dṛṣṭaṃ dharma|saṃśrayam a|nayam iti vyasanam iti ca rājñāṃ pracakṣate nīti|kuśalāḥ. tad alam anen' âsman|manas|tāpinā sv'|ârtha|nirapekṣeṇa te nirbandhena.

ath' âpy a|yaśasyaṃ, mārṣa, dharma|virodhi c' êti pratijñā|visaṃvādanam an|ucitatvān na vyavasyati te matiḥ, evam ap' îdaṃ tvad|vimokṣaṇ'|ârthaṃ samudyuktaṃ sajjam eva no hasty|aśva|ratha|patti|kāyaṃ sampannam anuraktaṃ kṛt'|âstra|śūra|puruṣam an|eka|samara|nīrājitaṃ mahan mah"|âugha|bhīmaṃ balam. tad anena parivṛtaḥ samabhigamy' âinaṃ vaśam a|vaśam† ānay' Ântaka|vaśaṃ vā prāpaya. evam a|vyartha|pratijñatā saṃpāditā syād ātma|rakṣā c' êti.»

31.80 Bodhisattva uvāca:

«n' ôtsahe, dev', ânyathā pratijñātum anyathā kartuṃ, śocyeṣu vā vyasana|paṅka|nimagneṣu narak'|âbhimukheṣu suhṛt|sva|jana†|parityakteṣv a|nātheṣu ca tad|vidheṣu prahartum.

api ca,

duṣ|karaṃ puruṣ'|âdo 'sāv
udāraṃ c' âkaron mayi,
mad|vacaḥ|pratyayād yo māṃ
vyasṛjad vaśam āgatam. [41]

one's life or to benefit elders. Why would you incur hardship by ignoring this teaching?

Experts in political science declare that it is wrong and disastrous for kings to subscribe to morality if it clearly conflicts with pragmatism or desire. So stop tormenting my heart and cease your stubborn disregard for your own welfare.

I appreciate, my son, that you cannot bring yourself to break this promise because you think it would be disreputable and immoral, and also because you are unused to such actions. But I have a huge army of elephants, horses, chariots and infantrymen, equipped and ready to rescue you, terrifying as a mighty flood. Accomplished and loyal, they are brave and skilled in weaponry. They have been consecrated by many battles.* Surrounded by these troops, approach the son of Sudása and force him against his will to submit to you or to Death. In this way you will fulfill your promise and also protect yourself."

The Bodhi·sattva replied: 31.80

"I could not bear to promise one thing but do another. Nor am I capable of harming people who are so helpless. Sinking into the mud of calamity and abandoned by their friends and relatives, they are heading for hell and deserve our pity.

Besides,

That man-eater performed
a difficult and noble deed for me.
Trusting my words, he released me,
even though I was in his power.

labdhaṃ tat|kāraṇāc c' êdaṃ mayā, tāta, su|bhāṣitam,
upakārī viśeṣeṇa so 'nukampyo mayā yataḥ. [42]

31.85 alaṃ c' âtra devasya mad|atyaya|śaṅkayā.† kā hi tasya śaktir asti mām evam abhigataṃ vihiṃsitum iti?»

evam anunīya ca Mahatmā pitaraṃ, vinivāraṇa|s'|ôdyamaṃ ca vinivartya praṇayi|janam anuraktaṃ ca bala|kāyam ekākī vigata|bhaya|dainayaḥ saty'|ânurakṣī loka|hit'|ârthaṃ Saudāsam abhivineṣyaṃs tan|niketam abhijagāma.

dūrād ev' âvalokya Saudāsas taṃ Mahā|sattvam ati|vismayād abhivṛddha|bahumāna|prasādaś cir'|âbhyāsa|virūḍha|krūratā|malina|matir api vyaktam iti cintām āpede:

«ahahahaha!

āścaryāṇāṃ bat' āścaryam!
adbhutānāṃ bat' âdbhutam!†
saty'|āudāryaṃ nṛ|pasy' êdam
ati|mānuṣa|daivatam! [43]

31.90 mṛtyu|raudra|svabhāvaṃ māṃ
vinīta|bhaya|saṃbhramaḥ
iti svayam upeto 'yaṃ.
hī dhairyaṃ! sādhu satyatā! [44]

It is because of him, father,
that I acquired these wise sayings.
In rendering this service,
he particularly deserves my compassion.

Nor should you worry that I may come to harm, divine lord. For how can he harm me if I go to him?" 31.85

Persuading his father this way, and turning away his loving friends and devoted army, despite their attempts to restrain him, the Great One set out alone for the dwelling of Sudása's son. Keeping his promise and devoid of fear or despair, he was determined to convert Kalmásha·pada for the benefit of the world.

When the son of Sudása saw the Great Being from afar, his feelings of utter amazement increased his respect and benevolence toward the prince. Although his mind was stained by a cruelty that had become rooted through long practice, he still had the following clear thought:

"Ah ha ha ha!

Wonder of wonders!
Miracle of miracles!
This prince's noble truthfulness
surpasses the human or divine!

Though I am as fierce as Death, 31.90
he returns to me of his own accord,
restraining all fear and worry.
What constancy! What veracity! How fine!

sthāne khalv asya vikhyātaṃ
satya|vāditayā yaśaḥ,
iti prāṇān sva|rājyaṃ ca
saty'|ârthaṃ yo 'yam atyajat.» [45]

atha Bodhisattvaḥ samabhigamy' âinaṃ vismaya|bahu-mān'|āvarjita|mānasam uvāca:

«prāptaṃ su|bhāṣita|dhanaṃ, pratipūjito 'rthī,
prītiṃ manaś ca gamitaṃ bhavataḥ prabhāvāt.
prāptas tad asmy ayam. aśāna yath"|ēpsitaṃ māṃ,
yajñāya vā mama paśu|vratam ādiśa tvam.» [46]

Saudāsa uvāca:

31.95 «n' âtyeti kālo mama khāditum tvāṃ.
dhūm'|ākulā tāvad iyaṃ cit" âpi
nirdhūma†|pakvaṃ piśitaṃ ca hṛdyaṃ.
śṛṇmas tad etāni su|bhāṣitāni.» [47]

Bodhisattva uvāca: «kas tav' ârtha itthaṃ|gatasya su|bhāṣita|śravanena?

imām avasthām udarasya hetoḥ
prāpto 'si saṃtyakta|ghṛṇaḥ prajāsu.
imāś ca dharmaṃ pravadanti gāthāḥ.
samety a|dharmeṇa yato na dharmaḥ. [48]

rakṣo|vikṛta|vṛttasya
saṃtyakt'|ārya†|pathasya te
n' âsti satyaṃ, kuto dharmaḥ.
kiṃ śrutena kariṣyasi?» [49]

How apt that he is renowned
widely for his truthfulness.
For he sacrificed his kingdom
and life for the sake of truth."

Approaching the son of Sudása, who was moved by wonder and respect, the Bodhi·sattva then said:

"Due to you, I attained valuable wise sayings,
honored a supplicant and gained a joyful mind.
So here I am, returned. Eat me if you like.
Or assign me as a victim for your sacrifice!"

The son of Sudása replied:

"It is not yet time for me to eat you. 31.95
The pyre still swirls with smoke.
Flesh is only tasty if cooked on a smokeless fire.
Let me hear these wise sayings instead."

"Why does a man such as you need to hear wise sayings?" the Bodhi·sattva replied.

"Casting aside compassion for your people,
you acquired this state because of your belly.
But these verses proclaim virtue,
and virtue does not fit well with vice.

You follow the warped life of a demon,
abandoning the path of noble men.
There is no truth in you, let alone virtue.
What use could you make of knowledge?"

atha Saudāsas tām avasādanām a|mṛṣyamāṇaḥ pratyuvāca:

31.100 «mā tāvad bhoḥ!

ko 'sau nṛ|paḥ, kathaya, yo na samudyat'|âstraḥ
krīḍā|vane vana|mṛgī|dayitān nihanti?
tadvan nihanmi manujān yadi vṛtti|hetor,
ādharmikaḥ kila tato 'smi, na te mṛga|ghnāḥ!» [50]

Bodhisattva uvāca:

«dharme sthitā na khalu te 'pi namanti yeṣāṃ
bhīta|druteṣv api mṛgeṣu śar'|âsanāni.
tebhyo 'pi nindyatama eva nar'|âśanas tu.
jāty|ucchritā hi puruṣā na ca bhakṣaṇīyāḥ.» [51]

atha Saudāsaḥ parikarkaś'|âkṣaram apy abhidhīyamāno Bodhisattvena tan|maitrī|guṇa|prabhāvād abhibhūta|raudra|svabhāvaḥ sukhāyamāna eva tad|vacanam abhiprahasann uvāca:

31.105 «bhoḥ Sutasoma!

mukto mayā nāma sametya geham
samantato rāja†|vibhūti|ramyam
yan mat|samīpaṃ punar āgatas tvaṃ,
na nīti|mārge kuśalo 'si tasmāt.» [52]

Bodhisattva uvāca: «n' âitad asti. aham eva tu kuśalo nīti|mārge, yad enaṃ na pratipattum icchāmi.

yan† nāma pratipannasya
dharmād aikāntikī cyutiḥ
na tu prasiddhiḥ saukhyasya,
tatra kiṃ nāma kauśalam? [53]

Unable to endure this criticism, the son of Sudása replied:
"Not so, sir! 31.100

Tell me the king who does not raise his bow
to kill a deer's mate in a pleasure park?
Likewise I kill men for my livelihood.
But it seems I am wrong but deer-killers are not!"

The Bodhi·sattva answered:

"Those who bend bows to shoot deer
fleeing in terror are also not right.
But much more culpable is the man-eater.
It is wrong to eat men due to their high birth."

Although addressed with these harsh words, the son of Sudása's vicious nature was suppressed by the Bodhi·sattva's friendliness and he remained calm. Laughing at the Bodhi·sattva's words, he said:
"My good fellow Suta·soma! 31.105

Released by me, you went home,
delightful royal riches surrounding you.
But now you have come back!
You are hardly skilled in pragmatism!"

"That is not so," the Bodhi·sattva replied. "In fact I am very skilled in the path of pragmatism, which is why I do not wish to practice it.

Why be skilled in something
if its practice only brings
a complete fall from virtue
and failure to gain happiness?

kiṃ ca bhūyaḥ,

31.110 ye nīti|mārga|pratipatti|dhīrāḥ,
prāyeṇa te pretya patanty apāyān.
apāsya jihmān iti nīti|mārgān
saty'|ânurakṣī punar āgato 'smi. [54]

ataś ca nītau kuśalo 'ham eva,
tyaktv" ân|ṛtaṃ yo 'bhirato 'smi satye.
na tat su|nītaṃ hi vadanti taj|jñā
yan n' ânubadhnanti yaśaḥ|sukh'|ârthāḥ.» [55]

Saudāsa uvāca:

«prāṇān priyān sva|janam aśru|mukhaṃ ca hitvā
rājy'|āśrayāṇi ca sukhāni mano|harāṇi,
kām artha|siddhim anupaśyasi satya|vākye
tad|rakṣaṇ'|ârtham iti† māṃ yad upāgato 'si?» [56]

Bodhisattva uvāca: «bahavaḥ satya|vacan'|āśrayā guṇ'|âtiśayāḥ. saṃkṣepatas† tu śrūyatām:

31.115 mālya|śriyaṃ hṛdyatay" âtiśete,
sarvān rasān svādutayā ca satyam,
śramād ṛte puṇya|guṇa|prasiddhyā
tapāṃsi tīrth'|âbhigama|śramāṃś ca. [57]

kīrter jagad|vyāpti|kṛta|kṣaṇāyā
mārgas tri|lok'|ākramaṇāya satyam,
dvāraṃ praveśāya sur'|ālayasya,
saṃsāra|dur|g'|ôttaraṇāya setuḥ.» [58]

Moreover,

31.110 Staunch followers of pragmatism
usually fall into a bad rebirth at death.*
So I have kept my promise and returned,
rejecting the path of pragmatism as crooked.

And in fact I show my skill in pragmatism
by rejecting lies and delighting in truth.
For experts say a good pragmatic action
brings fame, happiness and success."

The son of Sudása answered:

"You have sacrificed your dear life,
tearful kinsmen and attractive royal pleasures.
What benefit do you see in speaking the truth,
to protect which you have returned to me?"

"There are many excellent virtues that come from speaking the truth," the Bodhi·sattva replied. "Listen to a brief summary.

31.115 Truth surpasses beautiful garlands in charm
and every kind of flavor in relish.
Through its painless attainment of merit,
it exceeds austerities and the toil of visiting sacred sites.

Truth is the path by which fame covers
the three worlds, impatient to pervade mankind.
Truth is the door for entering the gods' abode,
the bridge for crossing samsara's perilous flood."

atha Saudāsaḥ «sādhu! yuktam!» ity abhipraṇamy' âinaṃ sa|vismayam abhivīkṣamāṇaḥ punar uvāca:

«anye narā mad|vaśa|gā bhavanti
dainy'|ârpaṇāt trāsa|vilupta|dhairyāḥ.
saṃtyajyase tvaṃ tu na dhairya|lakṣmyā.
manye na te mṛtyu|bhayaṃ nar'|êndra.» [59]

Bodhisattva uvāca:

31.120 «mahat" âpi prayatnena yac chakyaṃ n' âtivartitum
pratīkār'|â|samarthena bhaya|klaibyena tatra kim? [60]

iti pariganita|loka|sthitayo 'pi tu puruṣāḥ†

pāpa|prasaṅgād anutapyamānāḥ
śubheṣu karmasv a|kṛta|śramāś ca
āśaṅkamānāḥ† para|loka|duḥkhaṃ
martavya|saṃtrāsa|jaḍā bhavanti. [61]

tad eva kartuṃ na tu saṃsmarāmi
bhaved yato me manaso 'nutāpaḥ.
sātmī|kṛtaṃ karma ca śuklam, asmād
dharme sthitaḥ† ko maraṇād bibhīyāt? [62]

na ca smarāmy arthi|jan'|ôpayānaṃ
yan na praharṣāya mam' ârthināṃ vā.
iti pradānaiḥ samavāpta|tuṣṭir
dharme sthitaḥ ko maraṇād bibhīyāt? [63]

"Excellent! How right!" the son of Sudása exclaimed, bowing before the Bodhi·sattva. Gazing at him in wonder, he then addressed the Bodhi·sattva once more, saying:

"Fear makes the others in my power
lose all their bravery from despair.
But you never give up your glorious fortitude.
I believe you do not fear death, king of men."

The Bodhi·sattva said:

31.120 "It is impossible to avoid death,
however much one tries.
What is the use of cowardice
and other impotent remedies?

But even though they understand the condition of the world,
humans are numbed by the fear they must die,
tormented by remorse for their evil addictions.
Lacking perseverance in virtuous acts,
they worry about suffering in the next world.

But I do not recall committing a deed
for which I should feel remorse.
Pure conduct has become ingrained in me.
Who, established in virtue, would fear death?

I do not recall a petitioner's visit that
did not delight both me and them.
When satisfied this way by giving gifts,
who, established in virtue, would fear death?

31.125 ciraṃ vicinty' âpi ca n' âiva pāpe
manaḥ|pada|nyāsam api smarāmi.
viśodhita|svarga|patho 'ham evaṃ
mṛtyoḥ kim|arthaṃ bhayam abhyupeyām? [64]

vipreṣu bandhuṣu suhṛtsu samāśriteṣu
dīne jane yatiṣu c' āśrama|bhūṣaṇeṣu
nyastaṃ mayā bahu dhanaṃ dadatā yath"|ârhaṃ;
kṛtyaṃ ca yasya yad abhūt, tad akāri tasya. [65]

śrīmanti kīrtana|śatāni niveśitāni
sattr'|âjir'|āśramapadāni sabhāḥ prapāś ca.
mṛtyor na me bhayam atas tad|avāpta|tuṣṭer.
yajñāya tat samupakalpaya bhauṅkṣva vā mām!» [66]

tad upaśrutya Saudāsaḥ prasād' | âśru | vyāpta | nayanaḥ samudbhidyamāna|rom'|âñca|piṭako vismṛta|pāpa|svabhāva| tāmisraḥ sa|bahumānam avekṣya Bodhisattvam uvāca: «śāntaṃ pāpam!

31.130 adyād viṣaṃ sa khalu Hālahalaṃ prajānann
āśīviṣaṃ prakupitaṃ jvalad|āyasaṃ vā
mūrdh" âpi tasya śatadhā hṛdayaṃ ca yāyād,
yas tvad|vidhasya, nṛpa|puṅgava, pāpam icchet. [67]

tad arhati bhavāṃs tāny api me su | bhāṣitāni vaktum. anena hi te vacana|kusuma|varṣeṇ' âbhiprasādita|manasaḥ suṣṭhutaram abhivṛddhaṃ† teṣu me kautūhalam. api ca bhoḥ,

Even after long reflection,
I cannot recall ever bending toward evil.
My path to heaven has been cleared.
Why would I fear death?

31.125

I have given great wealth to brahmins,
relatives, friends, dependents, the wretched,
ascetics adorning hermitages, each as is due.
For all of them I did what was required.

I have had hundreds of monuments built:
hospitals, courtyards, hermitages, halls, watertanks.*
Content with this achievement, I do not fear death.
So prepare me for sacrifice, or eat me instead!"

When the son of Sudása heard these words, his eyes filled with tears of devotion. Breaking out in goose pimples, his hair bristled and the darkness of his wicked nature vanished into oblivion. Gazing at the Bodhi·sattva reverently, he said:

"Evil be pacified!

31.130

Whoever wishes evil on a man
like you, bull among kings,
may they knowingly eat
the poison Hálahala,
may they consume burning iron
or an enraged venomous snake,
may their head and heart
split into a hundred pieces!

Now please tell me the wise sayings. For, gladdened by the shower of your flower-like words, I feel even more curious to hear them. Furthermore, good sir,

dṛṣṭv" ātma|carita†|cchāyā|
vairūpyaṃ dharma|darpaṇe
api nām' āgat'|āvegaṃ
syān me dharm'|ôtsukaṃ manaḥ.» [68]

ath' âinaṃ Bodhisattvaḥ patrī|kṛt'|āśayaṃ dharma|śravaṇa|pravaṇa|mānasam avety' ôvāca:

«tena hi dharm'|ârthinā tad|anurūpa|samudācāra|sauṣṭhavena dharmaḥ śrotuṃ yuktaḥ.† paśya:

31.135 nīcaistar'|āsana|sthānād
vibodhya vinaya|śriyam,
prīty|arpitābhyāṃ cakṣurbhyāṃ
vāṅ|madhv āsvādayann iva, [69]

gaurav'|āvarjit'|âik'|âgra|
prasann'|âmala|mānasaḥ
sat|kṛtya dharmaṃ śṛṇuyād
bhiṣag|vākyam iv' āturaḥ.» [70]

atha Saudāsaḥ sven' ôttarīyeṇa samāstīry' ôccaistaraṃ śilā|talaṃ tatra c' âdhiropya Bodhisattvaṃ svayam an|āstaritāyām upaviśya bhūmau Bodhisattvasya purastāt tad†|ānan'|ôdvīkṣaṇa|vyāpṛta|nirīkṣaṇas taṃ Mahā|sattvam uvāca: «brūh' îdānīṃ, mārṣ'» êti. atha Bodhisattvo nav'|âmbhodhara|ninada|madhura|gambhīreṇ'† āpūrayann iva tad vanaṃ vyāpinā svareṇ' ôvāca:

«yad|ṛcchay" âpy upanataṃ†
sakṛt saj|jana|saṃgatam
bhavaty a|calam aty|antaṃ,
n' âbhyāsa|kramam īkṣate.» [71]

Now that I see my hideous conduct
reflected in the mirror of virtue,
I may feel a strong impulse
to yearn for morality."

The Bodhi·sattva realized that the son of Sudása had become a suitable vessel for instruction and that his mind had become inclined toward hearing the Teaching and so he said:

"A person who desires the Teaching should listen to it with proper deportment. Look here:

31.135

Reveal your fine modesty
by taking a lower seat,
as if relishing the honey-like words
with your eyes filled with joy.

With a pure and calm mind,
intent and moved by respect,
listen to the Teaching reverently
like a sick man listens to a doctor."

The son of Sudása then draped his cloak over a stone slab and, helping the Bodhi·sattva onto this higher seat, he sat down before him on the uncovered ground. Gazing earnestly up at his face, he then asked the Great Being to speak. As if filling the forest with his penetrating voice, deep and delightful like the rumbling of a fresh raincloud, the Bodhi·sattva then spoke:

"Even randomly meeting
a virtuous person just once
creates something firm and enduring,
requiring no constant attention."

tad upaśrutya Saudāsaḥ «sādhu! sādhv!» iti sa|śiraḥ|prakamp'|âṅgulī|vikṣepaṃ† saṃrādhya† Bodhisattvam uvāca: «tatas tataḥ?» atha Bodhisattvo dvitīyāṃ gāthām udājahāra:

31.140 «na saj|janād dūra|caraḥ kva cid bhaved.
bhajeta sādhūn vinaya|kram'|ânugaḥ.
spṛśanty a|yatnena hi tat|samīpa|gaṃ
visarpiṇas tad|guṇa|puṣpa|reṇavaḥ.» [72]

Saudāsa uvāca:

«su|bhāṣitāny arcayatā,
sādho, sarv'|ātmanā tvayā
sthāne khalu niyukto 'rthaḥ!
sthāne n' âvekṣitaḥ śramaḥ. [73]

tatas tataḥ?»
Bodhisattva uvāca:

31.145 «rathā nṛ|pāṇāṃ maṇi|hema|bhūṣaṇā
vrajanti dehāś ca jarā|virūpatām.
satāṃ tu dharmaṃ na jar" âtivartate.†
sthir'|ânurāgā hi guṇeṣu sādhavaḥ.» [74]

Saudāsa uvāca:† «amṛta|varṣaṃ khalv idam! aho samtarpitāḥ smaḥ! tatas tataḥ?»
Bodhisattva uvāca:

«nabhaś ca dūre vasudhā|talāc ca,
pārād a|pāraṃ† ca mah"|ârṇavasya,
ast'|âcal'|êndrād udayas, tato 'pi
dharmaḥ satāṃ dūratare '|satāṃ ca.» [75]

"Excellent! Excellent!" the son of Sudása exclaimed when he heard these words. Rocking his head in approval and making flourishing gestures with his hands, he then said to the Bodhi·sattva: "And next? And next?" Whereupon the Bodhi·sattva uttered the second verse:

"Never roam far from virtuous people. 31.140
Modest in conduct, frequent the good.
For their flower-like virtues spread pollen
which easily touches those nearby."

The son of Sudása replied:

"How right to use your wealth
to honor these sayings, virtuous prince,
dedicating yourself entirely,
without regard for hardship.

And next? And next?"

The Bodhi·sattva said:

"Royal chariots, adorned with gems and gold, 31.145
decay with old age just like bodies.
But age cannot surpass the merit of the good.
For good men have a strong love of virtue."*

"This is a veritable shower of ambrosia! Oh! How content I feel! And next? And next?" the son of Sudása exclaimed.

The Bodhi·sattva said:

"However far the sky is from the earth,
or the ocean's near shore from its far shore,
or the rising of the sun from Mount Sunset,
the morality of the good is further from the bad."

atha Saudāsaḥ prasāda|vismayābhyām āvarjita|prema|bahumāno Bodhisattvam uvāca:

31.150 «citr'|âbhidhān'|âtiśay'|ôjjval'|ârthā
gāthās tvad etā madhurā niśamya
ānanditas tat|pratipūjan'|ârthaṃ
varān ahaṃ te caturo dadāmi. [76]

tad vṛṇīṣva yad yan matto 'bhikāṅkṣas' îti.»
ath' âinaṃ Bodhisattvaḥ sa|vismaya|bahumāna uvāca:
«kas tvaṃ vara|pradānasya?

yasy' âsti n' ātmany api te prabhutvam
a|kārya|saṃrāga|parājitasya,
sa tvaṃ varaṃ dāsyasi kaṃ parasmai
śubha|pravṛtter apavṛtta|bhāvaḥ. [77]

31.155 ahaṃ ca deh' îti varaṃ vadeyam
manaś ca ditsā|śithilaṃ tava syāt.
tam atyayaṃ kaḥ sa|ghṛṇo 'bhyupeyād?
etāvad ev' âlam alaṃ yato naḥ.» [78]

atha Saudāsaḥ kiṃ cid vrīḍ"|âvanata|vadano Bodhisattvam uvāca: «alam atra|bhavato mām evaṃ viśaṅkitum.

prāṇān api parityajya
dāsyāmy etān† ahaṃ varān.
visrabdhaṃ tad vṛṇīṣva tvaṃ
yad yad icchasi, bhūmi|pa.» [79]

Feeling a mixture of affection and respect as well as devotion and wonder, the son of Sudása addressed the Bodhi·sattva, saying:

"The meaning of these delightful verses
blaze brightly with beautiful expression.
Filled with joy I will give you four boons
as a way of showing my reverence.

31.150

Please choose the boons you desire from me."

Feeling both surprise and admiration, the Bodhi·sattva replied:

"Who are you to give boons?

Conquered by your passion for evil,
you do not even have power over yourself.
What boon can you give to another,
removed as you are from moral conduct?

I might ask you for a boon that
your heart would be reluctant to grant.
What man of pity would risk such calamity?
You've done enough, more than enough for me."

31.155

His face lowered somewhat with shame, the son of Sudása then answered the Bodhi·sattva: "Do not hold such suspicions against me, good sir.

I will give you these boons
if it means sacrificing my life.
Choose what you desire
with confidence, lord of the earth."

Bodhisattva uvāca: «tena hi,

satya|vrato bhava. vivarjaya† sattva|hiṃsāṃ.
bandī|kṛtaṃ janam a|śeṣam imaṃ vimuñca.
adyā na c' âiva, nara|vīra, manuṣya|māṃsam.
etān varān an|avarāṃś caturaḥ prayaccha!» [80]

31.160 Saudāsa uvāca:

«dadāmi pūrvān bhavate varāṃs trīn;
anyaṃ caturthaṃ tu varaṃ vṛṇīṣva.
avaiṣi kiṃ na tvam idaṃ, yath" âham
īśo virantuṃ na manuṣya|māṃsāt?» [81]

Bodhisattva uvāca: «hanta! tad ev' âitat† saṃvṛttam! nan' ûktaṃ mayā: ‹kas tvaṃ vara|pradānasy'?› êti. api ca bhoḥ,

satya|vratatvaṃ ca kathaṃ syād a|hiṃsakatā ca te
a|parityajato, rājan, manuṣya|piśit'|âśitām? [82]

nan' ûktaṃ bhavatā pūrvaṃ dāsyāmy etān ahaṃ varān
prāṇān api parityajya? tad idaṃ jāyate 'nyathā.* [83]

31.165 a|hiṃsakatvaṃ ca kuto
māṃs'|ârthaṃ te ghnato narān?
saty evaṃ katame dattā
bhavatā syur varās trayaḥ?» [84]

"Well then," the Bodhi·sattva said:

"Take a vow of truth. Stop harming beings.
Release every one of your prisoners.
Cease eating human flesh, hero of men.
Grant me these four lofty boons!"

The son of Sudása replied: 31.160

"I grant you the first three boons,
but please choose another fourth.
Do you not understand that
I cannot desist from human meat?"

"Ha! It has turned out just as I said!" the Bodhi·sattva exclaimed. "Did I not tell you: 'Who are you to give boons?' What's more, sir,

How can you take a vow
to speak truth and not injure others,
if you are unwilling to renounce
eating human flesh, king?

Did you not say earlier that
you would grant these boons
if it meant sacrificing your life?
But things have turned out differently.

How can you stop harming others 31.165
if you kill men for their flesh?
In that case, what is the value
of the three boons you gave me?"

Saudāsa uvāca:

«tyaktvā rājyaṃ vane kleśo
yasya hetor dhṛto† mayā,
hato dharmaḥ, kṣatā kīrtis,
tyakṣyāmi tad ahaṃ katham?» [85]

Bodhisattva uvāca: «ata eva tad bhavāṃs tyaktum arhati.

dharmād arthāt sukhāt kīrter
bhraṣṭo yasya kṛte bhavān
an|arth'|āyatanaṃ tādṛk
kathaṃ na tyaktum arhasi? [86]

31.170 datt'|ânuśayitā c' êyam an|audārya|hate jane.
nīcatā sā kathaṃ nāma tvām apy abhibhaved iti? [87]

tad alaṃ te pāpmānam ev' ânubhrāmitum. avaboddhum arhasy ātmānam. Saudāsaḥ khalv atra|bhavān.

vaidy'|ēkṣitāni kuśalair upakalpitāni
grāmyāṇy anūpa|jala|jāny atha jāṅgalāni
māṃsāni santi. kuru tair hṛdayasya tuṣṭiṃ.
nind"|āvahād virama sādhu manuṣya|māṃsāt. [88]

The son of Sudása answered:

"How can I give up the thing
for which I renounced my kingdom,
sustained hardship in the forest,
destroyed virtue and crushed my fame?"

"That is exactly the reason why you should give it up," the Bodhi·sattva said.

"How could you not give up
the unbeneficial state
for which you fell from morality,
success, happiness and fame?

31.170 Only people afflicted with miserliness
regret a gift they have given.
How can that base quality
overtake a man such as you?

Cease your aimless wandering after evil. You should become aware of yourself. For you are, in fact, the son of Sudása.

There are meats and fish,
domestic and wild,
tested by physicians,
prepared by expert cooks.
Let your heart be
satisfied by them.
Cease the deplorable practice
of consuming human flesh.

tūrya|svanān sa|jala|toyada|nāda|dhīrān
gīta|svanaṃ ca niśi rājya|sukhaṃ ca tat tat
bandhūn sutān parijanaṃ ca mano|'nukūlaṃ
hitvā kathaṃ nu ramase 'tra vane vivikte? [89]

cittasya n' ârhasi, nar'|êndra, vaśena gantuṃ.
dharm'|ârthayor an|uparodha|pathaṃ bhajasva.
eko nṛ|pān yudhi vijitya samasta|sainyān
mā citta|vigraha|vidhau parikātaro bhūḥ! [90]

31.175 lokaḥ paro 'pi, manuj'|âdhipa, nanv avekṣyas?
tasmāt priyaṃ yad a|hitaṃ ca, na tan niṣevyam.
yat syāt tu kīrty|an|uparodhi manojña|mārgaṃ,
tad vi|priyaṃ sad api bheṣajavad bhajasva.» [91]

atha Saudāsaḥ prasād'|âśru|vyāpta|nayano gadgadāya-māna|kaṇṭhaḥ samabhisṛty' âiva Bodhisattvaṃ pādayoḥ saṃpariṣvajy' ôvāca:

How can you delight
in the secluded forest,
abandoning your relatives,
children and pleasant entourage,
leaving the music of instruments,
soft as rumbling rainclouds,
the sound of singing at night
and all your royal pleasures?

Do not be controlled
by your emotions, king.
Follow a path that conflicts
with neither morality nor profit.
You alone have conquered kings
and their entire armies in war.
Do not now be a coward
in battling your emotions!

Have you no regard
for the next world, king?
It is the reason not to pursue evil,
however much you may desire it.
Pursue instead, as if it were medicine,
a goal in harmony with fame
and whose path is attractive,
even though you may not like it."

31.175

The son of Sudása's eyes filled with tears of devotion. With a choked throat, he went straight up to the Bodhi·sattva and embraced his feet, saying:

«guṇa|kusuma|rajobhiḥ puṇya|gandhaiḥ samantāj
jagad idam avakīrṇaṃ kāraṇe tvad|yaśobhiḥ.
iti vicarati pāpe mṛtyu|dūt'|ôgra|vṛttau
tvam iva hi ka† iv' ânyaḥ s'|ânukampo mayi syāt? [92]

śāstā guruś ca mama daivatam eva ca tvaṃ!
mūrdhnā vacāṃsy aham amūni tav' ârcayāmi.
bhokṣye na c' âiva, Sutasoma, manuṣya|māṃsaṃ.
yan māṃ yathā vadasi, tac ca tathā kariṣye. [93]

nṛp'|ātmajā yajña|nimittam āhṛtā
mayā ca ye bandhana|kheda|pīḍitāḥ
hata|tviṣaḥ śoka|parīta|mānasās,
tad ehi, muñcāva sah' âiva tān api!» [94]

31.180 atha Bodhisattvas tath" êty asmai pratiśrutya yatra te nṛpati†|sutās ten' âvaruddhās tatr'† âbhijagāma. dṛṣṭv" âiva ca te nṛpati†|sutāḥ Sutasomaṃ «hanta! muktā vayam!» iti paraṃ harṣam upajagmuḥ.

virejire te Sutasoma|darśanān
nar'|êndra|putrāḥ sphuṭa|hāsa|kāntayaḥ,
śaran|mukhe candra|kar'|ôpabṛṃhitā
vijṛmbhamāṇāḥ kumud'|ākarā iva. [95]

ath' âinān abhigamya Bodhisattvaḥ samāśvāsayan priya|vacana|puraḥsaraṃ ca pratisaṃmodya Saudāsasy' â|drohāya śapathaṃ kārayitvā bandhanād vimucya sārdhaṃ Saudāsena taiś ca nṛ|pati|putrair anugamyamānaḥ svaṃ rājyam upetya

"How right that the world is
pervaded everywhere by your fame,
by the pollen of your flowery virtues
and the fragrance of your merit.
For who else but you
would feel pity for me,
a wandering criminal,
vicious as Death's messenger?

You are my teacher, guru and divinity!
I honor your words with bowed head.
I'll never again eat human flesh, Suta·soma.
I will do whatever you tell me.

The princes I brought here to be sacrificed,
men tormented by the anguish of captivity,
their splendor destroyed, stricken with grief:
come! Let us release them together!"

The Bodhi·sattva agreed and went over to where the princes were imprisoned. As soon as they saw Suta·soma, the princes were filled with great joy and exclaimed: "Hurrah! We have been freed!" 31.180

At the sight of Suta·soma,
the princes burst into delightful laughter,
gleaming like heaps of white lilies opening
at autumn's start when aroused by moonrays.

Approaching them, the Bodhi·sattva comforted the princes and returned their greetings, speaking to them with friendly words. After he had made them swear not to harm the son of Sudása, he and Sudása's son released them from

yath" | ârha | kṛta | satkārāṃs† tān rāja | putrān Saudāsaṃ ca sveṣu sveṣu rājyeṣu pratiṣṭhāpayām āsa.

tad evaṃ, śreyaḥ samādhatte yathā tath" âpy upanataḥ sat | saṃgama, iti śreyo | 'rthinā saj | jan' | âpāśrayeṇa† bhavitavyam.

«evam a | saṃstuta | suhṛt pūrva | janmasv apy upakāra | paratvād Buddho Bhagavān» iti Tathāgata | varṇe 'pi vācyam. «evaṃ sad | dharma | śravaṇam doṣ' | âpacayāya guṇa | samādhānāya ca bhavat'» îti sad | dharma | śravaṇa | varṇe† 'pi vācyam. śruta | praśaṃsāyām api vācyam: «evam an | ek' | ânuśaṃsaṃ śrutam» iti. satya | kathāyām api vācyam: «evaṃ saj | jan' | êṣṭaṃ puṇya | kīrty | ākara | bhūtaṃ† satya | vacanam» ity, «evaṃ sva | prāṇa | sukh' | āiśvarya | nirapekṣāḥ satyam anurakṣanti sat | puruṣā» iti satya | praśaṃsāyām apy upaneyaṃ. karuṇā|varṇe c' êti.†

their bonds. The Bodhi·sattva then returned to his kingdom, followed by the princes. After he had duly honored them, he re-established the princes and the son of Sudása in their respective kingdoms.

In this way, virtuous company produces felicity, however it comes about. Those who seek felicity should therefore associate with the good.

One should also narrate this story when praising the Tatha·gata, saying, "In this way, the Lord Buddha was so devoted to helping others that he was a friend to strangers even in his previous births." And when praising listening to the Good Teaching, one should narrate this story, saying, "In this way, listening to the Good Teaching results in a decrease in vice and the attainment of virtue." And one should also narrate it when praising knowledge, saying, "In this way, knowledge has several benefits." And it should also be narrated when discussing truth, saying, "In this way, the virtuous prize truthful speech as a treasure of merit and fame." And it should be cited when praising truth, saying, "In this way, good people protect the truth, disregarding their life, pleasures and kingship." And similarly when praising compassion.

AYOGṚHAJĀTAKAM

STORY 32

THE BIRTH-STORY OF AYO·GRIHA*

32.1 RĀJA|LAKṢMĪR API śreyo|mārgaṃ n' āvṛṇoti saṃvigna|manasām† iti saṃvega|paricayaḥ kāryaḥ.

tad|yath" ânuśrūyate.

Bodhisattva|bhūtaḥ kil' âyaṃ Bhagavān vyādhi|jarā|maraṇa|priya|viprayog'|ādi|vyasana|śat'|ôpanipāta|duḥkhitam† a|nātham a|trāṇam a|pariṇāyakaṃ lokam avekṣya karuṇayā samutsāhyamānas tat|paritrāṇa|vyavasita|matir ati|sādhu|svabhāvas, tat tat saṃpādayamāno vimukhasy' â|saṃstutasy' âpi ca lokasya hitaṃ sukha|viśeṣaṃ ca,

kadā cid anyatamasmin rāja|kule praj"|ânurāga|saumukhyād a|skhalit'|âbhivṛddhayā† ca samṛddhyā samānata|dṛpta|sāmantatayā† c' âbhivyajyamāna|mahā|bhāgye vinaya|ślāghini janma pratilebhe. sa jāyamāna eva tad rāja|kulaṃ tat|samāna|sukha|duḥkhaṃ ca pura|varaṃ paray" âbhyudaya|śriyā saṃyojayām āsa.

32.5 pratigraha|vyākula|tuṣṭa|vipraṃ
mad'|ôddhat'|âbhyujjvala|veṣa|bhṛtyam
an|eka|tūrya|svana|pūrṇa|kuñjam†
ānanda|nṛtt'|â|naya|vṛtta|bhāvam [1]

saṃsakta|gīta|drava|hāsa|nādaṃ
paras|par'|āśleṣa|vivṛddha†|harṣam,
naraiḥ priy'|ākhyānaka|dāna|tuṣṭair
āśāsyamān'|âbhyudayaṃ nṛ|pasya, [2]

For those who have been shaken by spiritual alarm,* not even the splendor of kingship can conceal the path to felicity. One should therefore intimately familiarize oneself with such spiritual realization. 32.1

Tradition has handed down the following story.

When our Lord was a Bodhi·sattva, he is said to have realized that the world was full of suffering. Afflicted by disease, old age, death, separation from loved ones and hundreds of other painful calamities, it had no protector, savior or guide. Driven by his compassion and extremely virtuous by nature, the Bodhi·sattva therefore set his heart on saving the world by creating well-being and exceptional happiness for people, even if they were enemies or strangers.

On one occasion he took his birth in a royal family. Famed for its disciplined conduct, the family's illustrious nature was obvious from the earnest devotion of its subjects, its ever-increasing wealth and the submissive attitude of proud neighboring kings. The mere event of the Bodhi·sattva's birth graced both the royal family and the city—companions in joy and sorrow—with festivities of magnificent splendor.

Brahmins were gratified by abundant gifts. 32.5
Servants in bright clothes were elated with pride.
Various instruments filled the bowers with music.
Unruly behavior mingled with dances of joy.

There was constant song, sport, laughter and noise.
Mutual embraces heightened feelings of joy
as people made wishes for the prince's welfare,
delighted by the gift of the good news.

vighaṭṭita†|dvāra|vimukta|bandhanaṃ
samucchrit'|âgrya†|dhvaja|citra|catvaram
vicūrṇa|puṣp'|āsava|sikta|bhū|talaṃ
babhāra ramyāṃ puram utsava|śriyam. [3]

mahā|gṛhebhyaḥ pravikīryamāṇair
hiraṇya|vastr'|ābharaṇ'|ādi|varṣaiḥ
lokaṃ tadā vyāptum iv' ôdyatā śrīr
unmatta|Gaṅgā|lalitaṃ cakāra. [4]

tena ca samayena tasya rājño jātā jātāḥ kumārā mriyante sma. sa taṃ vidhim a|mānuṣa|kṛtam iti manyamānas tasya tanayasya rakṣ"|ârthaṃ maṇi|kāñcana|rajata|bhakti|citre śrīmati sarv'|āyase prasūti|bhavane bhūta|vidyā|paridṛṣṭena Veda|vihitena ca krameṇa vihita|rakṣo|ghna|pratīkāre samucitaiś ca kautuka|maṅgalaiḥ kṛta|svastyayana|parigrahe jāta|karm'|ādi|saṃskāra|vidhiṃ saṃvardhanaṃ ca kārayām āsa.

32.10 tam api ca Mahā|sattvaṃ sattva|saṃpatteḥ puṇy'|ôpacaya|prabhāvāt su|saṃvihitatvāc ca rakṣāyā n' â|mānuṣāḥ prasehire. sa kāla|kramād avāpta|saṃskāra|karmā śrut'|âbhijan'|ācāra|mahadbhyo labdha|vidvad|yaśaḥ|sammānebhyaḥ† praśama|vinaya|medhā|guṇ'|āvarjitebhyo gurubhyaḥ samadhigat'|âneka|vidyaḥ pratyaham āpūryamāṇa|mūrtir yauvana|kāntyā nisarga|siddhena ca vinay'|ânurāgeṇa paraṃ prem'|āspadaṃ sva|janasya janasya ca babhūva.

The city displayed a delightful festivity:
prison doors opened, shackles were released;
squares glittered with flags raised high;
powder, flowers and wine sprinkled the ground.

Wealthy houses scattered showers of gold,
cloth, ornaments and other fineries,
as if Fortune sought to pervade the world,
imitating the Ganges in her frenzied play.

At that time, whenever the king fathered a child, it died. Believing this to be the act of some demon, the king had a nursery built to protect his son. Made entirely of iron, the splendid structure glittered with streaks of gems, gold and silver. Protective rites prescribed by the demonological sciences and ordained by the Vedas were performed to exorcise the demons. The normal auspicious ceremonies were also performed to ensure the welfare of the boy. So it was that the king had his son raised, consecrating him with the birth ceremony and other rites.

32.10 Due to the powerful merit that the Bodhi·sattva had accumulated through his good nature, as well as these carefully prepared safety measures, no demon had any power over the Great Being. As time passed, the Bodhi·sattva underwent all the due sacraments and rites and acquired various forms of knowledge from teachers who were renowned and honored for their wisdom and who were eminent in learning, noble birth and conduct, possessing virtues of serenity, modesty and intelligence. The Bodhi·sattva's looks developed every day in youthful beauty and he possessed a natural passion for discipline, both qualities making him an

a|saṃstutam a|saṃbaddhaṃ†
dūra|stham api saj|janam
jano 'nveti suhṛt|prītyā.
guṇa|śrīs tatra kāraṇam. [5]

hāsa|bhūtena nabhasaḥ śarad|vikaca|raśminā
saṃbandha|siddhir lokasya kā hi candramasā saha? [6]

atha sa Mahā|sattvaḥ puṇya|prabhāva|sukh'|ôpanatair divya|kalpair an|alpair api ca viṣayair upalālyamānaḥ sneha|bahumāna|sumukhena ca pitrā viśvāsana|nirviśaṅkaṃ dṛśyamānaḥ kadā cit svasmin pura|vare pravitata|ramaṇīya|śobhāṃ kāla|kram'|ôpanatāṃ Kaumudī|vibhūtiṃ didṛkṣuḥ kṛt'|âbhyanujñaḥ pitrā kāñcana|maṇi|rajata|bhakti|citr'|ālaṃkāraṃ samucchrita|nānā|vidha|rāga|pracal'†|ôjjvala|patākā†|dhvajaṃ haima|bhāṇḍ'|âbhyalaṃkṛta|vinīta|catura|turaṃgaṃ dakṣa|dākṣiṇya|nipuṇa|śuci|vinīta|dhīra|sārathiṃ citr'|ôjjvala|veṣa|praharaṇ'|āvaraṇ'|ânuyātraṃ ratha|varam abhiruhya,†

manojña|tūrya|svana|puraḥsaras tat pura|varam anuvicaraṃs tad|darśan'|ākṣipta|hṛdayasya kautūhala|lola|cakṣuṣaḥ stuti|sabhājan'|âñjali|pragraha|praṇām'|āśīr|vacana|prayoga|sa|vyāpārasy' ôtsava|ramyatara|veṣa|racanasya paura|jana-

object of deep affection to both his relatives and the general people.

Even if he is an unrelated stranger
living in a place far away,
people still follow a moral man with affection.
The reason is the glory of his virtues.

For when moonbeams glisten in autumn,
spreading a smile across the sky,
what forms the connection
between people and the moon?*

Feeling confident and no longer anxious, his father watched over the Great Being with affection and respect as he was pampered by various god-like pleasures that derived from the blissful power of his merit. One day, during the magnificent Káumudi festival, the prince felt an urge to see the splendor of the event extending delightfully across the city. With his father's permission, he mounted a fine chariot that was beautifully decorated with streaks of gold, gems and silver, its lofty banners and flags fluttering and glistening with various colors. The chariot's swift horses were well-trained and adorned with golden harnesses and its driver was skillful, dexterous, adept, honest, decent and reliable. A retinue followed behind, decked with colorful clothes and glittering weapons and armor.

Preceded by the delightful sounds of instruments, the Bodhi·sattva wandered through the capital city, observing the splendid crowd of citizens that had gathered there. The people's eyes flitted around with curiosity and their hearts became captivated when they caught sight of the prince.

sya† samudaya|śobhām ālokya labdha|praharṣ'|âvakāśe 'pi manasi kṛta|saṃvega|paricayatvāt pūrva|janmasu smṛtiṃ pratilebhe.

32.15 «kṛpaṇā bata lokasya
calatva|virasā sthitiḥ,
yad iyaṃ Kaumudī|lakṣmīḥ
smartavy" âiva bhaviṣyati! [7]

evaṃ|vidhāyāṃ ca jagat|pravṛttāv
aho yathā nirbhayatā janānām,
yan Mṛtyun" âdhiṣṭhita|sarva|mārgā
niḥ|saṃbhramā harṣam anubhramanti. [8]

a|vārya|vīryeṣv ariṣu sthiteṣu
jighāṃsayā vyādhi|jar"|ântakeṣu
avaśya|gamye para|loka|dur|ge,
harṣ'|âvakāśo 'tra sa|cetasaḥ kaḥ? [9]

svan'|ânukṛty" êva mah"|ârṇavānāṃ
saṃrambha|raudrāṇi jalāni kṛtvā
meghās taḍid|bhāsura|hema|mālāḥ
saṃbhūya bhūyo vilayaṃ vrajanti. [10]

taṭe† samantād† vinibaddha|mūlān
hṛtvā tarūṃl labdha|javaiḥ payobhiḥ
bhavanti bhūyaḥ saritaḥ kramena
śok'|ôpatāpād iva dīna|rūpāḥ. [11]

Dressed in delightful festive clothes, they praised and honored him enthusiastically, cupping their hands in respect, while making prostrations and uttering blessings. But despite the opportunity that this occasion afforded for joy, the Bodhi·sattva was so accustomed to spiritual alarm that he instead remembered his past lives.

"How pitiful is the state of this
distastefully changeable world!
This splendid Káumudi festival
will soon be but a memory! 32.15

But though this is the nature of the world,
the people still display such lack of fear,
wandering after pleasures without anxiety,
though Death rules over every path!

Disease, old age and death stand ready to strike,
enemies of unstoppable strength.
Who of sound mind can find room for joy,
when the perils of the next world must be met?

Though clouds pour rain of violent fury
as if imitating the roar of mighty oceans,
garlanded with golden flashes of lightning,
they rise up only to disperse again.

Though swift rivers remove trees
that are deeply rooted in banks,
in time they look pitiful again,
as if tormented by sorrow.

32.20 hṛtv" âpi śṛṅgāṇi mahī|dharāṇāṃ
vegena vṛndāni ca toya|dānām
vighūrṇya c' ôdvartya ca sāgar'|âmbhaḥ
prayāti nāśaṃ pavana|prabhāvaḥ. [12]

dīpt'|ôddhat'|ârcir vikasat|sphuliṅgaḥ
saṃkṣipya kakṣaṃ kṣayam eti vahniḥ.
krameṇa śobhāś ca van'|ântarāṇām
udyanti bhūyaś ca tiro|bhavanti. [13]

kaḥ saṃprayogo na viyoga|niṣṭhaḥ?
kāḥ saṃpado yā na vipat paraiti?
jagat|pravṛttāv iti cañcalāyām
a|pratyavekṣy' âiva janasya harṣaḥ.» [14]

iti sa parigaṇayan Mahātmā saṃvegād vyāvṛtta|pramod'|ôddhavena manasā ramaṇīyeṣv api pura | vara | vibhūṣ" | ârtham abhiprasāriteṣu† loka|citreṣv a|viṣajyamāna|buddhiḥ krameṇa sva|bhavanam anuprāptam ev' ātmānam apaśyat.

tad | abhivṛddha | saṃvegaś ca «viṣaya | sukheṣv an | āstho dharma ekaḥ śaraṇam» iti tat|pratipatti|niścita|matir yathā|prastāvam abhigamya rājānaṃ kṛt'|âñjalis tapo|vana|gamanāy' ânujñām ayācata:

32.25 «pravrajyā|saṃśrayāt kartum
icchāmi hitam ātmanaḥ,
kṛtāṃ tatr' âbhyanujñāṃ ca
tvay" ânugraha|paddhatim.» [15]

Though it churns and stirs the sea waters, 32.20
sweeping away mountain peaks
and forcefully dispelling cloud masses,
the powerful wind also dies.

With its bright towering flames and flying sparks,
fire consumes grass and then itself is destroyed.
Splendors arise in forest interiors
but in due course disappear again.

What meeting does not end in separation?
What success does not lead to calamity?
When fickleness is the way of the world,
the joy of these people lacks all reason."

As he pondered these thoughts, his feeling of spiritual alarm made the Great One become averse to the festive joys. His mind was no longer fixated by the colorful throngs of people who streamed forward to decorate the capital city, however delightful they looked, and in due course he noticed that he had arrived back at the palace.

But this increased his sense of spiritual alarm still further. And so, esteeming virtue alone as his refuge since it was unconcerned with sensual pleasures, he resolved to practice that way of life. As soon as the opportunity arose, he approached the king with hands cupped in respect and asked for permission to become an ascetic in the forest.

"I wish to bring myself benefit 32.25
by undertaking renunciation.
You would show me your favor
if you gave me your permission."

tac chrutvā priya|tanayaḥ sa tasya rājā
 digdhena dvi|rada iv' êṣuṇ" âbhividdhaḥ
gambhīro 'py uda|dhir iv' ânil'|âvadhūtas
 tac|choka|vyathita|manāḥ samācakampe. [16]

nivārayiṣyann atha taṃ sa rājā
 snehāt pariṣvajya sa|bāṣpa|kaṇṭhaḥ
uvāca: «kasmāt sahas" âiva, tāta,
 saṃtyaktum asmān matim ity akārṣīḥ? [17]

tvad|a|priyeṇ' ātma|vināśa|hetuḥ
 ken' âyam ity ākalitaḥ Kṛtāntaḥ?
śok'|âśru|paryākula|locanāni
 bhavantu kasya sva|jan'|ānanāni? [18]

ath' âpi kiṃ cit pariśaṅkitaṃ vā
 mayi vyalīkaṃ samupaśrutaṃ vā?
tad brūhi yāvad viramāmi tasmāt.
 paśyāmi na tv ātmani kiṃ cid īdṛk.» [19]

32.30 Bodhisattva uvāca:

«ity abhisneha|sumukhe
 vyalīkaṃ nāma kiṃ tvayi?
vi|priyeṇa samarthaḥ syān
 māṃ āsādayituṃ ca kaḥ?» [20]

«atha kiṃ tarhi naḥ parityaktum icchas'?» îti c' âbhihitaḥ s'|âśru|nayanena rājñā sa Mahā|sattvas tam uvāca: «mṛtyu| bhayāt. paśyatu devaḥ:

The king, who loved his son dearly, shook
like an elephant shot by a poisoned arrow,
or like the deep ocean churned by the wind,
his mind reeling with grief at these words.

Trying to stop him, his throat choked with tears,
the king embraced his son affectionately, saying:
"Why, my child, have you suddenly
made up your mind to abandon us?

What foe of yours has so stirred Death?
It will only bring ruin on him!
Whose relatives will find their eyes
become filled with tears of sorrow?

Do you suspect or have you heard
I have committed some offence?
Then tell me so I can cease it.
But I see no such crime in myself."

The Bodhi·sattva answered: 32.30

"What offence can you commit
when you are so earnest in affection?
And who has the power
to inflict harm on me?"

"Why, then, do you wish to abandon us?" asked the king, his eyes filling with tears. "Out of fear of death," the Great Being replied. "Consider this, Your Majesty.

yām eva rātriṃ prathamām upaiti
garbhe nivāsaṃ, nara|vīra, lokaḥ,
tataḥ prabhṛty a|skhalita|prayāṇaḥ
sa pratyahaṃ mṛtyu|samīpam eti. [21]

nītau su|yukto 'pi bale sthito 'pi
n' âtyeti kaś cin maraṇaṃ jarāṃ vā.
upadrutaṃ sarvam it' îdam ābhyāṃ.
dharm'|ârtham asmād vanam āśrayiṣye. [22]

32.35 vyūḍhāny udīrṇa|nara|vāji|ratha|dvipāni
sainyāni darpa|rabhasāḥ kṣiti|pā jayanti.
jetuṃ Kṛtānta|ripum ekam api tv a|śaktās.
tan me matir bhavati dharmam abhiprapattum. [23]

dṛpt'†|âśva|kuñjara|padāti|rathair anīkair
guptā vimokṣam upayānti nṛ|pā dviṣadbhyaḥ.
sārdhaṃ balair ati|balasya tu Mṛtyu|śatror
Manv|ādayo 'pi vi|vaśā vaśaṃ abhyupetāḥ. [24]

saṃcūrṇya danta|musalaiḥ pura|gopurāṇi
matta|dvipā† yudhi rathāṃś ca narān dvi|pāṃś ca.
n' âiv' Ântakaṃ pratimukh'|âbhigataṃ nudanti
vapr'|ânta|labdha|vijayair api tair viṣāṇaiḥ. [25]

From the first night a person
dwells in a womb, hero of men,
they daily draw closer to death,
advancing without deviation.

However skilled in politics or secure in might,
no-one eludes death or old age.
These two factors overrun the entire world.
So I will resort to the forest to practice virtue.

32.35

With furious pride,
kings defeat entire armies of incited
men, horses, chariots and elephants
drawn up in battle formation.
But they are unable to conquer
the solitary foe that is Death.
That is why my heart
wishes to practice virtue.

Protected by armies of proud horses,
elephants, infantrymen and chariots,
kings can find escape
from their enemies.
Yet from the time of Manu,*
they surrender themselves
and their troops to hostile Death,
helpless against his vast strength.

Frenzied elephants pulverize city-gates
with their club-like tusks in battle,
crushing chariots, men,
and other tuskers too.
Yet they cannot repel Death

dṛḍha|citra|varma|kavac'|āvaraṇān
yudhi dārayanty api vidūra|carān
iṣubhis tad|astra|kuśalā dviṣataś,
cira|vairiṇaṃ na tu Kṛtāntam arim. [26]

siṃhā vikartana|kharair† nakharair dvi|pānāṃ
kumbh'|âgra|magna|śikharaiḥ praśamayya tejaḥ
bhittv" âiva ca śruti†|manāṃsi ravaiḥ pareṣāṃ
Mṛtyuṃ sametya hata|darpa|balāḥ svapanti. [27]

32.40 doṣ'|ânurūpaṃ praṇayanti daṇḍaṃ
kṛt'|âparādheṣu nṛ|pāḥ pareṣu.
mah"|âparādhe 'pi tu† Mṛtyu|śatrau
na daṇḍa|nīti|pravaṇā bhavanti. [28]

nṛ|pāś ca sām'|ādibhir abhyupāyaiḥ†
kṛt'|âparādhān† vaśam ānayanti.
raudraś cir'|âbhyāsa|dṛḍh'|âvalepo
Mṛtyuḥ punar n' ânunay'|ādi|sādhyaḥ. [29]

krodh'|ânala|jvalita|ghora|viṣ'|âgni|garbhair
daṃṣṭr'|âṅkurair abhidaśanti narān bhujaṃ|gāḥ
daṃṣṭavya|yatna|vidhurās tu bhavanti Mṛtyau
vadhye 'pi nityam apakāra|vidhāna|dakṣe. [30]

when he advances upon them,
though previously they conquered
ramparts with the very same tusks.

Skilled archers pierce foes with arrows in war,
even if they are far away or protected
by strong and elaborate armor and mail.
Yet they cannot strike their old enemy Death.

Lions may quash
the might of elephants,
the tips of sharp slashing claws
sinking into upper foreheads.
Yet though their roars rupture
the ears and hearts of enemies,
they sleep on meeting Death,
their pride and strength destroyed.

Kings punish foes who wrong them
in accord with their offence.
Yet they show no desire to punish
the great criminal that is hostile Death.

32.40

Kings subdue enemies who wrong them
through ploys such as appeasement.*
But Death's pride is fortified by long experience.
Tactics like persuasion cannot affect his ferocity.

Snakes bite men
with pointed fangs,
packed with terrible burning poison
blazing with the fire of rage.
But they lack all endeavor

daṣṭasya kopa|rabhasair api panna|gaiś ca
mantrair viṣaṃ praśamayanty a|gadaiś ca vaidyāḥ.
āśī|viṣas tv ati|viṣo 'yam a|riṣṭa|daṃṣṭro
mantr'|â|gad'|ādibhir a|sādhya|viṣaḥ† Kṛtāntaḥ. [31]

pakṣ'|ânilair laḍita|mīna|kulaṃ vyudasya
megh'|âugha|bhīma|rasitaṃ jalam arṇavebhyaḥ
sarpān haranti vitat'|ôgra|phaṇān† Suparṇā;
Mṛtyuṃ punaḥ pramathituṃ na tath" ôtsahante. [32]

32.45 bhīta|drutān api jav'|âtiśayena jitvā
saṃsādya c' âika|bhuja|vajra|vilāsa|vṛttyā
vyāghrāḥ pibanti rudhirāṇi vane;†
n' âivaṃ pravṛtti|paṭavas tu bhavanti Mṛtyau. [33]

to sink their teeth into Death,
even though he deserves slaughter
for his constant skill in crime.

When a man is bitten
by snakes raging with fury,
doctors can quell the poison
using spells and medicines.
But Death is a snake of great venom,
wielding unbreakable fangs.
His poison cannot be affected
by spells, medicine and the like.

With the gust of their wings
Gárudas hurl water from oceans
teeming with playing fish,
their din terrifying as rainclouds.
They then grab snakes
bearing broad ferocious hoods.
Yet they never try
to destroy Death.

Tigers use their superior speed 32.45
to conquer deer fleeing in terror.
Subduing them playfully
with the thunderbolt of a paw,
they drink the blood
of the deer in the forest.
But they do not use their skill
to act this way against Death.

daṃṣṭrā|karālam api nāma mṛgaḥ sametya
vaiyāghram ānanam, upaiti punar vimokṣam.
Mṛtyor mukhaṃ tu pṛthu|roga|jar"|ārti|daṃṣṭraṃ
prāptasya kasya ca punaḥ śivatātir asti? [34]

pibanti nṛṇāṃ vikṛt'|ôgra|vigrahā
sah' âujas" āyūṃṣi dṛḍha|grahā grahāḥ.
bhavanti tu prastuta|Mṛtyu|vigrahā
vipanna|darp'|ôtkaṭatā|parigrahāḥ. [35]

pūjā|rata|droha|kṛte 'bhyupetān
grahān niyacchanti sa siddha|vidyāḥ
tapo|balaiḥ svastyayan'†|āuṣadhaiś ca.
Mṛtyu|grahas tv a|prativārya eva. [36]

māyā|vidhi|jñāś ca mahā|samāje
janasya cakṣūṃṣi vimohayanti.
ko 'pi prabhāvas tv ayam Antakasya,
yad bhrāmyate tair api n' âsya cakṣuḥ. [37]

32.50 hatvā viṣāṇi ca tapo|bala|siddha|mantrā
vyādhīn nṛṇām upaśamayya ca vaidya|varyāḥ
Dhanvantari|prabhṛtayo 'pi gatā vināśaṃ.
dharmāya me namati tena matir van'|ânte. [38]

āvir|bhavanti ca punaś ca tiro|bhavanti
gacchanti v" ânila|pathena mahīṃ viśanti
vidyā|dharā vividha|mantra|bala|prabhāvā.
Mṛtyuṃ sametya tu bhavanti hata|prabhāvāḥ. [39]

A deer may escape even if it encounters
the terrifying teeth of a tiger's mouth.
But who finds luck after entering Death's jaws
with its huge fangs of disease, age and anguish?

Demons drink the lifeforce and energy of men,
gripping them tightly with fierce, deformed bodies.
But when the battle with Death approaches,
they lose grip of their arrogance and pride.

Through ascetic powers, blessings and herbs,
men skilled in magic can restrain demons
who come to harm people devoted to worship.
But one cannot avert the demon that is Death.

Experts in the art of illusion
puzzle the eyes of large assemblies.
But Death has the power
to stop his eyes being confused.

Strengthened by asceticism, 32.50
some destroy poison with chants.
Eminent doctors quash
the diseases of men.
All these have perished,
from Dhanvan·tari* onwards.
That is why my heart seeks
a life of virtue in the forest.

Through the might of various spells,
vidya·dharas appear and disappear again.
They dwell on earth or follow the wind's path.
Yet they lose their powers on meeting Death.

dṛptān api pratinudanty asurān sur'|êndrā
dṛptān api pratinudanty asurāḥ surāṃś ca.
mān'|âdhirūḍha|matibhiḥ samudīrṇa|sainyais
taiḥ saṃhatair api tu Mṛtyur a|jayya eva. [40]

imām avety' â|prativārya|raudratāṃ
Kṛtānta|śatror bhavane na me ratiḥ.†
na manyunā sneha|parikṣayeṇa vā
prayāmi, dharmāya tu niścito vanam.» [41]

rāj" ôvāca:

32.55 «atha vane kas tav' āśvāsa† evam a|pratikriye mṛtyu|bhaye sati, dharma|parigrahe vā?†

kiṃ tvā vane na samupaiṣyati Mṛtyu|śatrur?
dharme sthitāḥ kim ṛṣayo na vane vinaṣṭāḥ?
sarvatra nāma niyataḥ krama eṣa tatra.
ko 'rtho vihāya bhavanaṃ vana|saṃśrayeṇa?» [42]

Bodhisattva uvāca:

«kāmaṃ sthiteṣu bhavane ca vane ca Mṛtyur
dharm'|ātmakeṣu viguṇeṣu ca tulya|vṛttiḥ.
dharm'|ātmanāṃ bhavati na tv anutāpa|hetur
dharmaś ca nāma vana eva sukhaṃ prapattum. [43]

The lordly gods repel the proud ásuras,
and the ásuras repel the proud gods.
Yet even if united, their stirred armies
brimming with pride could not defeat Death.

Realizing hostile Death's unstoppable ferocity,
I no longer take any delight in home.
Neither anger nor lack of affection drives me.
I go to the forest because I am intent on virtue."

The king replied:

"But if death's peril cannot be countered, what comfort is there for you in a life in the forest or in undertaking virtue? 32.55

Will the enemy that is Death
not also come to you in the forest?
Do ascetics, established in virtue,
not also die in the forest?
Surely the way of life there
can be practiced anywhere?
What need is there to abandon
your home and resort to the forest?"

The Bodhi·sattva answered:

"It is true that Death acts equally
toward the virtuous and immoral,
toward those who live in houses
and those who live in the forest.
But the virtuous have
no reason for remorse.
And it is definitely easier
to practice morality in the forest.

paśyatu devaḥ,

32.60 pramāda|mada|kandarpa|
lobha|dveṣ'|āspade gṛhe
tad|viruddhasya dharmasya
ko 'vakāśa|parigrahaḥ? [44]

vikṛṣyamāṇo bahubhiḥ ku|karmabhiḥ
parigrah'|ôpārjana|rakṣaṇ'|ākulaḥ
a|śānta|cetā vyasan'|ôday'|āgamaiḥ
kadā gṛha|sthaḥ śama|mārgam eṣyati? [45]

vane tu saṃtyakta|ku|kārya|vistaraḥ
parigraha|kleśa|vivarjitaḥ sukhī
śam'|âika|kāryaḥ parituṣṭa|mānasaḥ
sukhaṃ ca dharmaṃ ca yaśāṃsi c' ârcchati. [46]

dharmaś ca rakṣati naraṃ, na dhanaṃ balaṃ vā.
dharmaḥ sukhāya mahate, na vibhūti|siddhiḥ.
dharm'|ātmanaś ca mudam eva karoti Mṛtyur.
na hy asti dur|gati|bhayaṃ niratasya dharme. [47]

kriyā|viśeṣaś ca yathā vyavasthitaḥ
śubhasya pāpasya ca bhinna|lakṣaṇaḥ,
tathā vipāko 'py a|śubhasya dur|gatiś
citrasya dharmasya sukh'|āśrayā gatiḥ.» [48]

32.65 ity anunīya sa Mahātmā pitaraṃ kṛt'|âbhyanujñaḥ pitrā tṛṇavad apāsya rājya|lakṣmīṃ tapo|van'|āśrayaṃ cakāra. tatra ca dhyānāny a|pramāṇāni c' ôtpādya teṣu ca pratiṣṭhāpya lokaṃ Brahma|lokam adhiruroha.

Consider this, Your Majesty.

Houses are places of negligence, 32.60
pride, lust, greed and hatred.
What room does virtue have there,
the very opposite of such qualities?

Distracted by various evil activities,
householders fret over gaining and keeping possessions.
Arisen or imminent disasters make them uncalm.
When can one find peace if living in a house?
In the forest one rejects this array of evil acts.
Free from the toil of possessions, one is happy.
Content at heart, tranquility one's sole task,
one acquires happiness, virtue and fame.

Virtue protects a man, not riches or power.
Virtue brings great happiness, not wealth.
Death brings only joy to a man of virtue.
For a devotee of virtue never fears bad rebirth.

Good and evil have specific actions,
marked out by distinct characteristics.
The result of vice is a bad rebirth.
The result of radiant virtue is a happy one."

Persuading his father with these words, the Great Being 32.65
obtained his permission and resorted to the ascetic forest, discarding the splendors of kingship as if they were chaff. There he produced the dhyana meditations and the four immeasurables. After he had established the world in these states, he ascended to the Brahma Realm.*

tad evaṃ, saṃvigna | manasāṃ rāja | lakṣmīr api śreyo | mārgaṃ n' āvṛṇot', îti saṃvega|paricayaḥ kāryaḥ.

maraṇa | saṃjñā | varṇe 'pi vācyam: «evam āśu | maraṇa | saṃjñā saṃvegāya bhavat'» îti. tathā maraṇ'|ânusmṛti|varṇe '| nityatā | kathāyām apy upaneyam: «evam a | nityāḥ sarva | saṃskārā» iti. tathā sarva | loke 'n | abhirati | saṃjñāyām: «evam an|āśvāsikaṃ saṃskṛtam» iti. «evam a|trāṇo 'yam a| sahāyaś ca loka» ity evam api vācyam. «evaṃ vane sukhaṃ dharmaḥ† pratipattuṃ na geha» ity evam apy upaneyam.†

In this way, for those who have been shaken by spiritual alarm, not even the splendor of kingship can conceal the path to felicity. One should therefore intimately familiarize oneself with such spiritual realization.

One should also narrate this story when praising awareness of death, saying, "In this way, the thought of imminent death produces spiritual alarm." Likewise, one should cite this story when praising the recollection of death and discussing impermanence, saying, "In this way, all constructed phenomena are impermanent." One should also tell this story when discussing the notion of discontent with the entire world, saying: "In this way, constructed phenomena bring no solace." And one should also state: "In this way, the world has no protection or help." And one should also draw the following conclusion: "In this way, virtue can easily be practiced in the forest but not in a house."

MAHIṢAJĀTAKAM

STORY 33
THE BIRTH-STORY OF THE BUFFALO

33.1 SATI KṢANTAVYE kṣamā syān n' â|sat' îty apakāriṇam api sādhavo lābham iva bahu manyante.

tad|yath" ânuśrūyate.

Bodhisattvaḥ kil' ânyatamasminn araṇya|vana|pradeśe† paṅka|saṃparka|paruṣa|vapur† megha|viccheda† iva pāda|cārī vana|mahiṣa|vṛṣo babhūva. sa tasyāṃ dur|labha|dharma|saṃjñāyāṃ saṃmoha|bahulāyām api tiryag|gatau vartamānaḥ paṭu|vijñānatvān na dharma|caryā|nirudyoga|matir babhūva.

cir'|ânuvṛtty" êva nibaddha|bhāvā
 na taṃ kadā cit karuṇā mumoca.
ko 'pi prabhāvaḥ sa tu karmaṇāṃ† vā
 tasy' âiva vā, yat sa tathā babhūva. [1]

33.5 ataś ca nūnaṃ Bhagavān avocad
 a|cintyatāṃ karma|vipāka|yukteḥ
kṛp"|ātmakaḥ sann api yat sa bheje
 tiryag|gatiṃ tatra ca dharma|saṃjñām. [2]

vinā na karm' âsti gati|prabandhaḥ,
 śubhaṃ na c' ân|iṣṭa|vipākam asti.
sa dharma|saṃjño† 'pi tu karma|leśāṃs
 tāṃs tān samāsādya tathā tath" āsīt. [3]

ath' ânyatamo duṣṭa|vānaras tasya kāl'|ântar'|âbhivyaktāṃ prakṛti|bhadratāṃ day"|ânuvṛttyā ca vigata|krodha|saṃrambhatām avetya, «n' âsmād bhayam ast'» îti taṃ Mahā|sattvaṃ tena tena vihiṃsā|krameṇa bhṛśam† abādhata.

33.1

FORGIVENESS ONLY EXISTS if there is something to forgive, not otherwise. For this reason the virtuous esteem even those who wrong them as a gain.

Tradition has handed down the following story.

The Bodhi·sattva is said to have once been a wild buffalo who lived in a wild area of the forest. The mud that covered his body made him look fierce and he resembled a chunk of cloud as he walked along. Since their existence abounds with ignorance, it is difficult for animals to attain moral awareness. But despite this, the Bodhi·sattva's sharp acumen meant he was far from inactive in practicing virtue.

As though bound to him by long service,
compassion never left his side.
Some power had made him what he was,
deriving from past actions or his own nature.

33.5

For this reason the Lord said that the results
and methods of karma are incomprehensible.
For though compassionate, he was born an animal.
And despite that, he still had moral awareness.

Without karma there can be no connected births.
Good actions can also not have bad results.
But though morally aware, some trace of karma
must have affected him to be reborn this way.

The buffalo's innate goodness revealed itself over time and happened to be noticed by a wicked monkey. Observing that compassion made the buffalo devoid of anger and rage, the monkey concluded that there was nothing to fear from him. So he brutally began to torment the Great Being with various forms of injury.

dayā|mṛduṣu dur|janaḥ paṭutar'|âvalep'|ôddhavaḥ
parāṃ vrajati vikriyāṃ, na hi bhayaṃ tataḥ paśyati.
yatas tu bhaya|śaṅkayā su|kṛśay" âpi saṃspṛśyate
vinīta iva nīcakaiś carati tatra śānt'|ôddhavaḥ. [4]

sa kadā cit tasya Mahā|sattvasya visrabdha|suptasya† nidrā|vaśād vā pracalāyataḥ sahas" âiv' ôpari nipatati sma. drumam iva kadā cid enam abhiruhya† bhṛśaṃ saṃcālayām āsa. kṣudhitasy' âpi ca† kadā cid asya mārgam āvṛtya vyatiṣṭhata. kāṣṭheṇ' âpy enam kadā cic chravaṇayoś c' āghaṭṭayām† āsa. salil'|âvagāha†|samutsukasy' âpy asya kadā cic chiraḥ samadhiruhya† pāṇibhyāṃ nayane samāvavre. apy enam adhiruhya samudyata|daṇḍaḥ prasahy' âiva vāhayan Yamasya līlām anucakāra. Bodhisattvo 'pi tu† Mahā|sattvaḥ sarvaṃ tad asy' â|vinaya|viceṣṭitam† upakāram iva† niḥ|saṃkṣobha|saṃrambha|manyur marṣayām āsa.

33.10 sva|bhāva eva pāpānāṃ vinay'|ônmārga|saṃśrayaḥ
abhyāsāt tatra tu† satām upakāra iva kṣamā. [5]

ath'† ânyatamo yakṣas tam asya paribhavam a|mṛṣyamāno bhāvaṃ vā jijñāsamānas† tasya Mahā|sattvasya tena duṣṭa|kapinā vāhyamānaṃ taṃ mahiṣa|vṛṣaṃ sthitv" ânumārgam† uvāca:

A villain shows special gleeful insolence
toward those soft with compassion.
Seeing no danger in them,
he injures them greatly.
But if he suspects someone
even slightly of danger,
he will be servile and feign modesty,
his exuberance quelled.

Sometimes the monkey would suddenly leap onto the Great Being as he slumbered soundly and twitched his body under a spell of sleep. Sometimes he would clamber up the buffalo like a tree and shake him violently. Sometimes he would stand in front of him and block his path, just when he was hungry. Sometimes he rubbed the buffalo's ears with a stick. Sometimes he climbed onto the buffalo's head and covered his eyes with his hands, just as he yearned to plunge into water. Or otherwise he would mount him and playfully imitate Yama by wielding a stick and driving him forward by force.* But the Bodhi·sattva, that Great Being, endured all these indecent pranks without agitation, as if they were a service, and felt neither anger nor rage.

33.10

The wicked naturally follow
a path straying from decency.
But the good naturally tolerate this as a service,
so practiced are they in forbearance.*

Now a certain yaksha* who was unable to bear the insults suffered by the Great Being, or who perhaps wanted to test his character, blocked the path of the buffalo as the wicked monkey rode him and said:

«mā tāvad bhoḥ! kiṃ parikrīto 'sy anena duṣṭa|kapinā? atha dyūte parājitaḥ? ut' âho bhayam asmāt kiṃ cid āśaṅkase? ut' âho balam ātma|gataṃ n' âveṣi yad evam anena paribhūya vāhyase? nanu ca† bhoḥ,

veg'|āviddhaṃ tvad|viṣāṇ'|âgra|vajraṃ
bhindyād vajraṃ vajravad† vā nag'|êndrān.
pādāś c' ême roṣa|saṃrambha|muktā
majjeyus te paṅkavac chaila|pṛṣṭhe. [6]

idaṃ ca śail'|ôpama|saṃhataṃ sthiraṃ†
samagra|śobhaṃ bala|saṃpadā vapuḥ
svabhāva|saujaska|nirīkṣit'|ōrjitaṃ
dur|āsadaṃ kesariṇo 'pi te bhavet! [7]

33.15 mathāna dhṛtvā tad imaṃ khureṇa† vā!
viṣāṇa|koṭyā madam asya v" ôddhara!
kim asya jālmasya kaper a|śaktavat
prabādhanā|duḥkham idaṃ titikṣase? [8]

a|saj|janaḥ kutra yathā cikitsyate
guṇ'|ânuvṛttyā sukha|śīta†|saumyayā,
kaṭ'|ûṣṇa|rūkṣāṇi hi yatra siddhaye
kaph'|ātmake† roga iva prasarpati.» [9]

atha Bodhisattvas taṃ yakṣam avekṣamāṇaḥ kṣamā|pakṣa|patitam a|rūkṣ'|âkṣaram ity uvāca:

«avaimy enaṃ bala|nyūnaṃ† sadā c' â|vinaye ratam.
ata eva mayā tv asya yuktaṃ marṣayituṃ nanu? [10]

"Stop this, good fellow! Are you the hireling of this wicked monkey? Have you lost at dice? Do you fear some danger from him? Do you not know your own strength that you let him ride you in this humiliating way? Surely, good sir,

Wielded with force, the thunderbolt-tips of your horns
could pierce a bolt or cleave mountains like a bolt.
Kicked with furious rage, your hooves
could sink into a slab of rock like mud.

Your body is solid and as firm as a rock.
Its superb strength makes it entirely beautiful.
Beings powerful by nature gaze at your might.
Maned lions would find it hard to assail you!

So seize and crush him with your hoof! 33.15
Rip out his impudence with the tip of your horn!
Why do you act as if you were powerless,
enduring the torment inflicted by this rogue?

When is a criminal cured by being treated
with gentle, cool and soothing deeds of virtue?
Only bitter, hot, harsh herbs give a result,
as with the spread of a phlegmatic disease."

Looking at the yaksha, the Bodhi·sattva addressed him with gentle words that promoted forbearance:

"I know that he lacks strength
and always delights in indecency.
But is that not the reason
why I should put up with him?

pratikartum a|śaktasya kṣamā kā hi balīyasi?
vinay'|ācāra|dhīreṣu kṣantavyaṃ kiṃ ca sādhuṣu? [11]

33.20 śakta eva titikṣate dur|bala|skhalitaṃ yataḥ
varaṃ paribhavas tasmān na guṇānāṃ parābhavaḥ. [12]

a|sat|kriyā hīna|balāc ca nāma
nirveśa†|kālaḥ paramo guṇānām.
guṇa|priyas tatra kim ity avekṣya†
sva|dhairya|bhedāya parākrameta? [13]

nityaṃ kṣamāyāś ca nanu kṣamāyāḥ
kālaḥ par'|āyattatayā dur|āpaḥ.
pareṇa tasminn upapādite ca
tatr' âiva kopa|praṇaya|kramaḥ kaḥ? [14]

svāṃ dharma|pīḍām a|vicintya yo 'yaṃ
mat|pāpa|śuddhy|artham iva pravṛttaḥ,
na cet kṣamām apy aham atra kuryām
anyaḥ kṛta|ghno bata kīdṛśaḥ syāt?» [15]

yakṣa uvāca: «tena hi na tvam asya prabādhanāyāḥ kadā cin† mokṣyase.

33.25 guṇeṣv a|bahu|mānasya
dur|janasy' â|vinītatām
kṣamā|naibhṛtyam a|tyaktvā
kaḥ saṃkocayituṃ prabhuḥ?» [16]

What forbearance is it if one is powerless
to retaliate against those who are mightier?
And what is there to endure in good people
who are steadfast in decency and virtue?

Though one has the power to retaliate, 33.20
one should endure the wrongs of weaker beings.
For it is better to be insulted by them
than to ruin one's own virtues.

The best time to apply virtue is
when dishonored by someone weaker.
Why would a lover of virtue use violence,
only to destroy his own steadfastness?

There is never a wrong time for forbearance.
But the occasion is rare as it depends on others.
So if another person produces an opportunity,
why would one resort to anger?

If I did not show forbearance toward those
who disregard their violation of morality,
acting almost to purify my own bad karma,
would anyone exist less grateful than I?"

"In that case you will never escape from his torment," the yaksha replied.

"If you continue your passive tolerance, 33.25
who will be able to curb
the unruly conduct of this villain
who has no respect for virtue?"

Bodhisattva uvāca:

«parasya pīḍā|praṇayena yat sukhaṃ
  nivāraṇaṃ syād a|sukh'|ôdayasya vā,
sukh'|ârthinas tan na niṣevituṃ kṣamaṃ.
  na tad|vipāko hi sukha|prasiddhaye. [17]

kṣam"|āśrayād evam asau may" ârthataḥ
  prabodhyamāno yadi n' âvagacchati,
nivārayiṣyanti ta enam utpathād
  a|marṣiṇo yān ayam abhyupaiṣyati. [18]

a|sat|kriyāṃ prāpya ca tad|vidhāj janān
  na mādṛśe 'py evam asau kariṣyati.
na dṛṣṭa†|doṣo hi punas tathā cared,
  ataś ca muktir mama sā bhaviṣayti.» [19]

33.30 atha sa† yakṣas taṃ Mahā|sattvaṃ prasāda|vismaya|bahumān'|āvarjita|matiḥ «sādhu! sādhv!» iti sa|śiraḥ|prakamp'|āṅguli|vikṣepam abhisaṃrādhya tat tat priyam uvāca:

«kutas tiraścām iyam īdṛśī sthitir?
  guṇeṣv ayaṃ† c' ādara|vistaraḥ kutaḥ?
kay" âpi buddhyā tv idam āsthito vapus.
  tapo|vane ko 'pi bhavāṃs tapasyati!» [20]

ity enam abhipraśasya taṃ c' âsya duṣṭa|vānaraṃ pṛṣṭhād avadhūya samādiśya c' âsya rakṣā|vidhānaṃ tatr' âiv' ântar|dadhe.

The Bodhi·sattva answered:

"Those who seek happiness
should not pursue pleasure or avert pain
by injuring another person.
For this will not result in happiness.

I practice patience to make him aware.
If he still does not understand,
he will meet people intolerant of him.
They will make him cease his wicked ways.

When he is maltreated by these people,
he will stop tormenting those like me.
Seeing his crime, he will stop acting this way.
And that will then be my release."

"Excellent! Excellent!" the yaksha exclaimed, filled with devotion, wonder and reverence. Rocking his head and making flourishing gestures with his fingers, he applauded the Great Being with the following kind words: 33.30

"How can animals possess such conduct?
How can they have such wide regard for virtue?
Some design must lie behind your appearance.
You must practice asceticism in an ascetic grove!"

With these words of praise, the yaksha threw the wicked monkey off the buffalo's back and, after teaching the buffalo a protective spell, he disappeared there and then.

tad evaṃ, sati kṣantavye kṣamā syān n' â|sat' îty apakāriṇam api sādhavo lābham iva bahu|manyante.

iti kṣānti|kathāyāṃ vācyam. «evaṃ tiryag|gatānāṃ api† pratisaṃkhyāna | sauṣṭhavaṃ dṛṣṭam. ko nāma manuṣya | bhūtaḥ pravrajita|pratijño vā tad|vikalaḥ śobheta?» ity evam api vācyam. Tathāgata|varṇe sat|kṛtya dharma|śravaṇe c' êti.

In this way, forgiveness only exists if there is something to forgive, not otherwise. For this reason the virtuous esteem even those who wrong them as a gain.

One should tell this story when preaching forbearance. And one should also say: "In this way, even animals are shown to be capable of excellent mental strength. Who that is human or that has taken the vow of renunciation would wish to appear deficient in this regard?" One should also tell this story when praising the Tatha·gata or when listening to the Teaching with respect.

ŚATAPATTRAJĀTAKAM

STORY 34
THE BIRTH-STORY OF THE WOODPECKER

34.1 PROTSĀHYAMĀNO 'pi sādhur n' âlaṃ pāpe pravartitum an|abhyāsāt.

tad|yath" ânuśrūyate.

Bodhisattvaḥ kil' ânyatamasmin vana|pradeśe nānā|vidha|rāga|rucira|citra|pattraḥ śata|pattro babhūva. karuṇā|paricayāc ca tad|avastho 'pi na prāṇi|hiṃsā|kaluṣāṃ śata|patra|vṛttim anvavartata.†

bālaiḥ pravālaiḥ sa mahī|ruhāṇāṃ
puṣp'|âdhivāsair madhubhiś ca hṛdyaiḥ
phalaiś ca nānā|rasa|gandha|varṇaiḥ
saṃtoṣa|vṛttiṃ bibharāṃ cakāra. [1]

34.5 dharmaṃ parebhyaḥ pravadan yath"|ârham
ārtān yathā|śakti samuddharaṃś ca
nivārayaṃś c' â|vinayād an|āryān
udbhāvayām āsa par'|ârtha|caryām. [2]

iti sa† paripālyamānas tena Mahā|sattvena tasmin vana|pradeśe sattva|kāyaḥ s'|ācāryaka iva bandhumān iva sa|vaidya iva rājanvān iva ca† sukham abhyavardhata.

dayā|jananyā† paripālyamāno
vṛddhiṃ yath" âsau guṇato jagāma,
sa sattva|kāyo 'pi tath" âiva tena
saṃrakṣyamāṇo guṇa|vṛddhim āpa. [3]

EVEN WHEN PROVOKED, a virtuous man is incapable of turning to evil since it is contrary to his habit. 34.1

Tradition has handed down the following story.

The Bodhi·sattva is said to have once lived as a woodpecker* in an area of the forest, his wings glittering beautifully with various colors. But despite being born in that state, his ingrained compassion meant he lived off food that was different from other woodpeckers, since such subsistence is tainted by the sin of injuring living beings.

Instead he lived contentedly
off the young shoots of trees,
the sweet captivating scent of flowers,
and fruits of various tastes, smells and colors.

By duly preaching the Teaching to others, 34.5
helping those in distress as much as he could
and restraining the wicked from indecency,
he acted for the welfare of others.

Protected this way by the Great Being, the creatures in the forest area prospered happily, just as if they had a teacher, kinsman, doctor or king.

He increased in virtue,
protected by motherly compassion,
just as the creatures increased in virtue
from being protected by him.

atha kadā cit sa Mahā|sattvaḥ sattv'|ânukampayā van'|ântarāṇi samanuvicaraṃs tīvra|vedan"|âbhibhavād viceṣṭamānaṃ digdha|viddham iv' ânyatamasmin vana|pradeśe reṇu|saṃparka|vyākula|malina|kesara|saṭaṃ siṃhaṃ dadarśa. samabhigamya c' âinaṃ karuṇayā paricodyamānaḥ papraccha:

«kim idaṃ, mṛga|rāja? bāḍhaṃ khalv a|kalya|śarīraṃ tvāṃ paśyāmi.

34.10 dvi|peṣu darp'|âtiras'|ânuvṛttyā,
javа|prasaṅgād atha vā mṛgeṣu
kṛtaṃ tav' â|svāsthyam idaṃ śrameṇa,
vyādh'|êṣuṇā vā rujayā kayā cit. [4]

tad brūhi, vācyaṃ mayi ced idaṃ te.
yad eva vā kṛtyam ih' ôcyatāṃ tat.
mam' âsti yā mitra|gatā ca śaktis
tat|sādhya|saukhyaś ca† bhavān sukhī ca.» [5]

siṃha uvāca:

«sādho, pakṣi|vara, na me śrama|kṛtam† idam a|svāsthyaṃ rujayā vyādh'|êṣuṇā vā. idaṃ tv asthi|śakalaṃ gal'|ântara|vilagnaṃ† śalyam iva māṃ bhṛśaṃ dunoti. na hy enac† chaknomy abhyavahartum udgarituṃ vā. tad eṣa kālaḥ suhṛdām. yath" êdānīṃ jānāsi, tathā māṃ sukhinaṃ kuruṣv êti.»

One day, as he was wandering through the depths of the forest in his compassion for creatures, the woodpecker spotted a lion in an area of the jungle. The lion's matted mane was a filthy mess of dust and he was writhing around in intense pain, as if pierced by a poisoned arrow. Impelled by compassion, the woodpecker approached the lion and asked:

"What has happened here, king of beasts? You seem to be very sick.

Have you fallen ill from exhaustion,
indulging your pride against elephants
or swiftly chasing after deer?
Is a hunter's arrow the cause? Or a disease? 34.10

Speak if you think you can tell me.
Or state what needs to be done.
Whatever power my friendship offers,
I will use it to make you healthy and happy."

The lion answered:

"Virtuous and excellent bird, my sickness does not come from exhaustion, nor from a disease, nor a hunter's arrow. A chip of bone has stuck in my throat, tormenting me terribly like a barb. I cannot swallow it or spit it out. This is the moment for friends. Please heal me in whatever way you know best."

atha Bodhisattvaḥ paṭu|vijñānatvād vicintya śaly'|ôddharaṇ'|ôpāyaṃ tad|vadana|viṣkambhana†|pramāṇaṃ kāṣṭham ādāya taṃ siṃham uvāca: yā te śaktis tayā samyak tāvat sva|mukhaṃ nirvyādeh' îti. sa tathā cakāra. atha Bodhisattvas tad asya kāṣṭhaṃ danta|pālyor antare samyag niveśya praviśya c' âsya gala|mūlaṃ tat tiryag|avasthitam asthi|śakalaṃ vadan'|âgreṇ' âbhihṛty' âikasmin pradeśe samupapādita†|śaithilyam itarasmin parigṛhya paryante niścakarṣa.† nirgacchann eva ca† tat tasya vadana|viṣkambhaṇa|kāṣṭhaṃ nipātayām† āsa.

34.15 su|dṛṣṭa|karmā nipuṇo 'pi śalya|hṛn
na tat prayatnād api śalyam uddharet,
yad ujjahār' ân|abhiyoga|siddhayā
sa medhayā janma|śat'|ânubaddhayā. [6]

uddhṛtya śalyena sah" âiva tasya
duḥkhaṃ ca tat|saṃjanitāṃ śucaṃ ca
prītaḥ sa śaly'|ôddharaṇād yath" āsīt,
prītaḥ sa śaly'|ôddharaṇāt tath" āsīt. [7]

dharmatā hy eṣā saj|janasya:

prasādhya saukhyaṃ vyasanaṃ nivartya vā
sah' âpi duḥkhena parasya saj|janaḥ
upaiti tāṃ prīti|viśeṣa|saṃpadam
na yāṃ sva|saukhyeṣu sukh'|āgateṣv api. [8]

iti sa Mahā|sattvas tasya tad duḥkham upaśamayya pratīta†|hṛdayas tam āmantrya siṃhaṃ pratinanditas tena yath"|êṣṭaṃ jagāma.

Using his keen intelligence to consider how to extract the splinter, the Bodhi·sattva took a piece of wood that was wide enough to hold open the lion's mouth. He then told the lion to open his mouth as widely as he could. The lion obliged, whereupon the Bodhi·sattva inserted the piece of wood right between the lion's gums and entered deep into his throat. Using the tip of his beak, he took hold of the chip of bone that was lying across the lion's throat. After loosening it on one side he grabbed it by the other and pulled it out. Just as he was exiting, the woodpecker knocked down the piece of wood that held open the lion's mouth.

Not even an experienced and clever surgeon
could have removed the splinter, however they tried.
But he extracted it with an untrained intelligence
deriving from hundreds of past lives. 34.15

On extracting the splinter
and the pain and suffering it caused,
he felt as joyful as the lion
that the splinter was removed.

For the nature of a virtuous person is that:

Even if it involves pain,
to make others happy or avert their sorrow
gives a virtuous man a feeling of great joy
unfound in their own happiness, however easily gained.

Glad that he had quelled the lion's pain, the Great Being took leave of the lion, who bid him farewell in return, and then continued on his way.

34.20 atha kadā cit pravitata|rucira|citra|pattraḥ sa† śata|pattraḥ paribhraman kiṃ cit† tad|vidham āhāra|jātam an|āsādya kṣud|agni|parigata|tanus tam eva siṃham a|cira|hatasya hariṇa|taruṇasya māṃsam upabhuñjānaṃ tad|rudhir'|ânurañjita|vadana|nakhara|kesar'|âgraṃ saṃdhyā|prabhāsam ālabdhaṃ śaran|megha|vicchedam iva dadarśa.

kṛt'|ôpakāro 'pi tu na prasehe
vaktuṃ sa yācñā|viras'|âkṣaraṃ tam.
viśāradasy' âpi hi tasya lajjā
tat|kāla|mauna|vratam ādideśa. [9]

kāry'|ânurodhāt tu tath" âpi tasya
cakṣuṣ|pathe hrī|vidhuraṃ cacāra.
sa c' ânupaśyann api taṃ dur|ātmā
nimantraṇām apy akaron na tasya. [10]

śilā|tale bījam iva prakīrṇaṃ,
hutaṃ ca śānt'|ôṣmaṇi bhasma|puñje
sama|prakāraṃ phala|yoga|kāle
kṛtaṃ kṛta|ghne, vidule ca puṣpam. [11]

atha Bodhisattvo «nūnam ayaṃ na māṃ† pratyabhijānīta» iti nirviśaṅkataraḥ samabhigamy' âinam atithi†|vṛttyā prayukt'†|āśīr|vādaḥ saṃvibhāgam ayācata:

34.25 «pathyam astu mṛg'|êndrāya
vikram'|ārjita|vṛttaye!
arthi|saṃmānam icchāmi
tvad|yaśaḥ|puṇya|sādhanam!» [12]

Some time later, when he was flying around, spreading his beautiful glittering wings, the woodpecker was unable to find any appropriate food. His body had become afflicted by the fire of hunger when he spotted the same lion eating the meat of a freshly killed young antelope. The lion's mouth, claws and tips of his mane were dyed red with the animal's blood, making him resemble a piece of autumn cloud tinged by the glow of twilight. 34.20

But although he had done the lion a favor,
he dared not utter distasteful words of request.
For however eloquent he was, shame directed him
to undergo a vow of silence in the circumstance.

Instead his need for food made him wander
before the lion's eyes, painfully embarrassed.
But though the lion saw him,
he did not so much as greet him.

When it ripens, a deed done for an ingrate
is like a seed scattered on a slab of rock,
or an oblation poured on a cold pile of ash,
or the useless flower of a vídula tree.*

Concluding that the lion must not recognize him, the Bodhi·sattva approached him more confidently and asked him for a share of the food, blessing him with a benediction in the manner of a guest:

"May you be well, lord of beasts, 34.25
you who acquire food through bravery!
I wish for you to honor a petitioner,
so you can attain fame and merit!"

ity āśīr|vāda|madhuram apy ucyamāno 'tha sa† siṃhaḥ krauryal|mātsarya|paricayād an|ucit'|ārya|vṛttiḥ kop'|âgni| dīptay" âti|piṅgalayā didhakṣann iva vivartitayā dṛṣṭyā Bodhisattvam īkṣamāṇa uvāca:

«mā tāvad bhoḥ!

dayā|klaibyaṃ na yo veda khādan visphurato mṛgān,
praviśya tasya me vaktraṃ yaj jīvasi, na tad bahu? [13]

māṃ punaḥ paribhūy' âivam āsādayasi yācñayā?
jīvitena nu khinno 'si? paraṃ lokaṃ didṛkṣase?» [14]

34.30 atha Bodhisattvas tena tasya rūkṣ'|âkṣara|krameṇa pratyākhyāna|vacasā samupajāta|vrīḍas tata eva† nabhaḥ samutpapāta. «pakṣiṇo vayam» ity arthataḥ pakṣa|visphāra†|śabden' âinam uktv" âpacakrāma.†

ath' ânyatamā vana|devatā tasya tam a|sat|kāram a|sahamānā dhairya|prayāma|jijñāsayā vā samupetya† taṃ Mahā|sattvam uvāca:

«pakṣi|vara, kasmād imam a|sat|kāram asya dur|ātmanaḥ kṛt'|ôpakāraḥ san vidyamānāyāṃ† śaktāv api marṣayasi? ko 'rthaḥ kṛta|ghnen' ânen' âivam upekṣitena?

But although addressed with this delightful benediction, the lion was so instinctively cruel and selfish and so unused to noble behavior that he glared at the Bodhi·sattva, as if about to incinerate him with his bright red and rolling eyes that blazed with the fire of anger:

"Enough, sir!

I know nothing of cowardly compassion.
I eat up deer while they are still quivering!
Is it not already much that you live
after entering my mouth?

Do you impose more requests
out of contempt for me?
Are you tired of life?
Do you wish to see the next world?"

34.30 The Bodhi·sattva was filled with shame when he heard this cruel rejection and flew into the sky. Through the language of his extended wings, he expressed the sentiment "We are birds!"* and then flew away.

Now a certain forest deity, who was unable to endure the dishonor done to the Great Being, or who perhaps wished to know the extent of his fortitude, approached the bird and addressed him, saying:

"Finest of birds, why do you put up with the insults of this rogue, even though you have done him a favor and have the power to retaliate? Why show equanimity toward such an ungrateful being?

śaktas tvam asya nayane vadan'|âbhighātād
visphūrjitaḥ* pramathituṃ bala|śālino 'pi,
daṃṣṭr'|ântara|stham api c' āmiṣam asya hartuṃ.
tan mṛṣyate kim ayam asya bal'|âvalepaḥ?» [15]

atha Bodhisattvas tath" âpy a|sat|kāra|viprakṛtaḥ protsāhyamāno 'pi tayā vana|devatayā svāṃ prakṛti|bhadratāṃ vidarśayann† uvāca:

34.35 «alam† anena krameṇa! n' âiṣa mārgo 'smad|vidhānām!

ārte pravṛttiḥ sādhūnāṃ kṛpayā na tu lipsayā.
tām avaitu paro mā vā! tatra kopasya ko vidhiḥ? [16]

vañcanā sā ca tasy' âiva yan na vetti kṛtaṃ paraḥ.
ko hi pratyupakār'|ârthī tasya bhūyaḥ kariṣyati? [17]

upakartā tu dharmeṇa
paratas tat|phalena ca
yogam āyāti niyamād
ih' âpi yaśasaḥ śriyā. [18]

kṛtaṃ† ced dharma ity eva
kas tatr' ânuśayaḥ punaḥ?
atha pratyupakār'|ârtham
ṛṇa|dānaṃ na tat|kṛtam. [19]

He may be strong,
but you have the power
to wound his eyes,
bursting an attack at his face.
Or you could snatch the meat
from between his teeth.
So why do you put up with
his arrogance in his strength?"

But despite suffering this disrespectful insult and despite the exhortation of the forest deity, the Bodhi·sattva answered as follows, revealing his innate goodness:

"Speak not of such behavior! Beings such as I do not follow that path! 34.35

The virtuous help those in distress
from compassion, not desire for gain.
The other person can understand it or not!
What need is there to be angry about this?

By not realizing what others do for them,
people only cheat themselves.
For if someone seeks a return favor,
why would they help them again?

Through their self-restraint,
those who benefit others
gain virtue and virtue's fruit
as well as glory and prosperity.

If one acts this way, thinking it right,
why should one feel regret later?
If one does it to seek a favor in return,
then it is a loan, not a service.

34.40 upakṛtaṃ kila vetti na me paras
tad|apakāram iti prakaroti yaḥ,
nanu viśodhya guṇaiḥ sa yaśas|tanuṃ
dvirada|vṛttim abhipratipadyate. [20]

na vetti ced upakṛtam āturaḥ paro,
na yokṣyate nanu† guṇa|kāntayā śriyā.
sa|cetasaḥ punar atha ko bhavet kramaḥ
samucchritaṃ pramathitum ātmano yaśaḥ? [21]

idaṃ tv atra me yukta|rūpaṃ pratibhāti:

yasmin sādh'|ûpacīrṇe 'pi
mitra|dharmo na lakṣyate,
a|niṣṭhuram a|saṃrabdham
apayāyāc chanais tataḥ.» [22]

atha sā devatā tat | subhāṣita | prasādita | manāḥ «sādhu! sādhv!» iti punar uktam abhipraśasya tat tat priyam uvāca:

34.45 «ṛte jaṭā|valkala|dhāraṇa|śramād
bhavān ṛṣis tvaṃ vidit'|āyatir yatiḥ
na veṣa|mātraṃ hi munitva|siddhaye.
guṇair upetas tv iha tattvato muniḥ.» [23]

ity abhilakṣya pratipūjya c' âinaṃ† tatr' âiv' ântar|dadhe.

tad evaṃ, protsāhyamāno 'pi sādhur n' âlaṃ pāpe pravartitum an|abhyāsād.

If one harms others
for not recognizing a service,
it is like gaining a spotless fame through virtue,
only to dirty oneself like an elephant again!* 34.40

If the other is too sick to recognize a service,
they will never attain the lovely glory of virtue.
But why should a sensible person
destroy their lofty renown?

And the following point appears to me apt:

Those who do not display friendliness,
even after being helped by a good person,
should be quietly shunned,
without harshness or anger."

Gratified by the bird's wise words, the deity repeatedly praised him, saying, "Excellent! Excellent!" He then addressed him with the following kind words:

"Spared the toil of matted hair and bark robes, 34.45
you are a seer, an ascetic knowing the future!
Appearance is not enough to become a sage.
The real sage in the world has virtues."

After making this remark and honoring the woodpecker, the deity disappeared there and then.

In this way, even when provoked, a virtuous man is incapable of turning to evil since it is contrary to his habit.

iti saj|jana|praśaṃsāyāṃ vācyam. kṣānti|kathāyām† apy upaneyam: «evaṃ kṣamā|paricayān na vaira|bahulo bhavati. n' â|vadya|bahulo bahu|jana|priyo mano|jñaś c'» êti. «evaṃ pratisaṃkhyāna|bahulāḥ svāṃ guṇa|śobhām anurakṣanti paṇḍitā» iti pratisaṃkhyāna|varṇe 'pi† vācyam. Tathāgata|māhātmye ca bhadra|prakṛty|abhyāsa|varṇe ca: «evaṃ bhadra|prakṛtir abhyastā tiryag|gatānām api na nivartata» iti.

One should tell this story when praising the virtuous. And one should also cite this story when preaching forbearance, saying: “In this way, those who habitually practice forbearance will rarely have enemies. Seldom censured, they will be popular and liked by many people.” And one should narrate it when praising self-control, saying: “In this way, wise men who abound in self-control preserve the splendor of their virtue.” One should also narrate this story when discussing the majesty of the Tatha·gata or when praising a virtuous nature ingrained by practice, saying: “In this way, a good nature ingrained by habitual practice never lapses, even in the case of animals.”

NOTES

Bold *references are to the English text;* ***bold italic*** *references are to the Sanskrit text. An asterisk (*) in the body of the text marks the word or passage being annotated.*

21.3 **Great Being**: a translation of *mahā / sattva*. This important Buddhist term is often used for Bodhi·sattvas and may originally have been appropriated from non-Buddhist sources such as Brahmanical epic literature, where it often means someone who has great purity, character or courage, or simply a "hero." In the Brahmanical epics the compound is treated as a *bahuvrīhi* ("whose *sattva* is great"), whereas in Buddhist texts such as the "Garland of the Buddha's Past Lives" it tends to be treated as a *karmadhāraya* compound ("great being"), using the meaning of *sattva* as "being."

21.6 **Great One**: Literally meaning "great-spirited" or "he whose self is great," *mah"/ātmā* (Mahatma) is a pan-Indic term of respect, frequently found in both Buddhist and non-Buddhist literature. In Hindu epic, it often simply means "hero" and the example of Mahatma Gandhi illustrates how the term is still used in the modern day to refer to a person of high spiritual status. In the "Garland of the Buddha's Past Lives," *Mah"/ātmā* is used interchangeably with *mahā/sattva* ("Great Being"). I follow Khoroche's translation of "Great One" for *Mah"/ātmā*.

21.16 **Chakra·vaka birds** (*Anas casarca*) are renowned for their attachment to each other and are often used as symbols of conjugal love in Indian literature.

21.38 [18] **Quiet**: the Sanskrit here is *praśama*. The king assumes such quietness is negative, but thereby disregards the fact that it is precisely the ascetic quality of *praśama*, in the positive sense of "tranquility" or "calmness," that demonstrates the Bodhi·sattva's virtue.

21.64 For similar passages, see *Saṃyutta Nikāya* 1.162 and *Dīgha Nikāya* 2.136.

21.64 **Tatha·gata**: a common epithet of the Buddha. Buddhist traditions analyze the compound in various ways, depending on whether it is construed as *tathā/gata* ("thus-gone") or *tath"/āgata* ("thus-come"). At the end of a compound, *-gata* often simply means "is," resulting in the literal rendition of "is thus" for *tathā/gata*. The abstract nature of the phrase can be seen as an effective way of conveying the Buddha's transcendent state.

22.4 **Anánda**: one of the Buddha's main disciples, known for his devotional nature.

22.5 **Nagas** are semi-divine snakes. **Yakshas** are a type of semi-divine being (in other contexts demons). **Vidya·dharas** are divine beings known for their magical powers.

22.10 *Siddha*: a semi-divine being.

22.35 **Kadámba**: *Nauclea cadamba*. A large tree with orange fragrant flowers. **Sarja**: *Vatica robusta* A timber tree. **Árjuna**: *Terminalia arjuna*. Known for its medicinal properties, it has yellowish white flowers. **Kétaki**: *Pandanus fascicularis*, or *Pandanus odoratissimus*. A tree with fragrant flowers and pineapple-like fruits.

22.72 [38] **Hunter**: *niṣāda* is the name for a particular low caste in Indian society, often associated with hunters.

22.80 [43] **Twice-born**: birds are considered to be born first in an egg and then again when they hatch.

22.92 [51] The **king of stars** is the moon, and the **demon lord** is Rahu, who is said to swallow the moon during an eclipse.

23.3 **Lord**: a standard name for the Buddha, *Bhagavat* is notoriously difficult to translate. Literally meaning "he who has a share," the word is variously analyzed by Buddhist traditions but essentially refers to the sublime spiritual state that the Buddha has attained (or acquired a "share" of). The word *bhagavat* is also frequently found in non-Buddhist contexts to refer to God, as is illustrated by the famous Hindu text the *Bhagavadgītā* ("The Song of the Lord"). Due to its pan-Indic usage, I translate *Bhagavat* as "Lord" as a way of expressing the devotional connotations of the word, while at the same time avoiding doctrinally awkward translations such as "Blessed One."

23.3 **Moral treatises**: the *dharma/śāstras* are a category of Brahmanical text dealing with a wide range of issues, including caste practice, householder morality and the renunciate path.

23.14 **Kshatriya law**: the ideology of kings to attain and secure power and acquire profit. The *locus classicus* for such Machiavellian ideas is the treatise of the *Arthaśāstra* by Kauṭilya.

23.36 **Dhyanas**: four levels of meditation, each increasing in subtlety and concentration. The five transcendent knowledges (*abhijñā*) are: a divine eye, divine hearing, knowledge of other people's minds, an ability to recollect previous rebirths and supernatural powers. See EDGERTON s.v.

23.37 The Bodhi·sattva sees these events with his divine eye, which he acquires through the transcendent knowledges.

3.115 [60] **Look**: there is a pun here on the word *dṛṣṭi*, covering both the "look" of a poisonous snake but also the false "view" of the ministers' ideologies.

24.7 **Tínduki**: the fruits of the tínduki tree (*Diospyros embryopteris*), or Indian persimmon, are sour.

24.57 **Evil One**: Mara.

24.68 **Teaching**: the doctrine of Buddhism (the *dharma*). Also used with the meaning of truth or virtue.

25.3 *Shárabha*: although in later literature the *shárabha* is a mythical eight-legged animal, in the present context it appears to be a type of deer.

26.3 **Sala**: usually called shala (Sanskrit: *śāla*), *Shorea robusta*. A large timber tree. **Bákula**: *Mimusops elengi*. A tree with orange cherries. **Piyála**: *Buchanania latiifolia*. The fruit is edible and the kernel of the seed has an almond taste. **Hintála**: *Phoenix*, or *Elate paludosa*. A species of palm. Often called the mangrove date palm or marshy date tree. **Tamála**: *Xanthochymus pictorius*. A tree with dark bark and leaves, white blossoms and orange edible fruit. **Nakta·mala**: *Pongamia glabra* ("Indian beech"). Well known for its medicinal antiseptic properties, it has fragrant white flowers. **Vídula**: *Calamus rotang*. The rattan palm tree. **Níchula**: *Barringtonia acutangula*. Commonly called the Indian oak or itchy tree (due to hosting itchy caterpillars). The seeds are often used as a domestic remedy and the bark is used in India as a fish poison. It produces bright red flowers. **Shínshapa**: *Dalbergia sissoo*, or Indian redwood. An important timber tree in India. **Tínisha**: *Ougeinia dalbergioides*, or *Dalbergia oojeinensis*. A timber tree known for its toughness. It produces white-pink blossoms. **Shami**: *Prosopis spicigera*. A strong timber tree; used to kindle fire at sacrifice. **Palásha**: *Butea frondosa*. A timber tree with bright orange flowers used for dye. Its roots are used for rope and its wood is used on Hindu funeral pyres. **Shaka**: *Tectona grandis*. A teak tree. **Kasha**: *Saccharum spontaneum*, or Wild Sugarcane. A tall grass. **Kusha**: *Poa cynosuroides*. A sacred grass used in rituals. **Kadámba**: *Nauclea cadamba*. A large tree with orange fragrant flowers. **Sarja**: *Vatica robusta*. A timber tree. **Árjuna**: *Terminalia arjuna*. Known for its medicinal properties, it has yellowish white flowers. **Dhava**: *Anogeissus latifolia*. Its wood produces gum (ghatti gum) and its bark is known for medicinal properties. Its leaves contain a high amount of tannin. **Khádira**: *Acacia catechu*, or black cutch. A thorny tree used for timber. Its bark has medicinal properties and its heartwood is used for dye and tanning. **Kútaja**: *Wrightia antidysenterica*. A shrub that bears white, star-like flowers. Its bark and leaves are known for medicinal properties.

26.30 [15] **Deer Star**: the "Deer's Head" (*mṛga/śīrṣa*), or Capricorn constellation.

26.76 [38] **Three modes**: this refers to the categories of mind, speech and body.

27.12 [4] **Savoring a fine dramatic performance**: this refers to the aesthetic experience known as *rasa*.

28.13 [5] **Nándana garden**: a divine garden in the Trayas·trinsha heaven ruled over by Shakra.

28.54 [31] **Not a lady's man**: I follow MONIER-WILLIAMS, who notes that *kumbha* can mean "paramour of a harlot" or "fancy man." I am grateful to Andrew Skilton for his comments on this passage.

28.79 [47] The verse plays on the meaning of *kṣamā* as both "forbearance" and "earth."

29.3 **Brahma realm and dhyanas**: Each of the four *dhyānas* (meditative concentrations) has a corresponding group of heavens in which a person may be reborn. The deities born there are called Brahma (*Brahmā*) and their heaven is called a Brahma realm (*Brahma/loka*). In this story *Brahma/loka* appears to be used as an umbrella term covering the totality of the Brahma realms, thereby meaning the Brahma Realm. Brahma deities (masculine in gender) are to be differentiated from Brahman (neuter in gender), the impersonal absolute in Brahmanical thought.

29.5 **Sphere of Desire**: one of three spheres in Buddhist cosmology. The Sphere of Desire (*kāma/dhātu*) contains six heavens, the human world and the bad rebirths (*dur/gati*) of ghosts, animals and hell-beings. The two other spheres are the Sphere of (Pure) Form (*rūpa/dhātu*) and the Formless Sphere (*a/rūpa/dhātu*). The former is identified with the four *dhyāna* meditations and the latter with the four formless meditations (*samāpatti*).

29.24 [10] **Conception**: in Indian Buddhist thought, a person is "born" at conception with consciousness already in place.

29.35 [16] **Nishka**: a denomination of money. See MONIER-WILLIAMS S.V.

29.48 [28] **Sangháta**: a hell realm where two mountains converge to crush people in the middle. See *Mahāvastu* 1.21f.

29.54 [34] **Váitarani**: a river in hell. The *Mahāvastu* states that the river is "acrid" (*kṣāra/nadīṃ*, 1.7, *kṣār'/ôdakaṃ*, 1.12), and "hard" (*kaṭhināṃ*, 1.7). The *Bodhicaryāvatāra* states that its waters are like fire (*dahana/sama/jalāyāṃ Vaitaraṇyāṃ*, 10.10).

29.58 [38] Notice the poetic technique (*yamaka*) of repeating the same three syllables at the end of each quarter verse. Verses 29.72 [50] –29.76 [54] also offer fine examples; there the last two syllables of each quarter verse are repeated.

30.29 **Yójana**: a measurement of distance, originally marking the distance a person can travel without unyoking an animal. MONIER-WILLIAMS (see s.v.) states that texts differ over the exact distance of a yójana, ranging from 2.5 to 9 miles.

30.44 [22] **Floundering**: The Sanskrit word *magna* literally means "sunk" or "drowning." It recalls another common metaphor in Buddhism, whereby samsara is compared to an ocean and the Bodhi·sattva is a raft helping people to cross to the other side.

30.46 [23] **Mount Sunset**: a mountain in the West behind which the sun is supposed to set.

30.59 **Lordly elephants**: four elephants that are said to stand in the quarters of the sky, ridden by world-protectors (*loka/pāla*).

30.81 **Complete nirvana**: the Buddha's *parinirvāṇa*, acquired at death.

30.81 **This is not the way...** These words are uttered by the Buddha at his death-bed when he tells Anánda that the correct way to honor him is to practice the Dharma. See the *Mahāparinibbāna Sutta* (*Dīgha Nikāya* 2.138).

Soma: the god of the moon.

31.5 The **Vedas** are the most authoritative texts in Brahmanical thought, said to be direct hearings (*śruti*) of sacred truth. The four Vedas are: the *Ṛg Veda*, *Sāma Veda*, *Yajur Veda* and *Atharva Veda*. The **Vedángas** (*ved'/āṅgas*, literally "limbs of the Veda") are six subjects that are auxiliary to the Vedas. They include: phonetics (*śikṣā*), meter (*chandas*), grammar (*vyākaraṇa*), etymology (*nirukta*), astrology (*jyotiṣa*), and ritual (*kalpa*). See MONIER-WILLIAMS s.v. There are four *Upavédas* ("sub-Vedas"), each of which is linked to one of the four main Vedas. They are: the *Āyur/veda* (medicine), *Dhanur/veda* (archery), *Gāndharva/veda* (music), and *Śilpa/śāstra* (arts). In some texts the fourth *Upavéda* is *Śastra/śāstra* (weaponry) or *Sthāpatya/veda* (architecture). See MONIER-WILLIAMS s.v.

31.10 **Cuckoo**: the word *para/bhṛta* means "raised by another," referring to the way in which cuckoos have their eggs reared by other birds.

1.63 [28] **Kubéra**: the "lord of wealth" (*dhaneśvara*).

1.74 [38] **Three pursuits**: Brahmanical thought extols three different pursuits in life: *kāma* (desire or pleasure), *artha* (benefit or profit), and *dharma* (morality or righteousness). A fourth pursuit of "liberation" (*mokṣa*) is sometimes added to the list.

31.79 **Consecrated**: the notion that war is a form of sacrifice is constantly alluded to in martial literature such as the "Maha·bhárata."

.110 [54] **Bad rebirth**: the word *apāya* can refer to any of the three bad rebirths (a hell-being, ghost or animal). In the singular, it is often used for hell.

.127 [66] A few of these words are unclear. SPEYER translates *kīrtana* as "temple," and this is followed by KHOROCHE, but there seems little evidence for its precise meaning. I have opted for the more general word "monument." The word *sattra* is also vague. MONIER-WILLIAMS (see s.v.) lists various possible meanings, including house, asylum, and hospital. Originally, however, the word refers to a type of sacrifice. Therefore *sattr'/âjira* could mean a "sacrificial yard" or "sacrificial area." This mention of Vedic practice need not surprise the reader, as several *jātaka*s, including the present story, portray the Bodhi·sattva performing Brahmanical practices.

.145 [74] This verse is similar to *Dhammapada* v.151.

.164 [83] K has *āha* extra-metrically before the verse.

Story 32 **Ayo·griha**: "Iron-house." Although we are not explicitly told that this is the Bodhi·sattva's name, we can assume that this is the case from the passage following verse 4, in which we are told the Bodhi·sattva was reared in an iron nursery to protect him from demons. Furthermore, the Pali version of this story (*Jātaka* no. 510) explicitly states that this is his name (Pali: *Ayoghara*).

32.1 **Spiritual alarm**: the experience of saṃvega involves a type of spiritual shock whereby one's ordinary conceptions are "shaken up" through gaining an insight into impermanence. In Buddhist narratives, saṃvega often provides the trigger for the protagonist to embark on a path of renunciation.

32.12 [6] The meaning of the verse seems to be that people are attracted to the moon in the same way as they are to a virtuous person, even though they may not be acquainted.

32.36 [24] **Manu**: the father of mankind.

32.41 [29] **Ploys such as appeasement**: KHOROCHE (1989: 269, n.5) notes that four such ploys are listed in the *Arthaśāstra* (2.10) for dealing with an enemy: appeasement (*sāman*), bribery (*dāna*), sowing dissension (*bheda*) and armed force (*daṇḍa*).

32.50 [38] **Dhanvan·tari**: a divine physician, traditionally said to be the composer of the *Āyurveda*.

32.65 **Immeasurables**: the four mental attitudes of loving kindness, compassion, sympathetic joy and equanimity.

33.9 **Yama**, the god of death, is said to bear a staff and mount a buffalo.

33.10 [5] Following HAHN's interpretation of the second half of the verse (HAHN 2001: 384f.) based partly on the Tibetan translation.

33.11 The **yaksha** in this story is a semi-divine spirit, rather than a demon.

34.3 **Woodpecker**: the word *śata/pattra* literally means a bird with a hundred feathers.

34.23 [11] **Vídula**: *Calamus rotang*, the rattan palm. KHOROCHE (1989: 270, n.1) notes that, according to tradition, the flower of this tree cannot be used as an offering to gods.

34.30 HAHN (2001: 394) points out that the Tibetan translation has additional text here, which may indicate that some of the original Sanskrit is lost, thereby explaining the elliptical nature of the sentence. Hahn provides the following translation of the Tibetan: "Since we are birds there is nothing you can do to us!"

34.33 [15] HAHN (2001: 395) suggests the emendation of *visphūrjitaḥ* to *visphūrjinaḥ*, based on the Tibetan translation. This would then agree with *asya*: "when he (the lion) is opening (them) wide because of the attacks on (his) face" (HAHN's literal rendering).

34.40 [20] **To dirty oneself like an elephant again**: KHOROCHE (1989: 270, n.2) notes that this refers to an elephant's habit of spraying itself with water and then rolling in the dust.

EMENDATIONS TO THE SANSKRIT TEXT

This list is limited to the emendations that have been made of KERN's text. For a full record of variant readings, the reader is advised to consult KHOROCHE (1987).

Manuscripts and Editions Cited

A	Add. MS 1328, University Library, Cambridge. See KHOROCHE (1987: 6).
Asm	A, sec. manu
B	Add. MS 1415, University Library, Cambridge. See KHOROCHE (1987: 6).
Cb	MS G 9980, Asiatic Society, Calcutta. See KHOROCHE (1987: 8).
Em	Emendation
K	Edition of KERN (1891). KERN based his edition on MSS A, B, and P.
Kem	Emendation made by KERN (1891)
N	MS III.359.I, Durbar Library, Nepal. See KHOROCHE (1987: 9).
Nsm	N, sec. manu
P	MSS nos. 45/6, Fonds Sanscrit, Bibliothèque Nationale, Paris. See KHOROCHE (1987: 6).
T	MS 136, University Library, Tokyo. See KHOROCHE (1987: 8)
Toyoq	Fragments from Turfan. See edition of WELLER (1955) and comments by KHOROCHE (1987: 5f.).

Emendations Made

21 title	*cullabodhijātakam* N : *cullabodhisattvajātakam* T, *buddhabodhijātakam* A B P, *cuḍḍabodhijātakam* Kem
21.1	*krodhavijayāc* N T : *krodhavinayāc* A B K P
21.3	*daivavat* T : *daivata* K
21.4	*sa kālānām* A B N P T : *kālānām* K
21.4	*acireṇa* N T : *acireṇaiva* K
21.6	*kṛtapravrajyāparicayatvāt* T : *pravrajākṛtaparicayatvāt* K

21.6 *vairavairasya* N T : *madavairasya* K
21.9 *asmadanugamanavyavasāyena* T : *asmadanugamanaṃ pratyanena vyavasāyena* K
21.9 *bhavatyā* A B P : *bhavatyās* K
21.11 [3] *pariśrameṇa* A N P T : *paribhrameṇa* B K
21.15 *dvis trir* N T : *dvitrir* K
21.15 *naivecchati* A B N P T : *necchati* K
21.16 *dharaṇitale* A B N P T : *dharaṇitale* K
21.22 *atha tu* N : *atha* K
21.24 *upākrośa* A B N P T : *upakrośa* K
21.27 *pratipadyeya* N T : *prapadyeya* K
21.29 *strīsaṃdarśinaḥ* N T : *strīsaṃdarśanādhikṛtān* K
21.29 *emām* T : *aināṃ* A B N P : *aitāṃ* K
21.34 [15] *śailo 'pi yasya* N T : *syād yasya śailaḥ* K
21.34 [15] *jīvāmy atimandabhāgyā* N : *jīvāmi ca mandabhāgyā* K
21.35 [16] *cāham* A B N P T : *vāham* K
21.38 [18] *âbhinipīḍit'* N T : *âbhinipātit'* K
21.39 [19] *bhujapauruṣaṃ* A B N P T : *svāṃ bhujayo ruṣaṃ* K
21.41 [20] *ca* T : *tu* K
21.42 *avijñāya cāsmābhiś* N : *aparijñāyāsmābhiś* K
21.58 [33] *vidito* A B N P T : *viditaṃ* K
21.61 [35] *bahunātra* A B N P T : *bahunā tu* K
21.62 *nyapatad* N : *nyapatat tad atyaya* K
21.62 *vyasarjayat* N P T : *vyavasarjayat* K
21.63 *krodhavijayāc* N T : *krodhavinayāc* K
21.63 *krodhavijaye* N T : *krodhavinaye* K
22.1 *anukartum* N T : *anugantum* K
22.3 *sahasravipulasaṃkhyasya* A B N P : *sahasrasaṃkhyasya* K
22.4 *cāritraḥ śūraḥ* N T : *cāritraśūraḥ* K
22.4 *samaravidhiviśāradaḥ* N T : *samaravivadhaviśāradaḥ* K
22.4 *haṃsasenāpatir* N T : *senāpatir* K

22.5 *jvalitataraguṇaprabhāvāv* A B N T : *jvalitataraprabhāvāv* K
22.5 *ācārya* A N T : *ārya* K
22.5 *śeṣaṃ* N T : *śreṣṭhaśeṣaṃ* K
22.10 *sarvasattvahitapravṛttisumukhasya* A B N P T : *sarvasattvahitasumukhasya* K
22.13 *sasenāpater* A T : *sasenādhipater* K
22.13 *pratyayit'* T : *prātyayik'* K
22.13 *aneka* A N T : *naika* K
22.14 *prasṛtanipuṇaḥ* N T : *prasṛtanipuṇamatayaḥ* K
22.19 *mānasasaraḥpratispardhi* N T : *mānasasarasaḥ pratispardhi* K
22.19 *samupagūḍhavimalasalilam* N : *samupagūḍhaṃ vimalasalilam* K
22.20 [8] *opetaiḥ* N : *otpattra*
22.22 [10] *vicitraṃ kumudaiḥ* N T : *vicitra/kumudaiḥ* K
22.32 *taruṇahaṃsajanasaṃpāte* N T : *haṃsataruṇajanasaṃpāte* K
22.32 *viracana* N T : *vicaraṇa* K
22.32 *ca sitaiḥ* N T : *vikasitaiḥ* K
22.33 *abhivīkṣya paro vismayaḥ sva/yūth'/ânusmṛtiś ca prādurabhūt* A B N P T : *abhivīkṣya prādur abhūt* K
22.36 *saṃvarṇayām āsa* A B T : *varṇayām* K N.
22.37 *prakṣīṇa* N T : *prahīṇa* K
22.38 *pariprasnavyaktākāraṃ* N T : *praśnavyaktākāraḥ* K
22.39 *kena cid* N T : *kiṃ cid* K
22.39 *parihīyante* A B P T : *parihīyate* K
22.40 [19] *vāśitānvarthahṛdayāḥ* T : *vāśitārthasvahṛdayāḥ* K
22.43 *vibhūtirasaṃ* N T : *guṇavibhūtirasaṃ* K
22.44 *vibhūṣaṇāyāṃ* N T : *vibhūṣaṇarajanyāṃ*
22.47 *svasthatāṃ* N T : *svacchandatāṃ* K
22.48 *nyavedayanta* N T : *pratyavedayanta* K
22.49 *pramāṇasusaṃsthita* N : *pramāṇau susaṃsthita* K
22.50 *śākunikamanviṣya* N T : *śākunikagaṇe samanviṣya* K

22.50 *upalakṣya* A B N P : *upalabhya* K

22.52 [24] *ślakṣṇair* B N P T : *sūkṣmair* K

22.53 *cid atraivaṃvidho* N T : *cittatraivaṃvidho* K

22.53 *virutaviśeṣeṇa* B N T : *rutaviśeṣeṇa* K

22.53 *haṃsā* N T : *(haṃsā)* K

22.53 *diśaḥ* N T : *divaṃ* K

22.53 *haṃsasenāpatir* N T : *haṃsasenādhipatir* K

22.64 [32] *na ca* N T : *ca na* K

22.66 [33] *apacitaḥ* Em : *upacitaḥ* A B K N P T. Reading *apacitaḥ* with Speyer and Khoroche, as supported by the Pali parallel (Jātaka 5.339.22). All manuscripts, however, read *upacitaḥ*.

22.73 *taṃ* N T : om. K

22.73 *vidravantam* T : *vidrutam* K

22.73 *tatsamāsannau* N T : *tatsamāpannau* K

22.75 [40] *sajjapattraratho* A B N P T : *sajjapattrarathī* K

22.77 [41] *vihagaḥ* A N T : *vihaṃgaḥ* K

22.89 [48] *parīṇāhau* A B Cb P T : *pariṇāhau* K

22.90 [49] *muñca* Cb T : *muñced* K

22.93 *svajīvita* Cb T : *jīvita* K

22.93 *ālaṃkṛtena vacasā* Cb T : *ālaṃkṛtavacasā* K

22.93 *balāt* Cb T : *vaśāt* A B K P

22.95 [52] *vidarśitaḥ* Cb T : *pradarśitaḥ* K

22.98 [54] *evaṃ saha jñātigaṇena* A B Cb P T : *evaṃ suhṛjjñātigaṇena* K

22.101 *sa* Cb T : *atha* K

22.107 [60] *viśrambhaniḥśaṅkaṃ* Cb T : *viśrambhaniḥśaṅko* K

22.113 *prabhodbhāsurarucira* B Cb T : *prabhodbhāsurasurucira* K

22.113 *sukhāpāśraya* A B : *sukhopāśraya* K

22.116 [67] *samayānugrahanigrahapravṛttyā* A B Cb P T : *samayānugrahavigrahapravṛttyā* K

22.116 [67] *jagatāṃ* A B Cb P T : *jagato* K

22.118 [69] *dayāpravṛttiśobhāṃ* N T : *dayānuvṛttiśobhāṃ* K

2.121 [71] *sarvatraiva* N T : *sarvatra ca* K

2.130 [78] *ākāṅkṣitābhyāgamayoḥ* A B N P T : *ākāṅkṣitābhigamayoḥ* K

22.142 *praharṣa* A B N P T : *sapraharṣa* K

22.142 *vikasitanayanaḥ* N : *vadanaḥ* K

22.142 *ity* A B N P T : om. K

2.144 [88] *tathetaṃ mayi viśrambham* T : *tathaiva mayi visrambha* K

2.146 [89] *'bhinave* N T : *hi nave* K

2.147 [90] *kasya* N T : *kaś ca* K

2.147 [90] *āvalambeta* A B N P T : *āvalambyeta* K

2.147 [90] *saṃmāno vidhinā* T : *saṃmānavidhinā* K

2.150 [93] *vrajet* N T : *bhajet* K

22.157 *saṃmānana* N T : *saṃmāna* K

22.159 *anukartum* N T : *anugantum* K

22.160 *vācyam* N : om. K

22.160 *bhavad iti* N : *bhavatīti* K

23.3 *bodhir* N T : *mahābodhir* K

23.3 *kramaprayāmo* N T : *kramavyāyāmo* K

23.4 *rājamātrāṇāṃ* A B N P : om. K

23.6 *viṣayāntam* B N : *viṣayāntaram* A K P T

23.9 [3] *premaguṇonmukhe* N T : *premaguṇotsuke* K

23.10 *guṇavibhūtim* N T : *guṇasamṛddhim* K

23.10 *matitvān* N T : *buddhitvān* K

23.13 *pratāraṇā* N T : *pratāraṇa* K

23.13 *saṃcārahetu* N T : *saṃcāraṇahetu* K

23.14 *opagṛhṇīte* A B N P T : *opagṛṇīte* K

23.16 [5] *vāśani* N T : *cāśani* K

23.17 *tatsamīpaparivartināṃ* N T : *tatsamīpavartināṃ* K

23.17 *kāmavad* N T : *kāma iva tam* K

23.21 *ābhigatam* N T : *āgatam* K

23.25 *vrīḍāvanata* N T : *vrīḍāvanāmita* K

23.36 *pañca cābhijñāḥ* N T : *pañcābhijñāḥ* K

23.39 *svabuddhiracitam* N T : *svabuddhirucitam* K
23.43 *kāmopabhoga* N T : *kāmabhoga* K
23.46 [21] *upayoga/nayena* N : *upabhoganayena* K
23.47 *dṛṣṭigatonmārgeṇa* N : *dṛṣṭikṛtonmārgeṇa* K
23.48 *dṛṣṭigata* N : *dṛṣṭikṛta* K
23.48 *avetya* N T : *avekṣya* K
23.49 [22] *bhraśyate 'pakṛtaṃ* N T : *bhraśyaty apakṛtaṃ* K
23.52 *kṛtasaṃmodana* N T : *kṛtapratisaṃmodana* K
23.52 *ābhihāraś* N T : *ābhinirhāraś* K
23.54 *kuśatṛṇa* A B N P T : *kṛśatṛṇa* K
23.54 *gṛhītam* N T : *pragṛhītaṃ* K
23.55 *pravikasitasmitavadanā* A N T : *pravikasitavadanā* K
23.56 *vyavasāyasāmarthyam* N T : *vyavasāyasādhusāmarthyam* K
23.58 *atr' āsmān* A B N P : *asmān* K
23.58 *āyuṣmantaḥ* N : *atrabhavantaḥ* K
23.62 [25] *imam* N T : *idam* K
23.84 *śliṣṭair* N T : *suśliṣṭair* K
23.99 *amātyam āmantryovāca* N T : *amātyam uvāca* K
23.100 *manyate* N : *manyase* K
23.101 [51] *dharmaḥ* N T : *dharmaṃ* K
23.104 [53] *nu* N T : *na* K
23.106 [55] *aduṣṭam* A B N T : *adṛṣṭam* K
23.108 *naiva* N : *naiva ca* K
23.108 *grahītum* N T : *pratigrahītum* K
23.109 *ṛddhyabhisaṃskāraṃ* A N P T : *ṛddhyābhisaṃskāraṃ* K
23.109 *manasaṃ* N T : *mānasaṃ* K
23.127 [72] *badhāna* N P T : *bandhāna* K
23.129 *dṛṣṭigatakāpathād* N : *dṛśṭikṛtakāpathād* K
23.131 *pāpāśrayatvād* N T : °*nupāśrayatvād* K
24.7 *mārgapranaṣṭo* N T : *mārgāt pranaṣṭo* K

24.7 *digvibhāga* N T : *digbhāga* K
24.7 *prapātābhipranatām* N T : *prapātābhinatām* K
24.9 *vilalāpa* N T : *ārtivaśād vilalāpa* K
24.14 *samabhiruhya* N T : *abhiruhya* K
24.14 *prapātam* T : *tat prapātam* K
24.14 *īkṣamāṇo* A B N P T : *vīkṣamāṇo* K
24.16 *samabhipraṇamya sāñjalir udvīkṣamāṇa* N T : *samabhipraṇamyodvīkṣamāṇaḥ sāñjalir* K
24.23 *samāśvāsya* B N T : *āśvāsya* K
24.32 *'yam ahaṃ* N T : *'haṃ* K
24.38 *saumyabhāvaḥ* N T : *saumyasvabhāvaḥ* K
24.41 [23] *tu* N T : *ca* A B K P
24.41 [23] *kenāhato* A B N P T : *kena hato* K
24.51 [32] *me* A B N P T : *mām* K
24.55 [35] *etaṃ* T : *etat* K
24.57 *pāpaṃ karma* A B N P T : *pāpaṃ* K
24.57 *atibībhatsavikṛtadarśanaṃ* N : *atibībhatsavikṛtataradarśanaṃ* K
24.58 *nātivasanapraticchannakaupīnam* N T : *nātipracchannakaupīnam* K
24.64 [40] *amitracaritāṃ* A B N P T : *amitracaritaṃ* K
24.64 [40] *vṛttim* N T : *vṛttam* K
24.66 [42] *ime* A B P T : *imaṃ* K
24.66 [42] *prabhāvasiddhī* T : *prabhāvasiddhi* A B P : *prabhāvasiddhaṃ* N.
24.66 [42] *hy* A B N P T : om. K
24.68 *'pi* T : om. K
25.3 *bhūmibhāge* A B N P T : *bhūbhāge* K
25.4 *śarabhamṛgo* A B N P T : *śarabho mṛgo* K
25.6 *dūrāpasṛta* N : *dūrād apasṛta* K
25.7 *yena* N T : *yataḥ* K
25.7 *parameṇa* N T : *pareṇa* K

25.8 *ānumārgagataṃ* N T : *ānumārgāgataṃ* K
25.8 *sa turagas* N T : *turagavaras* K
25.10 [3] *saṃlakṣayām* A B N T : *saṃllakṣayām* K
25.10 [3] *rājāśva* N T : *drutāśva* K
25.12 *viśrāmahetoḥ* N T : *viśramahetoḥ* K
25.12 *vā* T : om. K
25.12 *araṇyamadhyam* N : *araṇyavanam* K
25.12 *utsṛjya* N T : *upasṛjya* K
25.15 [5] *rājya* A B N P : *rāja* K T
25.17 [7] *kiṇāṅkitānīva* A B N P T : *kīṇāṅkitānīva* K
25.22 [10] *vrajanti* A B N P T : *gacchanti* K
25.24 [12] *aimi* K T : *emi* A B N P
25.33 *sa* N : om. K
25.36 *adhyāruroha* A B N P T : *āruroha* K
25.50 [29] *sādhujana* A B N P T : *sādhu* K
25.50 [29] *niścalena* N T : *niścayena* K
25.50 [29] *hitasiddhibuddhyā* T : *hitabuddhisiddhyā* K
25.51 *dṛṣṭadhārmikasāmparāyikeṣv* N : *dṛḍham sāmparāyikeṣv* K
25.51 *avekṣyamāṇas* N T : *abhivīkṣyamāṇas* K
25.54 *anukrośapravṛttiṃ dṛṣṭvā* T : *api sānukrośā pravṛttirdṛṣṭā* K
25.54 *sānukrośena bhavitavyam* N T : *sānukrośenāryeṇa bhavitavyam* K
26.3 *kāśa* A B N P : om. K
26.4 *viṣāṇakhura* N T : *viṣāṇakṣura* K
26.5 *lobhanīyatāṃ* N T : *'tilobhanīyatāṃ* K
26.7 *atha kadācit sa* N : *atha sa kadācin* K
26.10 *bhayaviṣādaśramāpanodinīm* N T : *bhayaviṣādadainyaśramāpanodinīm* K
26.14 [7] *duḥkhaḥ* B N P T : *duḥkham* K
26.15 *ātyadbhutenā* N T : *ādbhutenā* K
26.15 *saumukhyena* N T : *saumukhena* K

26.21 *me rūpaṃ paśyāmi* N T : *me rūpam. paśya* K
26.27 *padavinyāsena* N T : *padanyāsena* K
26.27 *labdhapraṇayaprasarasaṃmānanā* N T : *labdhaprasarapraṇayasaṃmānā* K
26.35 *guṇān* N P T : *guṇaṃ* K
26.35 *anubhavāmy* N T : *anugacchāmy* K
26.35 *āho* N T : *utāho* K
26.35 *hriyam* N T : *śriyam* K
26.36 *rurumṛgasya mahopakāraṃ* N T : *mṛgasyopakāraṃ* K
26.38 *ādiśyamāna* N T : *ādeśyamāna* K
26.38 *ādiśyamāna* N T : *ādeśyamāna* K
26.38 *anuviveśa* N T : *anupraviveśa* K
26.40 [18] *onnamayato* N T : *onnāmayato* K
26.43 [20] *ābhrakuñje* A B N T : *ābhrakukṣe* K
26.44 [21] *vivyatsayā* N T : *bibhitsayā* K
26.48 *tena* A B N P T : om. K
26.48 *ātyadbhutena* N T : *ādbhutena* K
26.52 *vikutsayata* N T : *vijugupsata* K
26.53 [26] *tad* N : *tvad* K
26.60 *vaivarṇya* N T : *vaivarṇa* K
26.65 [32] *aiva* A B N P T : *eva* K
26.65 [32] *aiveha* A B N P T : *eveha* K
26.72 *ābhyāgamana* N T : *iha saṃgamana* K
26.73 *adhiropya* N T : *āropya* K
26.73 *niveśya* N T : *niveśya samutsāhayamānaḥ* K : *niveśya samutsāhamānaḥ* A B
26.76 [38] *trividhakriyam* A B N P T : *vividhakriyam* K
26.80 [41] *sā* A B N P T : *sa* K. Correcting KERN's misprint of *sa*.
26.81 [42] *vikṛtiṃ* N T : *vikṛtaṃ* K
26.81 [42] *prītyanusṛtā* N T : *prītyanusṛtān* K
26.83 [44] *sthiradayāḥ* N T : *sthiratayā* K

27 title *mahāvānarajātakam* T : *mahākapijātakam* K, *vānarajātakam* N

27.1 *manāṃsy* N : *mānasāny* K. Compare the same statement repeated at the end of the story.

27.8 *cakruḥ* A B N P T : om. K

27.8 *cohyamānaṃ* B N T : *vāhyamānaṃ* K

27.17 *nadītīre* T : *nadītīra°* K

27.18 *tāṃ* A B N P T : *taṃ* K. Correcting the misprint in KERN.

27.19 *vanyamṛgān* N T : *vanyagajamṛgān* K

27.21 *nirhāriṇā manojñena* N : *nirhāriṇātimanojñena* K

27.21 *anekair vānaraśatair* A B N P T : *anekavānaraśatair* K

27.22 *nāśayata* N T : *vināśayata* K

27.22 *samādideśa* N T : *ādideśa* K

27.24 *ca* B N T : om. K

27.24 *taṃ* N T : om. K

27.24 *śaraloṣṭadaṇḍavarṣeṇa* N T : *śaraloṣṭadaṇḍaśastravarṣeṇa* K

27.26 [9] *kṛpayā hi vivardhitaḥ* N T : *kṛpayābhivivardhitaḥ* K

27.26 [9] *evā* N T : *aivā* K

27.27 *tasya* A B N P T : om. K

27.28 [10] *abhiprayāta* N T : *abhiprayāyāt* K

27.29 *vetralatayā* A B N T : om. K

27.34 *parikṣobhita* N T : *kṣobhita* K

27.34 *cātaḥ* N : *cāyamataḥ* K

27.34 *iyaṃ* A B N P T : om. K

27.34 *yugapac chidyetām* T : *yugapat pracchidyetām* K

27.35 *vraṇān* N T : *vranāny* K

27.35 *abhigamya* N T : *abhyupagamya* K

27.37 [14] *prabhavanti* N T : *prataranti* K

27.43 *me* T : *māṃ* K

27.46 [20] *viniṣpatattīkṣṇaśilīmukhāni* N T : *viniṣpataddīptaśilīmukhāni* K

27.56 [28] *mamotsavābhyāgama* N T : *mahotsavābhyāgama* K
27.57 [29] *kṛtajñabhāvagrahaṇaṃ* B N T : *kṛtajñabhāvādgrahaṇaṃ* K
27.61 [33] *chramaṇadvijātīn* N T : *chramaṇānvijātīn* K
27.64 *āvarjayitukāmena* N : *samāvarjayitukāmena* K
28 title *kṣāntivādijātakam* N T : *kṣāntijātakam* K
28.3 *matsarādi* N T : *mātsaryādi* K
28.3 *gṛhavāsaṃ* K T : *gṛhāvāsaṃ* A B N P
28.5 *askhalitakṣāntisamādānaṃ* N T : *askhalitasamādānaṃ* K
28.7 [2] *kṣāntikathāḥ* N : *kṣāntikathāṃ* T
28.9 *sarvartu* N T : *samartu* K
28.9 *adhyāvasanāt* N : *adhyāsanāt* K
28.9 *upanināya* N T : *ānināya* K
28.12 *tatratyo* N T : *tatastyo* K
28.16 [8] *tāsāṃ* A B N P T : *nāsāṃ* K
28.17 [9] *vimānadeśeṣv avasajyamānā* N T : *vimānadeśeṣu viṣajyamānā* K
28.18 [10] *nṛttāni* N T : *nṛtyāni* K
28.25 *abhijagmuḥ* N T : *upajagmuḥ* K
28.25 *nainās* K N : *naitās* T
28.26 *api gāmbhīryātiśayād* T : *atigāmbhīryātiśayād* K
28.26 *maṅgalyapuṇyadarśanaṃ* N T : *maṅgalyaṃ puṇyadarśanaṃ* K
28.31 [17] *tu* N T : *hi* K
28.32 [18] *dhanodayasya* N T : *dhanocchrayasya* K
28.38 [24] *janayati na* N T : *na janayati* K
28.40 [25] *ātiśayaprasiddhiḥ* N P T : *ātiśayaḥ prasiddhaḥ* K
28.46 *yuvatividhṛtacchatracāmaravyajanottarīya* A B N P T : *yuvatidhṛtacchattravyajanottarīya* K
28.55 *pratihārī* K : *pratīhārī* N T
28.55 *ābhyāgamam* N T : *abhyāgamanam* K
28.58 *labdhatarapraṇayaprasarās* A B N T : *labdhatarapraṇaprasarās* K
28.60 *praduṣṭabhāvatvāt* A B N P : *praduṣṭabhāvāt* K

28.62 [34] *kaṣṭāśayaṃ* N T : *duṣṭāśayaṃ* K
28.63 *ṛṣivaraṃ* T : *ṛṣivaryaṃ* K
28.65 [36] *nihanyād* N T : *hi hanyād* K
28.66 *sasaṃrambhataram* T : *saṃrambhitaram* K
28.69 [38] *avamānayogaḥ* N P T : *apamānayogaḥ* K
28.72 [40] *viśeṣahetuṣu* A B N P T : *viśeṣahetubhiḥ* K
28.73 [41] *cārthataḥ* N T : *tattvataḥ* K
28.74 [42] *aticāpalāṃ* T : *aticāpalān* K
28.74 [42] *atiprathante* A B N P T : *abhiprathante* K
28.75 [43] *tad* A B N P T : *yad* K
28.77 [45] *kṣamātra* A B N P T : *kṣamā tu* K
28.79 [47] *abhyucitā* N T : *abhyuditā* K
28.81 [48] *asmān* N T : *asmād* K
28.84 [50] *svavṛttaṃ* N T : *svaṃ vṛttaṃ* K
28.85 [51] *śreyo'dhigamana* N T : *śreyo'bhigamana* K
28.92 *ca* N T : om. K
28.97 *imaṃ* N T : *idaṃ* K
28.97 *jātabhayaśaṅkāḥ* N T : *jātabhayāśaṅkāḥ* K
28.97 *vijñāpayām* A B N P T : *vijñāpayam* K. Correcting the misprint in Kern.
28.100 *athainān* A B N P T : *athaitān* K
28.108 [67] *asaṃkhyān* N T : *analpān* K
28.110 [69] *samamupanīya* K N : *samupanīya* A B P T
28.111 *kiṃcid astīti* N : *astīti* K
28.112 *vinipātagāmino* N T : *vinipātabhāgino* K
28.112 *anityatāpradarśane* N T : *anityatāsaṃdarśane* K
29.1 *viśeṣenānukampyāḥ* A B N P T : *viśeṣānukampyāḥ* K
29.3 *bodhisattvabhūtaḥ* N T : *bodhisattvaḥ* K
29.5 *utkṛṣṭa* N T : *utkliṣṭa* K
29.5 *avalokayan* N T : *vyavalokayan* K
29.6 *phalavipāka* A B N P T : *vipāka* K

29.7 [2] *śubhāśraye* A N T : *śubhāśrayo* K
29.11 [4] *cittasamādhāna* A B N P T : *cittasamādāna* K
29.13 *mārṣa* N T : *maharṣa* K. Compare 29.19.
29.14 [5] *aviṣajjamānaś* Em : *avisajjamānaś* N T : *aviṣajyamānaś*
29.26 [12] *prasūta* A B N T : *prasupta* K
29.29 [14] *siddham eṣām* N T : *siddhir eṣā* K
29.35 [16] *aiva* T : *aiṣa* K
29.37 [17] *tadantam eva* A B N P T : *tadantam eti* K
29.40 [20] *tadā* A B N P T : *tataḥ* K
29.43 [23] *kaṭu* N T : *paṭu* K
29.43 [23] *svavadhra* K N P : *vardhra* T
29.45 [25] *śitogra* A B N P T : *śitāgra* K
29.46 [26] *tathaivāpare* N T : *tathā cāpare* K
29.48 [28] *avirale* N T : *avikale* K
29.52 [32] *raudratarāyāṃ* N : *dīptatarāvāṃ* K
29.57 [37] *chidyante* N T : *pāṭhyante* K
29.59 [39] *yadā* A B N P T : om. K
29.60 [40] *durjanakaḍevara* A B T : *durjanakalevara* K
29.63 [43] *viśīryamāṇāsthi* N T : *vidīryamāṇāsthi* A B P : *vidāryamānaṃ*
29.63 [43] *śatārtinādinaṃ* A : *śatārtanādinaṃ* N : *śatārtanāditaṃ* T : *bhṛśam ārtinādinaṃ*
29.64 [44] *vā hṛta* N T : *vyāhṛta* K
29.64 [44] *tudet* A B P T : *nudet* K N
29.65 [45] *pāṭanatāḍanair* N T : *pāṭanair* K
29.67 [46] *nu* A B N P T : *na* K
29.71 [49] *sacchiṣya* N T : *suśiṣya* K
29.71 [49] *vivavruḥ* A B N P T : *vicakruḥ* K
29.81 *sugatigamanamārgaṃ* N T : *sugatimārgaṃ* K
29.83 *avasādanām* N T : *āsādanām* K
30.3 *tṛṇa* N T : *tarutṛṇa* K
30.5 *svayūtha* A B P T : *sayūtha* K

30.9 *dūrata* A B N P T : *dūra* K

30.9 *mandamandāni* N T : *mandāni* K

30.10 *ca* N : om. K

30.12 *ainān* N T : *aitān* K

30.22 [10] *'tra* N T : *tu* K

30.25 [11] *ghṛṇāviyuktā* N : *ghṛṇāvimuktā* K

30.29 *anekayojanaśatāyataṃ* N T : *anekayojanāyāmaṃ* K : *anekayojanāyataṃ*

30.29 *apathyadanāḥ* B N : *apathyādanāḥ* K

30.29 *śaknuyuḥ* N T : *śakyeyuḥ* K

30.34 *pānīyam* A B N P T : *panīyam* K. Correcting the misprint in Kern.

30.36 *durgottaraṇāya* N T : *durgottāraṇāya* K

30.41 *nīla* N T : om. K

30.41 *pātheyārtham* N T : *pātheyatām* K

30.41 *ādāya* A B N T : *ānīya* K

30.41 *ca* N T : om. K

30.42 *adhiruhya* A B P T : *āruhya* K

30.42 *janasya* N T : *janakāyasya* K

30.42 *svaṃ śarīraṃ* N T : *svaśarīraṃ* K

30.45 *aviganita* N T : *aganita* K

30.45 *duḥkhaḥ* N T : *duḥkhaṃ* K

30.45 *svaṃ śarīraṃ* A B N P T : *svaśarīraṃ* K

30.46 [23] *tārkṣyasya* N : *tārkṣasya* A B P T

30.47 [24] *sa* A B P T : *ca* K

30.47 [24] *drumalatā* N T : *vanalatā* K

30.51 [28] *puṣparajovikarṣiṇā* N T : *puṣparajovikarṣiṇāt* K

30.52 [29] *vyahāsayan* A B N T : *vyarāsayan* K

30.53 [30] *kutūhalotkampitavīcivikramaḥ* A B N P T : *kutūhalotkampitavīcivibhramaḥ* K

30.54 *aciramṛtaṃ* N T : *naciramṛtaṃ* K

30.56 [31] *tasyaiva* T : *tasyaiṣa* K
30.56 [31] *tathaiva* N T : *tasyaiva* K
30.59 *nistāraṇāvekṣayā* A B N P T : *nistāraṇāpekṣayā* K
30.62 [35] *sugandhicārv* B N T : *sugandhivāyv* K
30.67 [38] *sīdat* A B N P T : *sīṣat* K
30.67 [38] *uddharatīva* N T : *udvahatīva* K
30.69 [40] *yathārtha* A B N P T : *yathārha* K
30.73 [41] *etad* N T : *evam* K
30.74 [42] *tasya* N T : *tv asya* K
30.78 *āvekṣayā* A B N P T : *āpekṣayā* K
30.78 *ca* N T : om. K
30.80 *apy* N T : om. K
31.1 *śreyo'rthinā sajjanāpāśrayeṇa* N T : *sajjanāpāśrayeṇa śreyo'rthinā* K
31.3 *guṇaparigrahaprasaṅgāt* K N : *guṇaparigrahasaṅgāt* T
31.4 *somavat* N : *soma* K
31.5 *loke* A B N P : *lokaprema* K
31.6 [1] *anunnatihrīdyuti* B N : *anunnatihrīmati* K
31.9 [3] *cāsur* A B N T : *tvāsur* K
31.10 *kutha* N T : *kuthāstaraṇa* K
31.10 *nirmala* N T : *nirmalanīla* K
31.10 *anyatamad* A B T : *anyatamam* K
31.12 [5] *nṛttaiś* N T : *nṛtyaiś* K
31.12 [5] *lalitā* A B N P T : *lulitā* K
31.13 *kṛtopacāra* K N T : *kṛtopakāra* A B P
31.17 *'śvāpahṛto* N T : *'śvenāpahṛto* K
31.17 *saṃyogam* N T : *sārdhaṃ yogam* K
31.17 *suṣuve* N T : *prasuṣuve* K
31.18 *iti* T : *iti sa* K
31.18 *sa* A B K N P : om. T
31.18 *hatvā* N T : *ca hatvā hatvā* K

31.18 *tato* N T : *yato* K
31.18 *vo* N : om. K
31.18 *prasahya* N T : *prasahya prasahya* K
31.18 *bahurāja* N T : *rāja* K
31.19 *apahartum* N T : *upahartum* K
31.20 *atha* N T : *atha sa* K
31.20 *tacchīlavaikṛta* A B N P T Toyoq : *tacchīlavikṛta* K
31.20 *avocat* A B N P T Toyoq : *uvāca* K
31.25 *valkalapaṭṭaviniyatareṇu* A B N P T : *valkalapaṭṭaviniyataṃ roṣa* K
31.26 *ito* N T : *ita eva* K
31.26 *kadana* N : *kadanakaraṇa* K
31.29 [9] *kaḍevarā* A B N T : *kalevarā* K
31.29 [9] *paruṣam* T : *puruṣam* A B N P K
31.31 *īkṣamāṇo* Toyoq : *vīkṣamāṇo* K
31.31 *tadudyānanivartana* N Toyoq : *tadudyānavinivartana* K
31.31 *pratīkṣam* N : *pratīkṣiṇam* K
31.41 [15] *sutān* K N T Toyoq : *sutāṃ* A B P
31.43 [16] *cāpi* N T : *caiva* K
31.44 [17] *tan mām* T : *tasmād* K
31.50 *pratijñātam* N P T : *pratipannam* K
31.50 *khalajanasaṃbhāvanayā* N T : *khalajanasamatayā* K
31.50 *viśaṅkitum* N T : *pariśaṅkitum* K
31.52 [23] *tuṣṭi* N T : *stuti* K
31.56 *vikatthitam* N T : *vikalpitam* K
31.62 *kośasaṃpadavekṣiṇī* N : *kośasaṃpadapekṣiṇī* K
31.67 [31] *śreyo'nurāgasthiratāṃ* T : *śreyo'nurāgaḥ sthiratāṃ* K
31.67 [31] *prajñābhivṛddhyā* N T : *prajñā vivṛddhyā* K
31.71 [35] *asaṃstutair* N T : *asaṃskṛtair* K
31.76 [40] *nivṛttaśaṅkena* N T : *nivṛttasaṃketa* K
31.77 *evam* T : om. K

31.77 *cānṛtam āhur vedavida* N T : *cānṛtamārgo vedavihita* K

31.77 *te* N T : *tava*

31.78 *virodha* N T : *virodhi* K

31.79 *avaśam* N T : om. K

31.81 *suhṛtsvajana* N T : *suhṛtsu svajana* K

31.85 *madatyayaśaṅkayā* N T : *madatyayāśaṅkayā* K

31.89 [43] *batādbhutam* N T : *tathādbhutam* K

31.95 [47] *nirdhūma* N T : *vidhūma* K

31.98 [49] *saṃtyaktārya* A B N P T : *saṃtyaktārtha* K. Correcting the misprint in KERN.

31.106 [52] *rāja* N T : *rājya* K

31.108 [53] *yan* A B N P T : *yaṃ* K

31.113 [56] *iti* N T : *api* K

31.114 *saṃkṣepatas* B K N P T : *saṃkṣepas* A.

31.121 *puruṣāḥ* B N T : *kāpuruṣāḥ* K

31.122 [61] *āśaṅkamānāḥ* Em : *aśaṅkamānāḥ* K. Correcting the misprint in KERN.

31.123 [62] *dharme sthitaḥ* N T : *dharmasthitaḥ* K

31.131 *abhivṛddhaṃ* N T : *abhivṛddhaṃ ca* K

31.132 [68] *dṛṣṭvātmacarita* N T : *dṛṣṭvā me carita* K

31.134 *yuktaḥ* N : *yuktaṃ* K

31.137 *tad* A B P T : om. K

31.137 *madhuragambhīreṇā* N : *madhureṇa gambhīreṇā* K

31.138 [71] *upanataṃ* N T : *upānītaṃ* K

31.139 *saśiraḥprakampāṅgulīvikṣepaṃ* A N P : *svaśiraḥ prakampyāṅgulīvikṣepaṃ* K

31.139 *saṃrādhya* A B N P T : K

31.145 [74] *ātivartate* N T : *ābhivartate* K

31.146 *Saudāsa uvāca* A B N P T : om. K

31.148 [75] *apāraṃ* N T : *avāraṃ* K

31.157 [79] *etān* B N T : *tān* K

31.159 [80] *vivarjaya* N T : *visarjaya* K
31.162 *tadevaitat* T : *tavaitat* K
31.167 [85] *dhṛto* K N : *vṛto* A B P
31.177 [92] *ka* A B N P T : *kva* K
31.180 *nṛpati* N T : *nṛpa* K
31.180 *tatrā* N T : *tatraivā* K
31.180 *nṛpati* N : *nṛpa* K
31.182 *yathārhakṛtasatkārāṃs* A N T : *saṃskārāṃs* K
31.183 *sajjanāpāśrayeṇa* N : *sajjanasamāśrayeṇa* K
31.184 *saddharmaśravaṇavarṇe* N T : *saddharmaśravaṇe* K
31.184 *puṇyakīrtyākarabhūtaṃ* N T : *puṇyakīrtyākaraṃ* K
31.184 *ceti* N T : *'pi ceti* K
32.1 *saṃvignamanasām* N T : *saṃvignamānasānām* K
32.3 *opanipātaduḥkhitam* N T : *opanipātaṃ duḥkhitam* K
32.4 *askhalitābhivṛddhayā* N T : *askhalitābhivṛddhyā* K
32.4 *samānatadṛptasāmantatayā* N P : *samānatadṛptasāmantayā* K
32.5 [1] *anekatūryasvanapūrṇakuñjam* A N T : *anekatūryasvanapūrṇakūjam* K
32.6 [2] *vivṛddha* N T : *vivṛtta* K
32.7 [3] *vighaṭṭita* K T : *vighāṭita* K
32.7 [3] *samucchritāgrya* N T : *samucchritāgra* K
32.10 *saṃmānebhyaḥ* N T : *saṃmānanebhyaḥ* K
32.11 [5] *asaṃbaddhaṃ* N T A : *asaṃbandhaṃ* K
32.13 *pracal'* N T : *pracalit'* K
32.13 *patākā* A B N T : *patāka* K
32.13 *abhiruhya* N T : *adhiruhya* K
32.14 *paurajanasya* A B N T : *paurajānapadasya* K
32.19 [11] *taṭe* N T : *taṭaiḥ* K
32.19 [11] *samantād* A B N P T : *samaṃ* K
32.23 *abhiprasāriteṣu* N T : *abhiprasāriṣu* K

32.36 [24] *dṛptā* N T : *hṛṣṭā* K
32.37 [25] *mattadvipā* A B N P T : *mattā dvipā* K
32.39 [27] *vikartanakharair* A B N P T : *vikartanakarair* K
32.39 [27] *śruti* A B N P T : *śruta* K
32.40 [28] *'pi tu* N T : *yadi* K
32.41 [29] *abhyupāyaiḥ* N T : *apyupāyaiḥ* K
32.41 [29] *kṛtāparādhān* N T : *kṛtāparādhaṃ* K
32.43 [31] *asādhyaviṣaḥ* N : *asādhyabalaḥ* K
32.44 [32] *vitatographaṇān* N T : *vitatagrahaṇāḥ* K
32.45 [33] *vane mṛgāṇām* A B N P T : *vanamṛgāṇāṃ* K
32.48 [36] *tapobalaiḥ svastyayanau* N T : *tapobalasvastyayanau* K
32.53 [41] *ratiḥ* A B N P : *matiḥ* K
32.55 *atha vane kastavāśvāsa* N T : *atha vane tava ka āśvāsa* K
32.55 *vā* B T : om. K
32.67 *sukhaṃ dharmaḥ* N T : *dharmaḥ sukhaṃ* K
32.67 *upaneyam* N T : *unneyam* A B K P
33.3 *araṇyavanapradeśe* N T : *araṇyapradeśe* K
33.3 *paṅkasaṃparkaparuṣavapur* N T : *paṅkasaṃparkātparuṣavapur* K
33.3 *meghaviccheda* T : *meghanīlaviccheda* K. Following T and the Tibetan translation (see HAHN 2001).
33.4 [1] *karmaṇāṃ* N T : *karmaṇo* K
33.6 [3] *dharmasaṃjño* A B N P T : *dharmasaṃjñī* K. Correcting the misprint in KERN.
33.7 *bhṛśam* N : *bhṛśataram* K
33.9 *visrabdhasuptasya* N : *visrabdhaprasuptasya* K. Following N (HAHN 2001).
33.9 *abhiruhya* N : *adhiruhya* K
33.9 *ca* N : om. K
33.9 *cicchravaṇayoścāghaṭṭayām* N : *śravaṇayorghaṭṭayām* K. Following HAHN's (2001) conjectural emendation based on the Tibetan translation and N.

33.9 *salilāvagāha* N : *salilāvagāhana* K

33.9 *samadhiruhya* N : *samabhiruhya* K

33.9 *tu* N : om. K

33.9 *āvinayaviceṣṭitam* N : *āvinayaceṣṭitam* K

33.9 *iva* N : *iva manyamāno* K. Following the Tibetan translation (HAHN 2001) and N.

33.10 [5] *tu* N : *ca* K

33.11 *athā* N : *atha kilā* K

33.11 *jijñāsamānas* : *jijñāsayamānas* K. Following KHOROCHE's (1987) emendation.

33.11 *mahiṣavṛsaṃ sthitvānumārgam* N : *mahiṣavṛṣabhaṃ mārge sthitvedam* K. Following N (see HAHN 2001).

33.12 *ca* N : om. K. Following N (see HAHN 2001).

33.13 [6] *vajraṃ vajravad* N : *vajravad* K

33.14 [7] *śailopamasaṃhataṃ sthiraṃ* N : *śailopamasaṃhatasthiraṃ* K. Following N (see HAHN 2001).

33.15 [8] *khureṇa* N : *kṣureṇa* K

33.16 [9] *sukhaśīta* N : *sukhaśīla* K. Following N and the Tibetan translation (see HAHN 2001).

33.16 [9] *kaphātmake* A B N : *kaphātmako* K

33.18 [10] *balanyūnaṃ* N : *balanūnaṃ* K. Following HAHN's (2001) emendation based on N and the Tibetan translation.

33.21 [13] *nirveśa* A B N : *nirdeśa* K. See also HAHN 2001 for a discussion.

33.21 [13] *avekṣya* N : *apekṣya* K

33.24 *asya prabādhanāyāḥ kadā cin* N T : *asyāḥ kadācit prabādhanāyā* K. Following HAHN's (2001) emendation based on the Tibetan translation; already suggested by GAWRONSKI.

33.29 [19] *dṛṣṭa* N T : *labdha* K. Following N T and the Tibetan translation (HAHN 2001).

33.30 *sa* N : om. K. Following N and the Tibetan translation (HAHN 2001).

33.31 [20] *ayaṃ* N T : *asau* K

33.34 *api* N : *bodhisattvānāṃ* K. Following N and the Tibetan translation (HAHN 2001).

34.3 *anvavartata* N : *anuvavarta* K

34.6 *sa* A B T : om. K. Following A B T and the Tibetan translation (HAHN 2001).

34.6 *ca* N : om. K

34.7 [3] *dayājananyā* T : *dayāmahattvāt* K. See HAHN (2001) for a discussion.

34.11 [5] *saukhyaś ca* N : *saukhyasya* K

34.13 *śramakṛtam* N : *saukhyaś* K

34.13 *galāntaravilagnaṃ* N : *galāntare vilagnaṃ* K

34.13 *enac* : *enaṃ* A B N P

34.14 *viṣkambhaṇa* N : *viṣkambha* K

34.14 *samupapādita* N : *samutpādita* K

34.14 *niścakarṣa* N : *vicakarṣa* K

34.14 *ca* N : om. K. Following N and the Tibetan translation (HAHN 2001).

34.14 *nipātayām* A B N P T : *nipātayam* K. Correcting the misprint in KERN.

34.19 *pratīta* N : *prīta* K

34.20 *atha kadā cit pravitataruciracitrapattraḥ sa* N : *atha sa kadā cit pravitataruciracitrapattraḥ* K

34.20 *kiṃ cit* N : *kiṃ cit kva cit* K

34.24 *na māṃ* N : *māṃ na* K. Following N (see HAHN 2001).

34.24 *atithi* N : *arthi* K. Following N and the Tibetan translation (HAHN 2001).

34.24 *prayuktā* N : *prayuktayuktā* K. Following N and the Tibetan translation (HAHN 2001) in omitting *-yukta-* after *prayukta-*.

34.26 *sa* N : om. K. Following N and the Tibetan translation.

34.30 *tata eva* A B N : *tatraiva* K. Following A B N and the Tibetan translation (HAHN 2001).

34.30 *visphāra* N : *visphāraṇa* K

34.30 *āpacakrāma* N : *pracakrāma* K

34.31 *samupetya* N : *samutpatya* K

34.32 *vidyamānāyāṃ* N : *saṃvidyamānāyāṃ* K. Following N (see HAHN 2001).

34.34 *vidarśayann* N : *pradarśayann* K

34.35 *alam* N : *alam alam* K

34.39 [19] *kṛtaṃ* A B N : *kṛtaś* K

34.41 [21] *nanu* N : *'pi sa* K. Following N and the Tibetan translation (HAHN 2001).

34.46 *pratipūjya cainaṃ* A B P : *pratipūjyainaṃ* K

34.48 *kṣāntikathāyām* Toyoq : *evaṃ kṣāntikathāyām* K. Following Toyoq fragment xiv in omitting *evaṃ*. HAHN (2001: 397) also suggests further emendations based on the Tibetan translation.

34.48 *'pi* Toyoq : om. K. Following Toyoq fragment xiv and the Tibetan translation.

GLOSSARY OF COMMON NAMES, TERMS, AND EPITHETS

ANÁNDA a chief disciple of the Buddha, known for his devoted nature.

ÁSURA a class of demon or anti-god.

AYO·GRIHA a prince who becomes an ascetic. The Bodhi·sattva in story 32.

BODHI an ascetic. The name of the Bodhi·sattva in stories 21 and 23.

BODHI·SATTVA "Awakening Being." A person who has made a vow to practice the perfections (*pāramitā*) and become a fully awakened Buddha (*samyak/saṃbuddha*). The Buddha in his past lives.

BRAHMA a type of deity living in the Sphere of Pure Form (*rūpa/dhātu*). The Bodhi·sattva is a Brahma deity in story 29.

BRAHMA·DATTA a king of Varánasi.

BRAHMAN the absolute principle of the universe in Brahmanical thought.

DHANVAN·TARI a divine physician.

DHRITA·RASHTRA a royal goose. The Bodhi·sattva in story 22.

GANGES (*Gaṅgā*) a river in North India.

GÁRUDA a divine bird. The enemy of snakes.

GREAT BEING (*Mahā/sattva*) an epithet of the Bodhi·sattva.

GREAT ONE (*mahātmā*) an epithet of the Bodhi·sattva, used synonymously with Great Being (*Mahā/sattva*).

HÍMAVAT the Himálaya mountains.

INDRA the king of the gods in the Trayas·trinsha heaven in the Sphere of Desire (*kāma/dhātu*).

KALMÁSHA·PADA a cannibal (story 31).

KÁUMUDI the goddess of moonlight. The Káumudi festival is held in October to November.

KÁURAVA "descendant of Kuru." A royal dynasty.

KSHANTI·VADIN an ascetic. The Bodhi·sattva in story 28.

MADRI the wife of Vishvan·tara.

MÁNASA a lake.

MANU the father of mankind.

MARA a demonic figure hostile to the Buddha.

MOUNT SUNSET a mountain in the West behind which the sun is believed to set.

NAGA a semi-divine snake.

NÁNDANA a divine park.

SANGHÁTA a hell realm of clashing mountains.

SIDDHA a semi-divine being.

SOMA the god Moon.

SUDÁSA a king. Father of Kalmásha·pada.

SÚMUKHA the general of the royal goose in story 22.

SUTA·SOMA a prince. The Bodhi·sattva in story 31.

TATHA·GATA an epithet of the Buddha ("Thus-gone").

TEACHING the Dharma, or teaching of the Buddha.

TREATISES the Brahmanical shastra (*śāstra*) texts.

VÁITARANI a river in hell.

VARÁNASI a city in North India.

VIDYA·DHARA a divine being wielding magical powers.

VISHVAN·TARA a prince noted for his generosity. The Bodhi·sattva in story 9.

YAKSHA a demon or type of divine spirit.

YAMA the god of the dead.

THE CLAY SANSKRIT LIBRARY

The volumes in the series are listed here in order of publication.
Titles marked with an asterisk* are also available in the
Digital Clay Sanskrit Library (eCSL).
For further information visit www.claysanskritlibrary.org

1. The Emperor of the Sorcerers (*Bṛhatkathāślokasaṃgraha*) (vol. 1 of 2) by *Budhasvāmin*. Sir James Mallinson
2. Heavenly Exploits (*Divyāvadāna*). Joel Tatelman
3. Maha·bhárata III: The Forest (*Vanaparvan*) (vol. 4 of 4)* William J. Johnson
4. Much Ado about Religion (*Āgamaḍambara*) by *Bhaṭṭa Jayanta*. Csaba Dezső
5. The Birth of Kumára (*Kumārasaṃbhava*) by *Kālidāsa*. David Smith
6. Ramáyana I: Boyhood (*Bālakāṇḍa*) by *Vālmīki*. Robert P. Goldman
7. The Epitome of Queen Lilávati (*Līlāvatīsāra*) (vol. 1 of 2) by *Jinaratna*. R.C.C. Fynes
8. Ramáyana II: Ayódhya (*Ayodhyākāṇḍa*) by *Vālmīki*. Sheldon I. Pollock
9. Love Lyrics (*Amaruśataka, Śatakatraya & Caurapañcāśikā*) by *Amaru, Bhartṛhari & Bilhaṇa*. Greg Bailey & Richard Gombrich
10. What Ten Young Men Did (*Daśakumāracarita*) by *Daṇḍin*. Isabelle Onians
11. Three Satires (*Kaliviḍambana, Kalāvilāsa & Bhallaṭaśataka*) by *Nīlakaṇṭha, Kṣemendra & Bhallaṭa*. Somadeva Vasudeva
12. Ramáyana IV: Kishkíndha (*Kiṣkindhākāṇḍa*) by *Vālmīki*. Rosalind Lefeber
13. The Emperor of the Sorcerers (*Bṛhatkathāślokasaṃgraha*) (vol. 2 of 2) by *Budhasvāmin*. Sir James Mallinson
14. Maha·bhárata IX: Shalya (*Śalyaparvan*) (vol. 1 of 2)* Justin Meiland

15. Rákshasa's Ring (*Mudrārākṣasa*)*
    by *Viśākhadatta*. Michael Coulson
16. Messenger Poems (*Meghadūta, Pavanadūta & Haṃsadūta*)
    by *Kālidāsa, Dhoyī & Rūpa Gosvāmin*. Sir James Mallinson
17. Ramáyana III: The Forest (*Araṇyakāṇḍa*)
    by *Vālmīki*. Sheldon I. Pollock
18. The Epitome of Queen Lilávati (*Līlāvatīsāra*) (vol. 2 of 2)
    by *Jinaratna*. R.C.C. Fynes
19. Five Discourses on Worldly Wisdom (*Pañcatantra*)*
    by *Viṣṇuśarman*. Patrick Olivelle
20. Ramáyana V: Súndara (*Sundarakāṇḍa*) by *Vālmīki*.
    Robert P. Goldman & Sally J. Sutherland Goldman
21. Maha·bhárata II: The Great Hall (*Sabhāparvan*)
    Paul Wilmot
22. The Recognition of Shakúntala (*Abhijñānaśākuntala*) (Kashmir Recension) by *Kālidāsa*. Somadeva Vasudeva
23. Maha·bhárata VII: Drona (*Droṇaparvan*) (vol. 1 of 4)*
    Vaughan Pilikian
24. Rama Beyond Price (*Anargharāghava*)
    by *Murāri*. Judit Törzsök
25. Maha·bhárata IV: Viráta (*Virāṭaparvan*)
    Kathleen Garbutt
26. Maha·bhárata VIII: Karna (*Karṇaparvan*) (vol. 1 of 2)
    Adam Bowles
27. "The Lady of the Jewel Necklace" & "The Lady who Shows her Love" (*Ratnāvalī & Priyadarśikā*) by *Harṣa*.*
    Wendy Doniger
28. The Ocean of the Rivers of Story (*Kathāsaritsāgara*) (vol. 1 of 7)
    by *Somadeva*. Sir James Mallinson
29. Handsome Nanda (*Saundarananda*)*
    by *Aśvaghoṣa*. Linda Covill
30. Maha·bhárata IX: Shalya (*Śalyaparvan*) (vol. 2 of 2)*
    Justin Meiland
31. Rama's Last Act (*Uttararāmacarita*) by *Bhavabhūti*.
    Sheldon Pollock. Foreword by Girish Karnad

32. "Friendly Advice" (*Hitopadeśa*) by *Nārāyaṇa* &
"King Víkrama's Adventures" (*Vikramacarita*). Judit Törzsök

33. Life of the Buddha (*Buddhacarita*)
by *Aśvaghoṣa*. Patrick Olivelle

34. Maha·bhárata V: Preparations for War (*Udyogaparvan*) (vol. 1 of 2)
Kathleen Garbutt. Foreword by Gurcharan Das

35. Maha·bhárata VIII: Karna (*Karṇaparvan*) (vol. 2 of 2)
Adam Bowles

36. Maha·bhárata V: Preparations for War (*Udyogaparvan*) (vol. 2 of 2)
Kathleen Garbutt

37. Maha·bhárata VI: Bhishma (*Bhīṣmaparvan*) (vol. 1 of 2)*
Including the "Bhagavad Gita" in Context
Alex Cherniak. Foreword by Ranajit Guha

38. The Ocean of the Rivers of Story (*Kathāsaritsāgara*) (vol. 2 of 7)
by *Somadeva*. Sir James Mallinson

39. "How the Nagas were Pleased" (*Nāgānanda*) by *Harṣa* &
"The Shattered Thighs" (*Ūrubhaṅga*) by *Bhāsa*.*
Andrew Skilton

40. Gita·govínda: Love Songs of Radha and Krishna (*Gītagovinda*)*
by *Jayadeva*. Lee Siegel. Foreword by Sudipta Kaviraj

41. "Bouquet of Rasa" & "River of Rasa" (*Rasamañjarī & Rasataraṅgiṇī*) by *Bhānudatta*. Sheldon Pollock

42. Garland of the Buddha's Past Lives (*Jātakamālā*) (vol. 1 of 2)*
by *Āryaśūra*. Justin Meiland

43. Maha·bhárata XII: Peace (*Śāntiparvan*) (vol. 3 of 5)*
"The Book of Liberation" (*Mokṣadharma*). Alexander Wynne

44. The Little Clay Cart (*Mṛcchakaṭikā*) by *Śūdraka*.
Diwakar Acharya. Foreword by Partha Chatterjee

45. Bhatti's Poem: The Death of Rávana (*Bhaṭṭikāvya*)*
by *Bhaṭṭi*. Oliver Fallon

46. "Self-Surrender," "Peace," "Compassion," and "The Mission of the Goose": Poems and Prayers from South India (*Ātmārpaṇastuti, Śāntivilāsa, Dayāśataka & Haṃsasaṃdeśa*) by *Appayya Dīkṣita, Nīlakaṇṭha Dīkṣita & Vedānta Deśika*. YIGAL BRONNER & DAVID SHULMAN Foreword by GIEVE PATEL
47. Maha·bhárata VI: Bhishma (*Bhīṣmaparvan*) (vol. 2 of 2)* ALEX CHERNIAK
48. How Úrvashi Was Won (*Vikramorvaśīya*) by *Kālidāsa* VELCHERU NARAYANA RAO & DAVID SHULMAN
49. The Quartet of Causeries (*Caturbhāṇī*) by *Śūdraka, Śyāmilaka, Vararuci & Īśvaradatta*. CSABA DEZSŐ & SOMADEVA VASUDEVA
50. Garland of the Buddha's Past Lives (*Jātakamālā*) (vol. 2 of 2)* by *Āryaśūra*. JUSTIN MEILAND
51. Princess Kadámbari (*Kādambarī*) (vol. 1 of 3) by *Bāṇa*. DAVID SMITH
52. The Rise of Wisdom Moon (*Prabodhacandrodaya*)* by *Kṛṣṇamiśra*. MATTHEW T. KAPSTEIN Foreword by J.N. MOHANTY
53. Maha·bhárata VII: Drona (*Droṇaparvan*) (vol. 2 of 4)* VAUGHAN PILIKIAN
54. Maha·bhárata X & XI: Dead of Night & The Women (*Sauptikaparvan & Strīparvan*).* KATE CROSBY
55. Seven Hundred Elegant Verses (*Āryāsaptaśatī*)* by *Govardhana*. FRIEDHELM HARDY
56. Málavika and Agni·mitra (*Mālavikāgnimitram*) by *Kālidāsa*. DÁNIEL BALOGH & ESZTER SOMOGYI